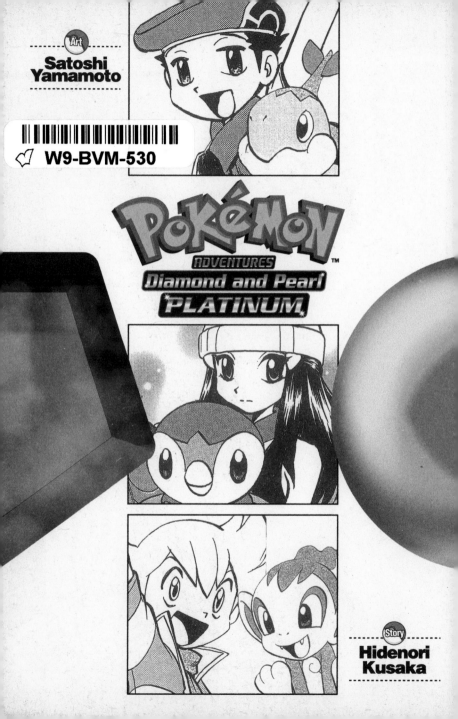

Art

Satoshi Yamamoto

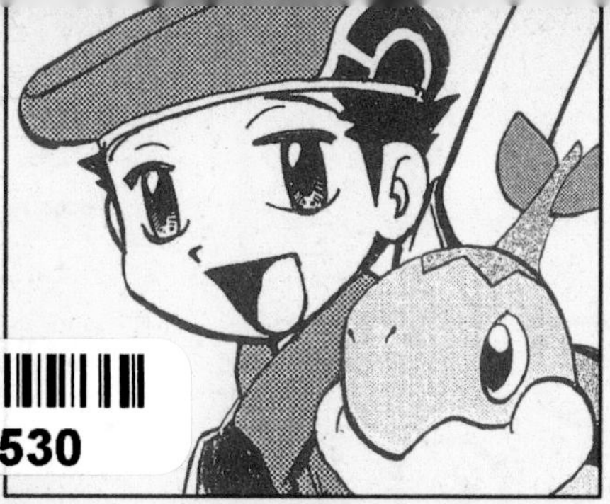

Pokémon Adventures™
Diamond and Pearl Platinum

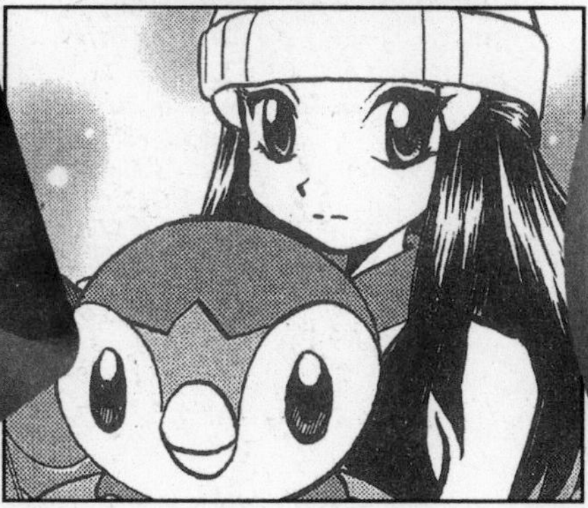

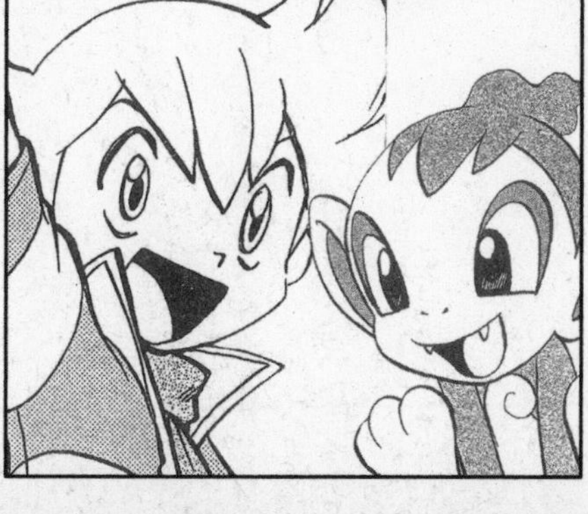

Story

Hidenori Kusaka

Our Story So Far…

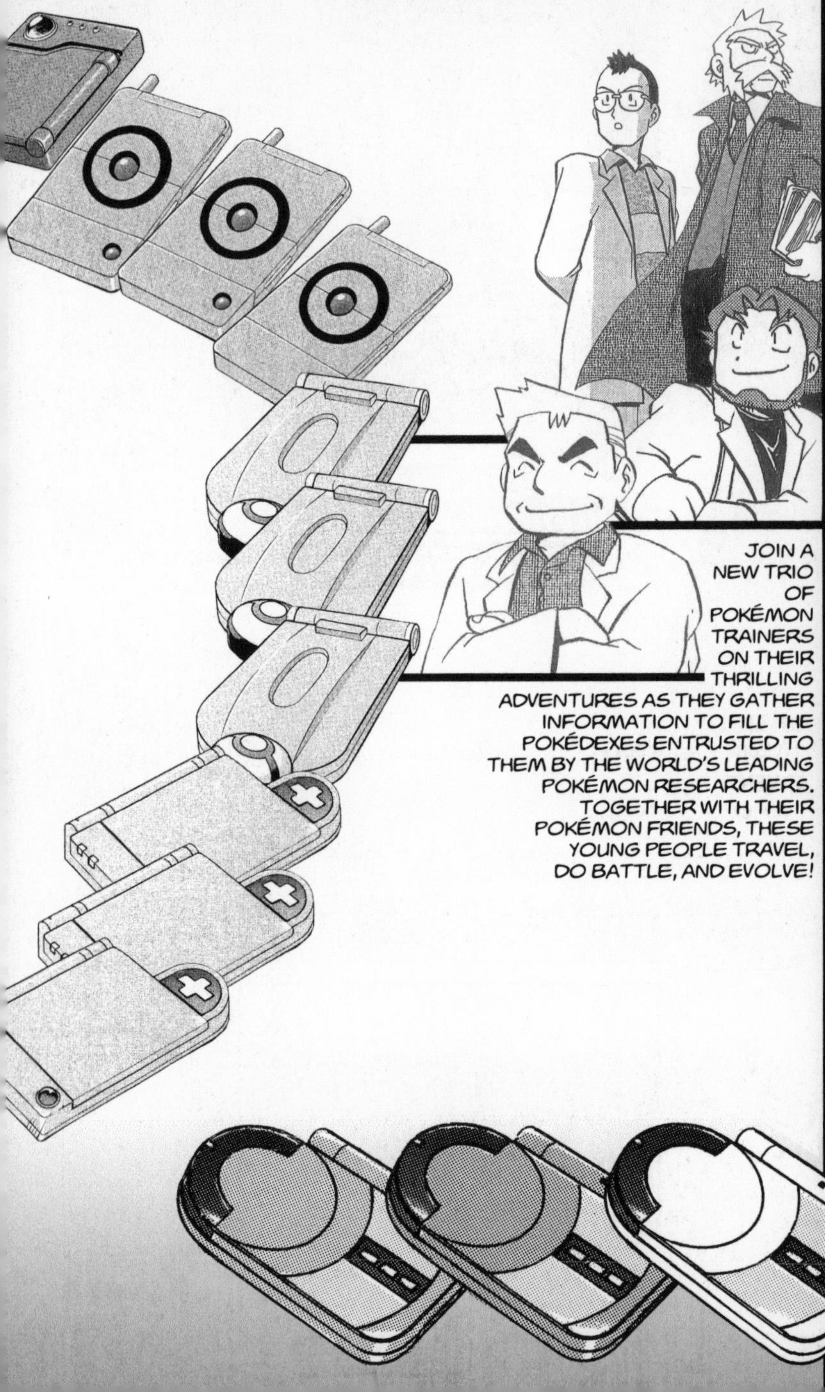
JOIN A NEW TRIO OF POKÉMON TRAINERS ON THEIR THRILLING ADVENTURES AS THEY GATHER INFORMATION TO FILL THE POKÉDEXES ENTRUSTED TO THEM BY THE WORLD'S LEADING POKÉMON RESEARCHERS. TOGETHER WITH THEIR POKÉMON FRIENDS, THESE YOUNG PEOPLE TRAVEL, DO BATTLE, AND EVOLVE!

Pokémon Adventures Diamond and Pearl Platinum

1

CONTENTS

7
The Seventh Chapter

DIAMOND ✶ PEARL

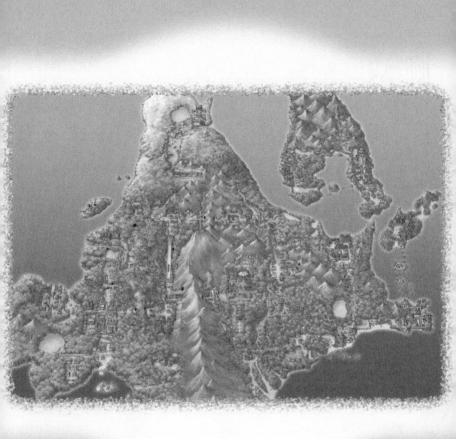

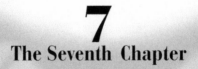

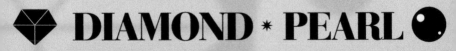

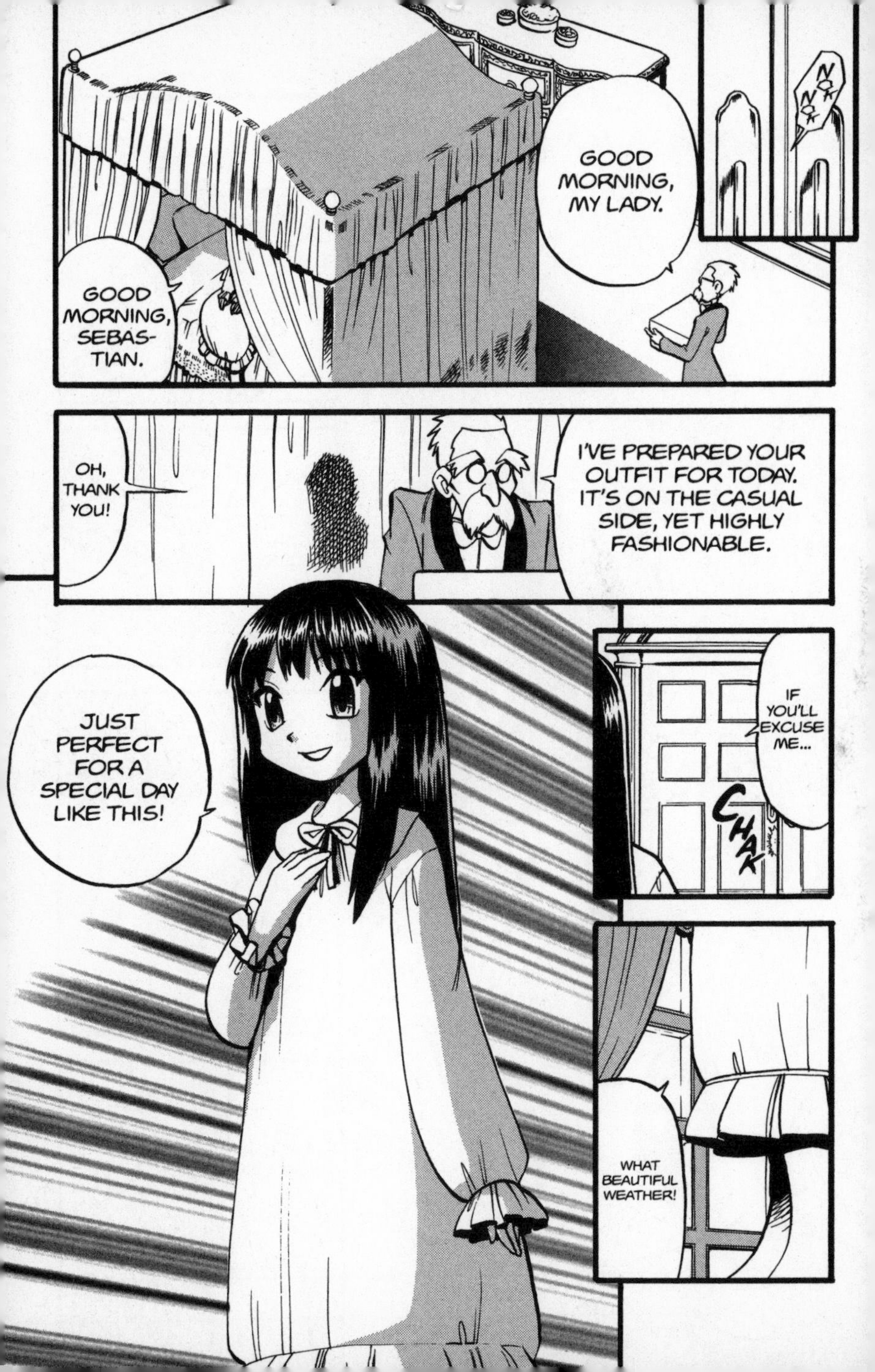
NOK NOK
GOOD MORNING, MY LADY.
GOOD MORNING, SEBAS-TIAN.
I'VE PREPARED YOUR OUTFIT FOR TODAY. IT'S ON THE CASUAL SIDE, YET HIGHLY FASHIONABLE.
OH, THANK YOU!
IF YOU'LL EXCUSE ME...
CHAK
WHAT BEAUTIFUL WEATHER!
JUST PERFECT FOR A SPECIAL DAY LIKE THIS!

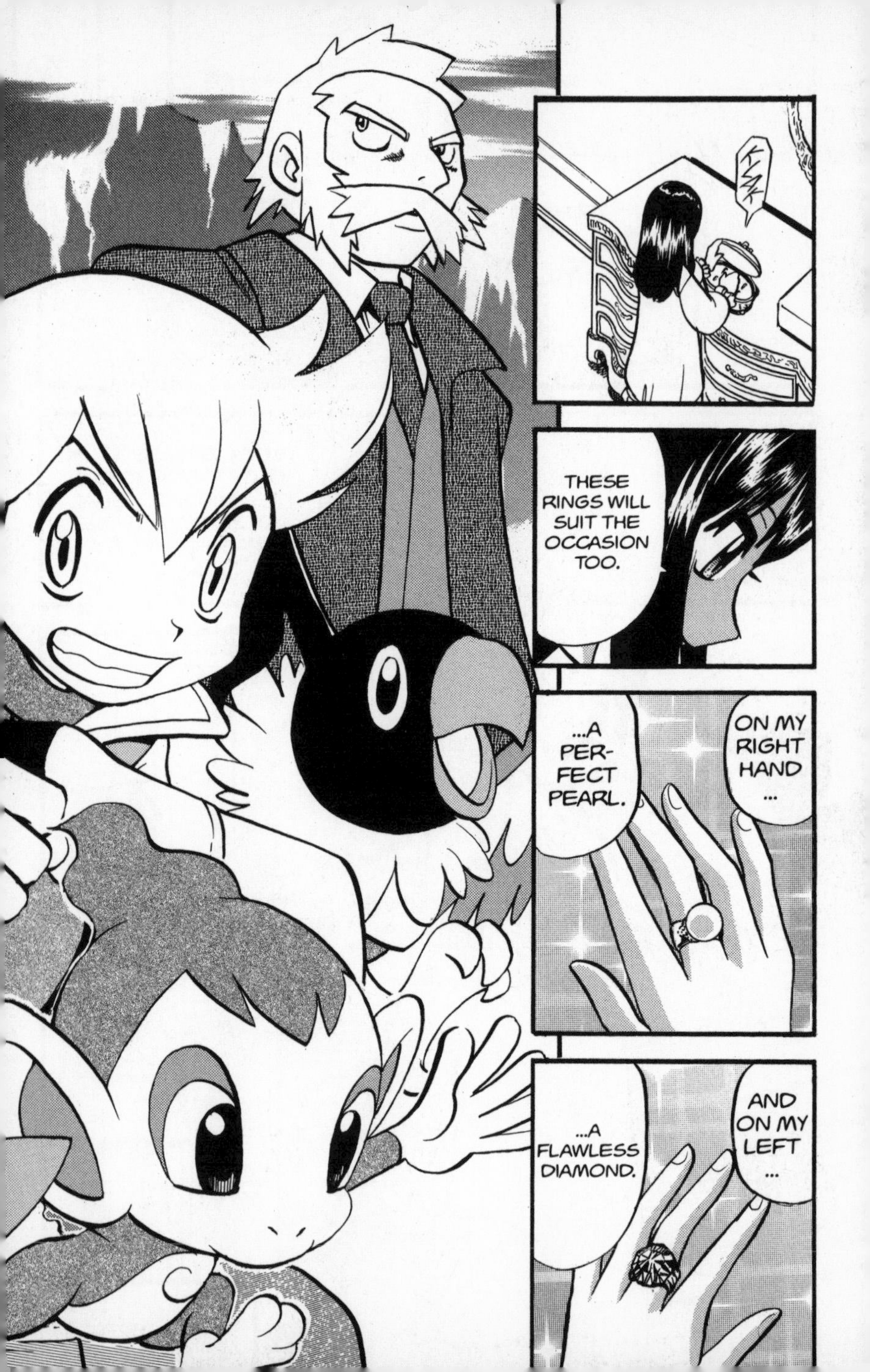
KLAK
THESE RINGS WILL SUIT THE OCCASION TOO.
ON MY RIGHT HAND ...
...A PER-FECT PEARL.
AND ON MY LEFT ...
...A FLAWLESS DIAMOND.

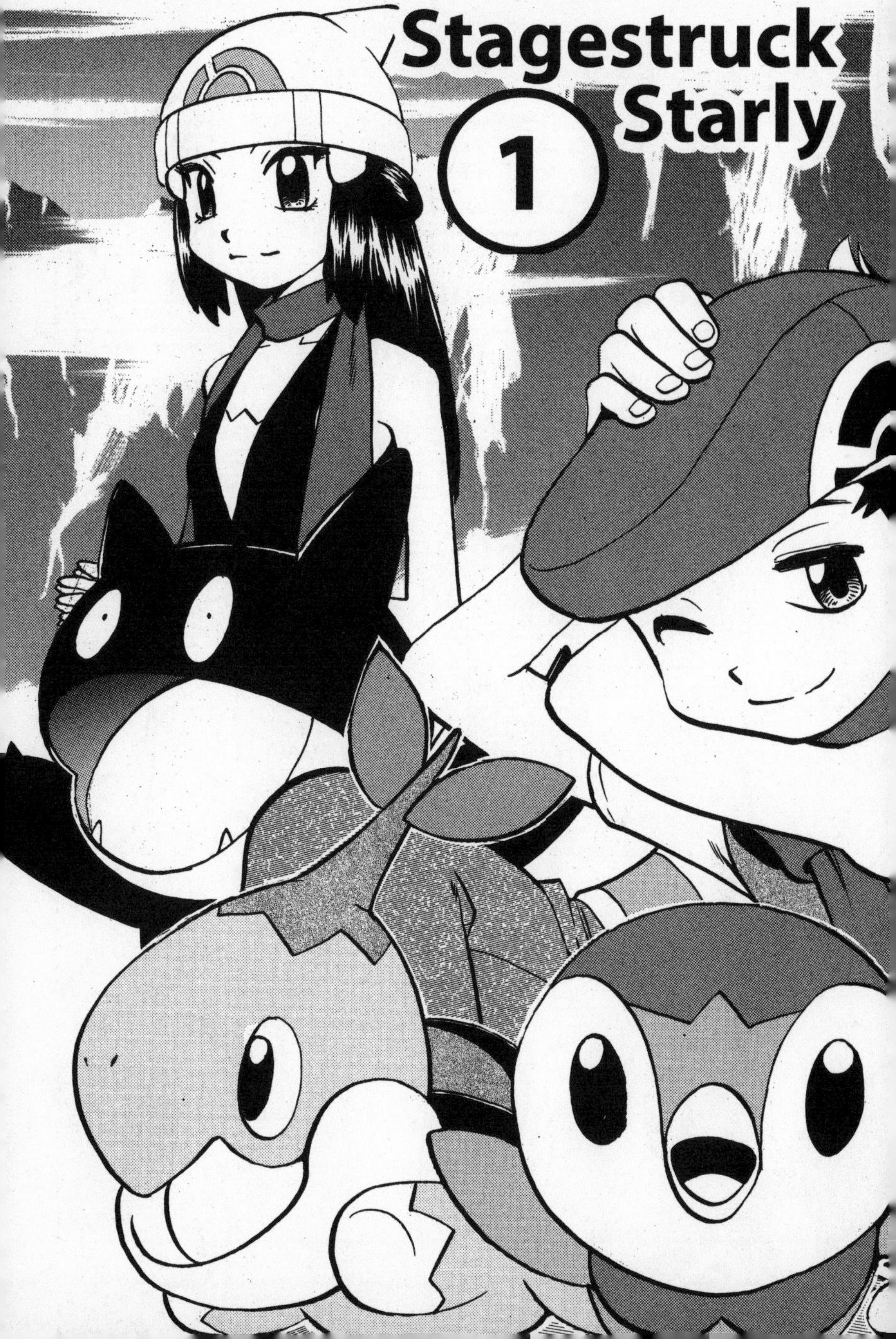
Stagestruck Starly
1

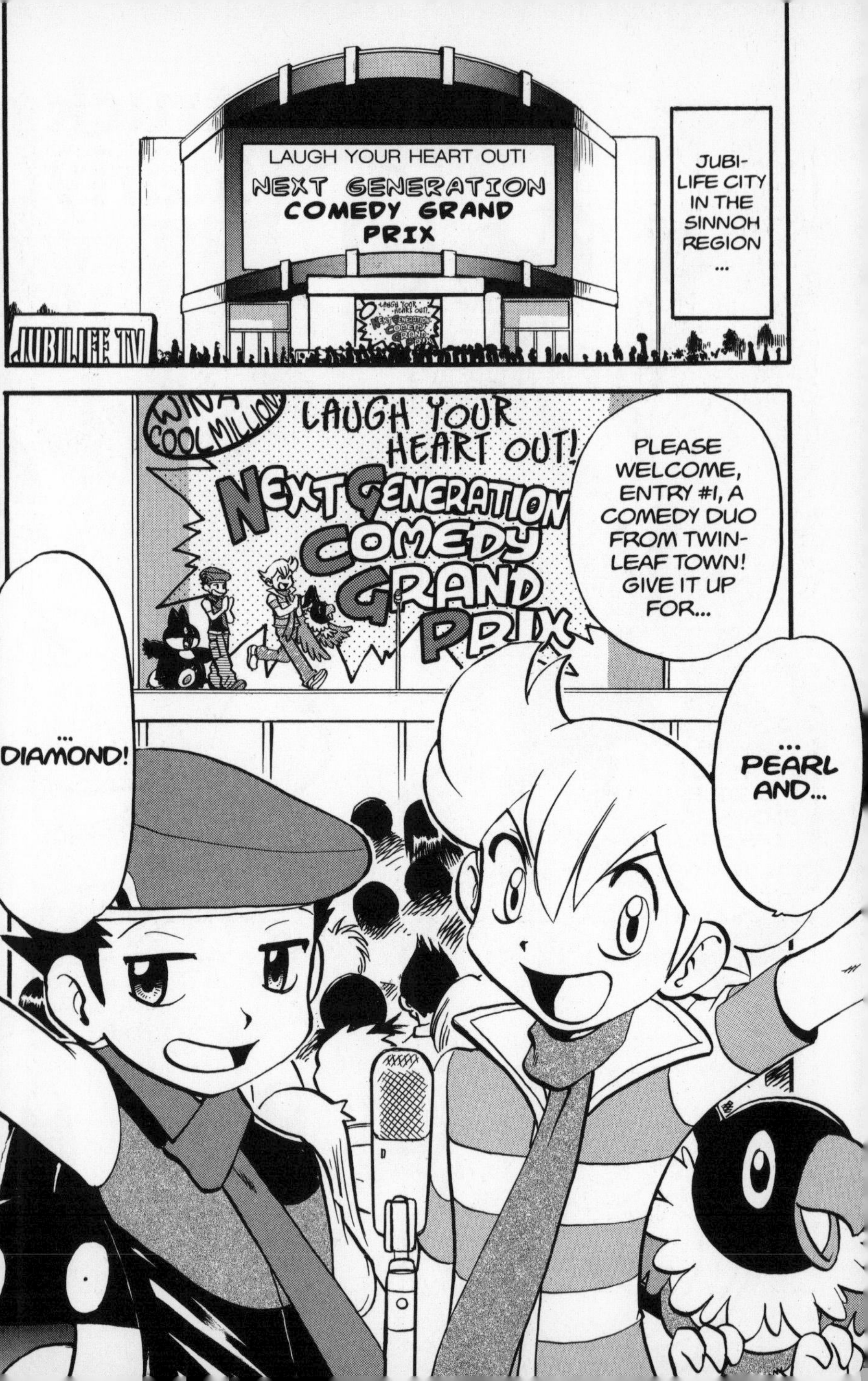
JUBI-LIFE CITY IN THE SINNOH REGION ...
LAUGH YOUR HEART OUT!
NEXT GENERATION COMEDY GRAND PRIX
JUBILIFE TV
WIN A COOL MILLION
LAUGH YOUR HEART OUT!
NEXT GENERATION COMEDY GRAND PRIX
PLEASE WELCOME, ENTRY #1, A COMEDY DUO FROM TWIN-LEAF TOWN! GIVE IT UP FOR...
... PEARL AND...
... DIAMOND!

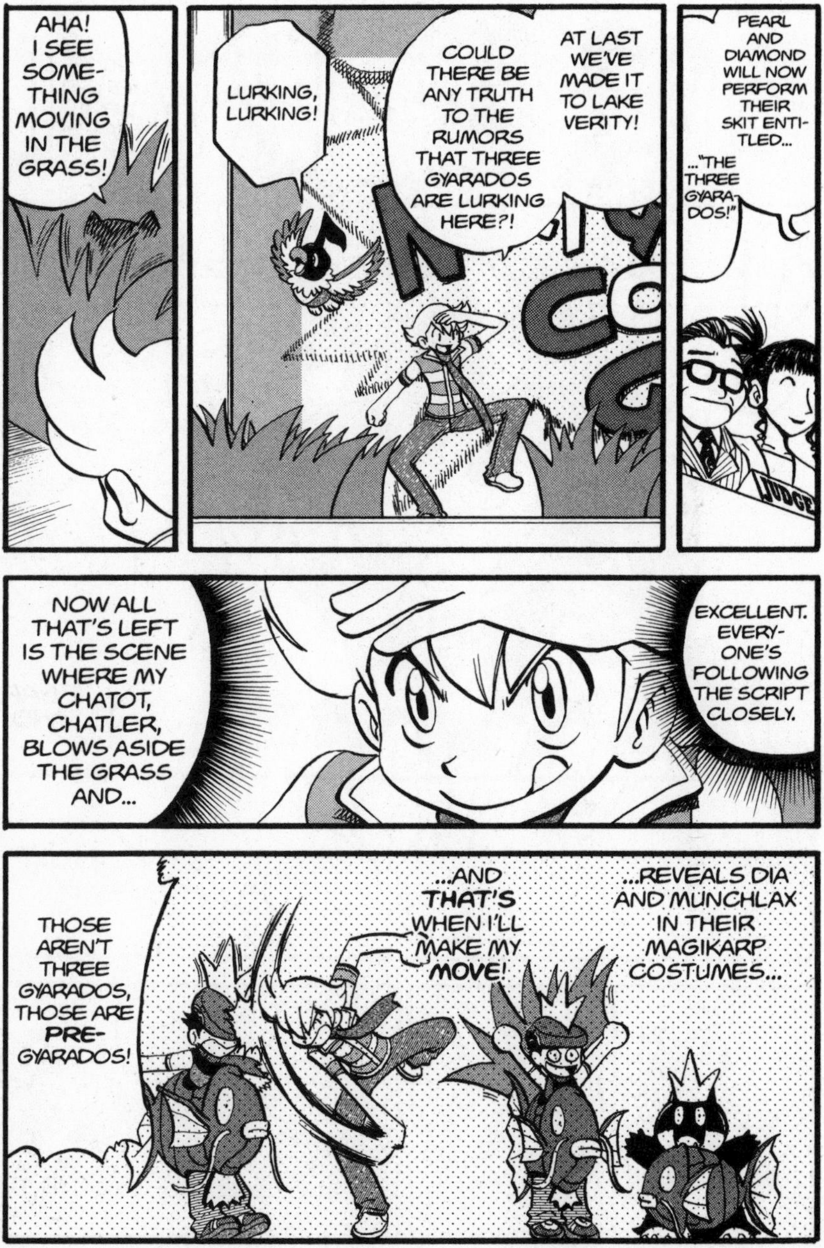
PEARL AND DIAMOND WILL NOW PERFORM THEIR SKIT ENTITLED...
..."THE THREE GYARADOS!"
JUDGE
AT LAST WE'VE MADE IT TO LAKE VERITY!
COULD THERE BE ANY TRUTH TO THE RUMORS THAT THREE GYARADOS ARE LURKING HERE?!
LURKING, LURKING!
AHA! I SEE SOMETHING MOVING IN THE GRASS!
EXCELLENT. EVERYONE'S FOLLOWING THE SCRIPT CLOSELY.
NOW ALL THAT'S LEFT IS THE SCENE WHERE MY CHATOT, CHATLER, BLOWS ASIDE THE GRASS AND...
...REVEALS DIA AND MUNCHLAX IN THEIR MAGIKARP COSTUMES...
...AND THAT'S WHEN I'LL MAKE MY MOVE!
THOSE AREN'T THREE GYARADOS, THOSE ARE PRE-GYARADOS!

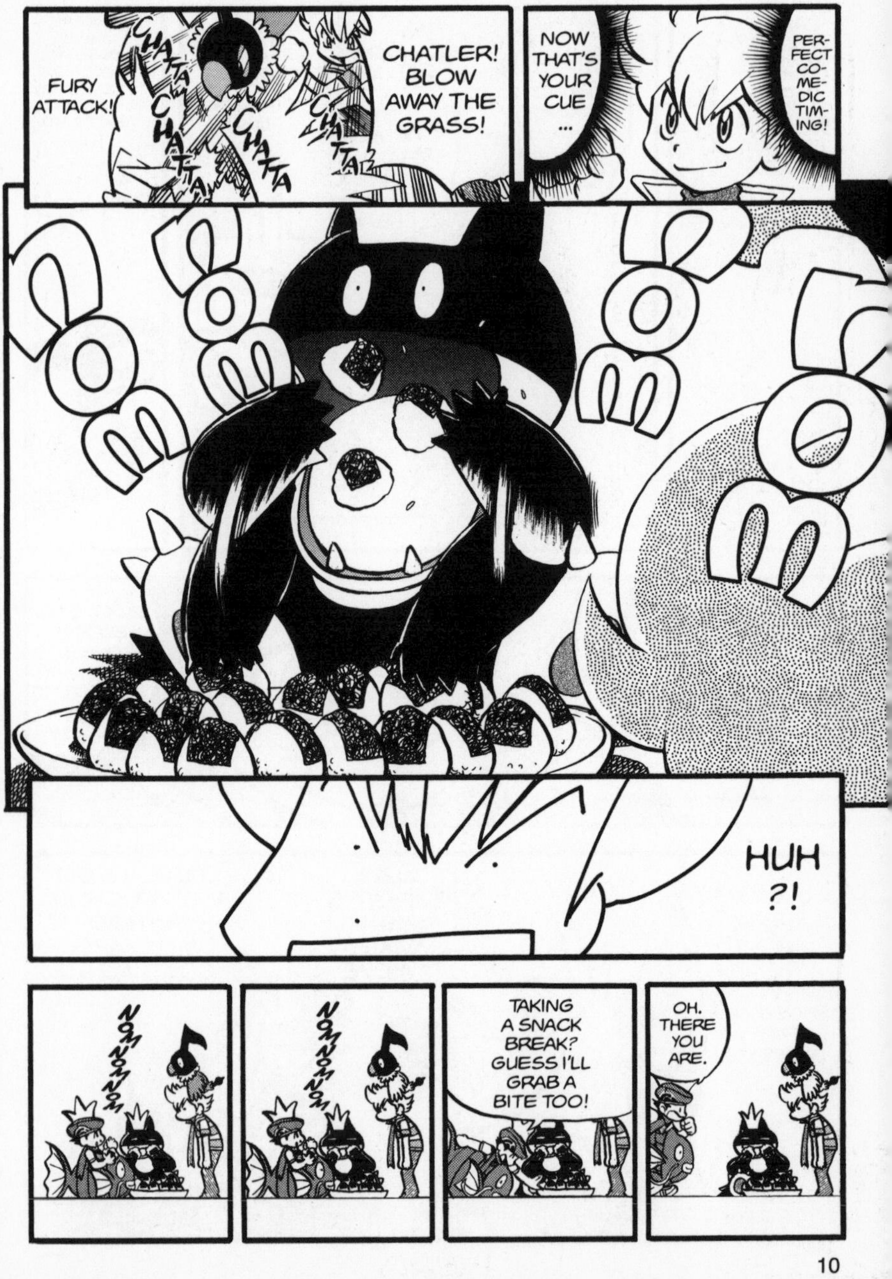
FURY ATTACK!
CHATLER! BLOW AWAY THE GRASS!
NOW THAT'S YOUR CUE ...
PERFECT COMEDIC TIMING!
HUH ?!
NOM NOM NOM
NOM NOM NOM
TAKING A SNACK BREAK? GUESS I'LL GRAB A BITE TOO!
OH. THERE YOU ARE.

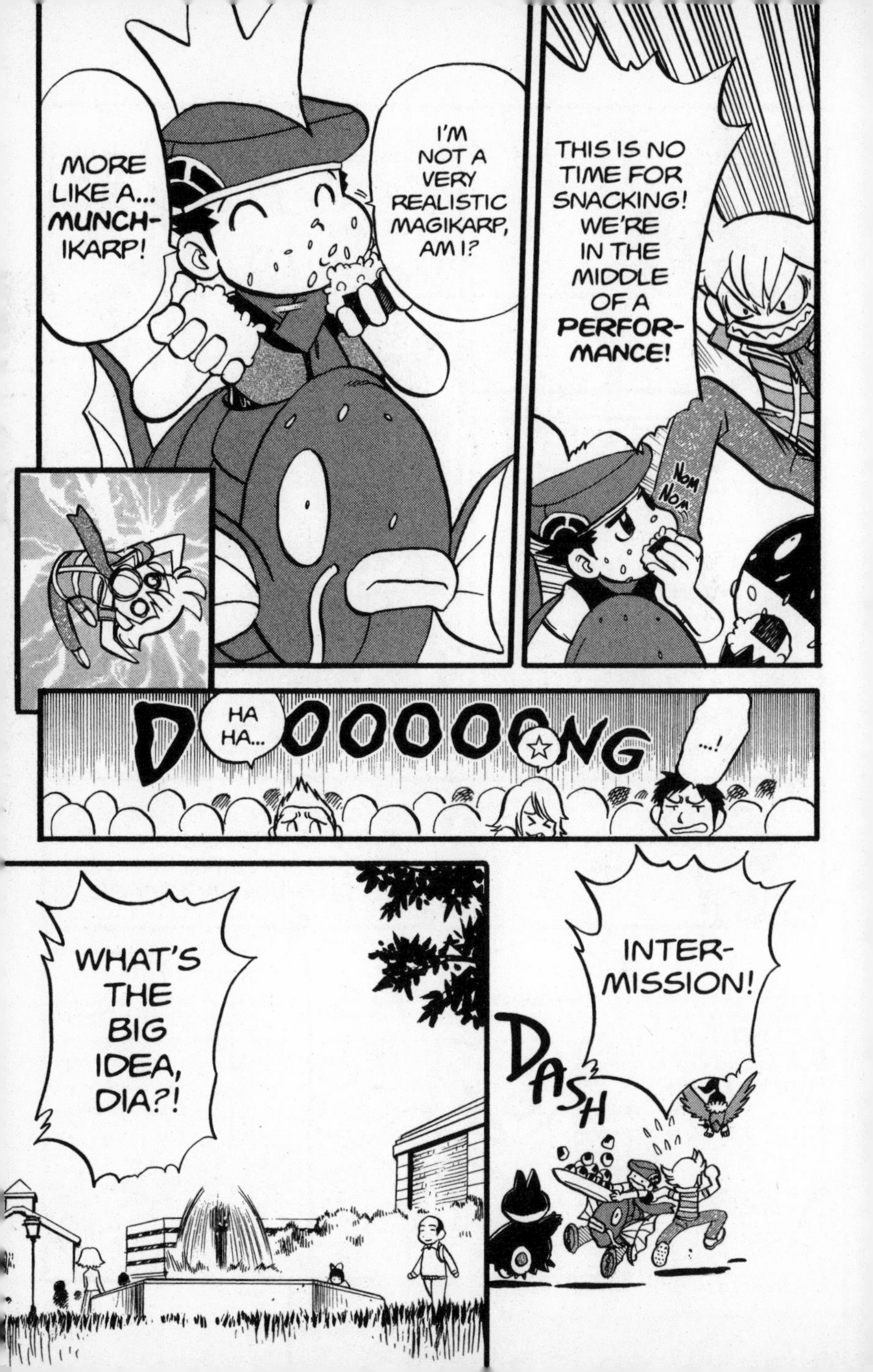
I'M NOT A VERY REALISTIC MAGIKARP, AM I?
MORE LIKE A... MUNCH-IKARP!
THIS IS NO TIME FOR SNACKING! WE'RE IN THE MIDDLE OF A PERFORMANCE!
NOM NOM
DOOOOOONG
HA HA...
...!
INTER-MISSION!
WHAT'S THE BIG IDEA, DIA?!
DASH

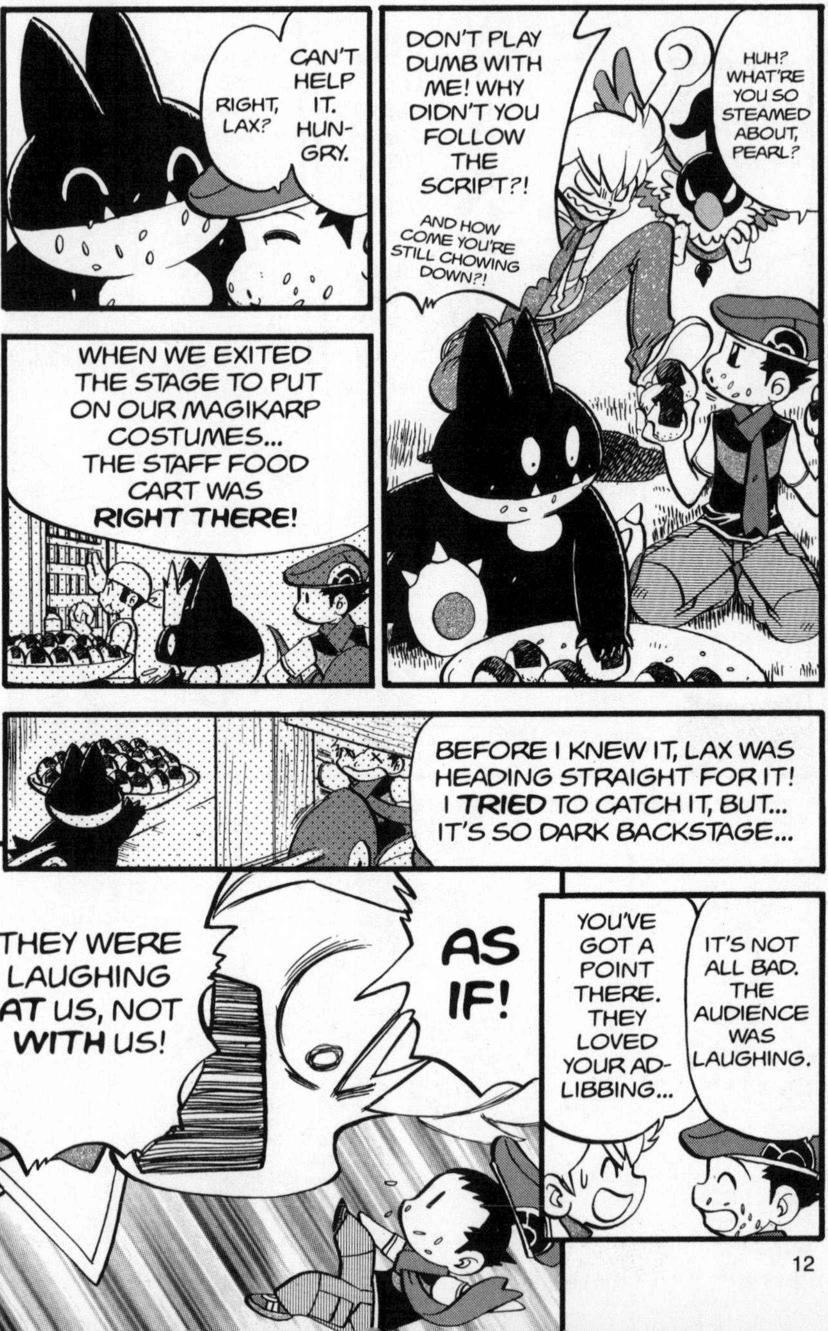
RIGHT, LAX?
CAN'T HELP IT. HUN-GRY.
DON'T PLAY DUMB WITH ME! WHY DIDN'T YOU FOLLOW THE SCRIPT?!
AND HOW COME YOU'RE STILL CHOWING DOWN?!
HUH? WHAT'RE YOU SO STEAMED ABOUT, PEARL?
WHEN WE EXITED THE STAGE TO PUT ON OUR MAGIKARP COSTUMES... THE STAFF FOOD CART WAS RIGHT THERE!
BEFORE I KNEW IT, LAX WAS HEADING STRAIGHT FOR IT! I TRIED TO CATCH IT, BUT... IT'S SO DARK BACKSTAGE...
YOU'VE GOT A POINT THERE. THEY LOVED YOUR AD-LIBBING...
IT'S NOT ALL BAD. THE AUDIENCE WAS LAUGHING.
AS IF!
THEY WERE LAUGHING AT US, NOT WITH US!

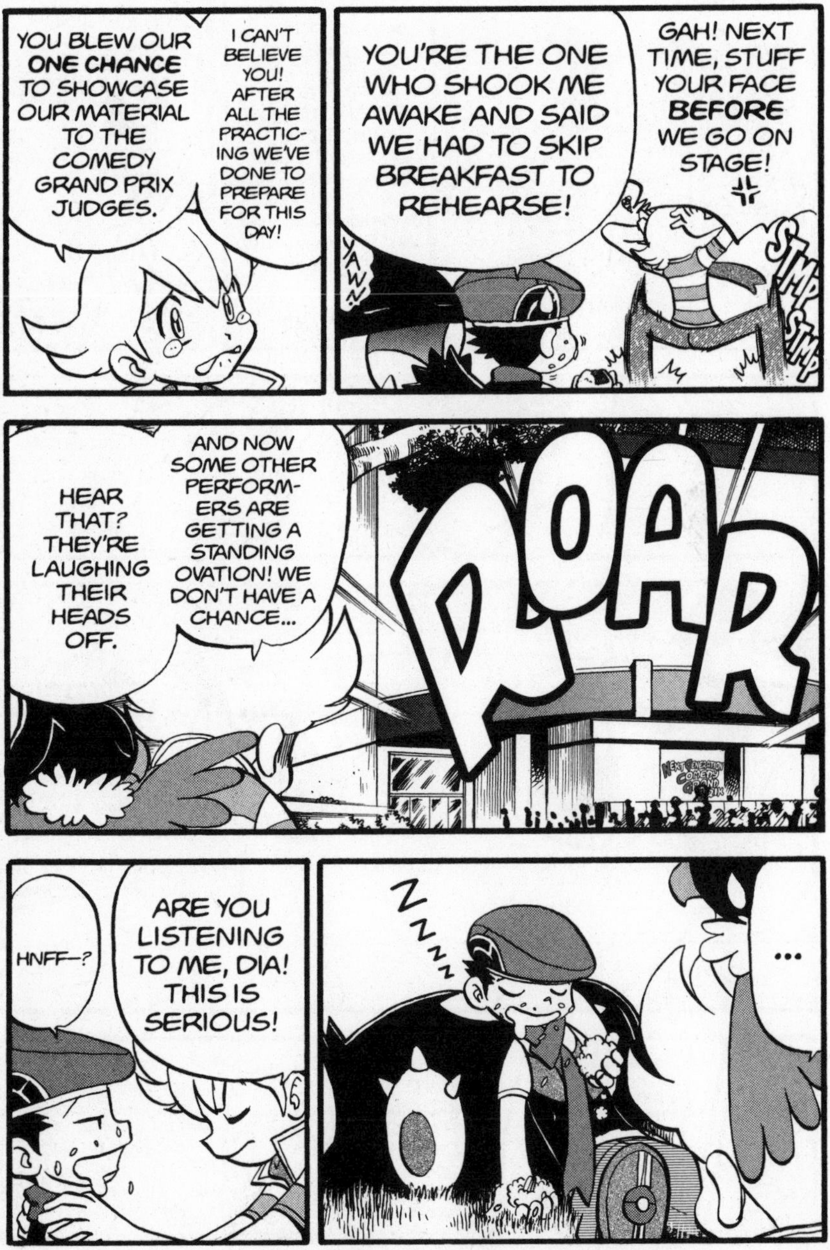
YOU BLEW OUR **ONE CHANCE** TO SHOWCASE OUR MATERIAL TO THE COMEDY GRAND PRIX JUDGES.
I CAN'T BELIEVE YOU! AFTER ALL THE PRACTIC-ING WE'VE DONE TO PREPARE FOR THIS DAY!
YOU'RE THE ONE WHO SHOOK ME AWAKE AND SAID WE HAD TO SKIP BREAKFAST TO REHEARSE!
GAH! NEXT TIME, STUFF YOUR FACE **BEFORE** WE GO ON STAGE!
YAWN
STMP STMP
AND NOW SOME OTHER PERFORM-ERS ARE GETTING A STANDING OVATION! WE DON'T HAVE A CHANCE...
HEAR THAT? THEY'RE LAUGHING THEIR HEADS OFF.
ROAR
NEXT GENERATION COMEDY GRAND PRIX
HNFF—?
ARE YOU LISTENING TO ME, DIA! THIS IS SERIOUS!
ZZZZ
...

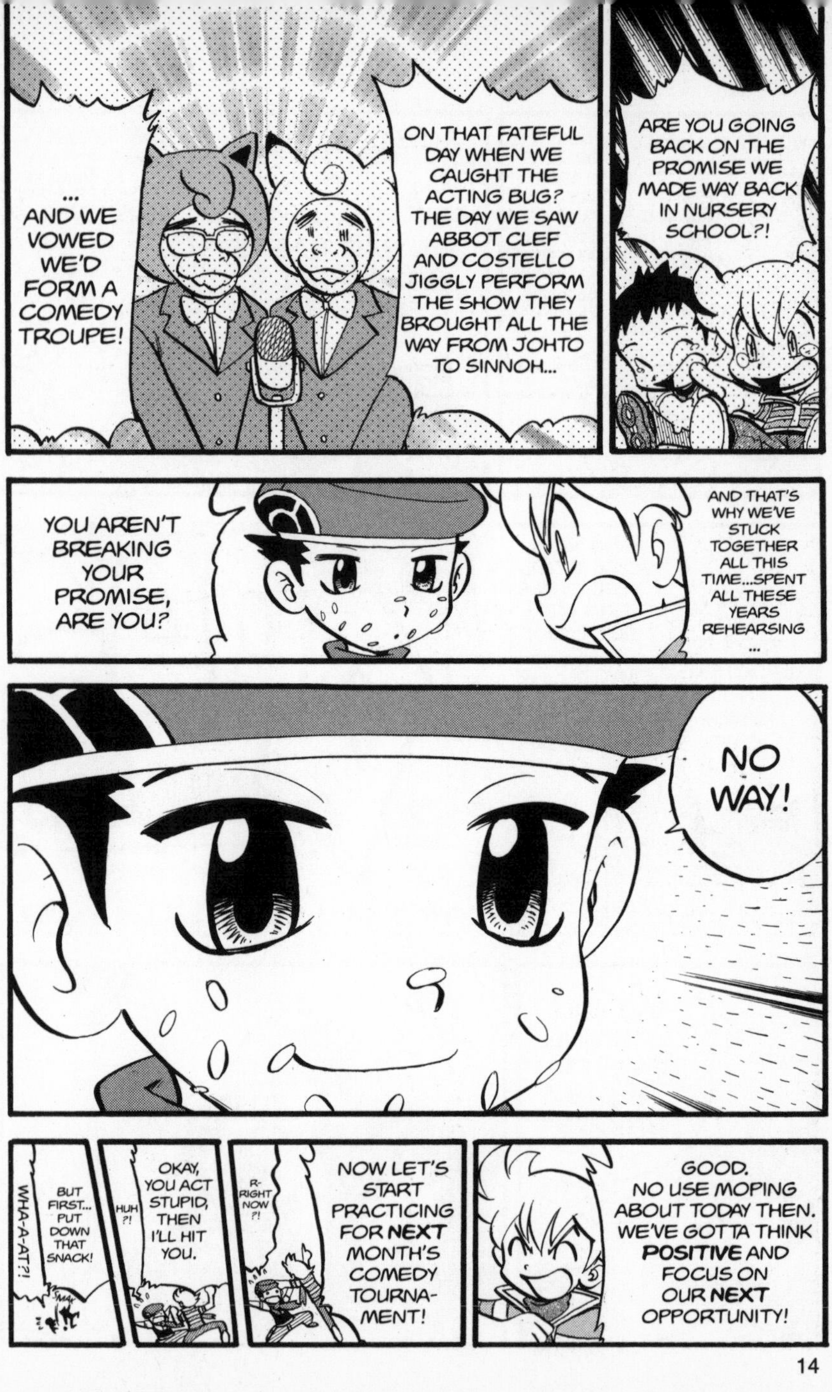
ARE YOU GOING BACK ON THE PROMISE WE MADE WAY BACK IN NURSERY SCHOOL?!
ON THAT FATEFUL DAY WHEN WE CAUGHT THE ACTING BUG? THE DAY WE SAW ABBOT CLEF AND COSTELLO JIGGLY PERFORM THE SHOW THEY BROUGHT ALL THE WAY FROM JOHTO TO SINNOH...
...AND WE VOWED WE'D FORM A COMEDY TROUPE!
AND THAT'S WHY WE'VE STUCK TOGETHER ALL THIS TIME...SPENT ALL THESE YEARS REHEARSING...
YOU AREN'T BREAKING YOUR PROMISE, ARE YOU?
NO WAY!
GOOD. NO USE MOPING ABOUT TODAY THEN. WE'VE GOTTA THINK **POSITIVE** AND FOCUS ON OUR **NEXT** OPPORTUNITY!
NOW LET'S START PRACTICING FOR **NEXT** MONTH'S COMEDY TOURNA-MENT!
R-RIGHT NOW?!
OKAY, YOU ACT STUPID, THEN I'LL HIT YOU.
HUH?!
BUT FIRST... PUT DOWN THAT SNACK!
WHA-A-AT?!

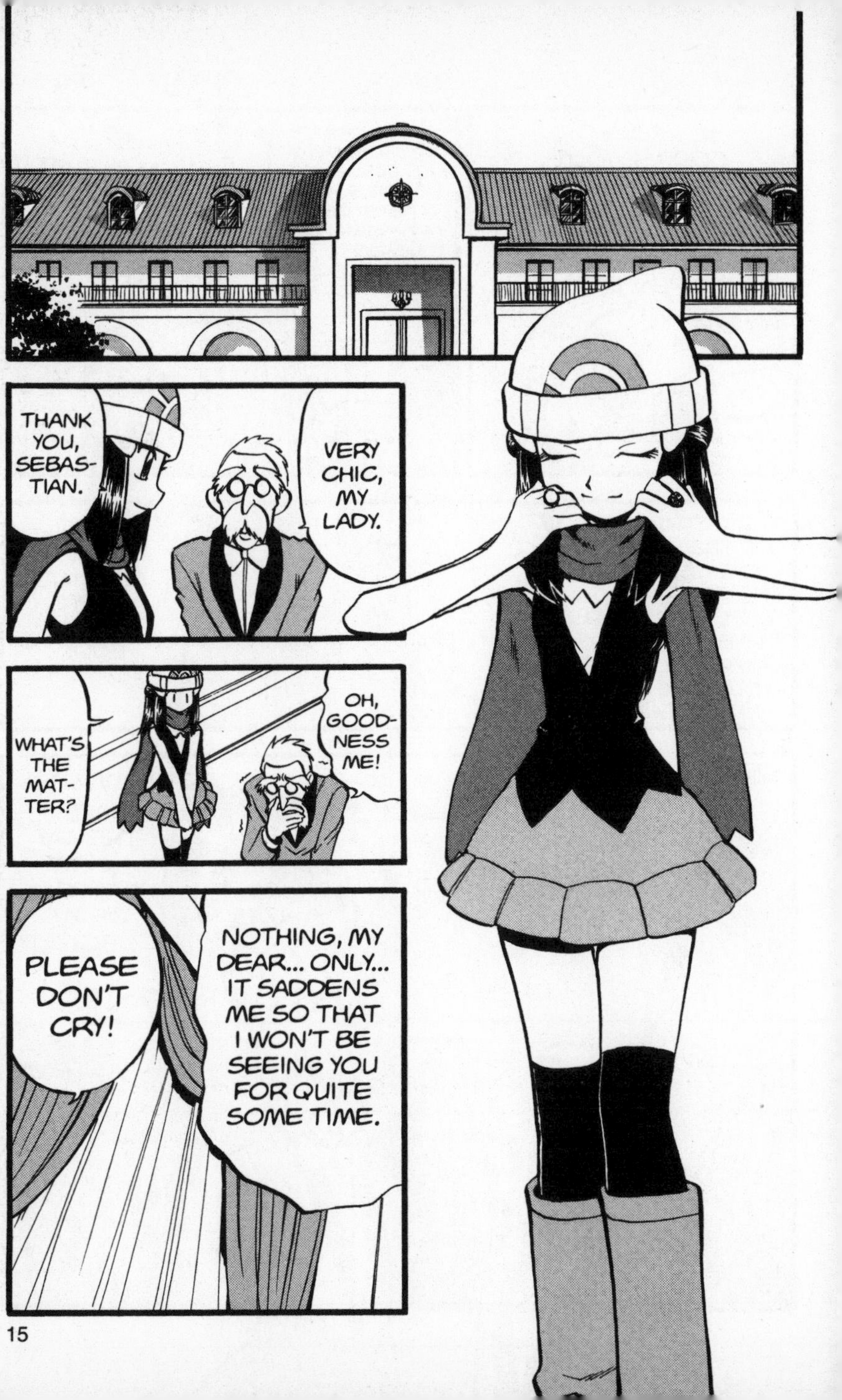
VERY CHIC, MY LADY.
THANK YOU, SEBASTIAN.
OH, GOODNESS ME!
WHAT'S THE MATTER?
NOTHING, MY DEAR... ONLY... IT SADDENS ME SO THAT I WON'T BE SEEING YOU FOR QUITE SOME TIME.
PLEASE DON'T CRY!

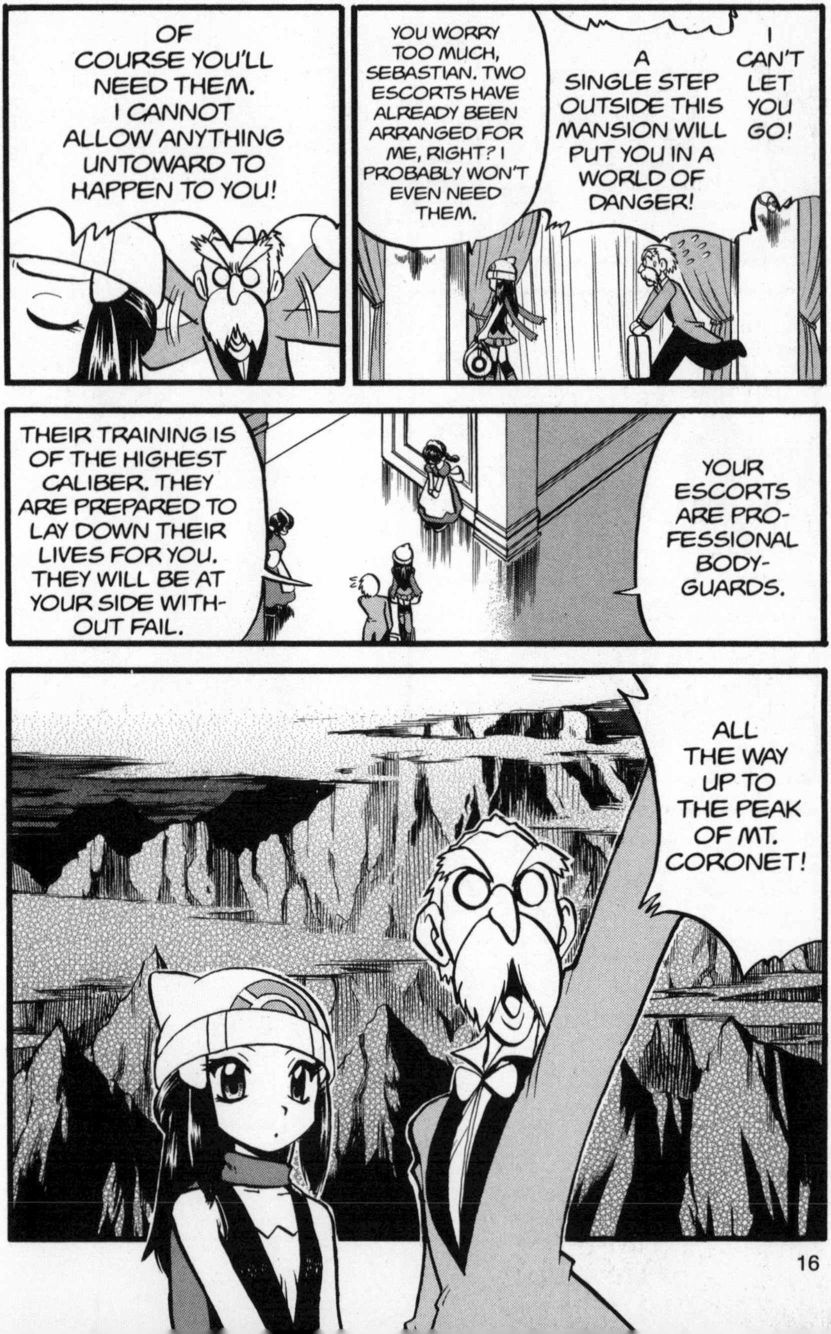
I CAN'T LET YOU GO!
A SINGLE STEP OUTSIDE THIS MANSION WILL PUT YOU IN A WORLD OF DANGER!
YOU WORRY TOO MUCH, SEBASTIAN. TWO ESCORTS HAVE ALREADY BEEN ARRANGED FOR ME, RIGHT? I PROBABLY WON'T EVEN NEED THEM.
OF COURSE YOU'LL NEED THEM. I CANNOT ALLOW ANYTHING UNTOWARD TO HAPPEN TO YOU!
YOUR ESCORTS ARE PRO-FESSIONAL BODY-GUARDS.
THEIR TRAINING IS OF THE HIGHEST CALIBER. THEY ARE PREPARED TO LAY DOWN THEIR LIVES FOR YOU. THEY WILL BE AT YOUR SIDE WITH-OUT FAIL.
ALL THE WAY UP TO THE PEAK OF MT. CORONET!

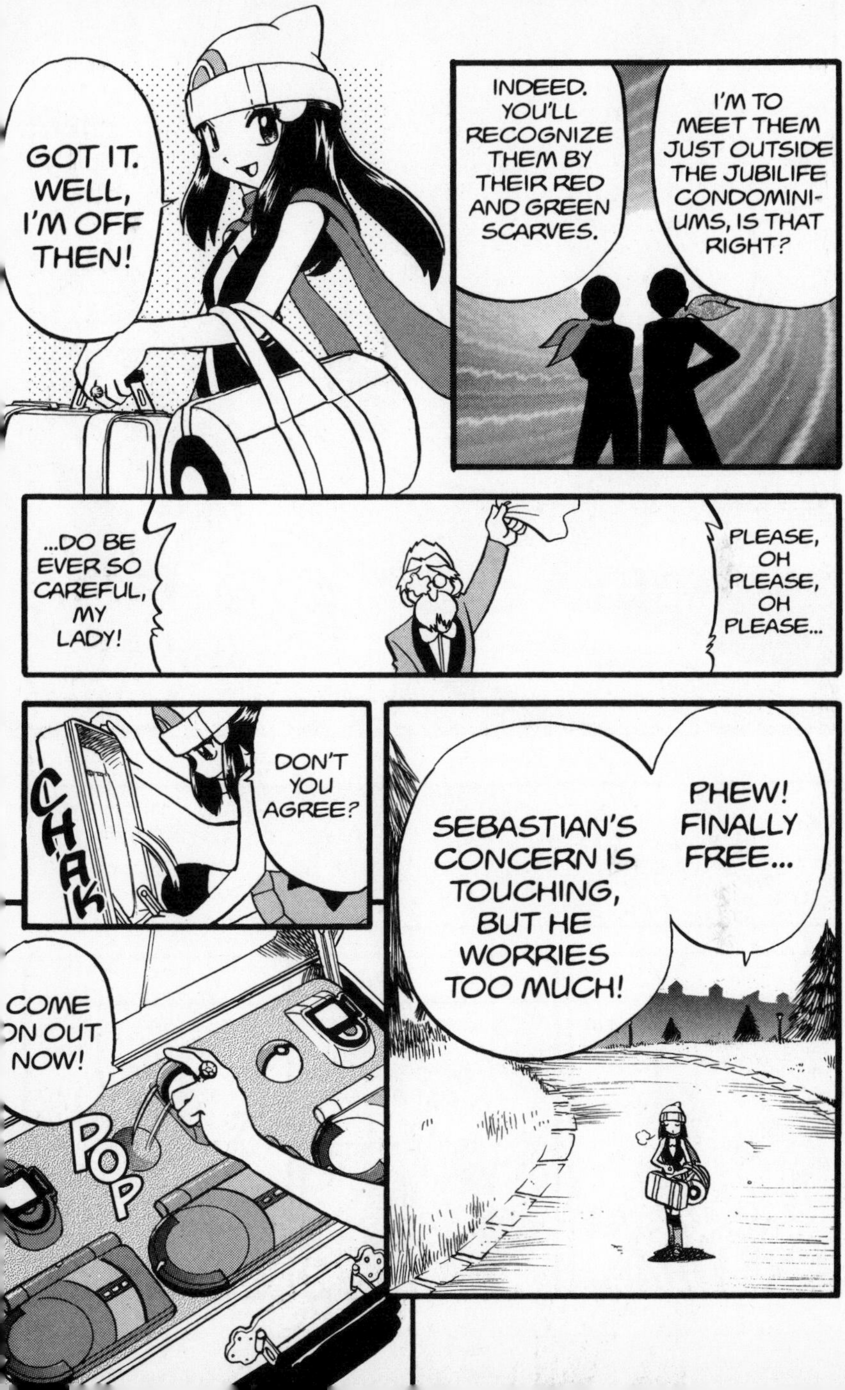
I'M TO MEET THEM JUST OUTSIDE THE JUBILIFE CONDOMINI-UMS, IS THAT RIGHT?
INDEED. YOU'LL RECOGNIZE THEM BY THEIR RED AND GREEN SCARVES.
GOT IT. WELL, I'M OFF THEN!
PLEASE, OH PLEASE, OH PLEASE...
...DO BE EVER SO CAREFUL, MY LADY!
PHEW! FINALLY FREE...
SEBASTIAN'S CONCERN IS TOUCHING, BUT HE WORRIES TOO MUCH!
DON'T YOU AGREE?
CHAK
COME ON OUT NOW!
POP

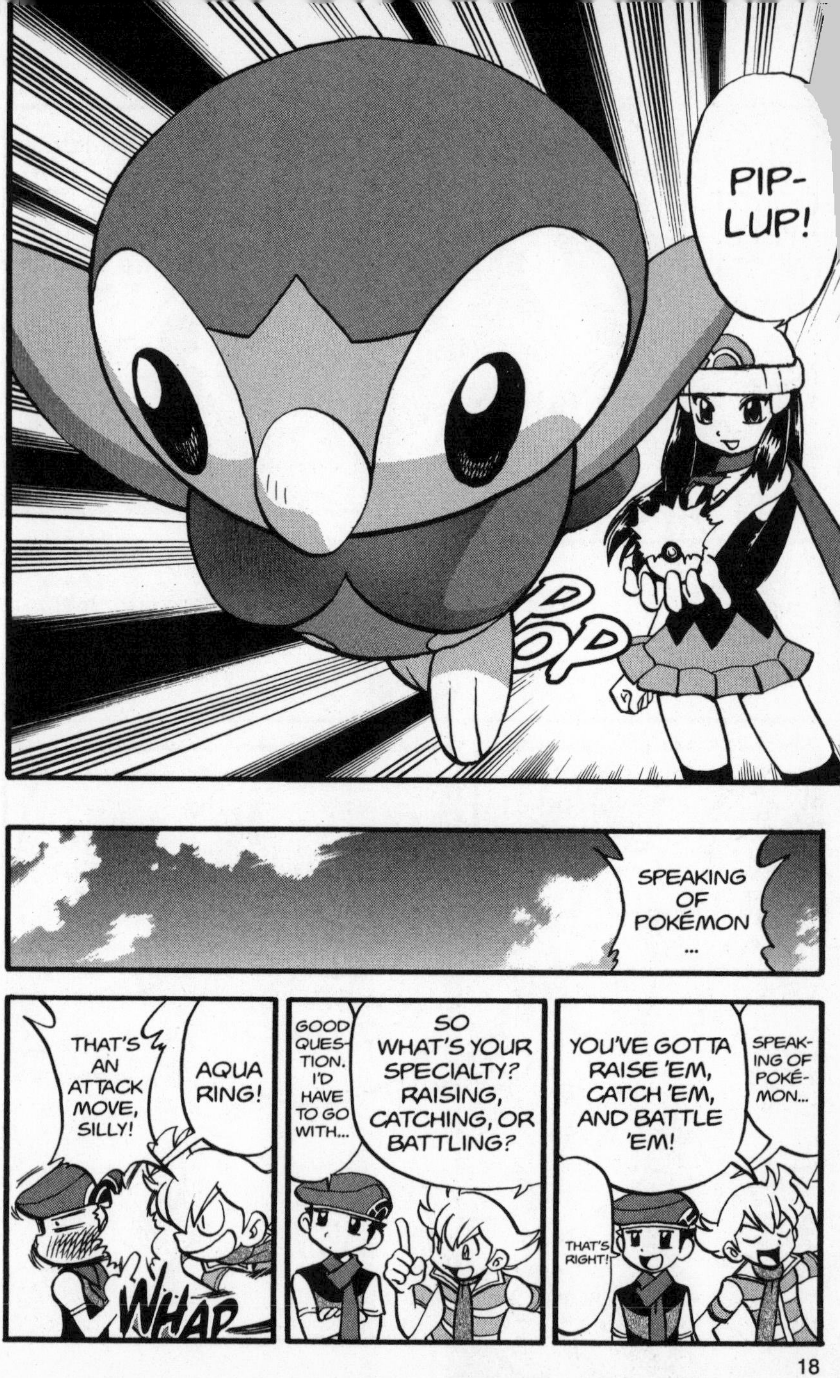
PIP-LUP!
POP
SPEAKING OF POKÉMON ...
SPEAK-ING OF POKÉ-MON...
YOU'VE GOTTA RAISE 'EM, CATCH 'EM, AND BATTLE 'EM!
THAT'S RIGHT!
SO WHAT'S YOUR SPECIALTY? RAISING, CATCHING, OR BATTLING?
GOOD QUES-TION. I'D HAVE TO GO WITH...
AQUA RING!
THAT'S AN ATTACK MOVE, SILLY!
WHAP

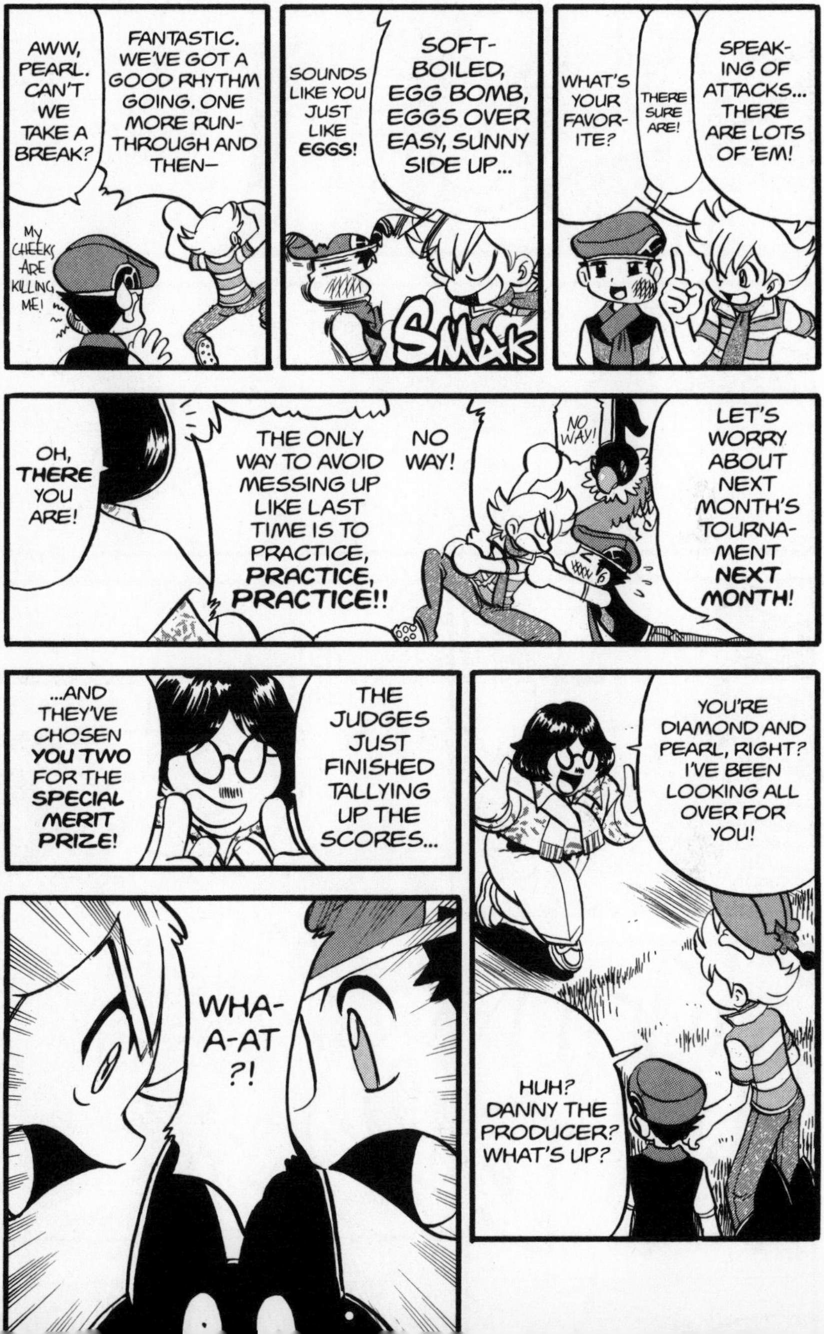

FANTASTIC. WE'VE GOT A GOOD RHYTHM GOING. ONE MORE RUN-THROUGH AND THEN—
AWW, PEARL. CAN'T WE TAKE A BREAK?
MY CHEEKS ARE KILLING ME!
SOFT-BOILED, EGG BOMB, EGGS OVER EASY, SUNNY SIDE UP...
SOUNDS LIKE YOU JUST LIKE EGGS!
SMAK
SPEAKING OF ATTACKS... THERE ARE LOTS OF 'EM!
THERE SURE ARE!
WHAT'S YOUR FAVORITE?
LET'S WORRY ABOUT NEXT MONTH'S TOURNAMENT NEXT MONTH!
NO WAY!
NO WAY!
THE ONLY WAY TO AVOID MESSING UP LIKE LAST TIME IS TO PRACTICE, PRACTICE, PRACTICE!!
OH, THERE YOU ARE!
HUH? DANNY THE PRODUCER? WHAT'S UP?
YOU'RE DIAMOND AND PEARL, RIGHT? I'VE BEEN LOOKING ALL OVER FOR YOU!
THE JUDGES JUST FINISHED TALLYING UP THE SCORES...
...AND THEY'VE CHOSEN YOU TWO FOR THE SPECIAL MERIT PRIZE!
WHA-A-AT?!

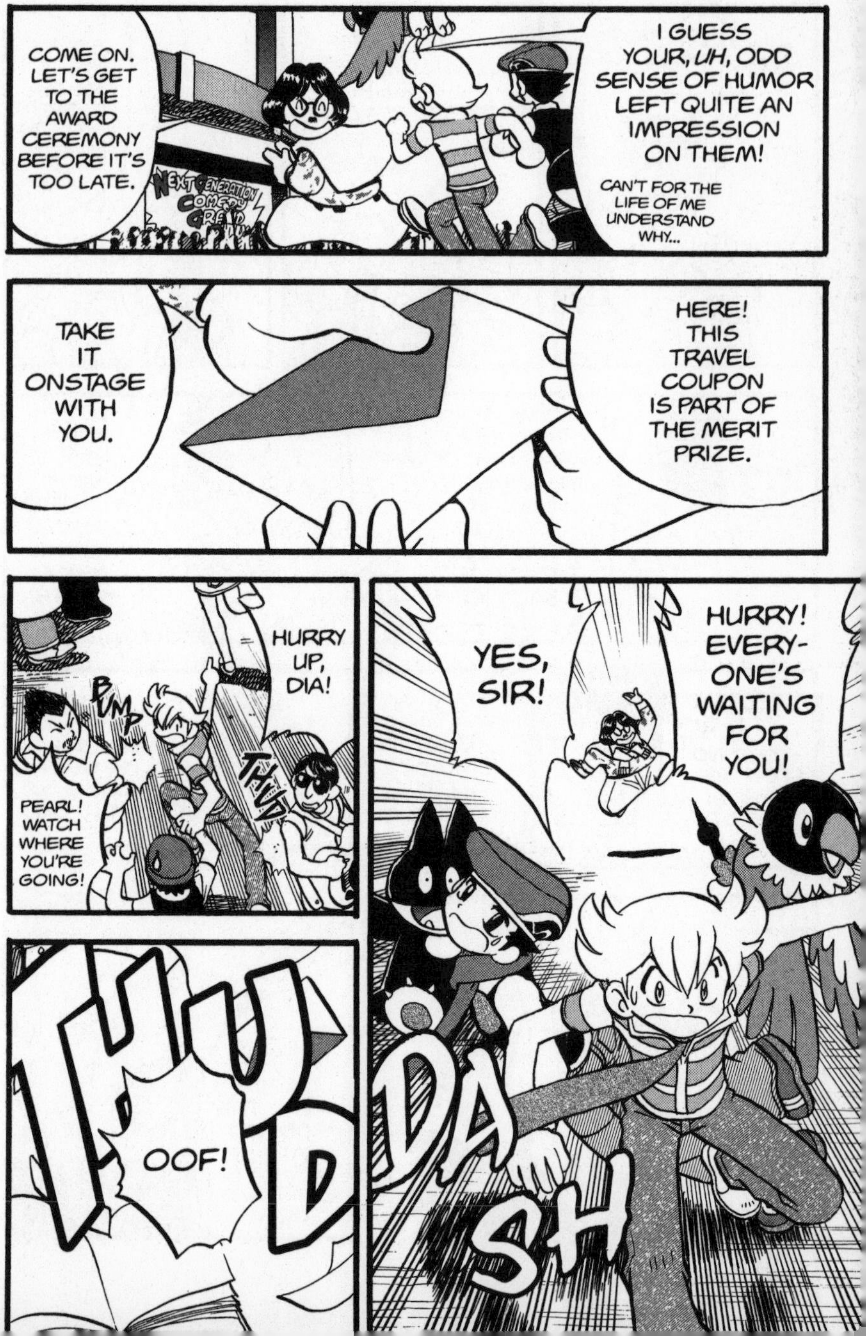
I GUESS YOUR, UH, ODD SENSE OF HUMOR LEFT QUITE AN IMPRESSION ON THEM!
CAN'T FOR THE LIFE OF ME UNDERSTAND WHY...
COME ON. LET'S GET TO THE AWARD CEREMONY BEFORE IT'S TOO LATE.
NEXT GENERATION COMEDY GRAND
HERE! THIS TRAVEL COUPON IS PART OF THE MERIT PRIZE.
TAKE IT ONSTAGE WITH YOU.
HURRY! EVERY-ONE'S WAITING FOR YOU!
YES, SIR!
DASH
HURRY UP, DIA!
BUMP
THUD
PEARL! WATCH WHERE YOU'RE GOING!
THUD
OOF!

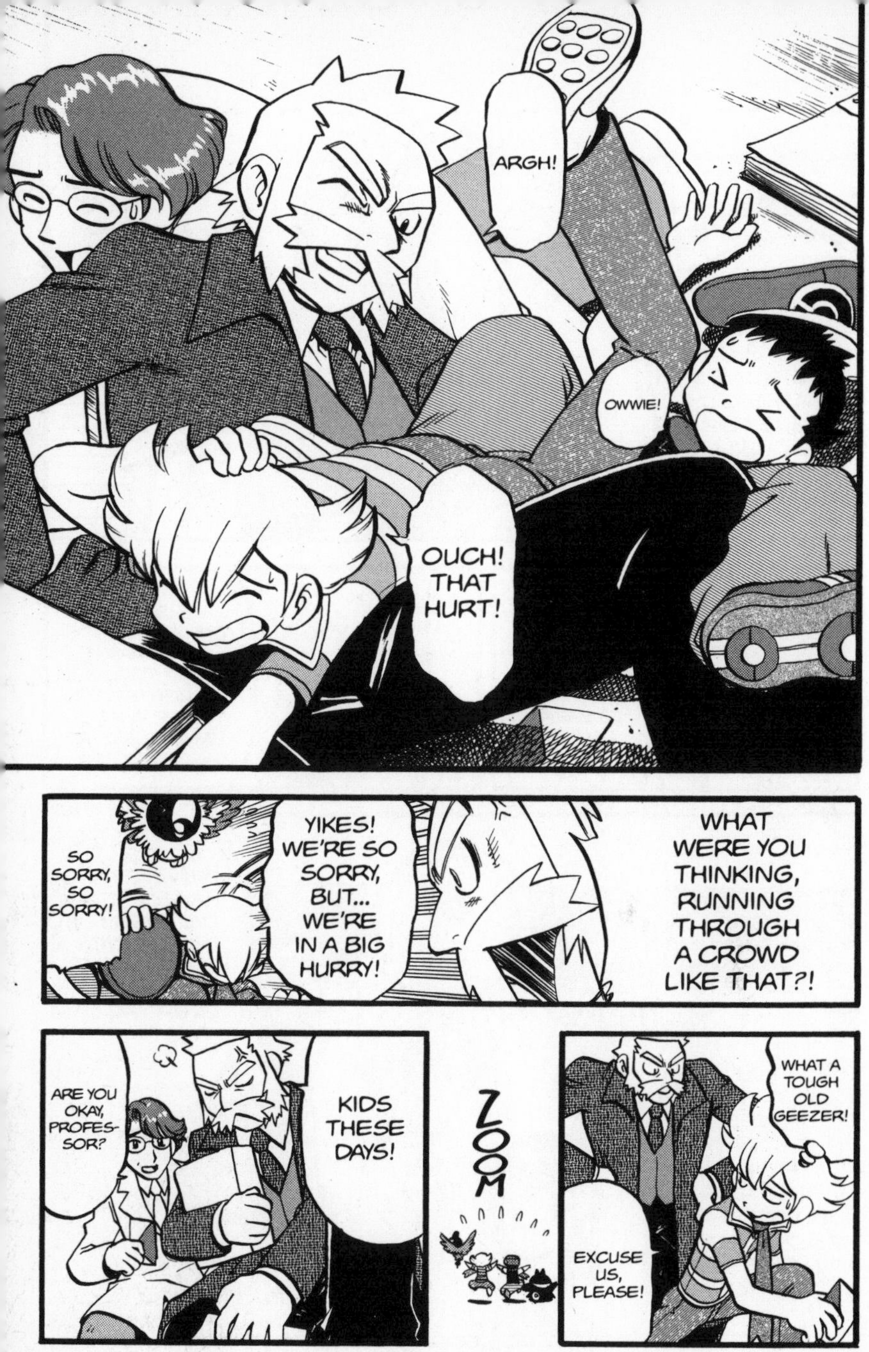
ARGH!
OWWIE!
OUCH! THAT HURT!
WHAT WERE YOU THINKING, RUNNING THROUGH A CROWD LIKE THAT?!
YIKES! WE'RE SO SORRY, BUT... WE'RE IN A BIG HURRY!
SO SORRY, SO SORRY!
WHAT A TOUGH OLD GEEZER!
EXCUSE US, PLEASE!
ZOOM
KIDS THESE DAYS!
ARE YOU OKAY, PROFES-SOR?

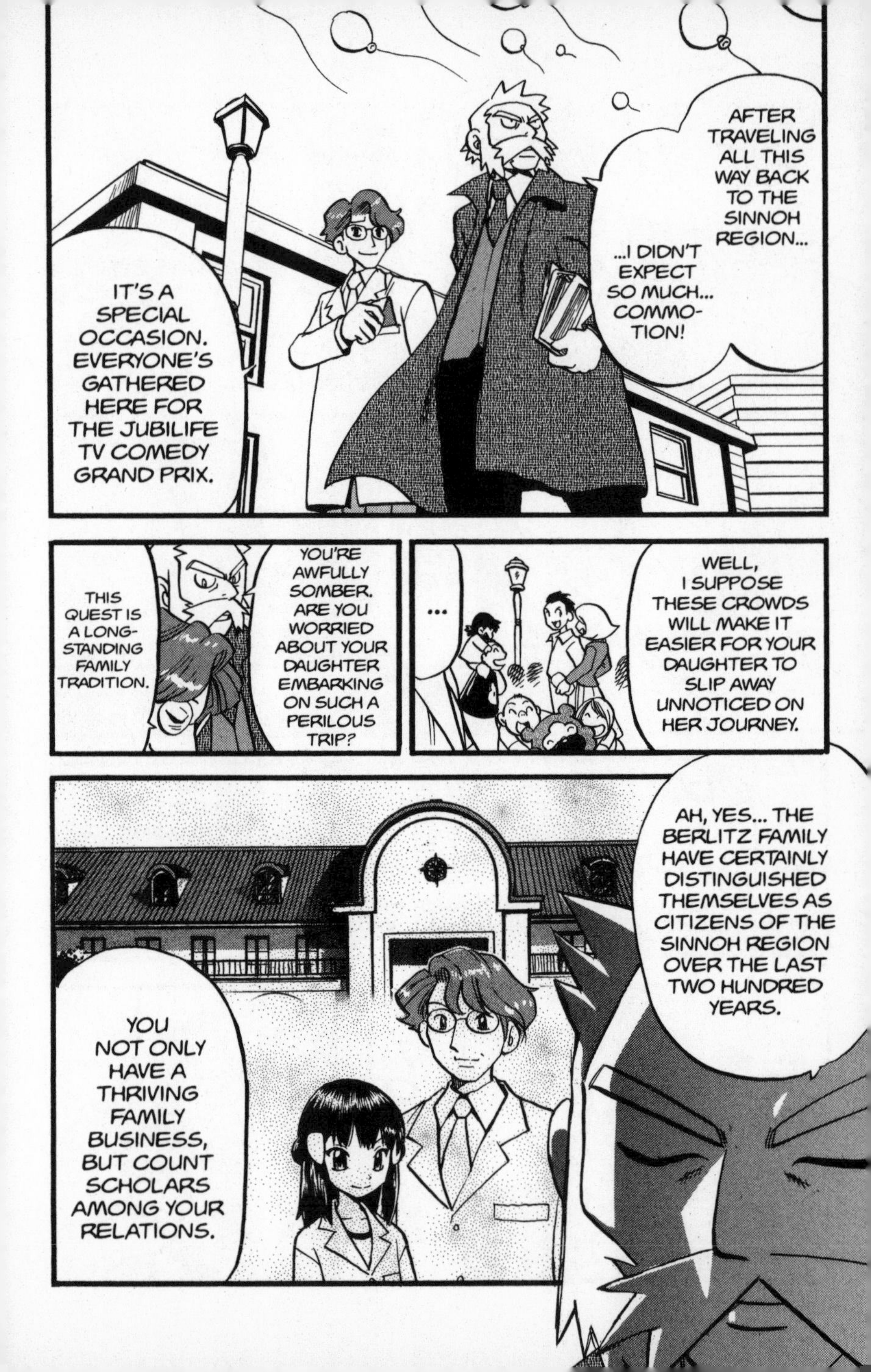
AFTER TRAVELING ALL THIS WAY BACK TO THE SINNOH REGION...
...I DIDN'T EXPECT SO MUCH... COMMO-TION!
IT'S A SPECIAL OCCASION. EVERYONE'S GATHERED HERE FOR THE JUBILIFE TV COMEDY GRAND PRIX.
WELL, I SUPPOSE THESE CROWDS WILL MAKE IT EASIER FOR YOUR DAUGHTER TO SLIP AWAY UNNOTICED ON HER JOURNEY.
...
YOU'RE AWFULLY SOMBER. ARE YOU WORRIED ABOUT YOUR DAUGHTER EMBARKING ON SUCH A PERILOUS TRIP?
THIS QUEST IS A LONG-STANDING FAMILY TRADITION.
AH, YES... THE BERLITZ FAMILY HAVE CERTAINLY DISTINGUISHED THEMSELVES AS CITIZENS OF THE SINNOH REGION OVER THE LAST TWO HUNDRED YEARS.
YOU NOT ONLY HAVE A THRIVING FAMILY BUSINESS, BUT COUNT SCHOLARS AMONG YOUR RELATIONS.

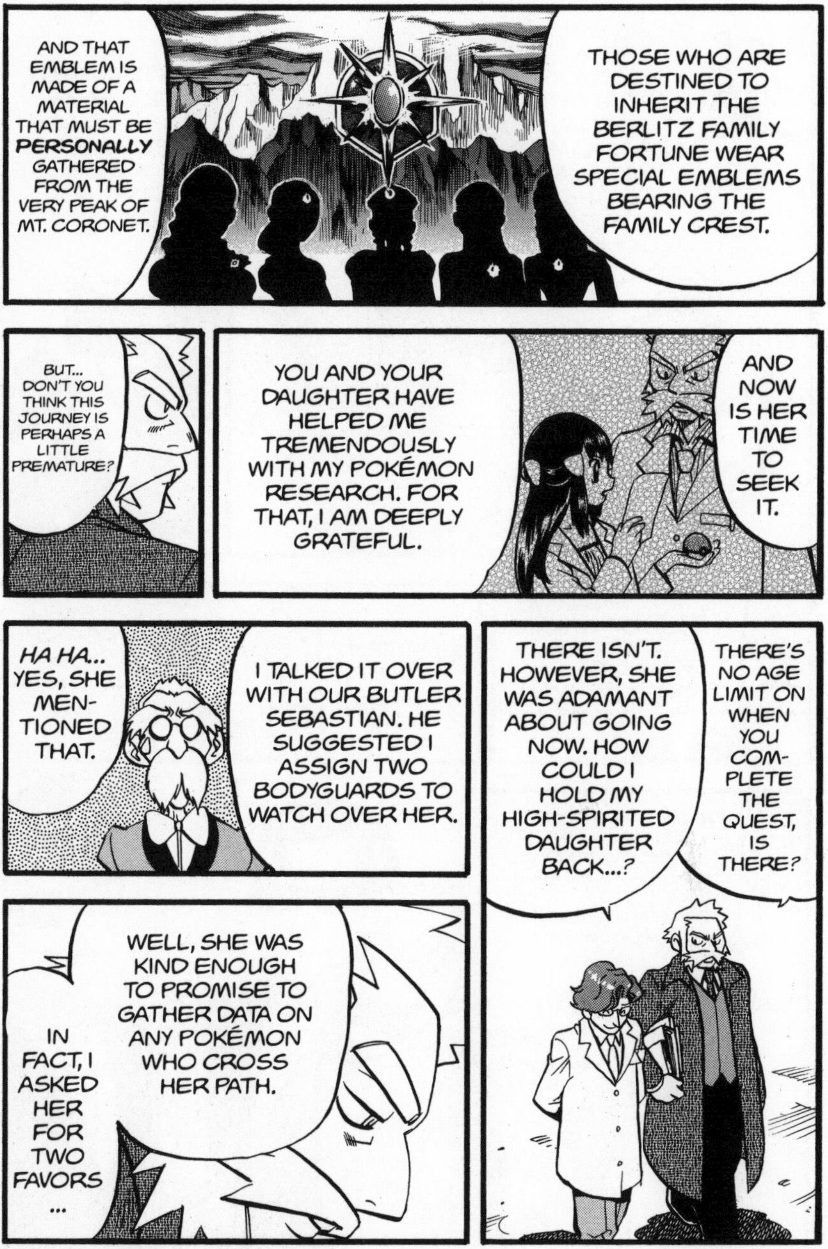
THOSE WHO ARE DESTINED TO INHERIT THE BERLITZ FAMILY FORTUNE WEAR SPECIAL EMBLEMS BEARING THE FAMILY CREST.
AND THAT EMBLEM IS MADE OF A MATERIAL THAT MUST BE **PERSONALLY** GATHERED FROM THE VERY PEAK OF MT. CORONET.
AND NOW IS HER TIME TO SEEK IT.
YOU AND YOUR DAUGHTER HAVE HELPED ME TREMENDOUSLY WITH MY POKÉMON RESEARCH. FOR THAT, I AM DEEPLY GRATEFUL.
BUT... DON'T YOU THINK THIS JOURNEY IS PERHAPS A LITTLE PREMATURE?
THERE'S NO AGE LIMIT ON WHEN YOU COMPLETE THE QUEST, IS THERE?
THERE ISN'T. HOWEVER, SHE WAS ADAMANT ABOUT GOING NOW. HOW COULD I HOLD MY HIGH-SPIRITED DAUGHTER BACK...?
I TALKED IT OVER WITH OUR BUTLER SEBASTIAN. HE SUGGESTED I ASSIGN TWO BODYGUARDS TO WATCH OVER HER.
HA HA... YES, SHE MENTIONED THAT.
WELL, SHE WAS KIND ENOUGH TO PROMISE TO GATHER DATA ON ANY POKÉMON WHO CROSS HER PATH.
IN FACT, I ASKED HER FOR TWO FAVORS...

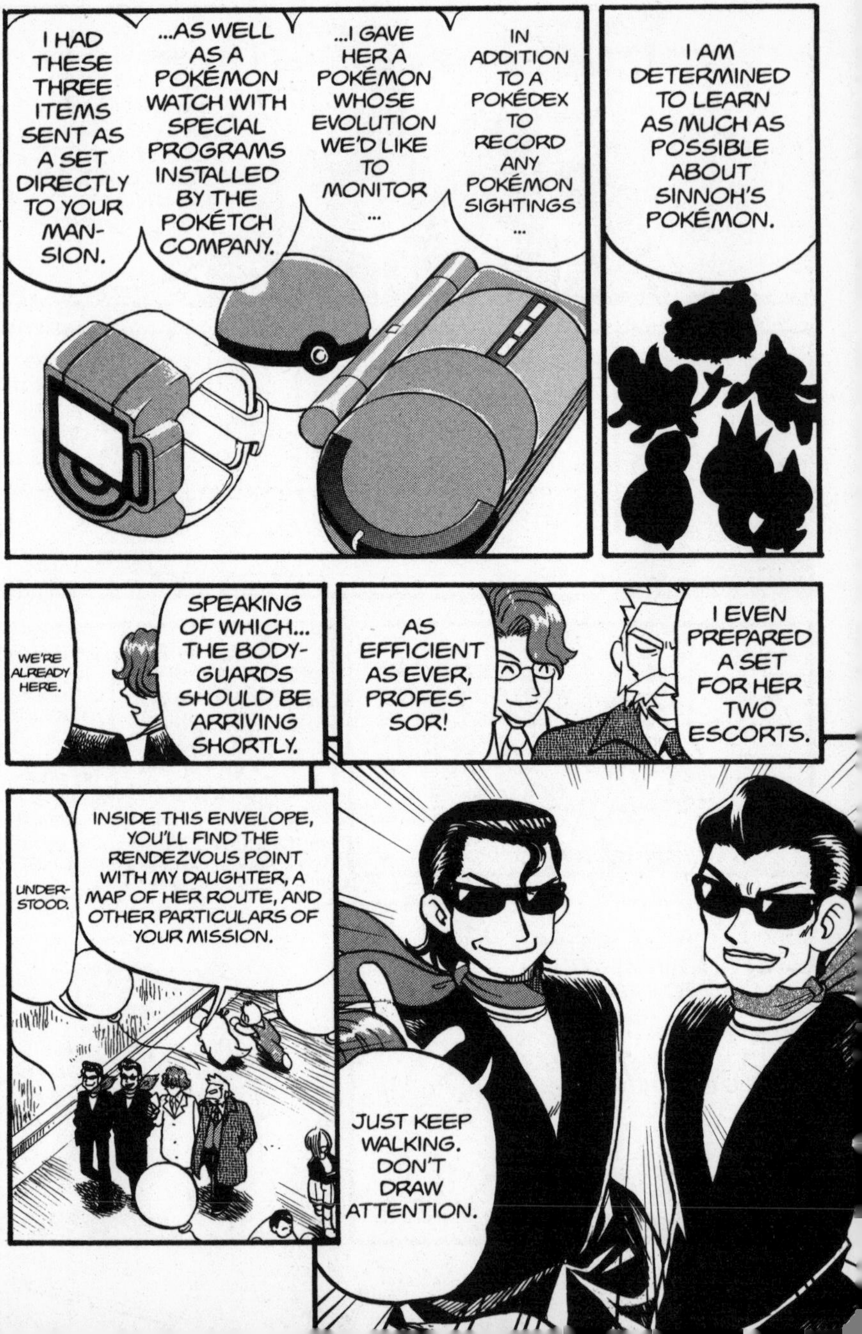
I HAD THESE THREE ITEMS SENT AS A SET DIRECTLY TO YOUR MANSION.
...AS WELL AS A POKÉMON WATCH WITH SPECIAL PROGRAMS INSTALLED BY THE POKÉTCH COMPANY.
...I GAVE HER A POKÉMON WHOSE EVOLUTION WE'D LIKE TO MONITOR...
IN ADDITION TO A POKÉDEX TO RECORD ANY POKÉMON SIGHTINGS...
I AM DETERMINED TO LEARN AS MUCH AS POSSIBLE ABOUT SINNOH'S POKÉMON.
I EVEN PREPARED A SET FOR HER TWO ESCORTS.
AS EFFICIENT AS EVER, PROFESSOR!
SPEAKING OF WHICH... THE BODYGUARDS SHOULD BE ARRIVING SHORTLY.
WE'RE ALREADY HERE.
JUST KEEP WALKING. DON'T DRAW ATTENTION.
INSIDE THIS ENVELOPE, YOU'LL FIND THE RENDEZVOUS POINT WITH MY DAUGHTER, A MAP OF HER ROUTE, AND OTHER PARTICULARS OF YOUR MISSION.
UNDERSTOOD.

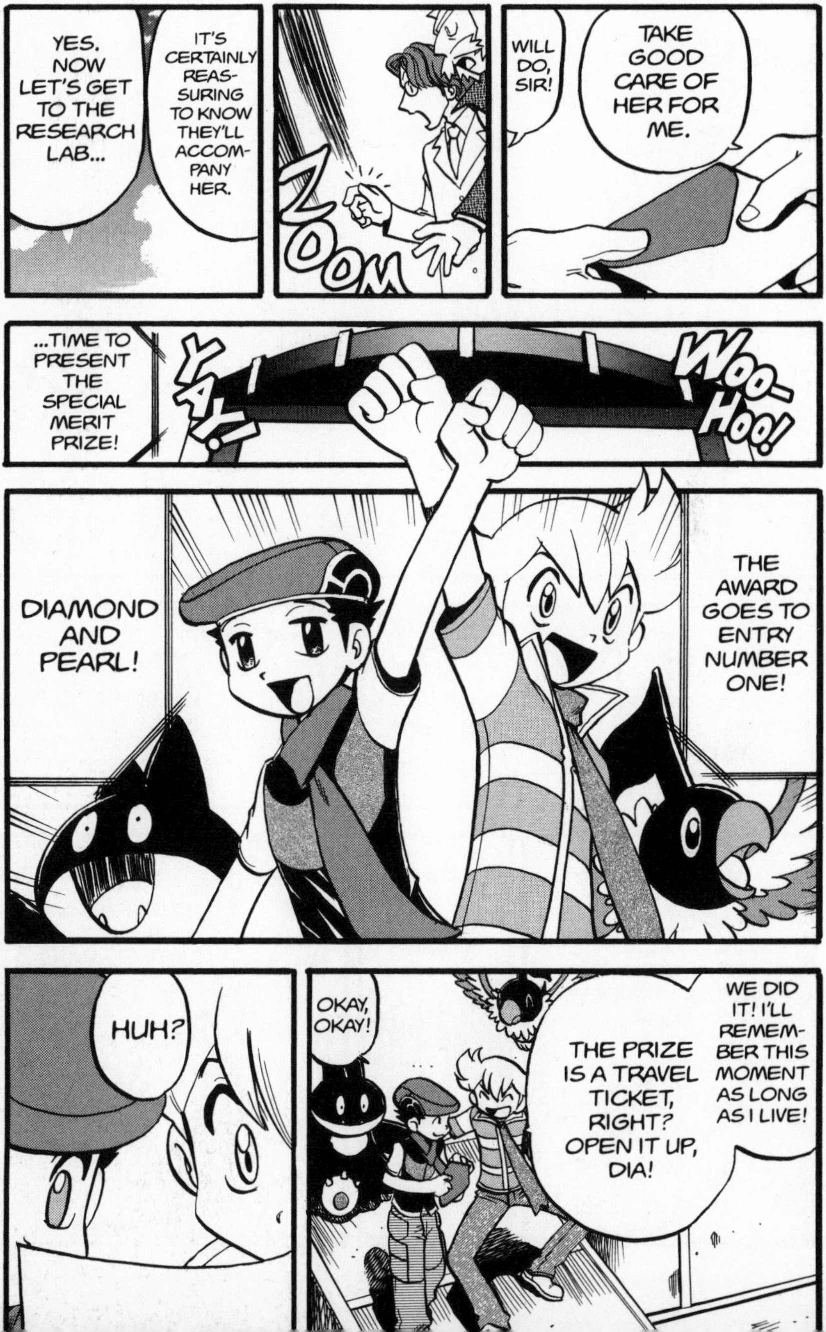
TAKE GOOD CARE OF HER FOR ME.
WILL DO, SIR!
ZOOM
IT'S CERTAINLY REAS-SURING TO KNOW THEY'LL ACCOM-PANY HER.
YES. NOW LET'S GET TO THE RESEARCH LAB...
WOO-HOO!
YAY!
...TIME TO PRESENT THE SPECIAL MERIT PRIZE!
THE AWARD GOES TO ENTRY NUMBER ONE!
DIAMOND AND PEARL!
WE DID IT! I'LL REMEM-BER THIS MOMENT AS LONG AS I LIVE!
THE PRIZE IS A TRAVEL TICKET, RIGHT? OPEN IT UP, DIA!
OKAY, OKAY!
HUH?

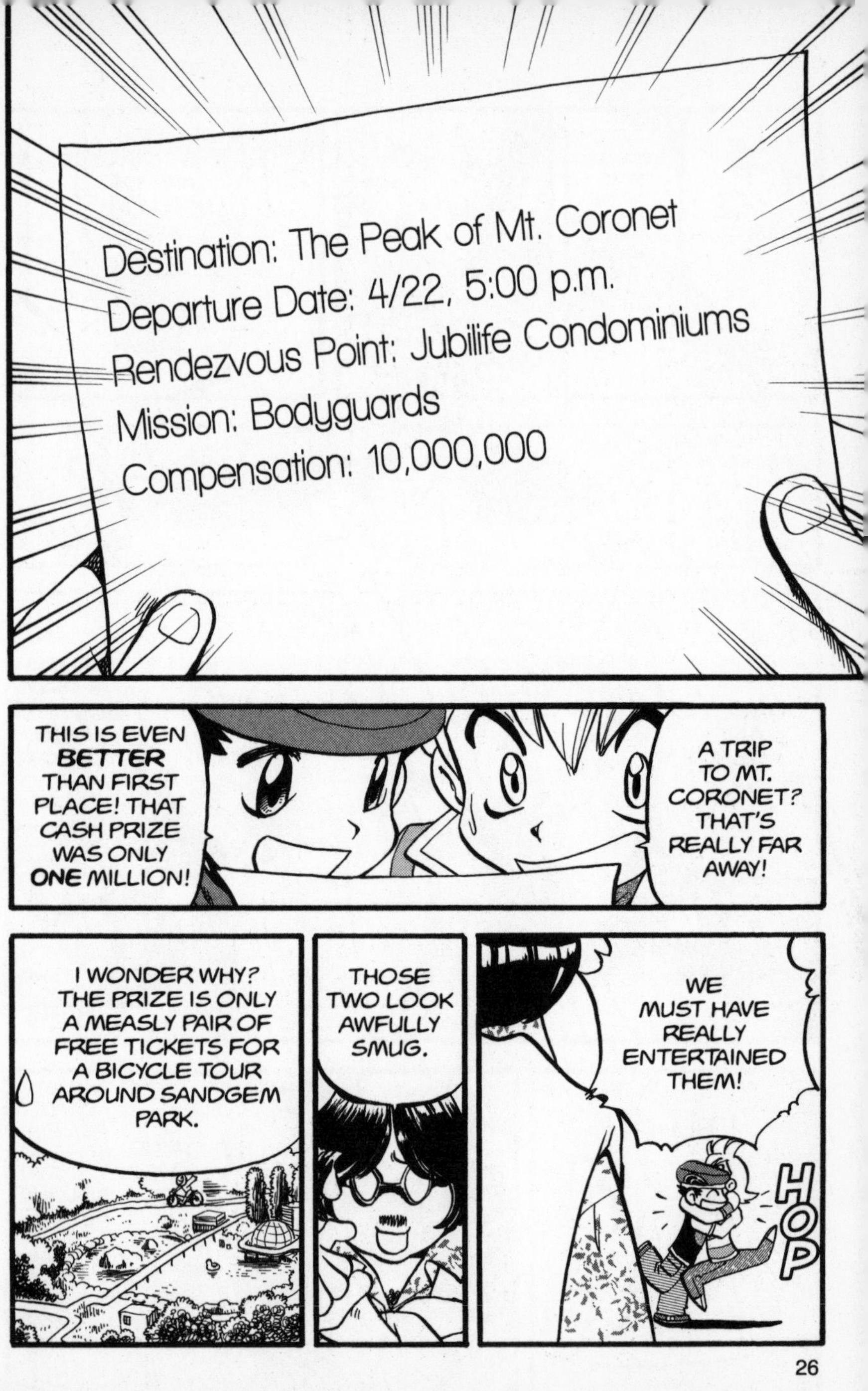
Destination: The Peak of Mt. Coronet
Departure Date: 4/22, 5:00 p.m.
Rendezvous Point: Jubilife Condominiums
Mission: Bodyguards
Compensation: 10,000,000
THIS IS EVEN BETTER THAN FIRST PLACE! THAT CASH PRIZE WAS ONLY ONE MILLION!
A TRIP TO MT. CORONET? THAT'S REALLY FAR AWAY!
I WONDER WHY? THE PRIZE IS ONLY A MEASLY PAIR OF FREE TICKETS FOR A BICYCLE TOUR AROUND SANDGEM PARK.
THOSE TWO LOOK AWFULLY SMUG.
WE MUST HAVE REALLY ENTERTAINED THEM!
HOP

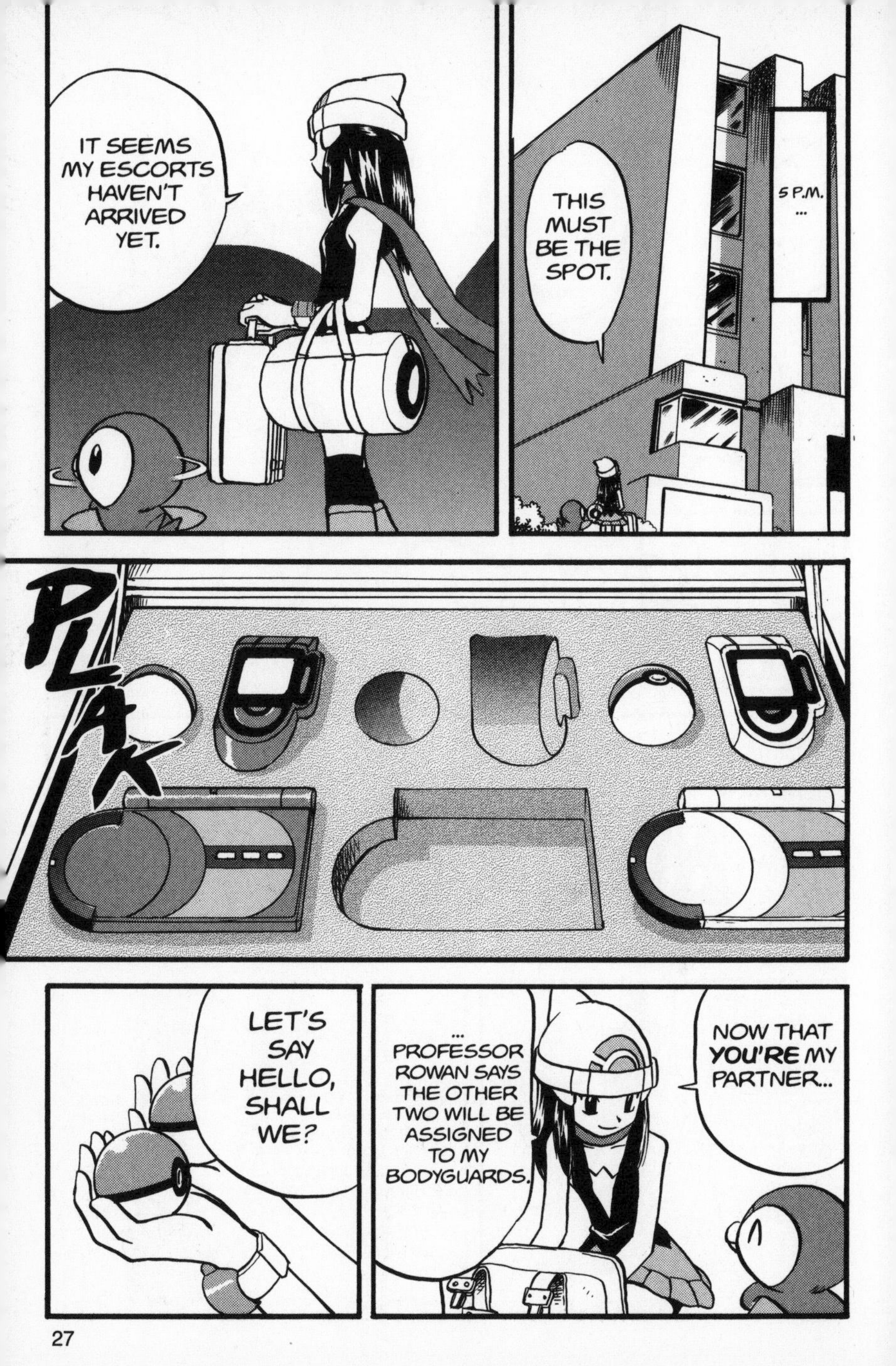
IT SEEMS MY ESCORTS HAVEN'T ARRIVED YET.
THIS MUST BE THE SPOT.
5 P.M. ...
PLAK
LET'S SAY HELLO, SHALL WE?
NOW THAT **YOU'RE** MY PARTNER...
... PROFESSOR ROWAN SAYS THE OTHER TWO WILL BE ASSIGNED TO MY BODYGUARDS.

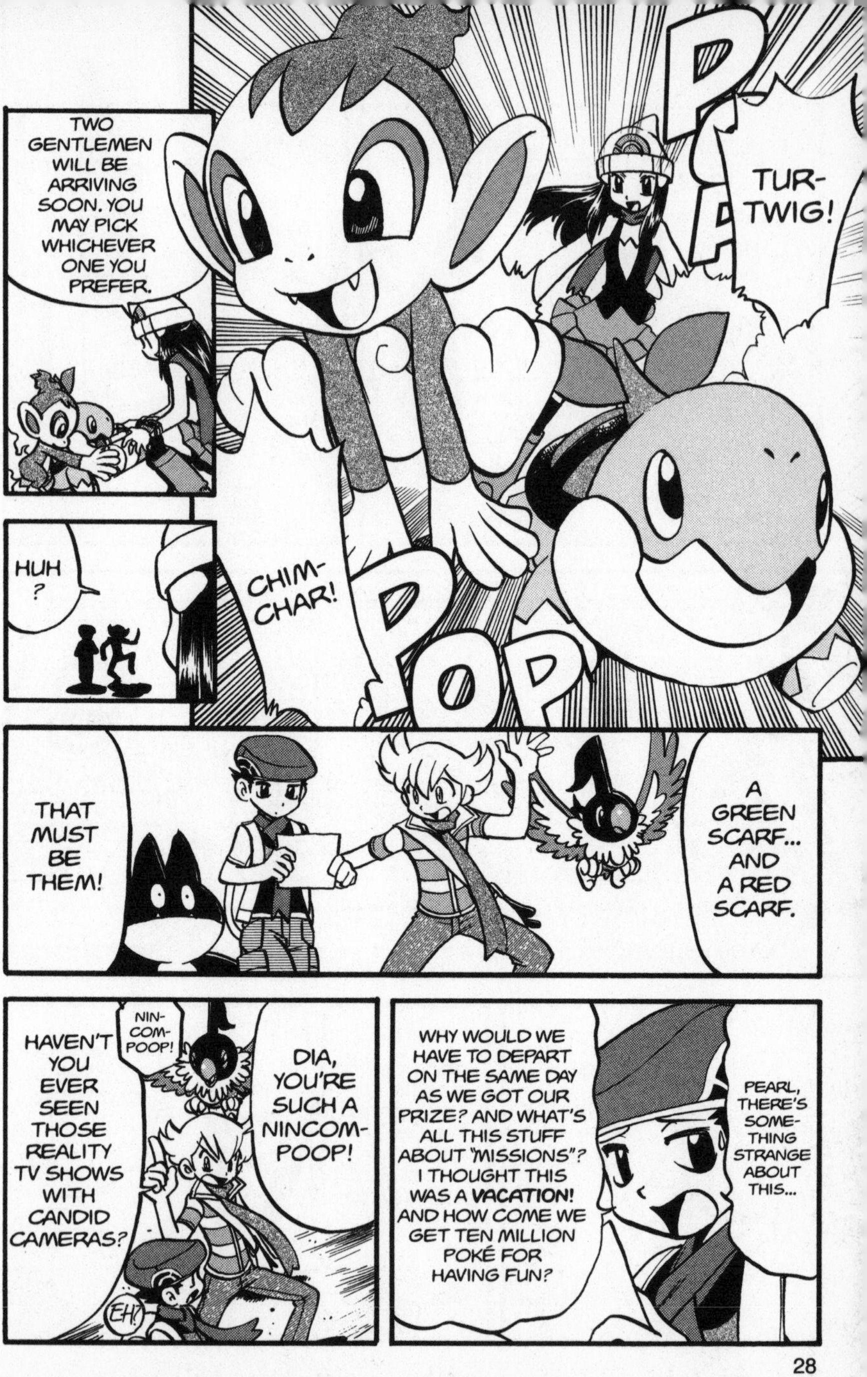
TWO GENTLEMEN WILL BE ARRIVING SOON. YOU MAY PICK WHICHEVER ONE YOU PREFER.
HUH ?
CHIM-CHAR!
TUR-TWIG!
POP
POP
THAT MUST BE THEM!
A GREEN SCARF... AND A RED SCARF.
HAVEN'T YOU EVER SEEN THOSE REALITY TV SHOWS WITH CANDID CAMERAS?
NIN-COM-POOP!
DIA, YOU'RE SUCH A NINCOM-POOP!
EH?
WHY WOULD WE HAVE TO DEPART ON THE SAME DAY AS WE GOT OUR PRIZE? AND WHAT'S ALL THIS STUFF ABOUT "MISSIONS"? I THOUGHT THIS WAS A **VACATION**! AND HOW COME WE GET TEN MILLION POKÉ FOR HAVING FUN?
PEARL, THERE'S SOME-THING STRANGE ABOUT THIS...

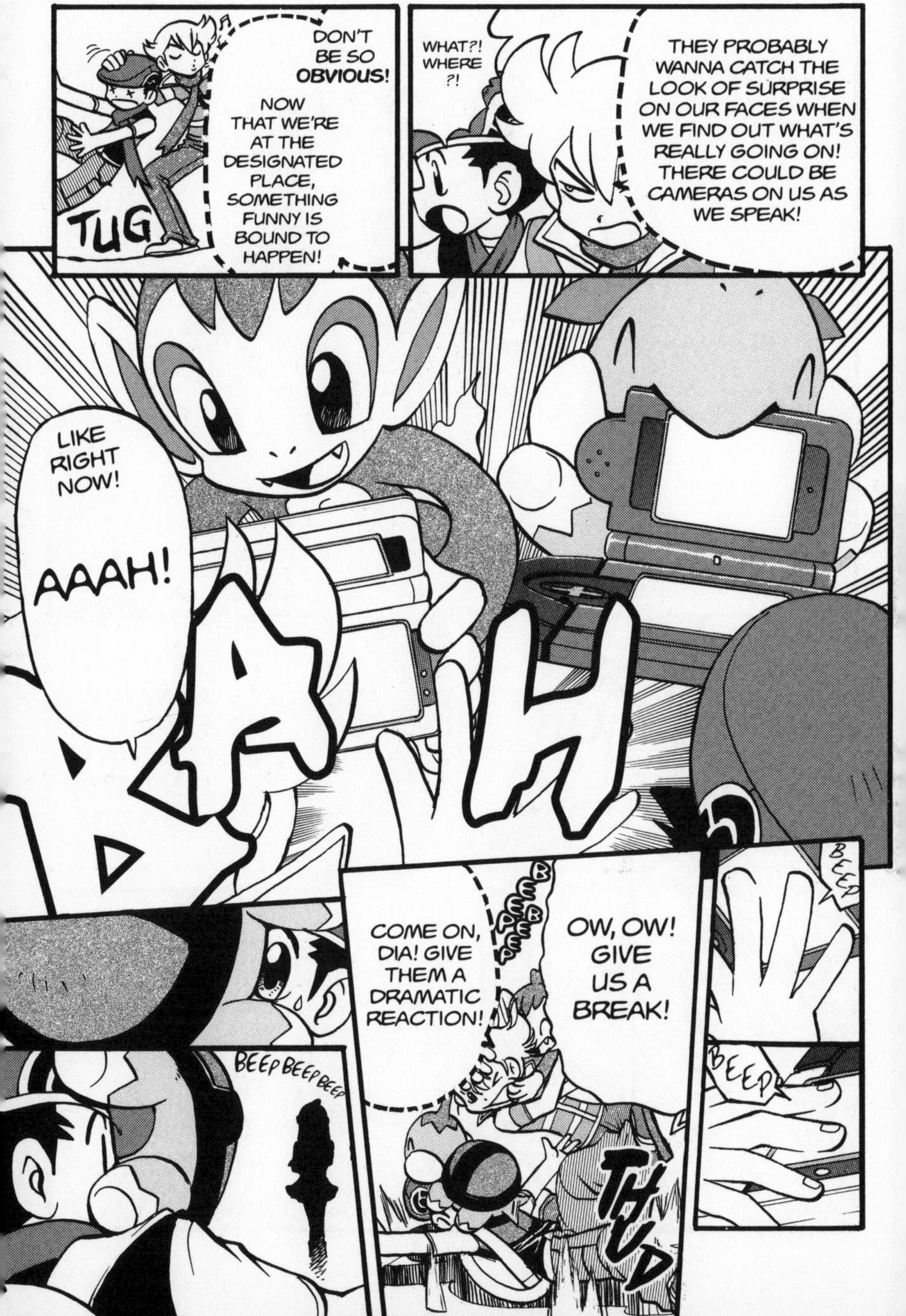

TUG
DON'T BE SO **OBVIOUS**!
NOW THAT WE'RE AT THE DESIGNATED PLACE, SOMETHING FUNNY IS BOUND TO HAPPEN!
WHAT?! WHERE ?!
THEY PROBABLY WANNA CATCH THE LOOK OF SURPRISE ON OUR FACES WHEN WE FIND OUT WHAT'S REALLY GOING ON! THERE COULD BE CAMERAS ON US AS WE SPEAK!
LIKE RIGHT NOW!
AAAH!
BEEP
COME ON, DIA! GIVE THEM A DRAMATIC REACTION!
OW, OW! GIVE US A BREAK!
BEEP BEEP BEEP
BEEP
THUD

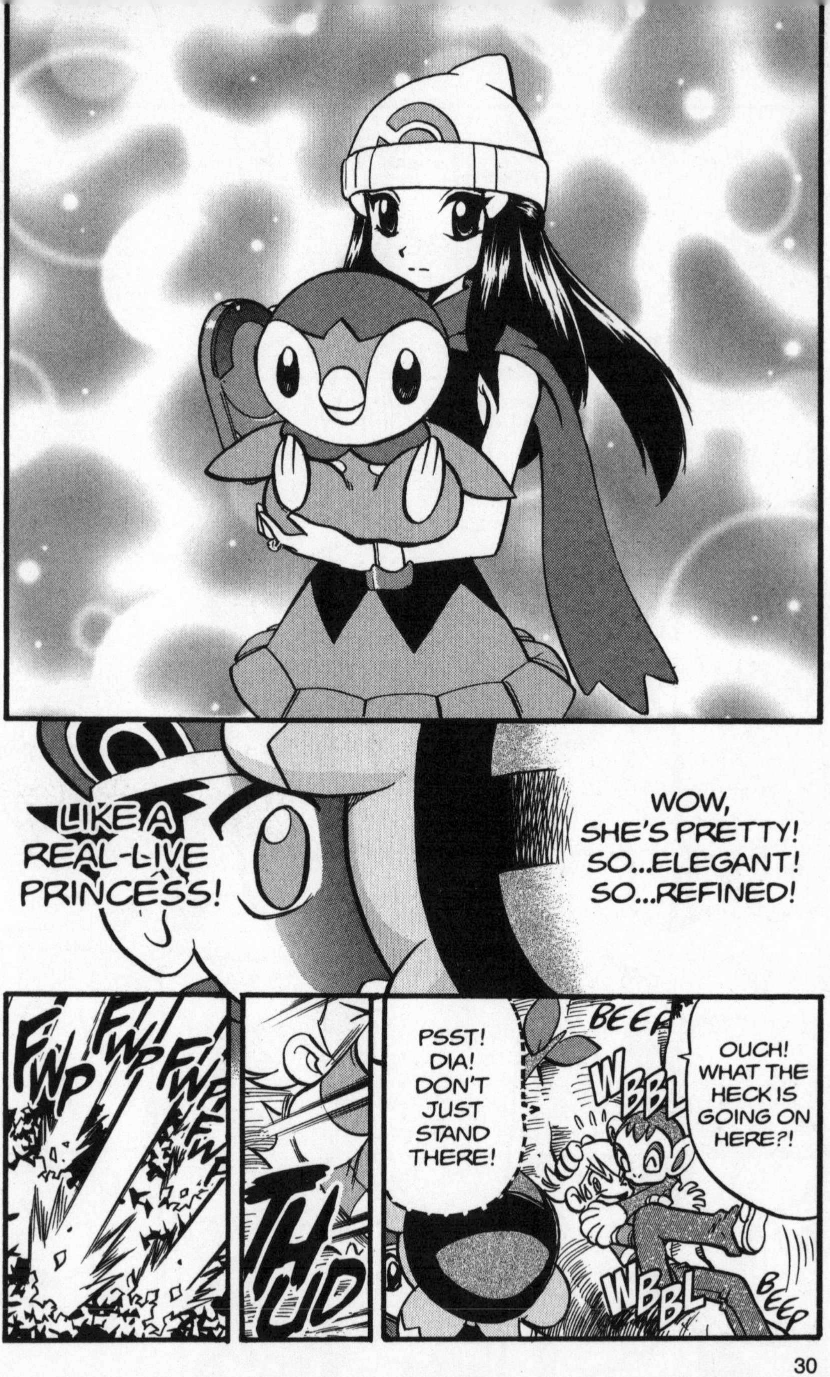

WOW, SHE'S PRETTY! SO...ELEGANT! SO...REFINED!
LIKE A REAL-LIVE PRINCESS!
FWP FWP FWP FWP
THD
PSST! DIA! DON'T JUST STAND THERE!
BEEP
WBBL
OUCH! WHAT THE HECK IS GOING ON HERE?!
WBBL
BEEP

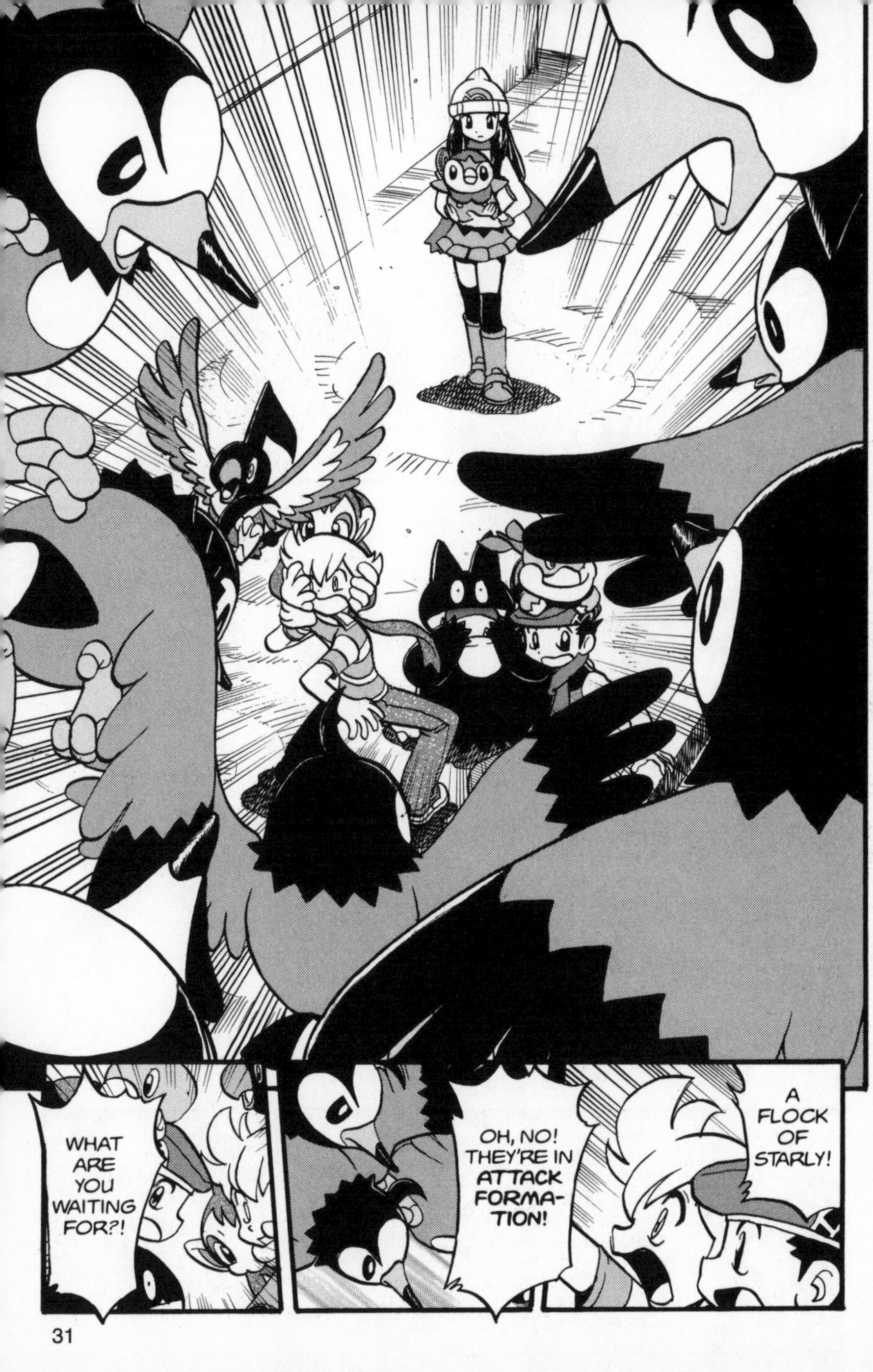
A FLOCK OF STARLY!
OH, NO! THEY'RE IN ATTACK FORMA-TION!
WHAT ARE YOU WAITING FOR?!

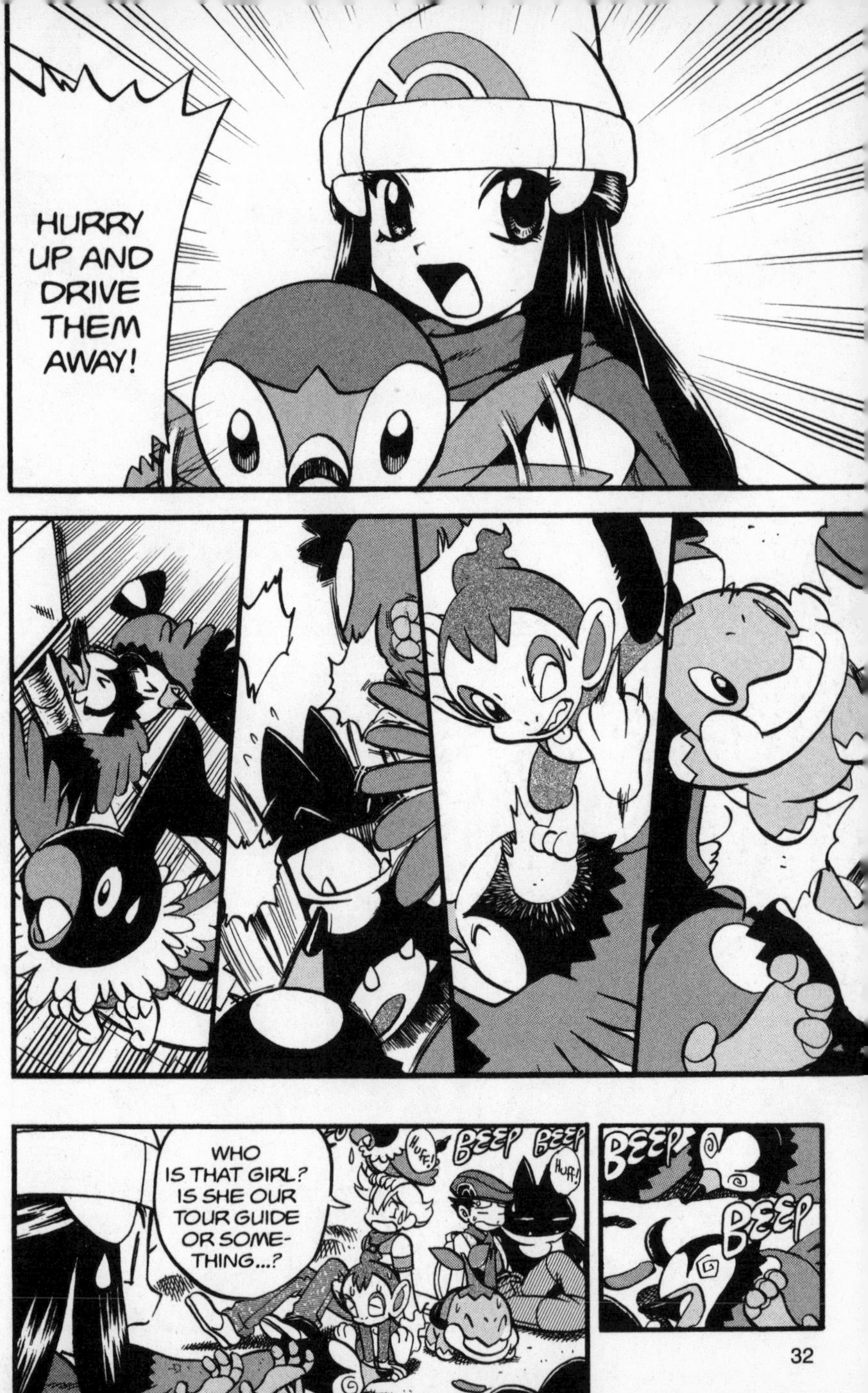
HURRY UP AND DRIVE THEM AWAY!
WHO IS THAT GIRL? IS SHE OUR TOUR GUIDE OR SOME-THING...?
HUFF!
HUFF!
BEEP BEEP
BEEP
BEEP

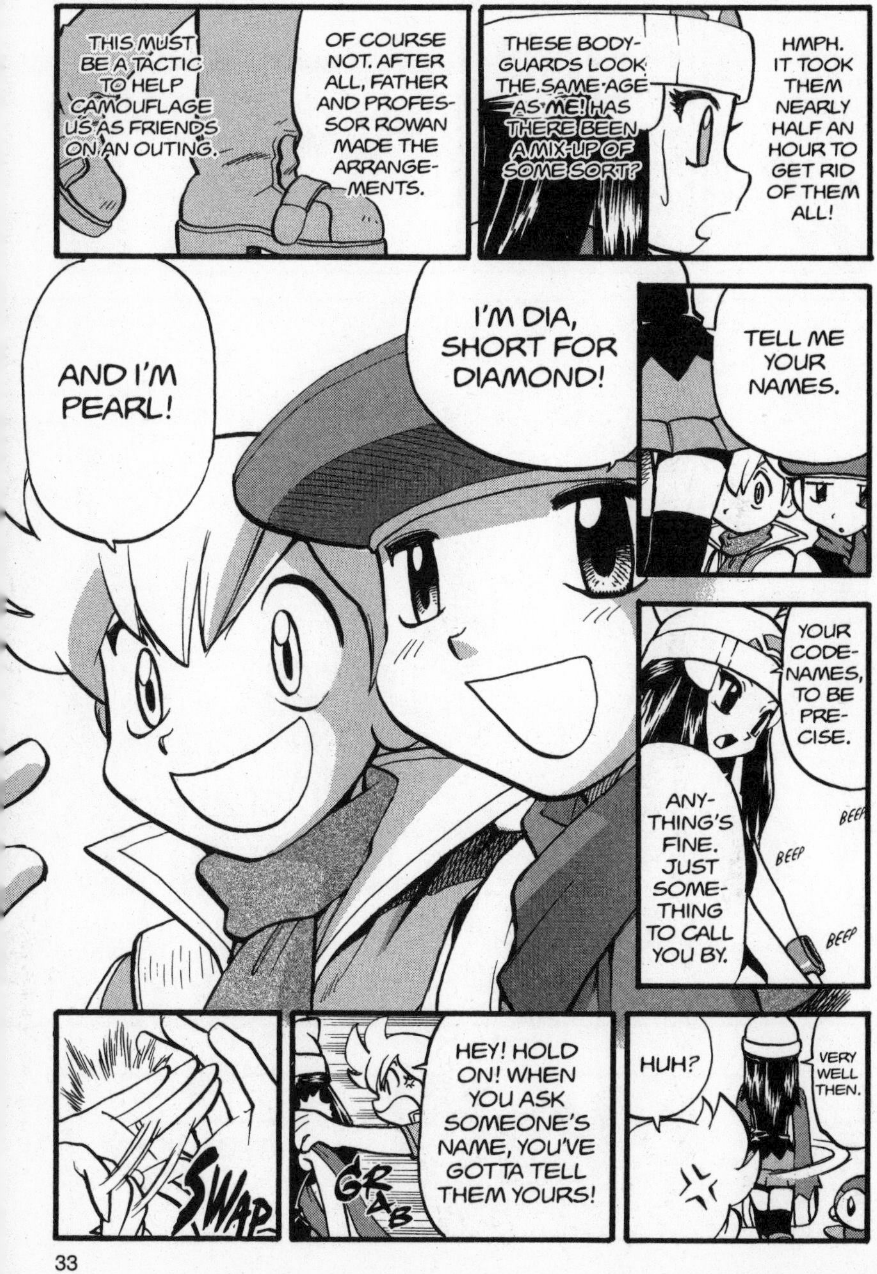
THIS MUST BE A TACTIC TO HELP CAMOUFLAGE US AS FRIENDS ON AN OUTING.
OF COURSE NOT. AFTER ALL, FATHER AND PROFESSOR ROWAN MADE THE ARRANGEMENTS.
THESE BODY-GUARDS LOOK THE SAME AGE AS ME! HAS THERE BEEN A MIX-UP OF SOME SORT?
HMPH. IT TOOK THEM NEARLY HALF AN HOUR TO GET RID OF THEM ALL!
AND I'M PEARL!
I'M DIA, SHORT FOR DIAMOND!
TELL ME YOUR NAMES.
YOUR CODE-NAMES, TO BE PRECISE.
ANYTHING'S FINE. JUST SOMETHING TO CALL YOU BY.
BEEP
BEEP
BEEP
SWAP
GRAB
HEY! HOLD ON! WHEN YOU ASK SOMEONE'S NAME, YOU'VE GOTTA TELL THEM YOURS!
HUH?
VERY WELL THEN.

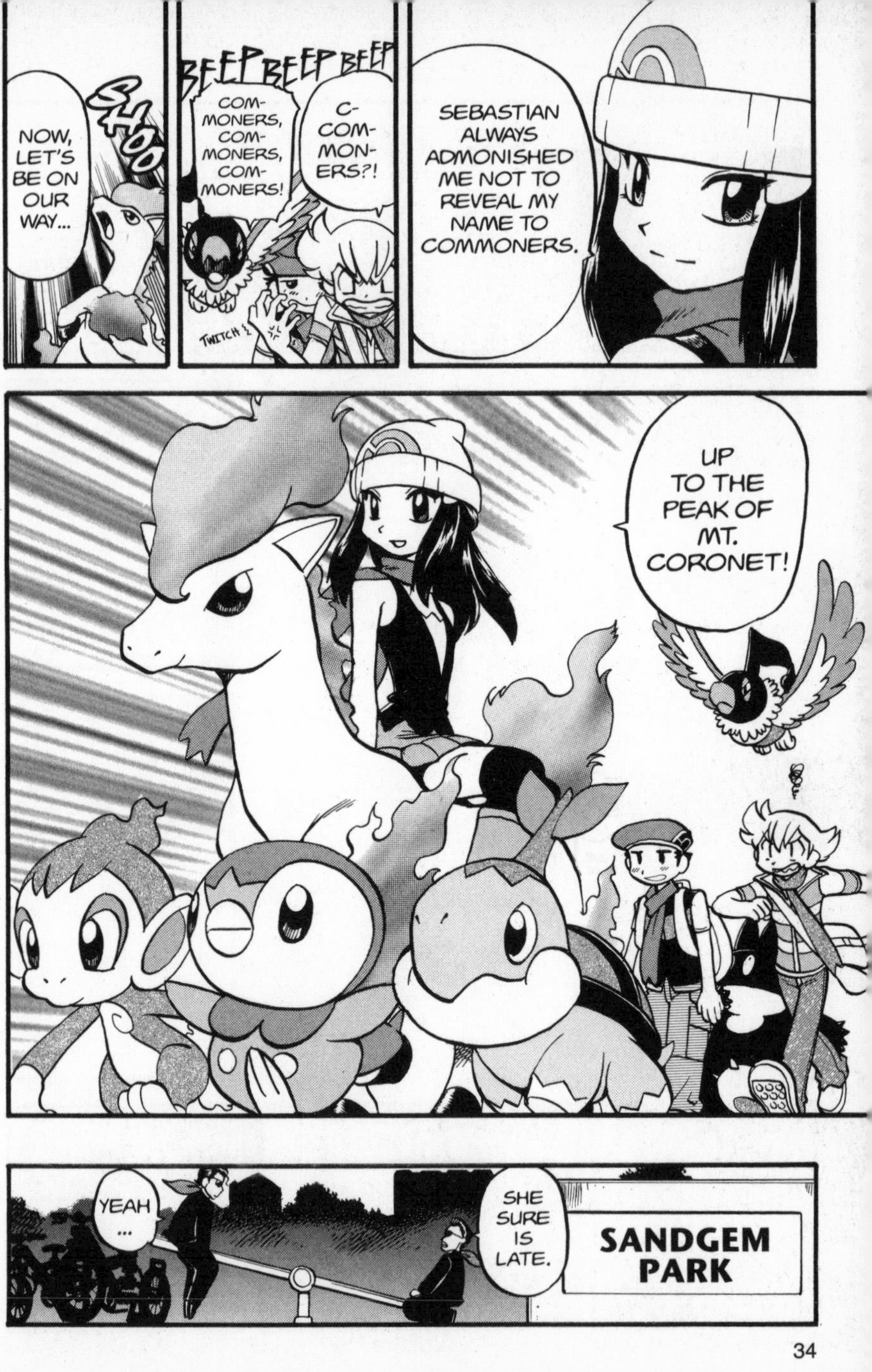
SEBASTIAN ALWAYS ADMONISHED ME NOT TO REVEAL MY NAME TO COMMONERS.
BEEP BEEP BEEP
C-COM-MON-ERS?!
COM-MONERS, COM-MONERS, COM-MONERS!
TWITCH
SHOO
NOW, LET'S BE ON OUR WAY...
UP TO THE PEAK OF MT. CORONET!
SANDGEM PARK
SHE SURE IS LATE.
YEAH ...

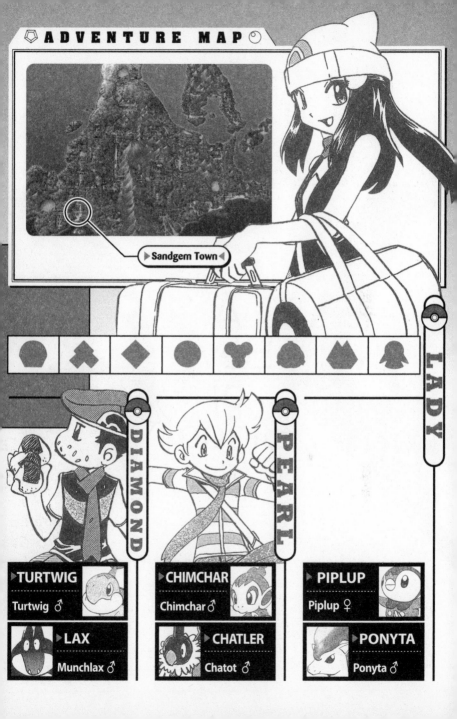

ADVENTURE MAP

▶ Sandgem Town ◀

DIAMOND

PEARL

LADY

▶ **TURTWIG**
Turtwig ♂

▶ **LAX**
Munchlax ♂

▶ **CHIMCHAR**
Chimchar ♂

▶ **CHATLER**
Chatot ♂

▶ **PIPLUP**
Piplup ♀

▶ **PONYTA**
Ponyta ♂

2

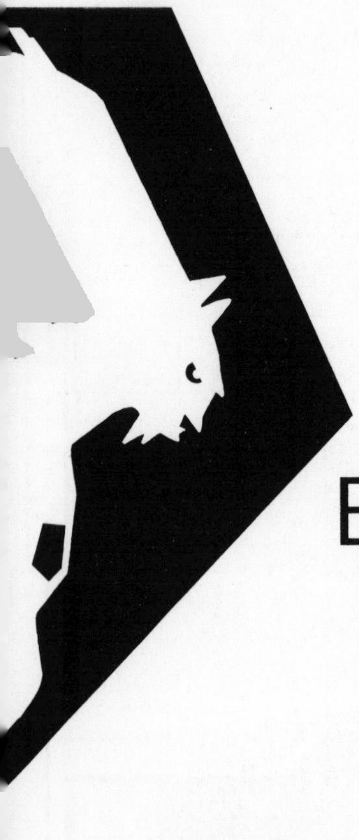

A Bevy of Bidoof

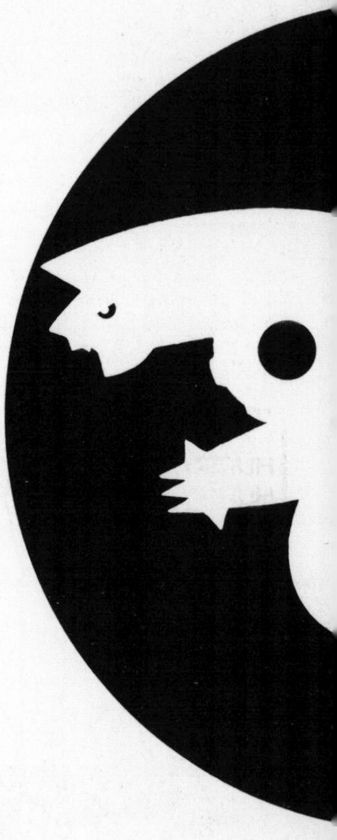

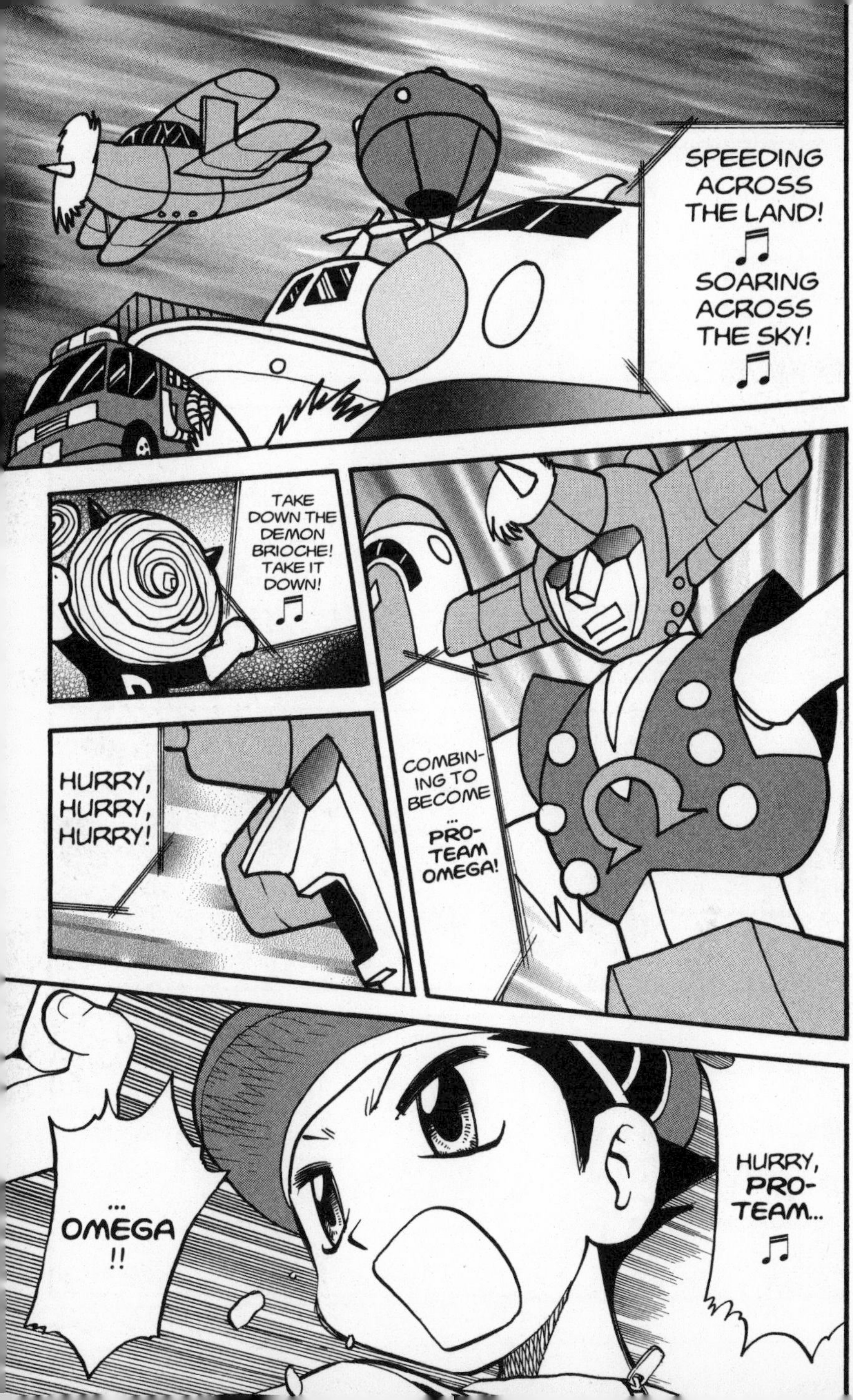
SPEEDING ACROSS THE LAND! ♫
SOARING ACROSS THE SKY! ♫
COMBINING TO BECOME ... PRO-TEAM OMEGA!
TAKE DOWN THE DEMON BRIOCHE! TAKE IT DOWN! ♫
HURRY, HURRY, HURRY!
HURRY, PRO-TEAM... ♫
... OMEGA !!

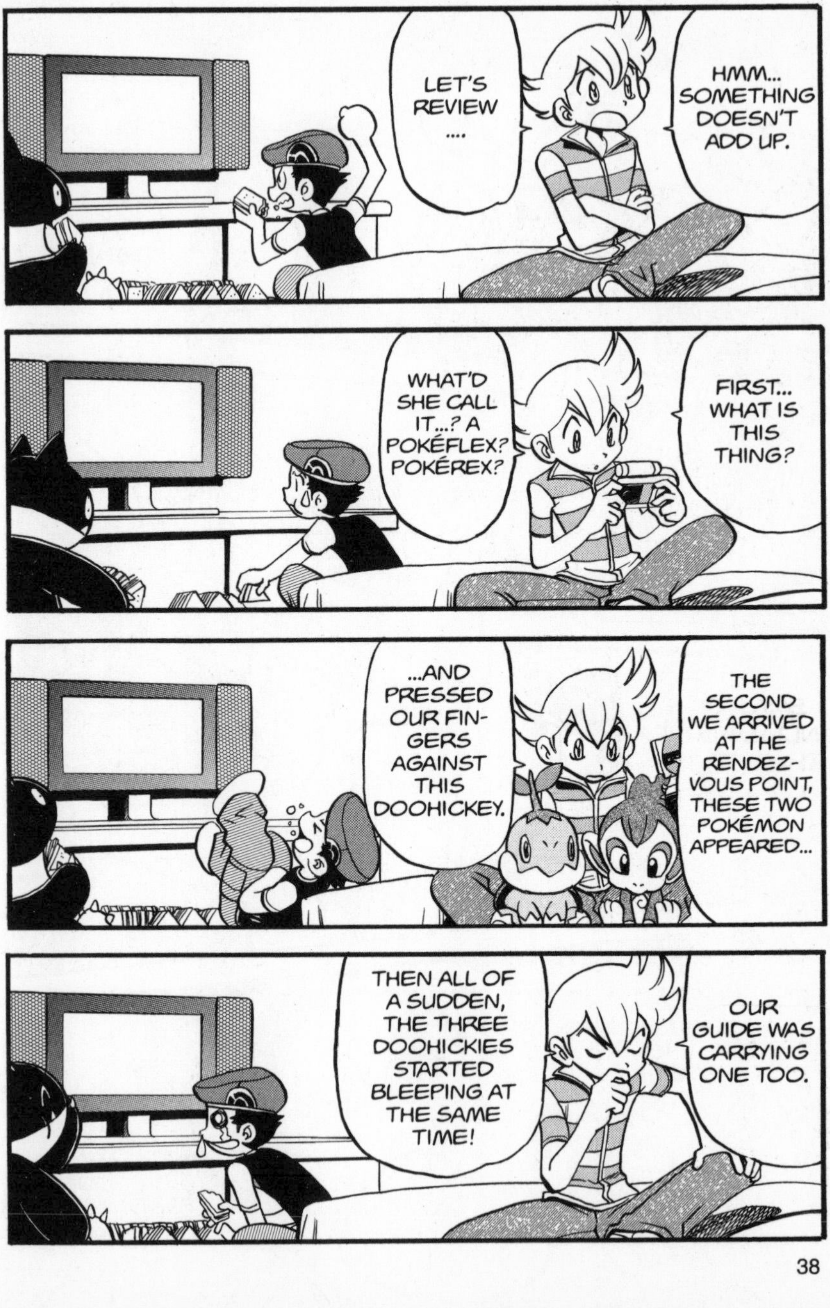
HMM... SOMETHING DOESN'T ADD UP.
LET'S REVIEW ....
FIRST... WHAT IS THIS THING?
WHAT'D SHE CALL IT...? A POKÉFLEX? POKÉREX?
THE SECOND WE ARRIVED AT THE RENDEZ-VOUS POINT, THESE TWO POKÉMON APPEARED...
...AND PRESSED OUR FIN-GERS AGAINST THIS DOOHICKEY.
OUR GUIDE WAS CARRYING ONE TOO.
THEN ALL OF A SUDDEN, THE THREE DOOHICKIES STARTED BLEEPING AT THE SAME TIME!

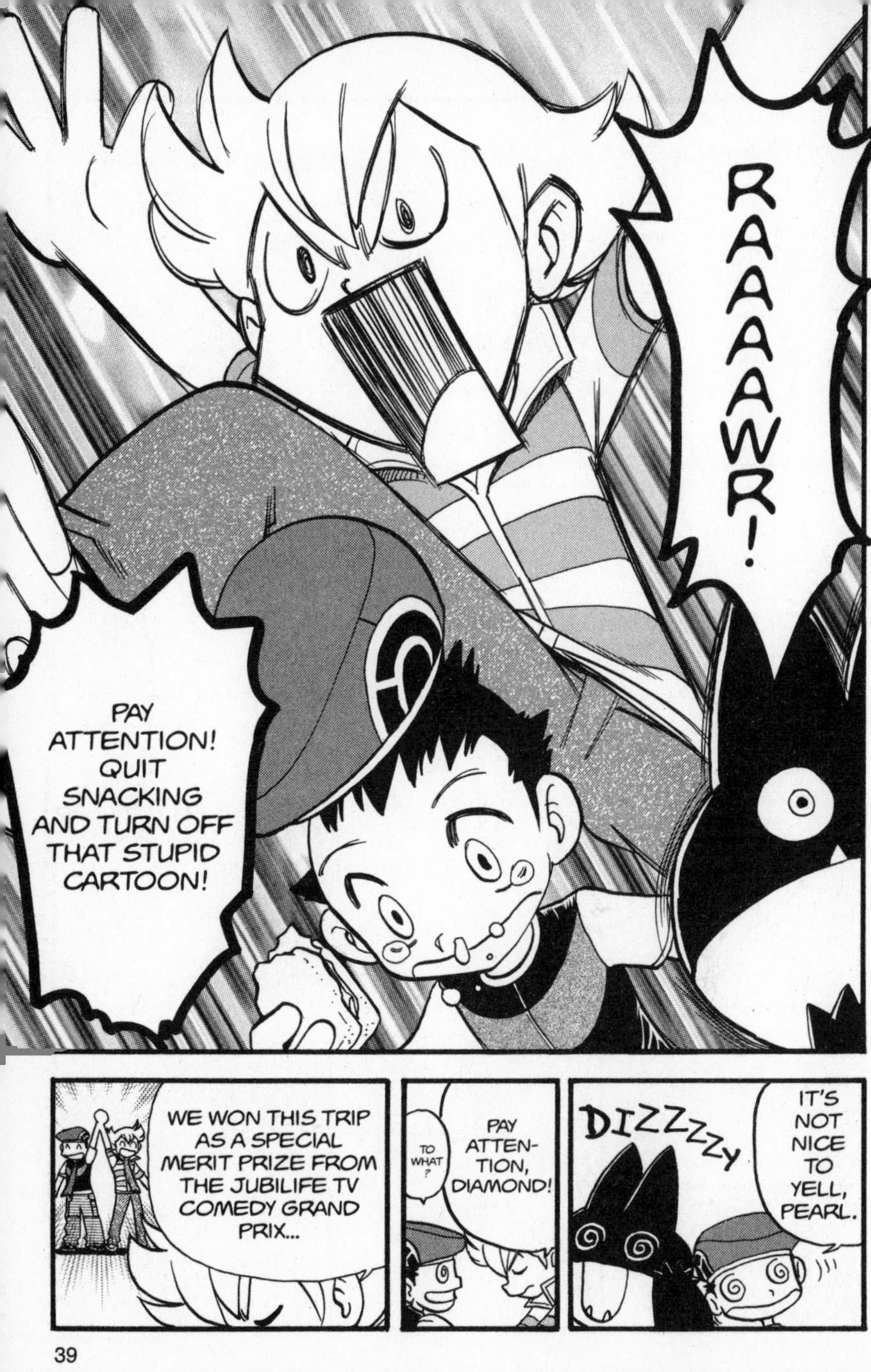
RAAAAWR!
PAY ATTENTION! QUIT SNACKING AND TURN OFF THAT STUPID CARTOON!
WE WON THIS TRIP AS A SPECIAL MERIT PRIZE FROM THE JUBILIFE TV COMEDY GRAND PRIX...
PAY ATTEN-TION, DIAMOND!
TO WHAT?
IT'S NOT NICE TO YELL, PEARL.
DIZZZZZY

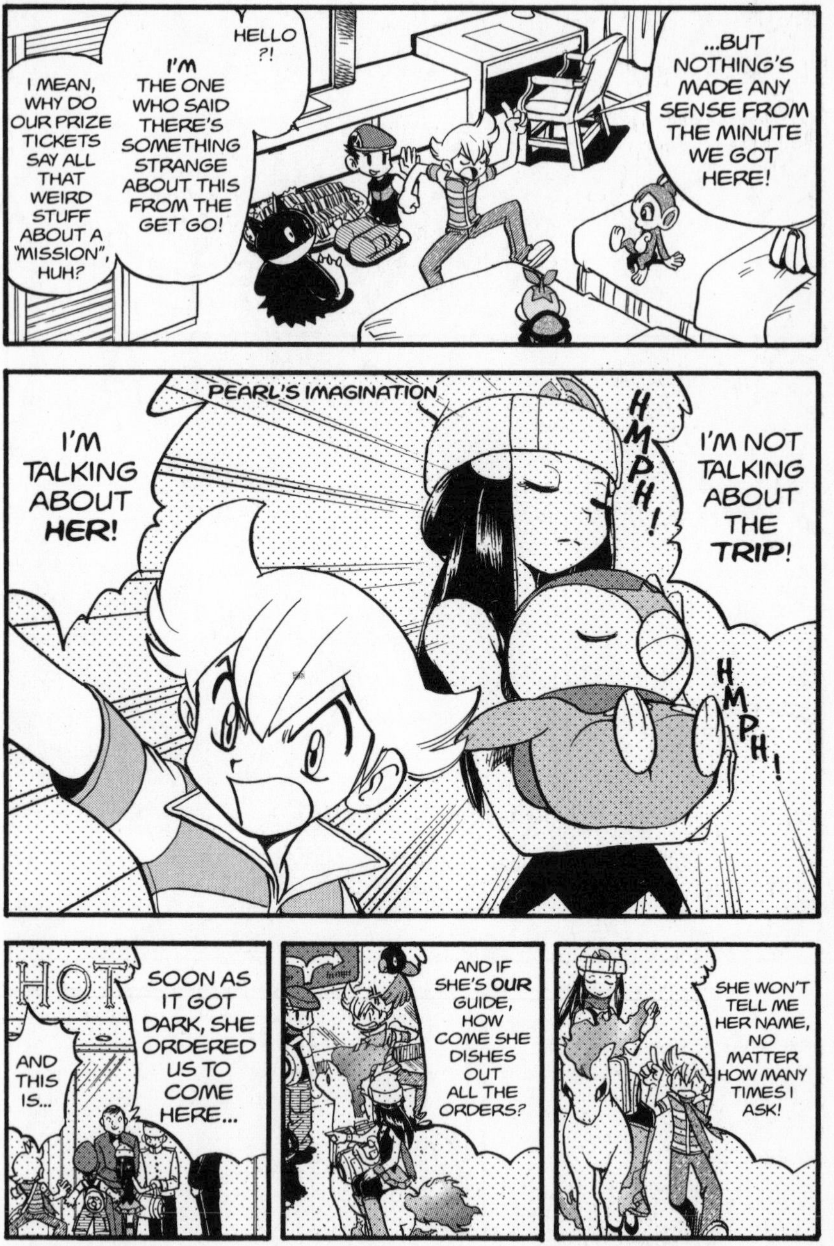
...BUT NOTHING'S MADE ANY SENSE FROM THE MINUTE WE GOT HERE!
HELLO ?!
I'M THE ONE WHO SAID THERE'S SOMETHING STRANGE ABOUT THIS FROM THE GET GO!
I MEAN, WHY DO OUR PRIZE TICKETS SAY ALL THAT WEIRD STUFF ABOUT A "MISSION", HUH?
PEARL'S IMAGINATION
I'M NOT TALKING ABOUT THE TRIP!
HMPH!
HMPH!
I'M TALKING ABOUT HER!
SHE WON'T TELL ME HER NAME, NO MATTER HOW MANY TIMES I ASK!
AND IF SHE'S OUR GUIDE, HOW COME SHE DISHES OUT ALL THE ORDERS?
SOON AS IT GOT DARK, SHE ORDERED US TO COME HERE...
AND THIS IS...
HOT

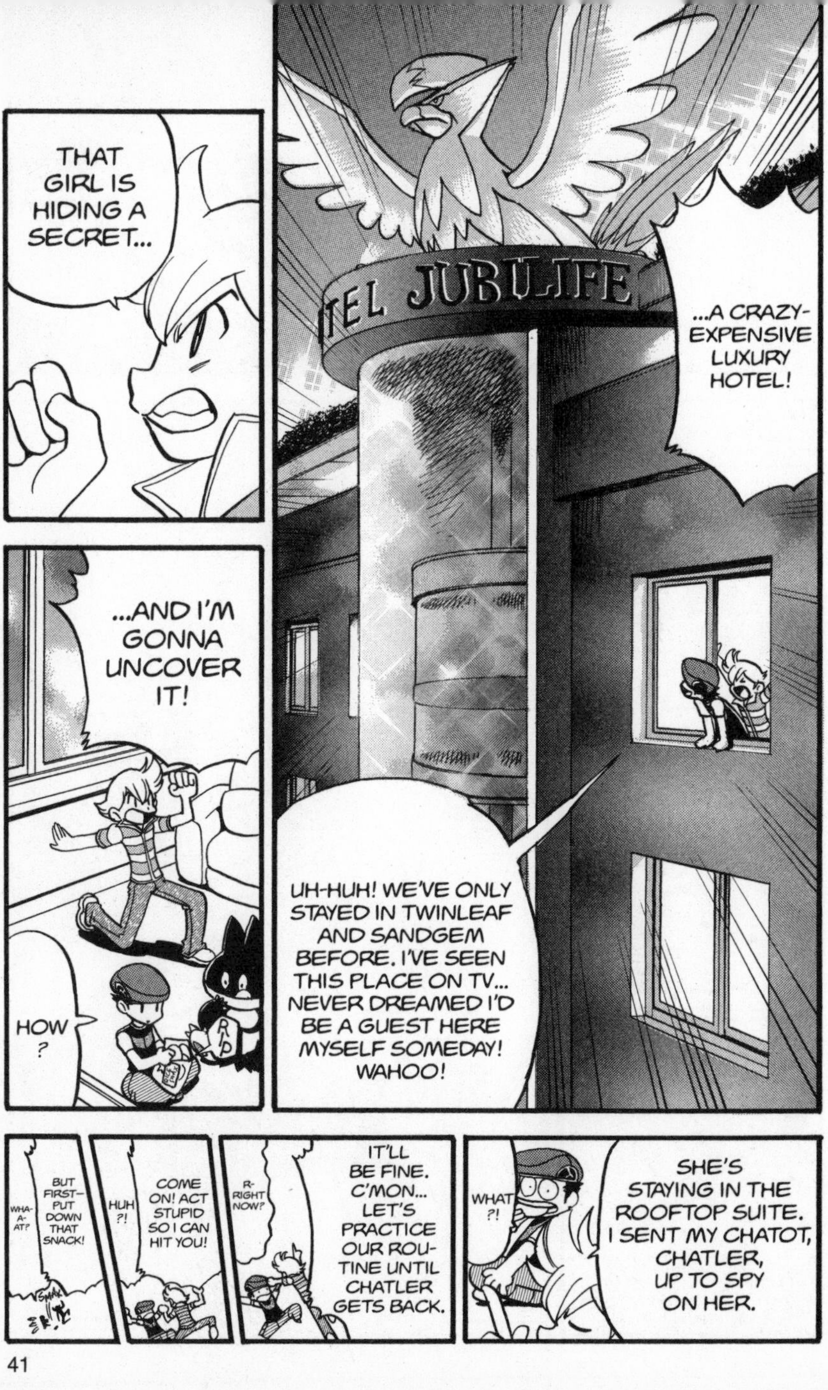

...A CRAZY-EXPENSIVE LUXURY HOTEL!
UH-HUH! WE'VE ONLY STAYED IN TWINLEAF AND SANDGEM BEFORE. I'VE SEEN THIS PLACE ON TV... NEVER DREAMED I'D BE A GUEST HERE MYSELF SOMEDAY! WAHOO!
TEL JUBILIFE
THAT GIRL IS HIDING A SECRET...
...AND I'M GONNA UNCOVER IT!
HOW?
SHE'S STAYING IN THE ROOFTOP SUITE. I SENT MY CHATOT, CHATLER, UP TO SPY ON HER.
WHAT?!
IT'LL BE FINE. C'MON... LET'S PRACTICE OUR ROUTINE UNTIL CHATLER GETS BACK.
R-RIGHT NOW?
COME ON! ACT STUPID SO I CAN HIT YOU!
HUH?!
BUT FIRST—PUT DOWN THAT SNACK!
WHA-A-AT?

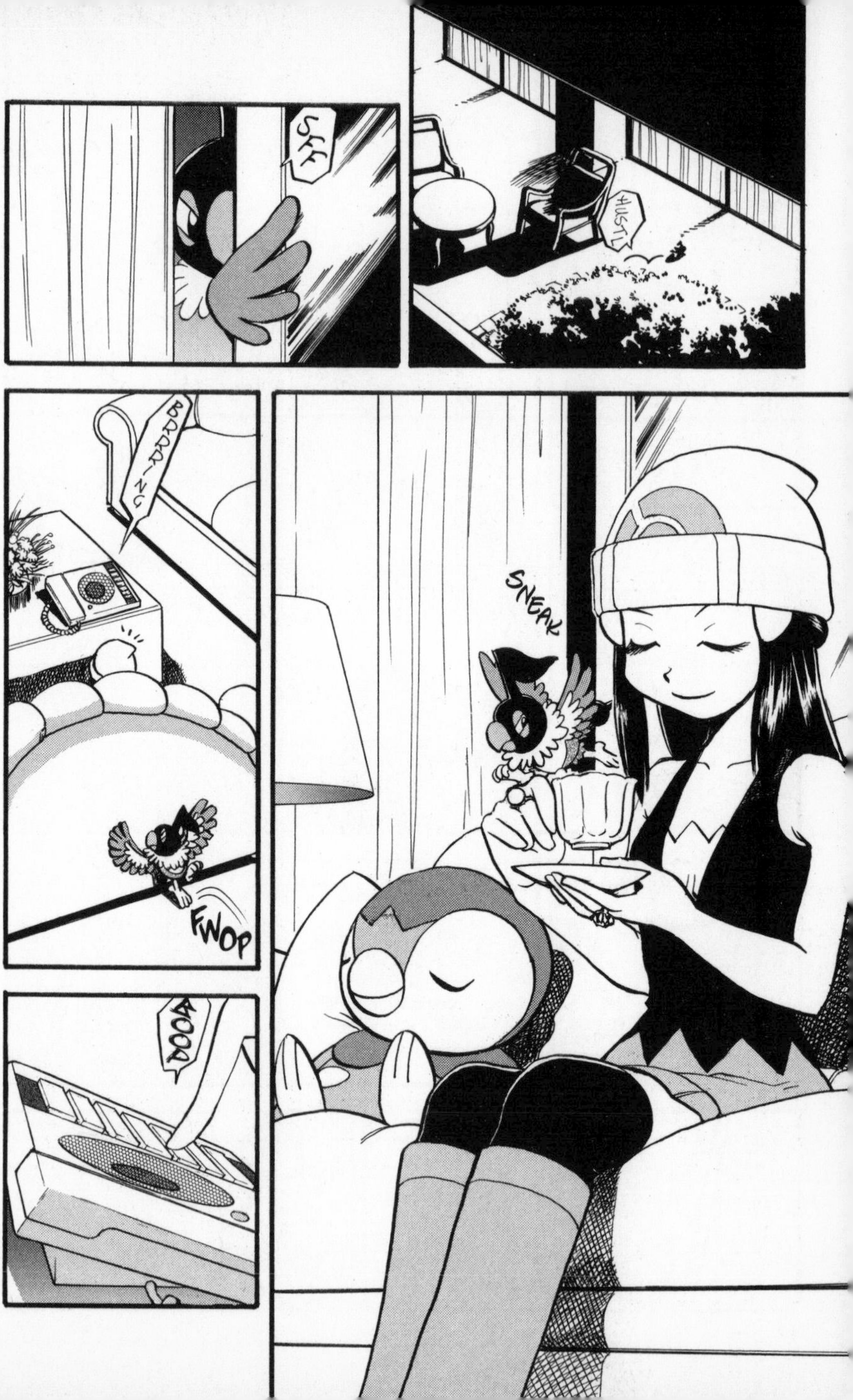
HUSTL
SFF
SNEAK
BRRRING
FWOP
BOOP

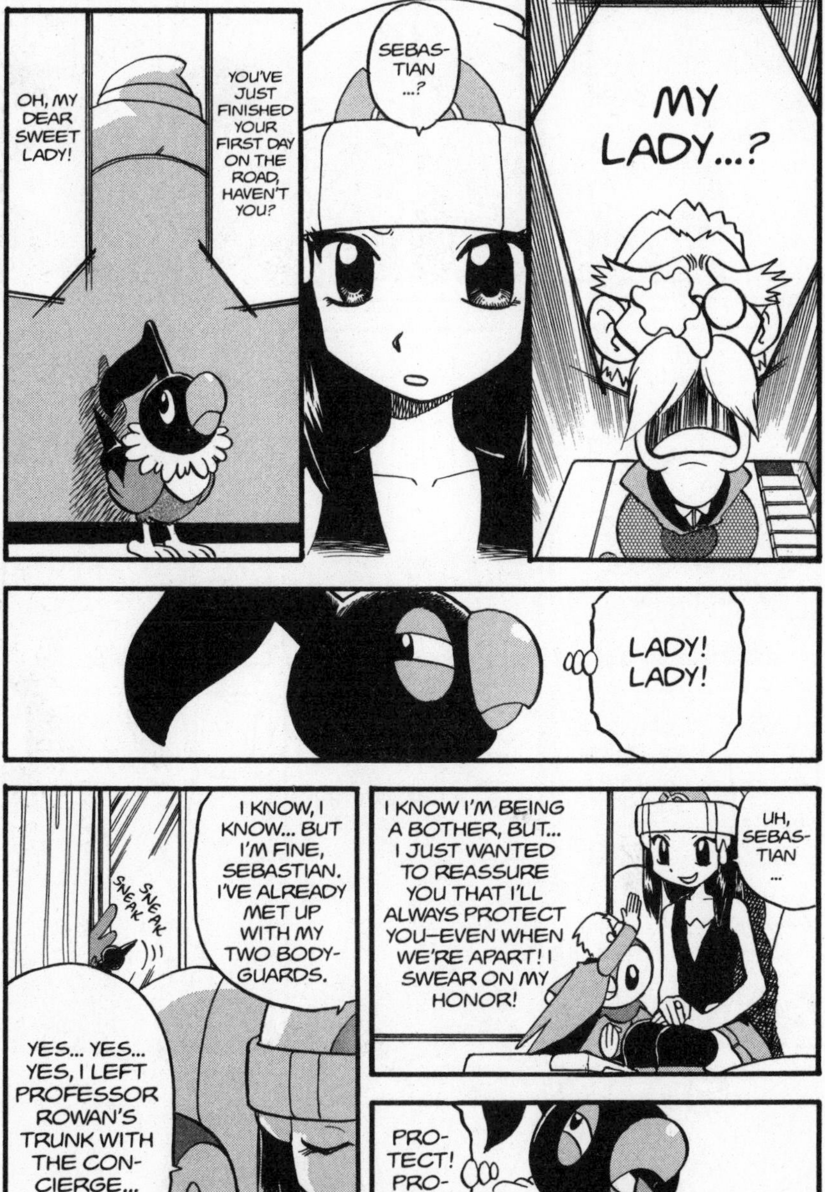
OH, MY DEAR SWEET LADY!
YOU'VE JUST FINISHED YOUR FIRST DAY ON THE ROAD, HAVEN'T YOU?
SEBASTIAN...?
MY LADY...?
LADY! LADY!
YES... YES... YES, I LEFT PROFESSOR ROWAN'S TRUNK WITH THE CONCIERGE...
I KNOW, I KNOW... BUT I'M FINE, SEBASTIAN. I'VE ALREADY MET UP WITH MY TWO BODYGUARDS.
SNEAK SNEAK
I KNOW I'M BEING A BOTHER, BUT... I JUST WANTED TO REASSURE YOU THAT I'LL ALWAYS PROTECT YOU—EVEN WHEN WE'RE APART! I SWEAR ON MY HONOR!
UH, SEBASTIAN...
PROTECT! PROTECT!

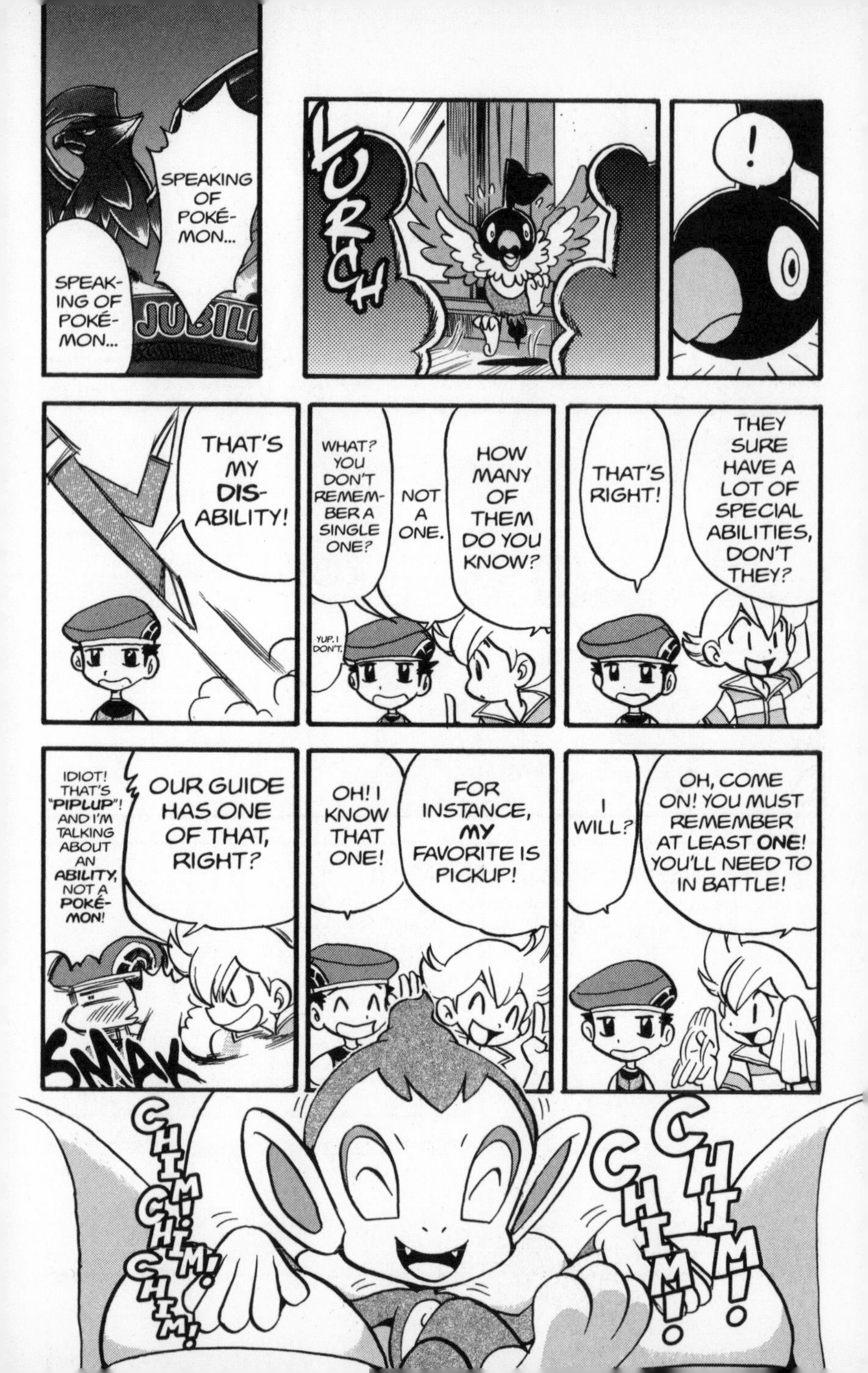

SPEAKING OF POKÉMON...
SPEAK-ING OF POKÉ-MON...
JUBILI
VORCH
!
THEY SURE HAVE A LOT OF SPECIAL ABILITIES, DON'T THEY?
THAT'S RIGHT!
HOW MANY OF THEM DO YOU KNOW?
NOT A ONE.
WHAT? YOU DON'T REMEMBER A SINGLE ONE?
YUP. I DON'T.
THAT'S MY DIS-ABILITY!
OH, COME ON! YOU MUST REMEMBER AT LEAST ONE! YOU'LL NEED TO IN BATTLE!
I WILL?
FOR INSTANCE, MY FAVORITE IS PICKUP!
OH! I KNOW THAT ONE!
OUR GUIDE HAS ONE OF THAT, RIGHT?
IDIOT! THAT'S "PIPLUP"! AND I'M TALKING ABOUT AN ABILITY, NOT A POKÉMON!
SMAK
CHIM! CHIM! CHIM!
CHIM! CHIM! CHIM!

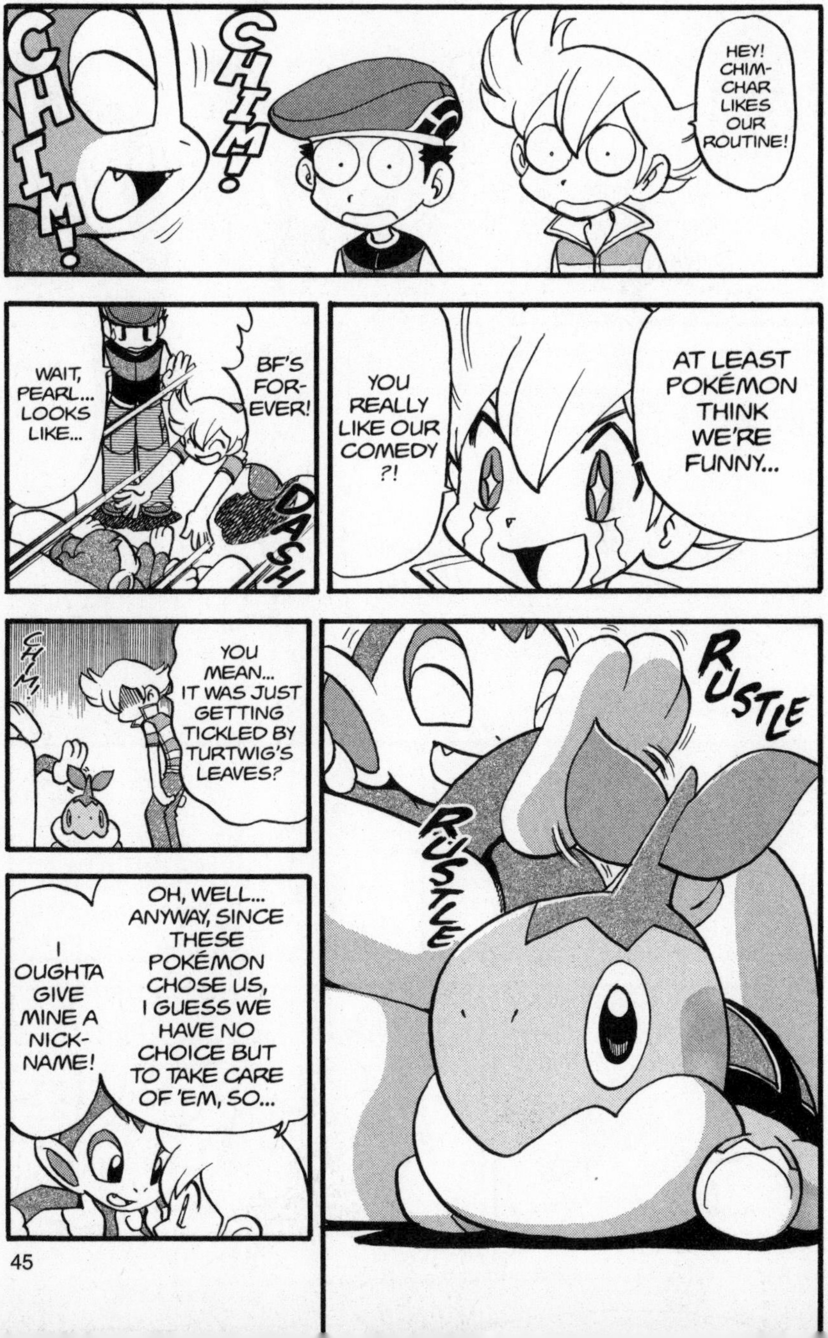
HEY! CHIMCHAR LIKES OUR ROUTINE!
CHIM!
CHIM!
AT LEAST POKÉMON THINK WE'RE FUNNY...
YOU REALLY LIKE OUR COMEDY?!
BF'S FOREVER!
WAIT, PEARL... LOOKS LIKE...
DASH
RUSTLE
RUSTLE
YOU MEAN... IT WAS JUST GETTING TICKLED BY TURTWIG'S LEAVES?
CHIM!
OH, WELL... ANYWAY, SINCE THESE POKÉMON CHOSE US, I GUESS WE HAVE NO CHOICE BUT TO TAKE CARE OF 'EM, SO...
I OUGHTA GIVE MINE A NICKNAME!

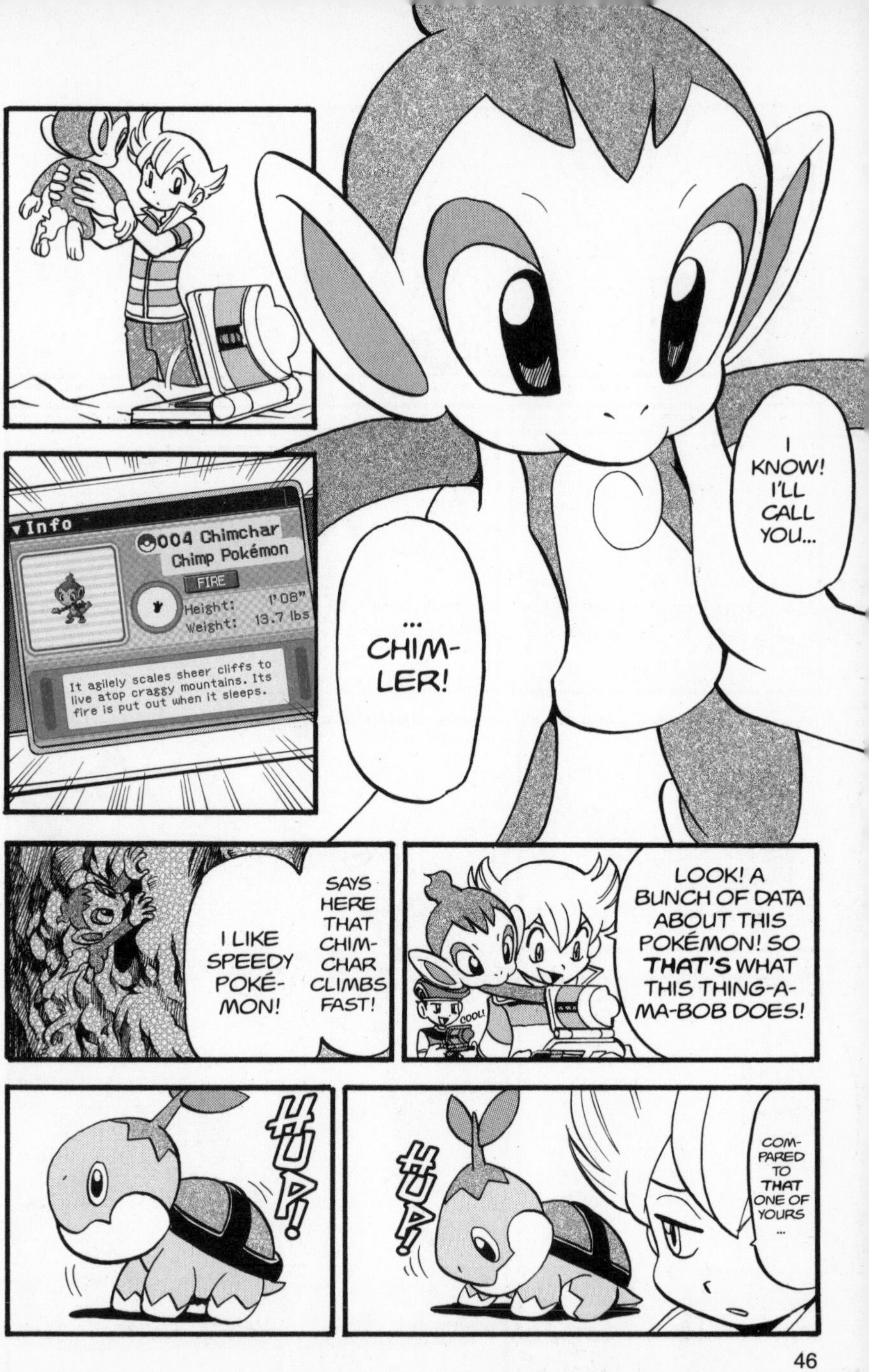
I KNOW! I'LL CALL YOU...
... CHIMLER!
Info
004 Chimchar
Chimp Pokémon
FIRE
Height: 1'08"
Weight: 13.7 lbs
It agilely scales sheer cliffs to live atop craggy mountains. Its fire is put out when it sleeps.
LOOK! A BUNCH OF DATA ABOUT THIS POKÉMON! SO THAT'S WHAT THIS THING-A-MA-BOB DOES!
COOL!
SAYS HERE THAT CHIMCHAR CLIMBS FAST!
I LIKE SPEEDY POKÉMON!
HUP!
COMPARED TO THAT ONE OF YOURS...
HUP!

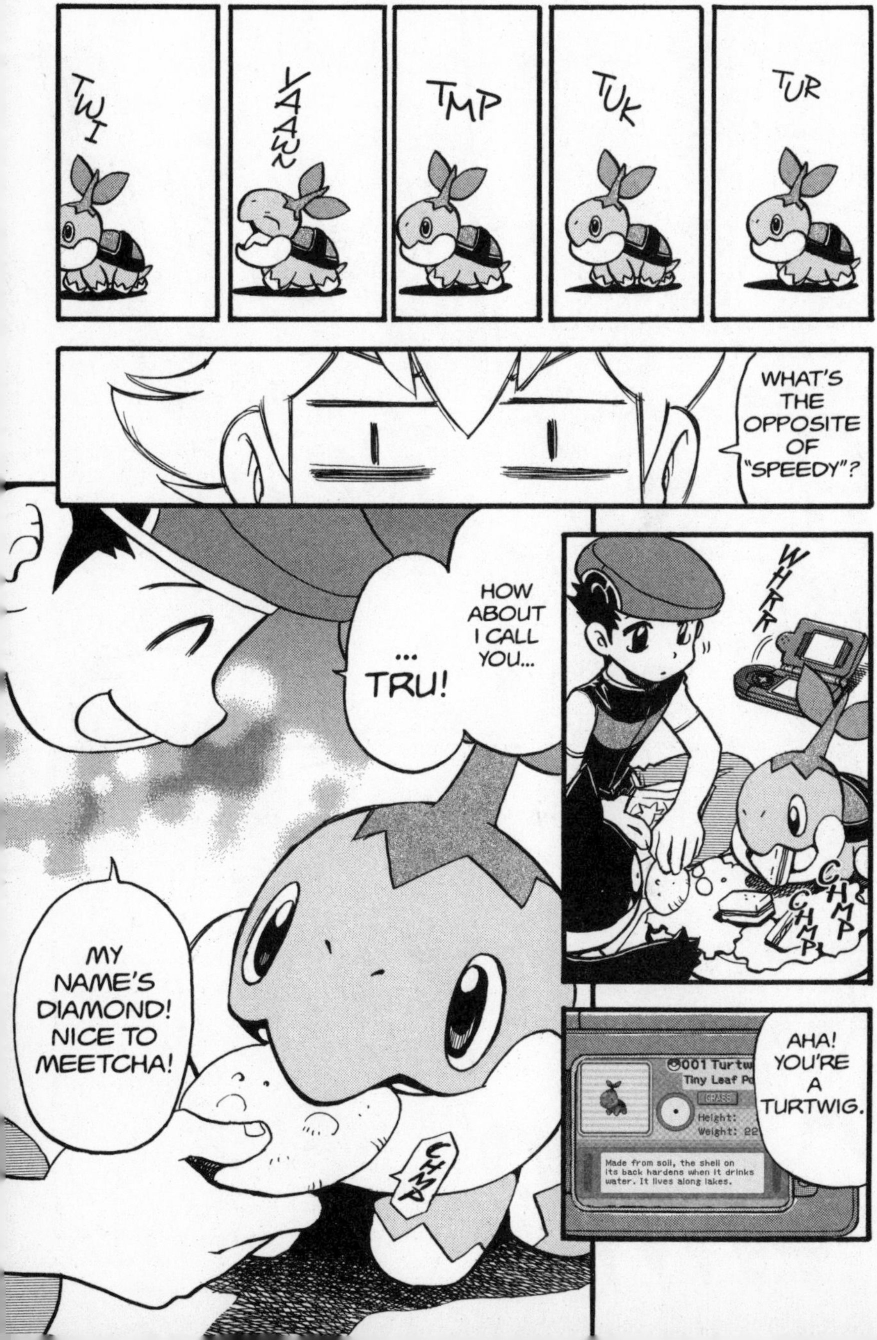
TWI
YAAWN
TMP
TUK
TUR
WHAT'S THE OPPOSITE OF "SPEEDY"?
WHHRR
CHMP
CHMP
001 Turtw
Tiny Leaf Po
GRASS
Height:
Weight: 22
Made from soil, the shell on its back hardens when it drinks water. It lives along lakes.
AHA! YOU'RE A TURTWIG.
HOW ABOUT I CALL YOU...
... TRU!
MY NAME'S DIAMOND! NICE TO MEETCHA!
CHMP

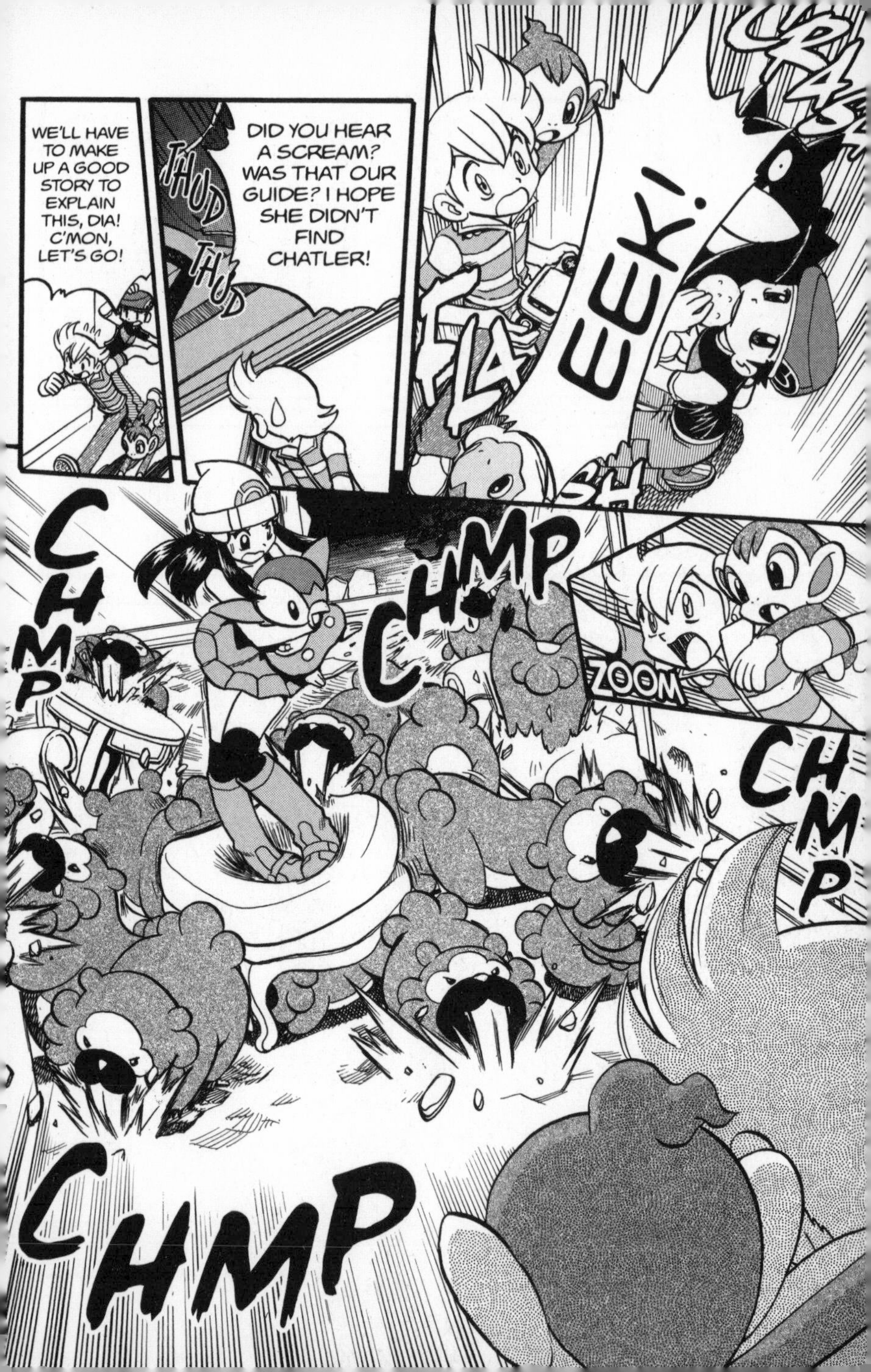
WE'LL HAVE TO MAKE UP A GOOD STORY TO EXPLAIN THIS, DIA! C'MON, LET'S GO!
THUD THUD
DID YOU HEAR A SCREAM? WAS THAT OUR GUIDE? I HOPE SHE DIDN'T FIND CHATLER!
CRASH
EEK!
FLASH
CHMP
CHMP
ZOOM
CHMP
CHMP

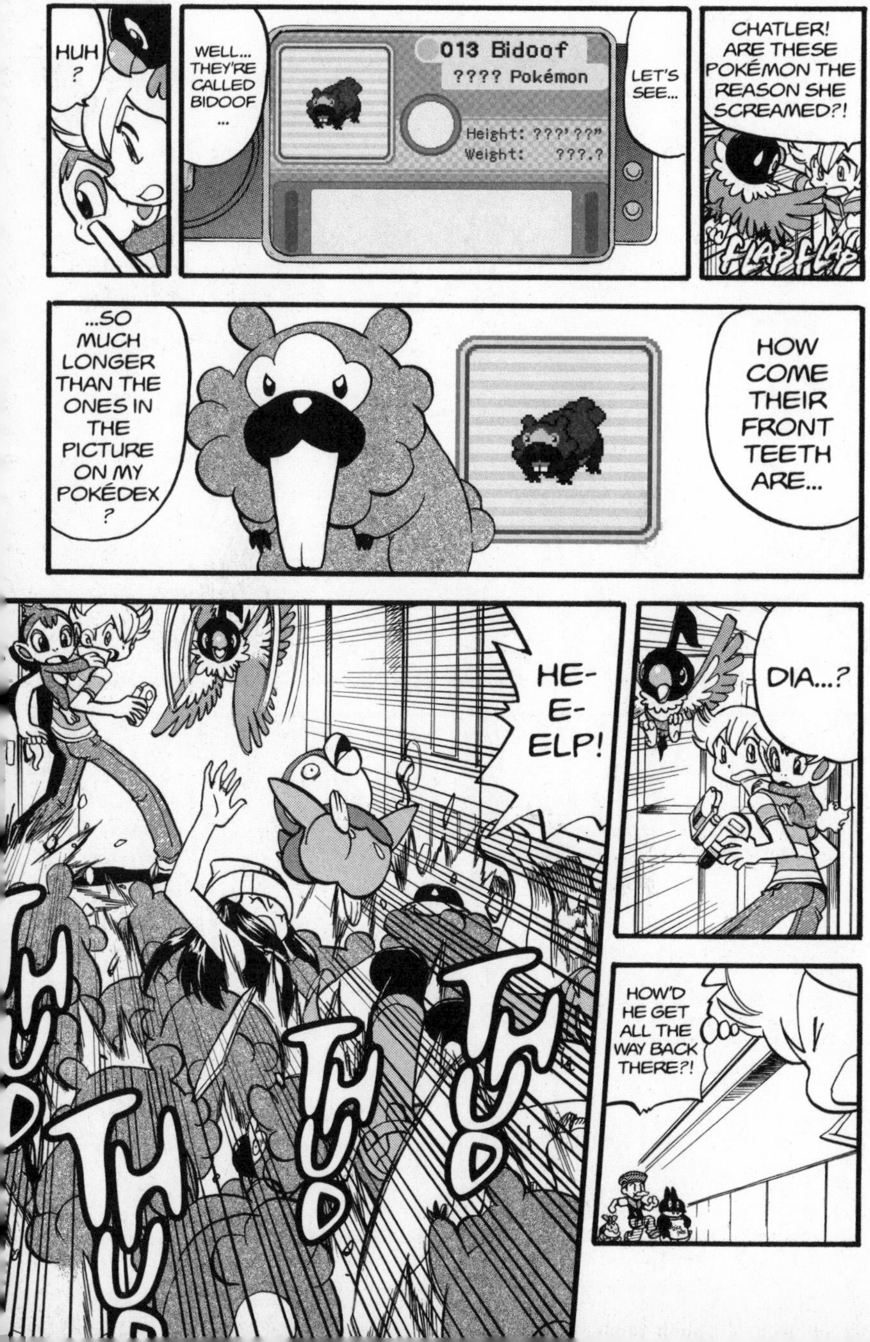
CHATLER! ARE THESE POKÉMON THE REASON SHE SCREAMED?!
FLAP FLAP
LET'S SEE...
013 Bidoof
???? Pokémon
Height: ???'??"
Weight: ???.?
WELL... THEY'RE CALLED BIDOOF...
HUH?
HOW COME THEIR FRONT TEETH ARE...
...SO MUCH LONGER THAN THE ONES IN THE PICTURE ON MY POKÉDEX?
DIA...?
HOW'D HE GET ALL THE WAY BACK THERE?!
HE-E-ELP!
THUD
THUD
THUD

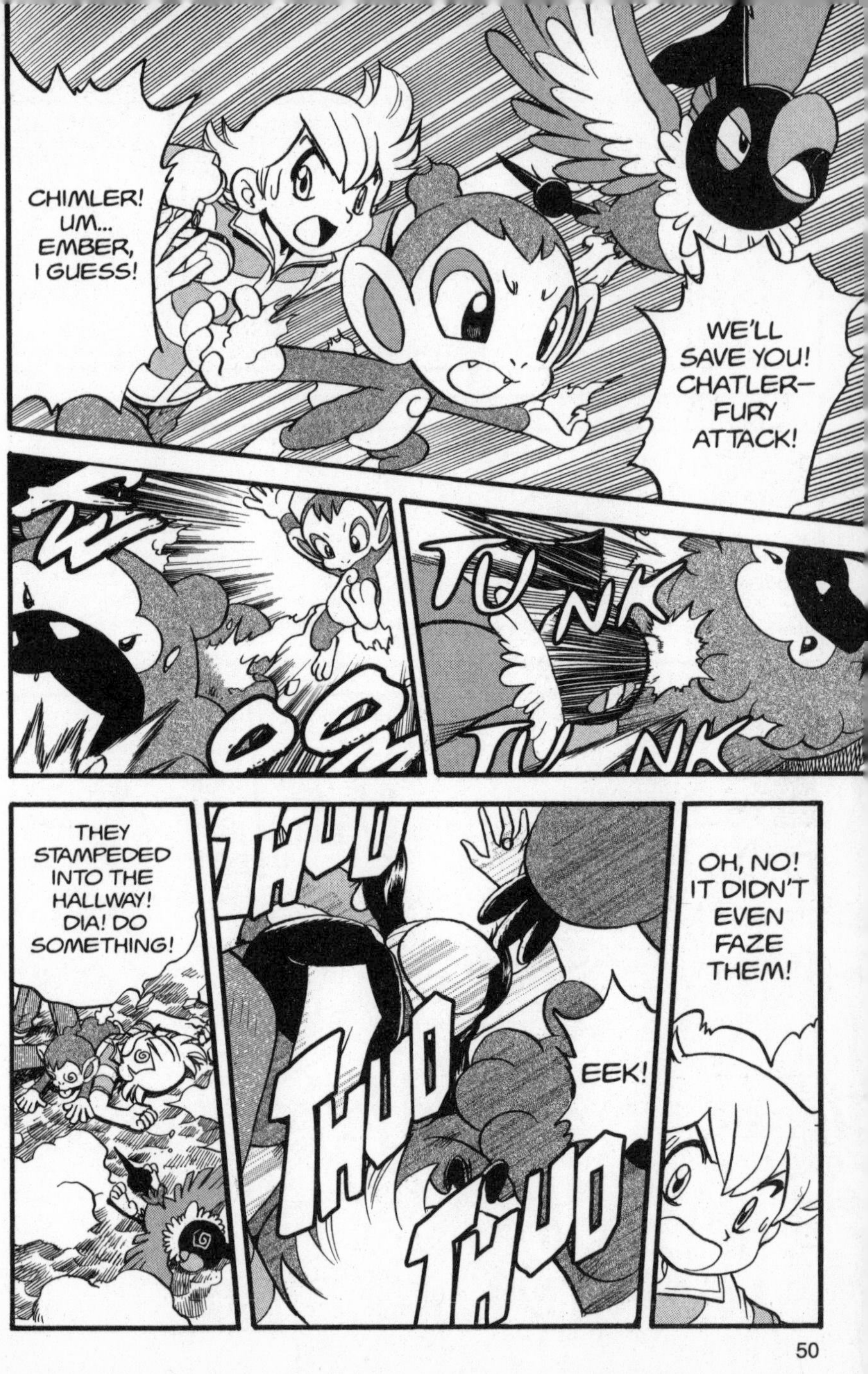

CHIMLER! UM... EMBER, I GUESS!
WE'LL SAVE YOU! CHATLER— FURY ATTACK!
TUNK
TUNK
THEY STAMPEDED INTO THE HALLWAY! DIA! DO SOMETHING!
THUD
THUD
THUD
EEK!
OH, NO! IT DIDN'T EVEN FAZE THEM!

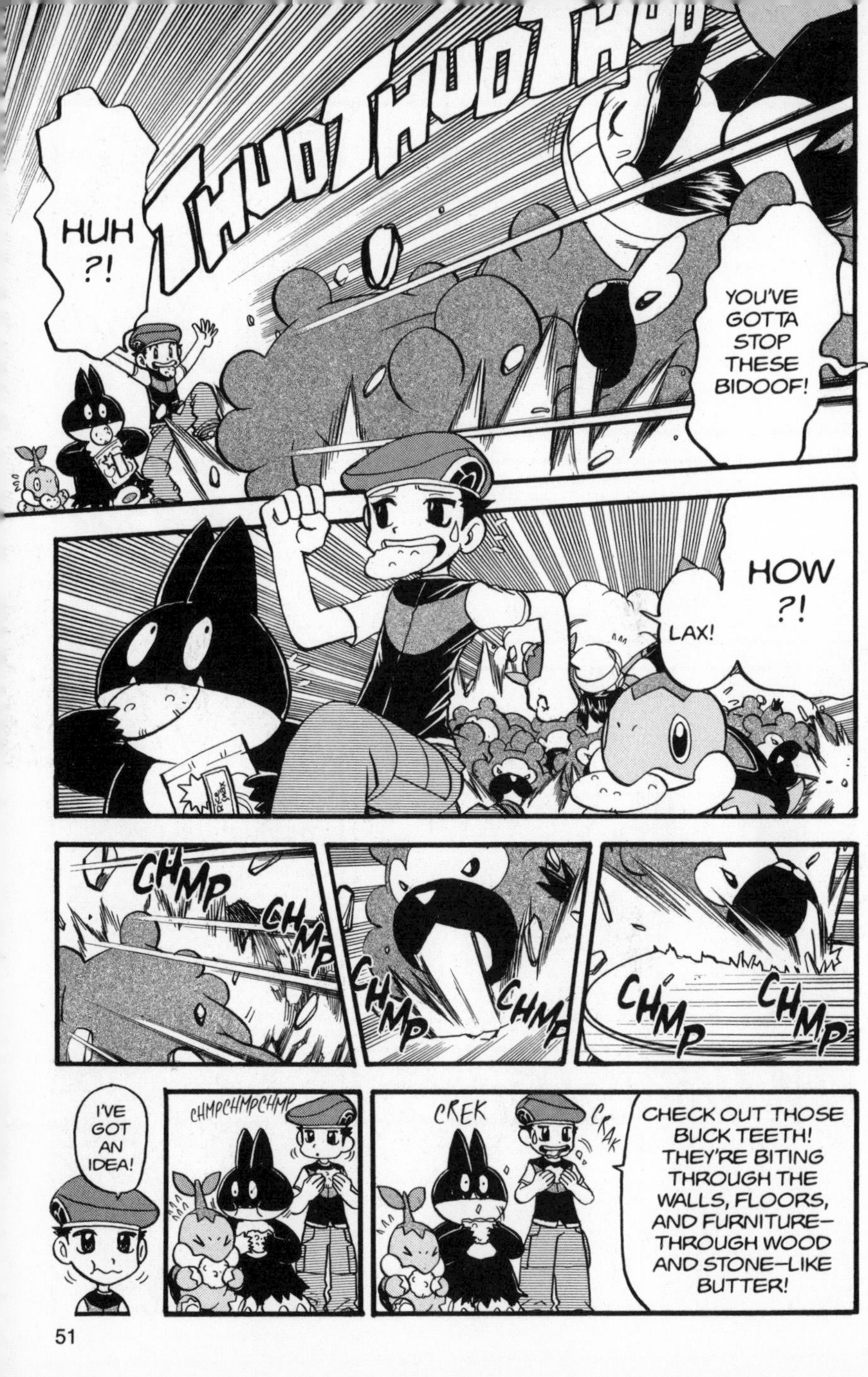
THUD THUD THU
HUH ?!
YOU'VE GOTTA STOP THESE BIDOOF!
HOW ?!
LAX!
CHMP CHMP
CHMP CHMP
CHMP CHMP
I'VE GOT AN IDEA!
CHMPCHMPCHMP
CREK
CRAK
CHECK OUT THOSE BUCK TEETH! THEY'RE BITING THROUGH THE WALLS, FLOORS, AND FURNITURE—THROUGH WOOD AND STONE—LIKE BUTTER!

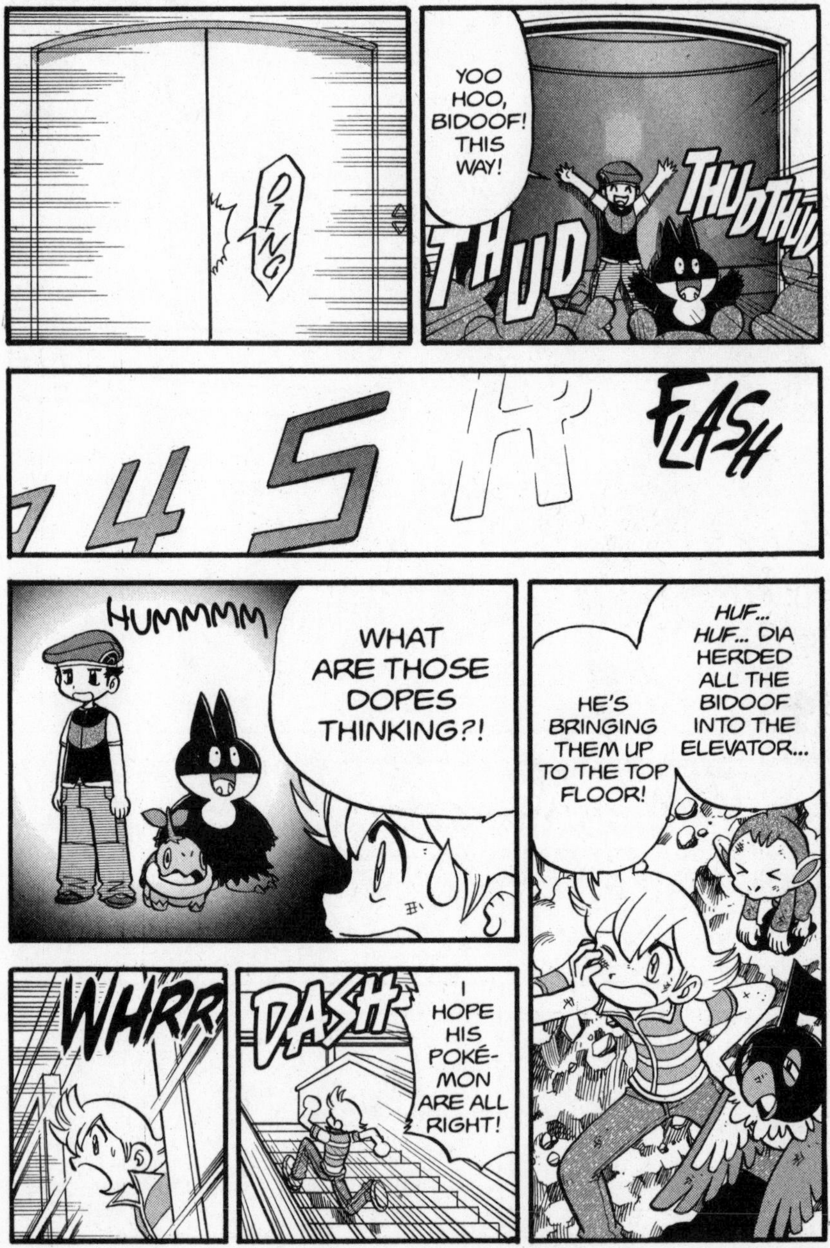
DING
YOO HOO, BIDOOF! THIS WAY!
THUD
THUDTHUD
4
5
FLASH
HUMMMM
WHAT ARE THOSE DOPES THINKING?!
HUF... HUF... DIA HERDED ALL THE BIDOOF INTO THE ELEVATOR...
HE'S BRINGING THEM UP TO THE TOP FLOOR!
WHRR
DASH
I HOPE HIS POKÉMON ARE ALL RIGHT!

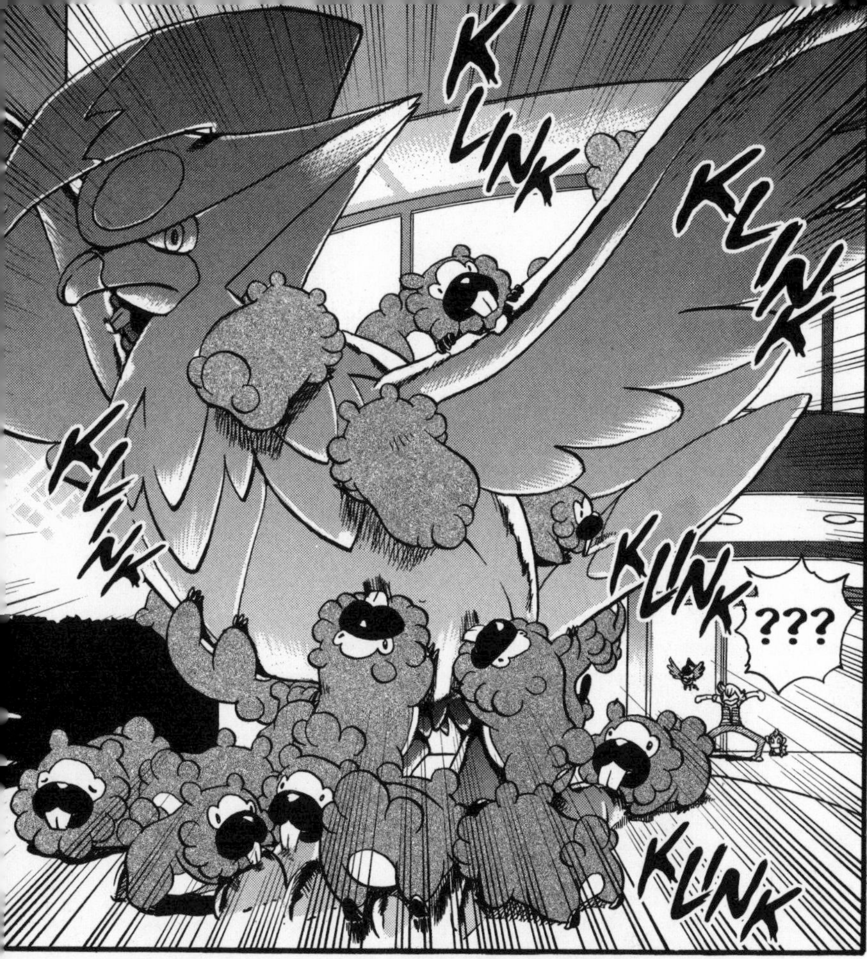
KLINK
KLINK
KLINK
KLINK
???
KLINK

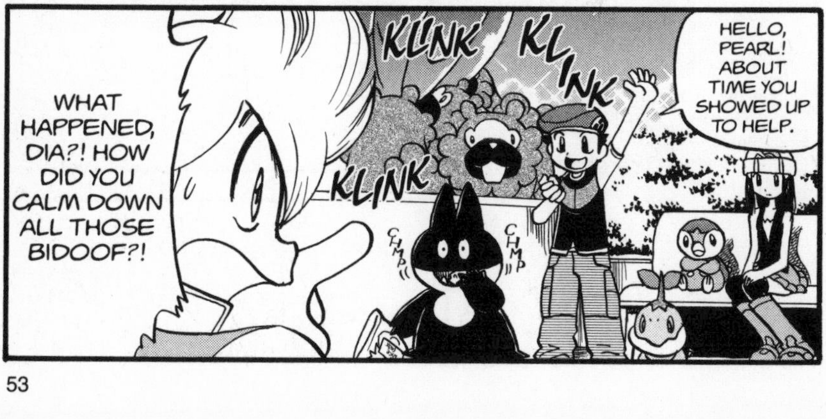
HELLO, PEARL! ABOUT TIME YOU SHOWED UP TO HELP.
KLINK
KLINK
WHAT HAPPENED, DIA?! HOW DID YOU CALM DOWN ALL THOSE BIDOOF?!
KLINK
CHMP
CHMP

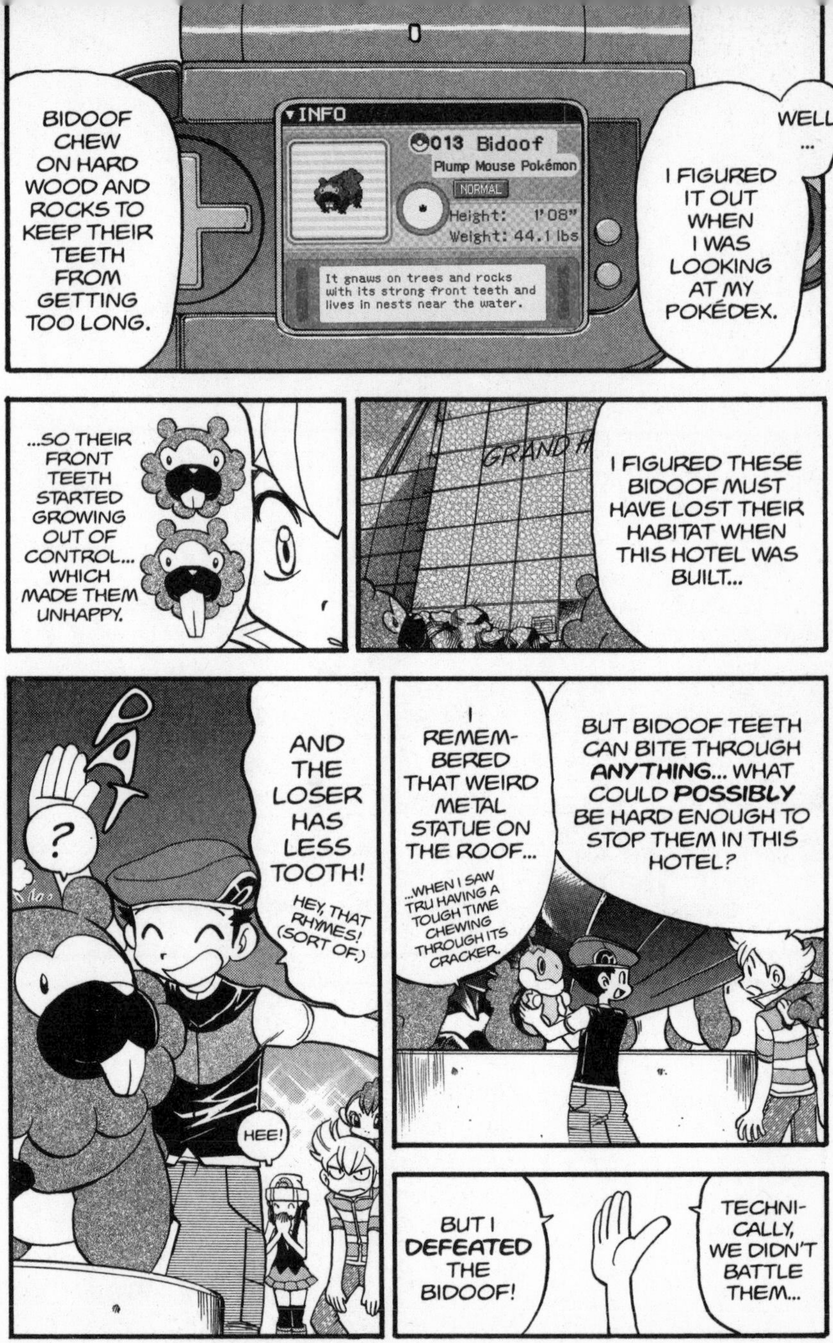
WELL ... I FIGURED IT OUT WHEN I WAS LOOKING AT MY POKÉDEX.
INFO
013 Bidoof
Plump Mouse Pokémon
NORMAL
Height: 1'08"
Weight: 44.1 lbs
It gnaws on trees and rocks with its strong front teeth and lives in nests near the water.
BIDOOF CHEW ON HARD WOOD AND ROCKS TO KEEP THEIR TEETH FROM GETTING TOO LONG.
I FIGURED THESE BIDOOF MUST HAVE LOST THEIR HABITAT WHEN THIS HOTEL WAS BUILT...
GRAND H
...SO THEIR FRONT TEETH STARTED GROWING OUT OF CONTROL... WHICH MADE THEM UNHAPPY.
BUT BIDOOF TEETH CAN BITE THROUGH **ANYTHING**... WHAT COULD **POSSIBLY** BE HARD ENOUGH TO STOP THEM IN THIS HOTEL?
I REMEMBERED THAT WEIRD METAL STATUE ON THE ROOF...
...WHEN I SAW TRU HAVING A TOUGH TIME CHEWING THROUGH ITS CRACKER.
TECHNICALLY, WE DIDN'T BATTLE THEM...
BUT I **DEFEATED** THE BIDOOF!
AND THE LOSER HAS LESS TOOTH!
HEY, THAT RHYMES! (SORT OF.)
?
HEE!

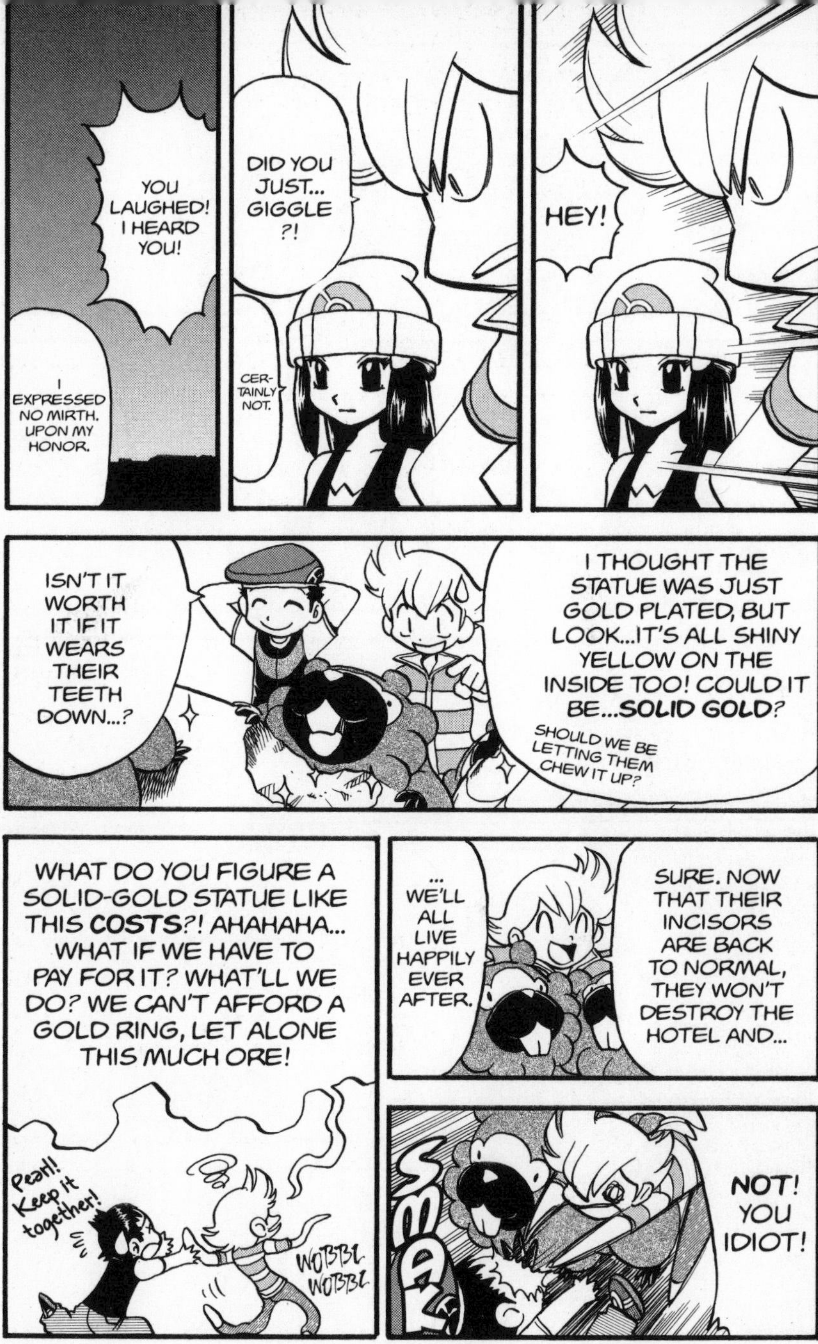
YOU LAUGHED! I HEARD YOU!
I EXPRESSED NO MIRTH. UPON MY HONOR.
DID YOU JUST... GIGGLE?!
CERTAINLY NOT.
HEY!
ISN'T IT WORTH IT IF IT WEARS THEIR TEETH DOWN...?
I THOUGHT THE STATUE WAS JUST GOLD PLATED, BUT LOOK...IT'S ALL SHINY YELLOW ON THE INSIDE TOO! COULD IT BE...**SOLID GOLD**?
SHOULD WE BE LETTING THEM CHEW IT UP?
WHAT DO YOU FIGURE A SOLID-GOLD STATUE LIKE THIS **COSTS**?! AHAHAHA... WHAT IF WE HAVE TO PAY FOR IT? WHAT'LL WE DO? WE CAN'T AFFORD A GOLD RING, LET ALONE THIS MUCH ORE!
Pearl! Keep it together!
WOBBL WOBBL
SURE. NOW THAT THEIR INCISORS ARE BACK TO NORMAL, THEY WON'T DESTROY THE HOTEL AND...
... WE'LL ALL LIVE HAPPILY EVER AFTER.
SMAK
NOT! YOU IDIOT!

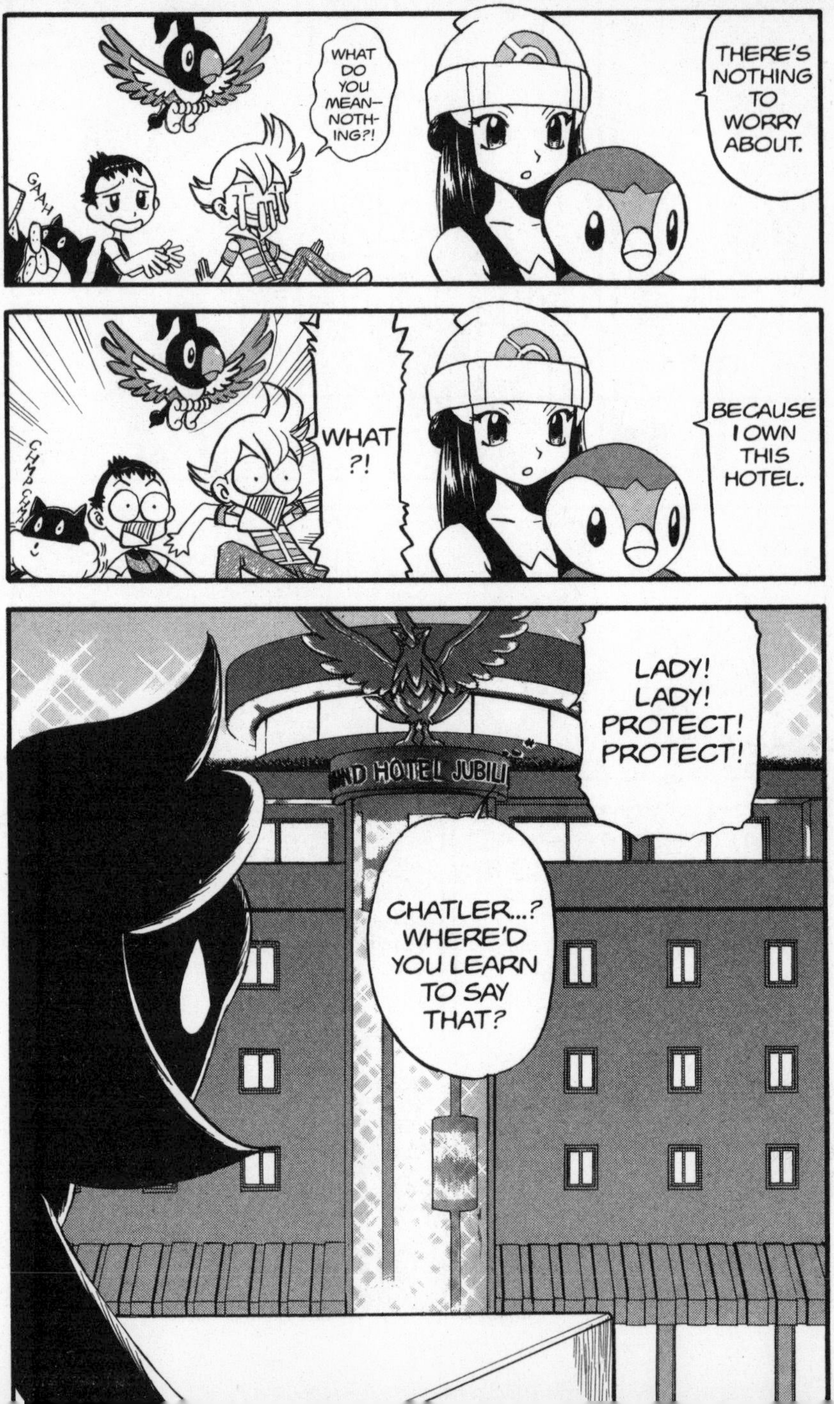
THERE'S NOTHING TO WORRY ABOUT.
WHAT DO YOU MEAN—NOTHING?!
GAAAH
BECAUSE I OWN THIS HOTEL.
WHAT?!
CHMP CHMP
LADY! LADY! PROTECT! PROTECT!
ND HOTEL JUBILI
CHATLER...? WHERE'D YOU LEARN TO SAY THAT?

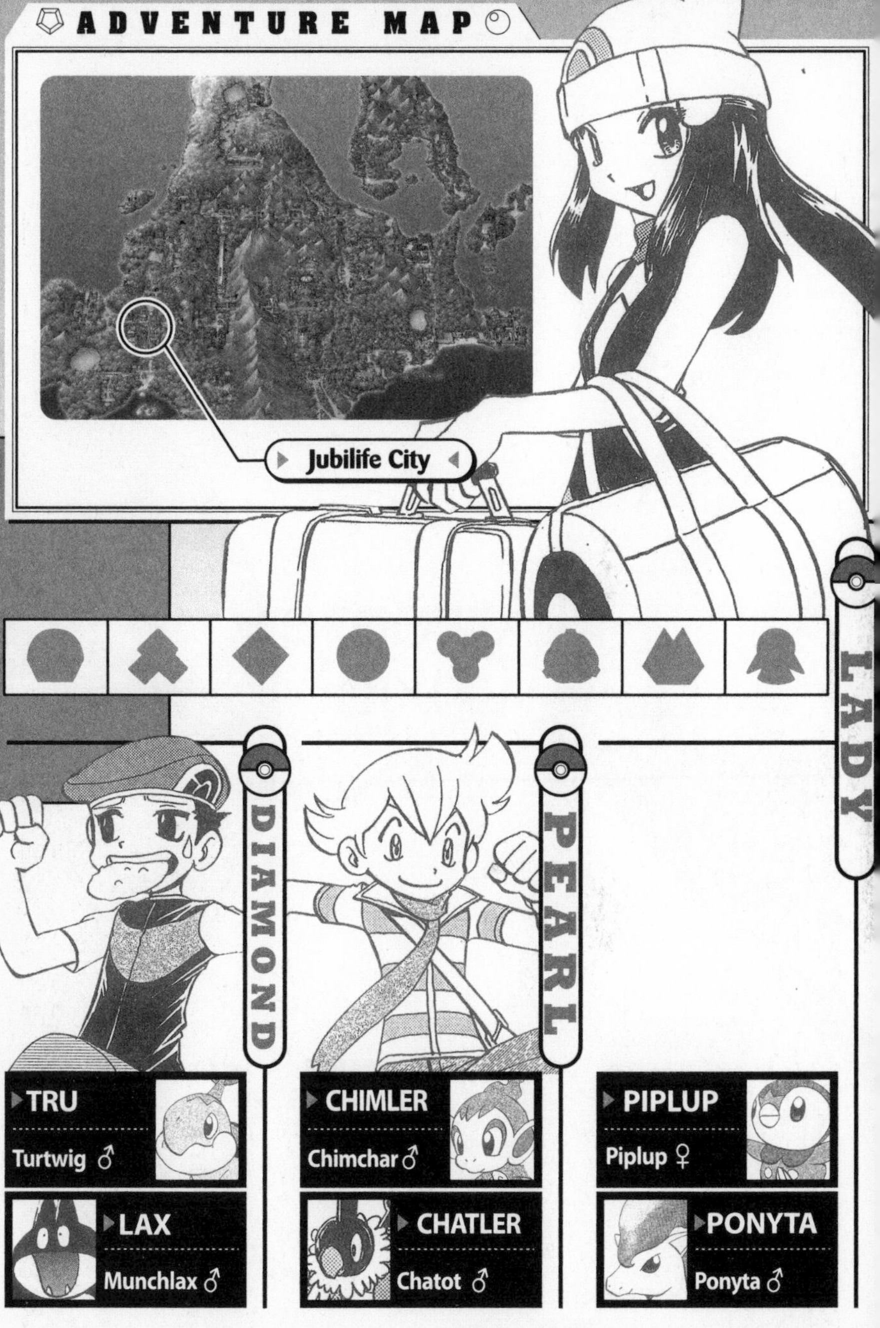
ADVENTURE MAP
Jubilife City
LADY
DIAMOND
PEARL
TRU
Turtwig ♂
LAX
Munchlax ♂
CHIMLER
Chimchar ♂
CHATLER
Chatot ♂
PIPLUP
Piplup ♀
PONYTA
Ponyta ♂

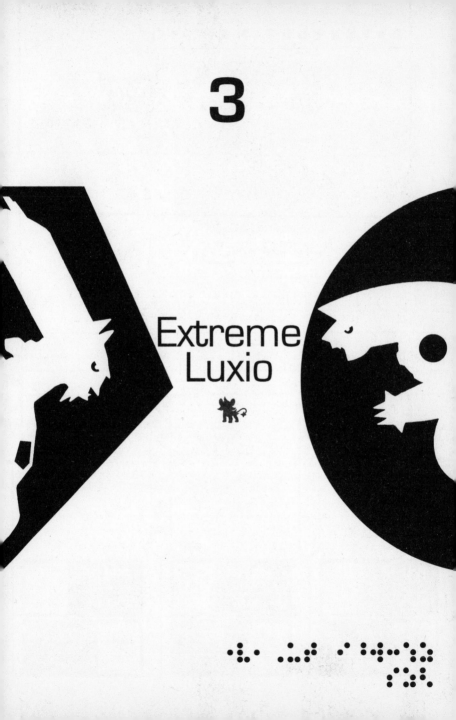

3

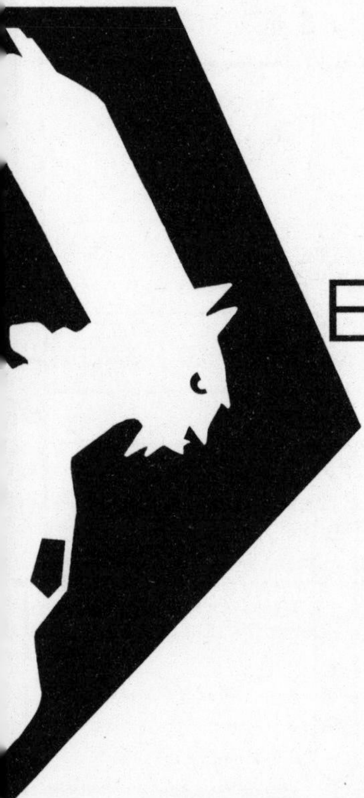

Extreme Luxio

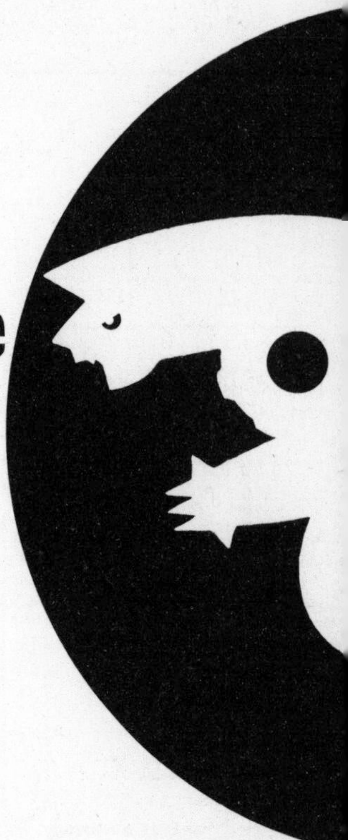

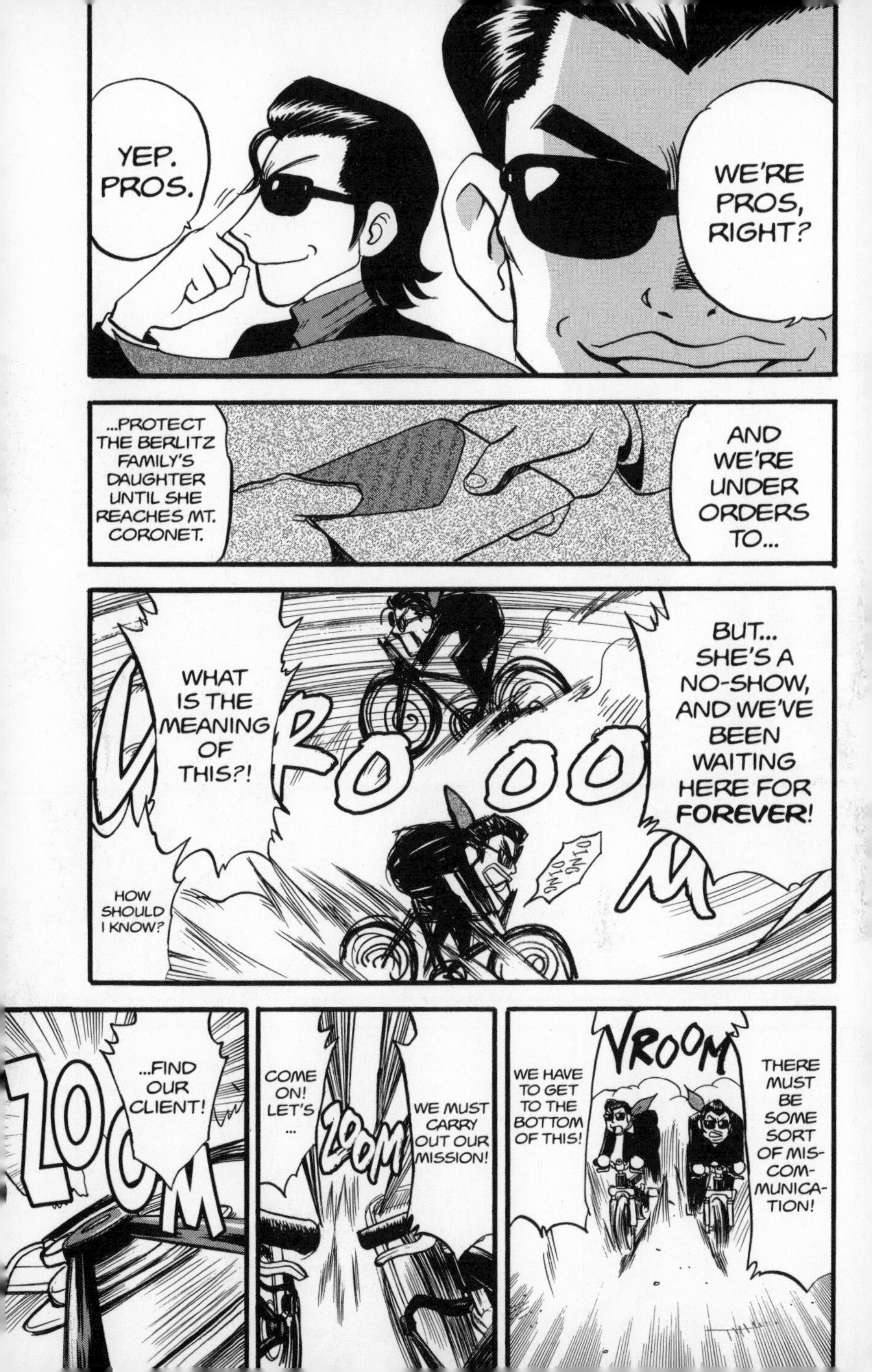
WE'RE PROS, RIGHT?
YEP. PROS.
AND WE'RE UNDER ORDERS TO...
...PROTECT THE BERLITZ FAMILY'S DAUGHTER UNTIL SHE REACHES MT. CORONET.
BUT... SHE'S A NO-SHOW, AND WE'VE BEEN WAITING HERE FOR **FOREVER**!
ROOOM
WHAT IS THE MEANING OF THIS?!
DING DING
HOW SHOULD I KNOW?
THERE MUST BE SOME SORT OF MIS-COMMUNICATION!
VROOM
WE HAVE TO GET TO THE BOTTOM OF THIS!
WE MUST CARRY OUT OUR MISSION!
ZOOM
COME ON! LET'S ...
...FIND OUR CLIENT!
ZOOOM

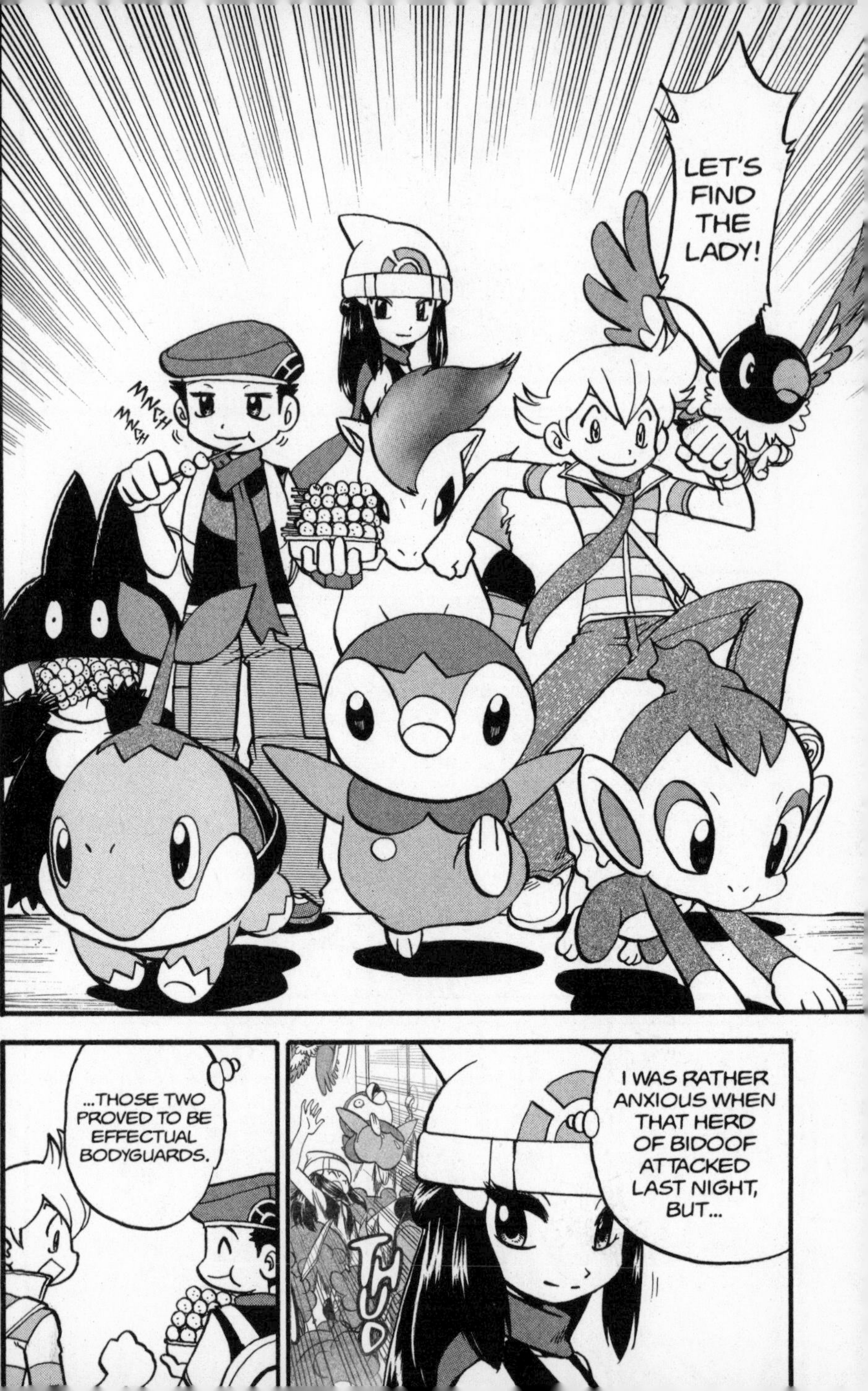
LET'S FIND THE LADY!
MNCH MNCH
I WAS RATHER ANXIOUS WHEN THAT HERD OF BIDOOF ATTACKED LAST NIGHT, BUT...
...THOSE TWO PROVED TO BE EFFECTUAL BODYGUARDS.

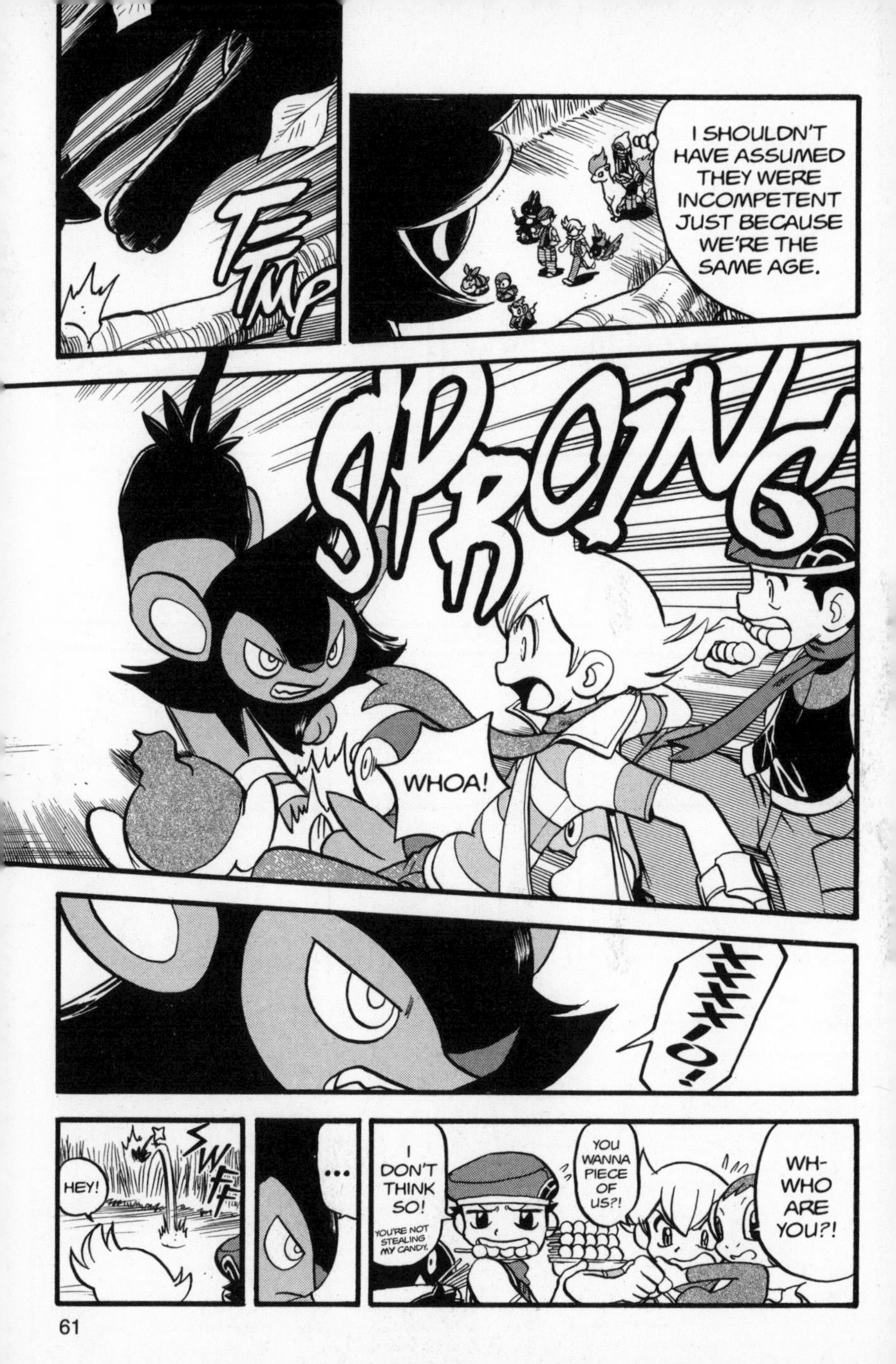
FMP
I SHOULDN'T HAVE ASSUMED THEY WERE INCOMPETENT JUST BECAUSE WE'RE THE SAME AGE.
SPROING
WHOA!
HHHH-O?!
HEY!
SWFF
...
I DON'T THINK SO!
YOU'RE NOT STEALING MY CANDY.
YOU WANNA PIECE OF US?!
WH-WHO ARE YOU?!

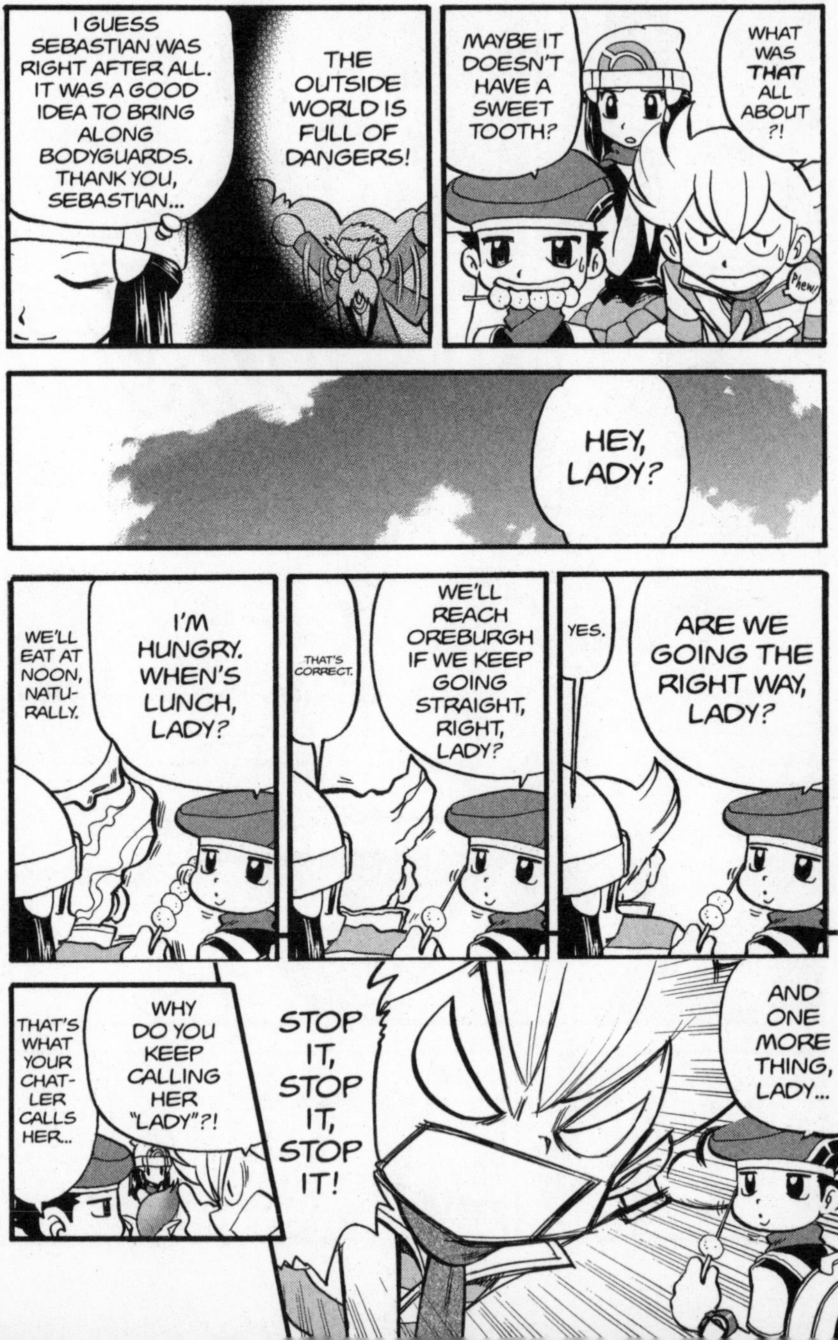
WHAT WAS THAT ALL ABOUT?!
Phew!
MAYBE IT DOESN'T HAVE A SWEET TOOTH?
THE OUTSIDE WORLD IS FULL OF DANGERS!
I GUESS SEBASTIAN WAS RIGHT AFTER ALL. IT WAS A GOOD IDEA TO BRING ALONG BODYGUARDS. THANK YOU, SEBASTIAN...
HEY, LADY?
ARE WE GOING THE RIGHT WAY, LADY?
YES.
WE'LL REACH OREBURGH IF WE KEEP GOING STRAIGHT, RIGHT, LADY?
THAT'S CORRECT.
I'M HUNGRY. WHEN'S LUNCH, LADY?
WE'LL EAT AT NOON, NATU-RALLY.
AND ONE MORE THING, LADY...
STOP IT, STOP IT, STOP IT!
WHY DO YOU KEEP CALLING HER "LADY"?!
THAT'S WHAT YOUR CHAT-LER CALLS HER...

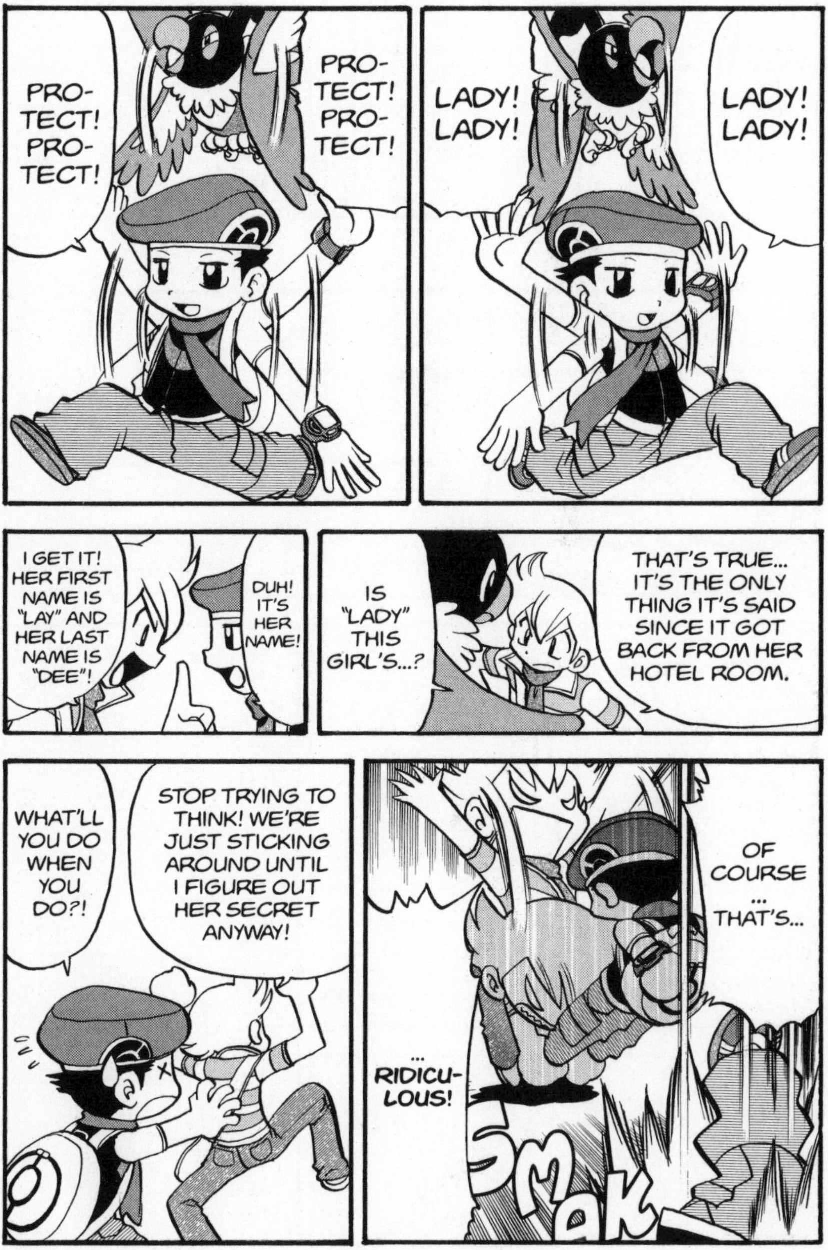
LADY! LADY!
LADY! LADY!
PRO-TECT! PRO-TECT!
PRO-TECT! PRO-TECT!
THAT'S TRUE... IT'S THE ONLY THING IT'S SAID SINCE IT GOT BACK FROM HER HOTEL ROOM.
IS "LADY" THIS GIRL'S...?
DUH! IT'S HER NAME!
I GET IT! HER FIRST NAME IS "LAY" AND HER LAST NAME IS "DEE"!
OF COURSE ... THAT'S...
...RIDICULOUS!
SMAK
STOP TRYING TO THINK! WE'RE JUST STICKING AROUND UNTIL I FIGURE OUT HER SECRET ANYWAY!
WHAT'LL YOU DO WHEN YOU DO?!

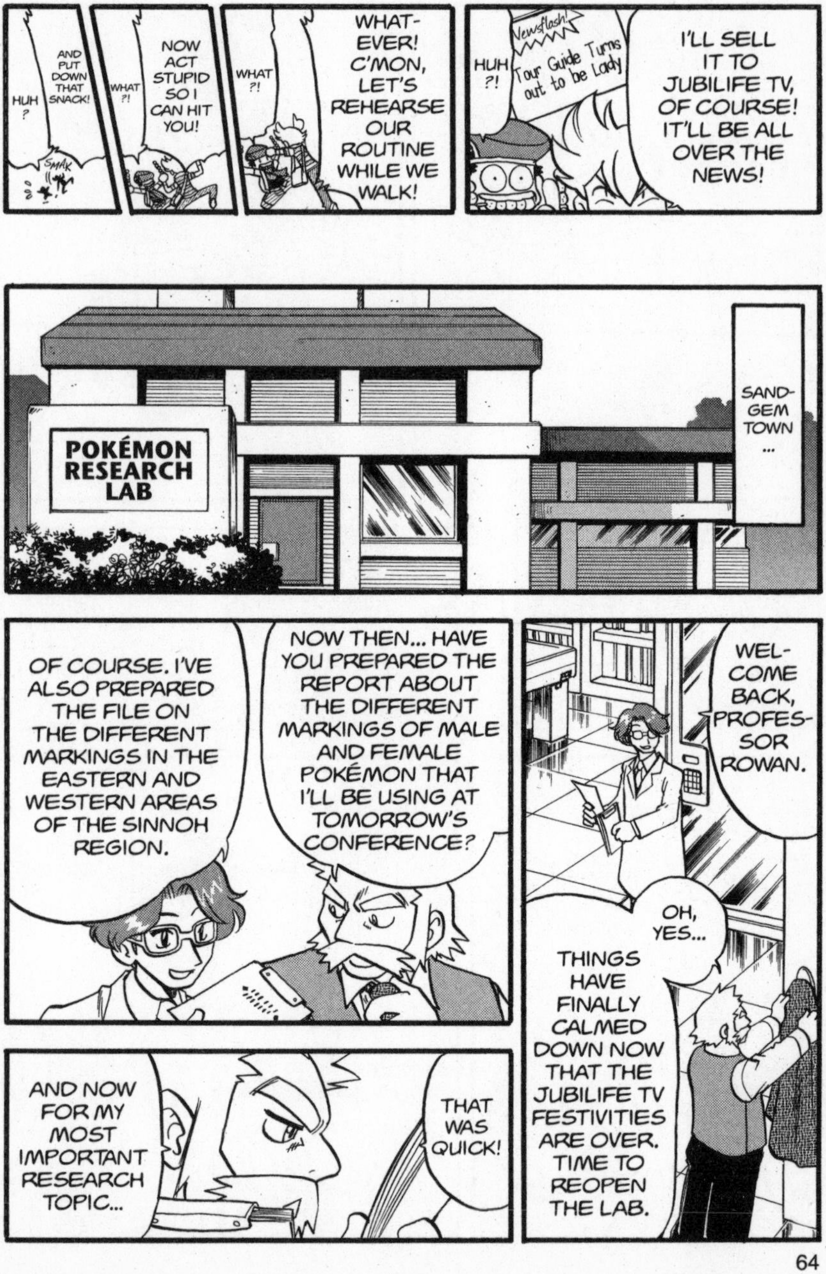
HUH ?
AND PUT DOWN THAT SNACK!
SMAK
WHAT ?!
NOW ACT STUPID SO I CAN HIT YOU!
WHAT ?!
WHAT-EVER! C'MON, LET'S REHEARSE OUR ROUTINE WHILE WE WALK!
HUH ?!
Newsflash! Tour Guide Turns out to be Lady
I'LL SELL IT TO JUBILIFE TV, OF COURSE! IT'LL BE ALL OVER THE NEWS!
SAND-GEM TOWN ...
POKÉMON RESEARCH LAB
WEL-COME BACK, PROFES-SOR ROWAN.
OH, YES...
THINGS HAVE FINALLY CALMED DOWN NOW THAT THE JUBILIFE TV FESTIVITIES ARE OVER. TIME TO REOPEN THE LAB.
NOW THEN... HAVE YOU PREPARED THE REPORT ABOUT THE DIFFERENT MARKINGS OF MALE AND FEMALE POKÉMON THAT I'LL BE USING AT TOMORROW'S CONFERENCE?
OF COURSE. I'VE ALSO PREPARED THE FILE ON THE DIFFERENT MARKINGS IN THE EASTERN AND WESTERN AREAS OF THE SINNOH REGION.
THAT WAS QUICK!
AND NOW FOR MY MOST IMPORTANT RESEARCH TOPIC...

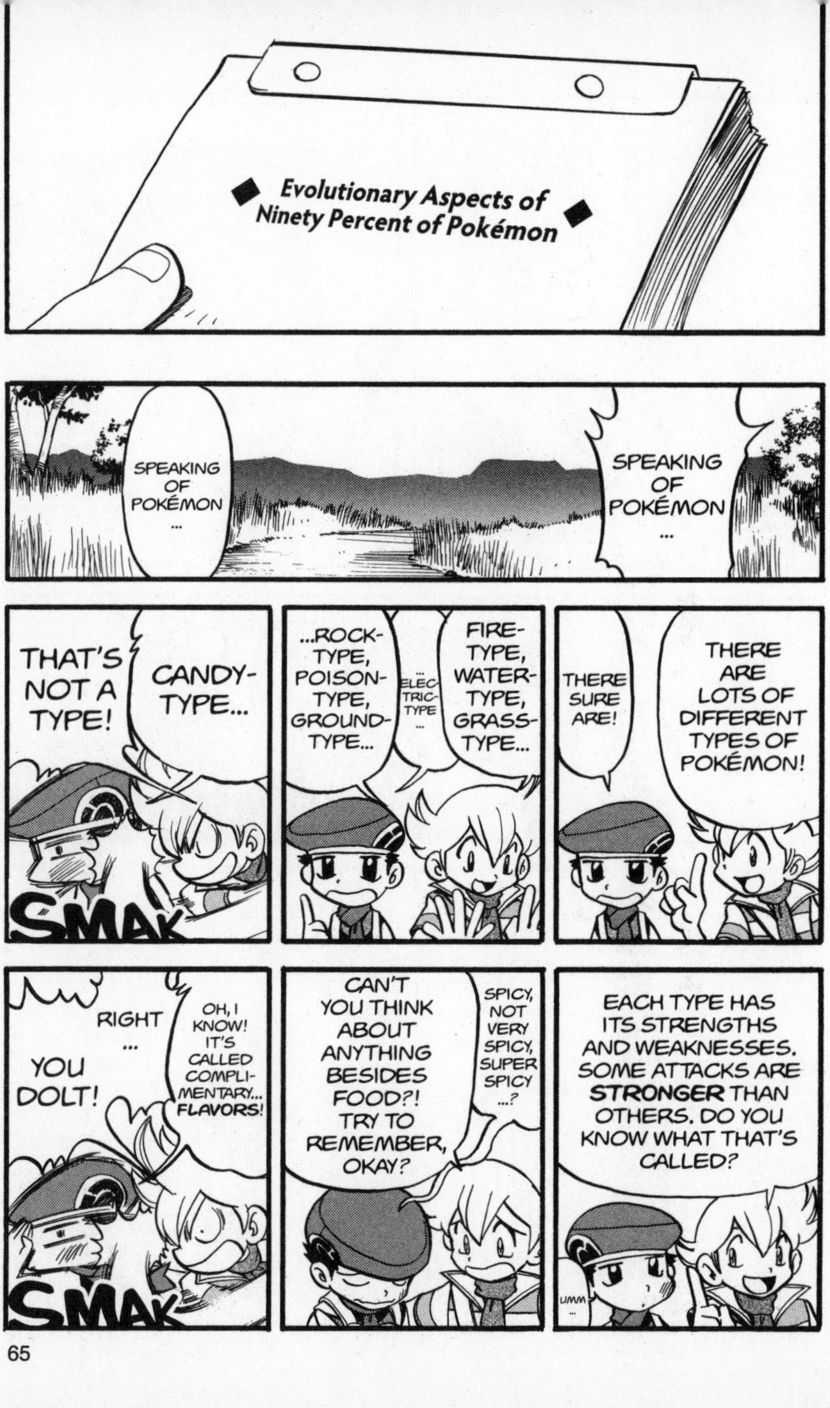
Evolutionary Aspects of Ninety Percent of Pokémon
SPEAKING OF POKÉMON...
SPEAKING OF POKÉMON...
THERE ARE LOTS OF DIFFERENT TYPES OF POKÉMON!
THERE SURE ARE!
FIRE-TYPE, WATER-TYPE, GRASS-TYPE...
...ELECTRIC-TYPE...
...ROCK-TYPE, POISON-TYPE, GROUND-TYPE...
CANDY-TYPE...
THAT'S NOT A TYPE!
SMAK
EACH TYPE HAS ITS STRENGTHS AND WEAKNESSES. SOME ATTACKS ARE **STRONGER** THAN OTHERS. DO YOU KNOW WHAT THAT'S CALLED?
UMM...
SPICY, NOT VERY SPICY, SUPER SPICY...?
CAN'T YOU THINK ABOUT ANYTHING BESIDES FOOD?! TRY TO REMEMBER, OKAY?
OH, I KNOW! IT'S CALLED COMPLIMENTARY... **FLAVORS**!
RIGHT... YOU DOLT!
SMAK

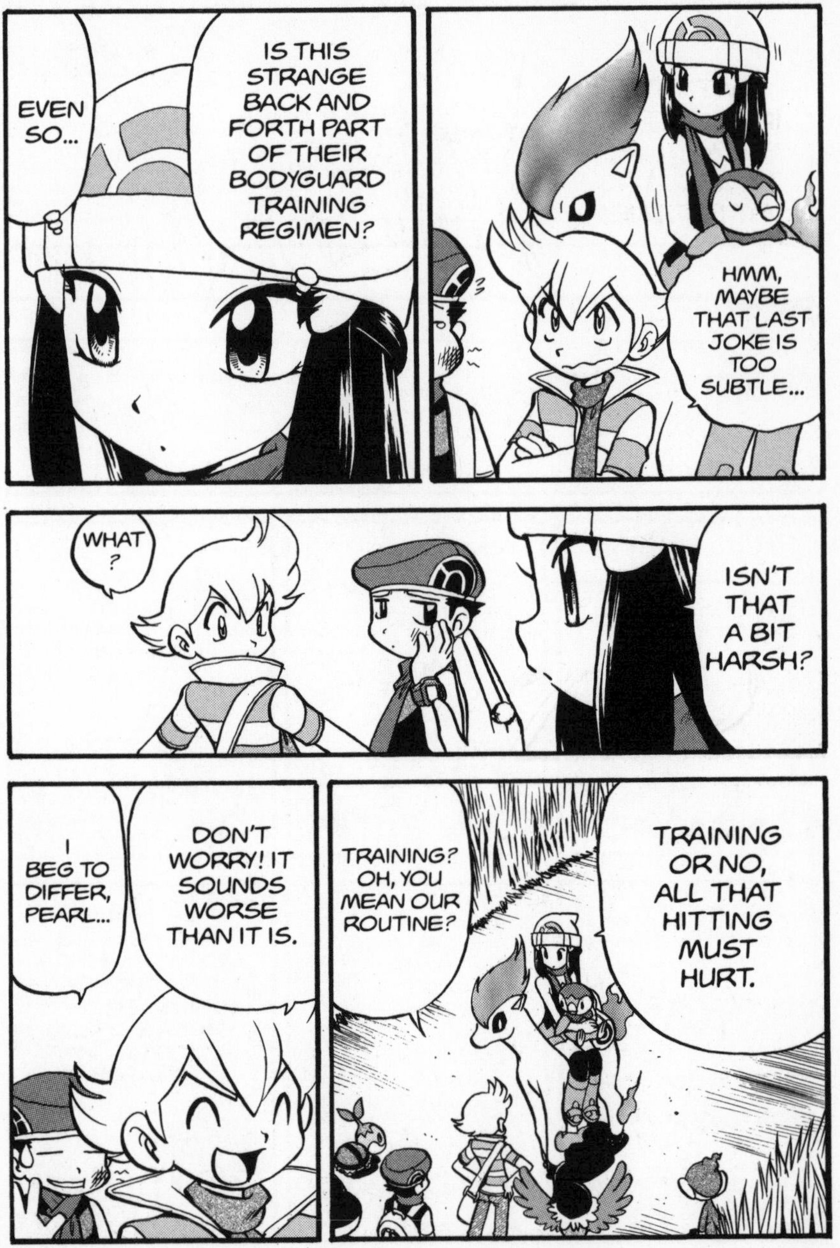
EVEN SO...
IS THIS STRANGE BACK AND FORTH PART OF THEIR BODYGUARD TRAINING REGIMEN?
HMM, MAYBE THAT LAST JOKE IS TOO SUBTLE...
WHAT?
ISN'T THAT A BIT HARSH?
I BEG TO DIFFER, PEARL...
DON'T WORRY! IT SOUNDS WORSE THAN IT IS.
TRAINING? OH, YOU MEAN OUR ROUTINE?
TRAINING OR NO, ALL THAT HITTING MUST HURT.

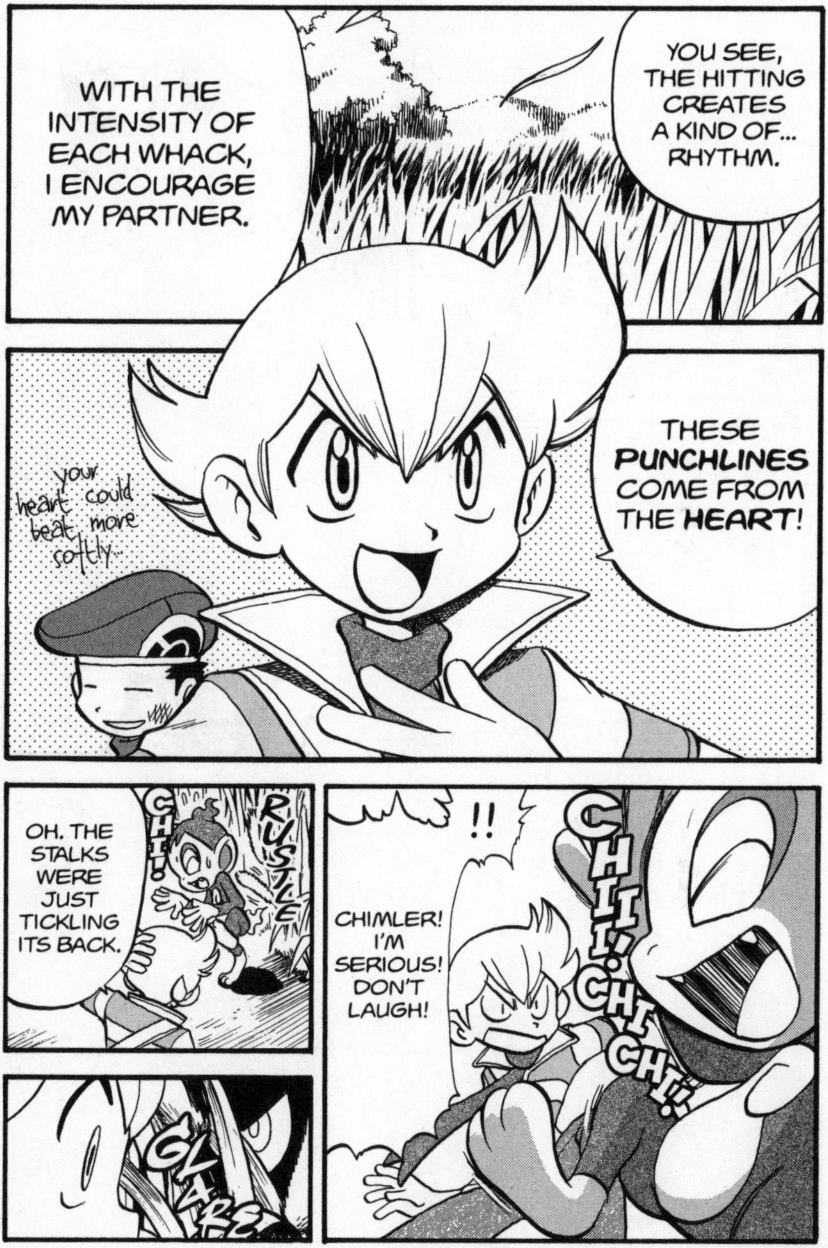
WITH THE INTENSITY OF EACH WHACK, I ENCOURAGE MY PARTNER.
YOU SEE, THE HITTING CREATES A KIND OF... RHYTHM.
THESE PUNCHLINES COME FROM THE HEART!
your heart could beat more softly...
OH. THE STALKS WERE JUST TICKLING ITS BACK.
CHI!
RUSTLE
!!
CHIMLER! I'M SERIOUS! DON'T LAUGH!
CHIII, CHI CHI CHI!!
GLARE

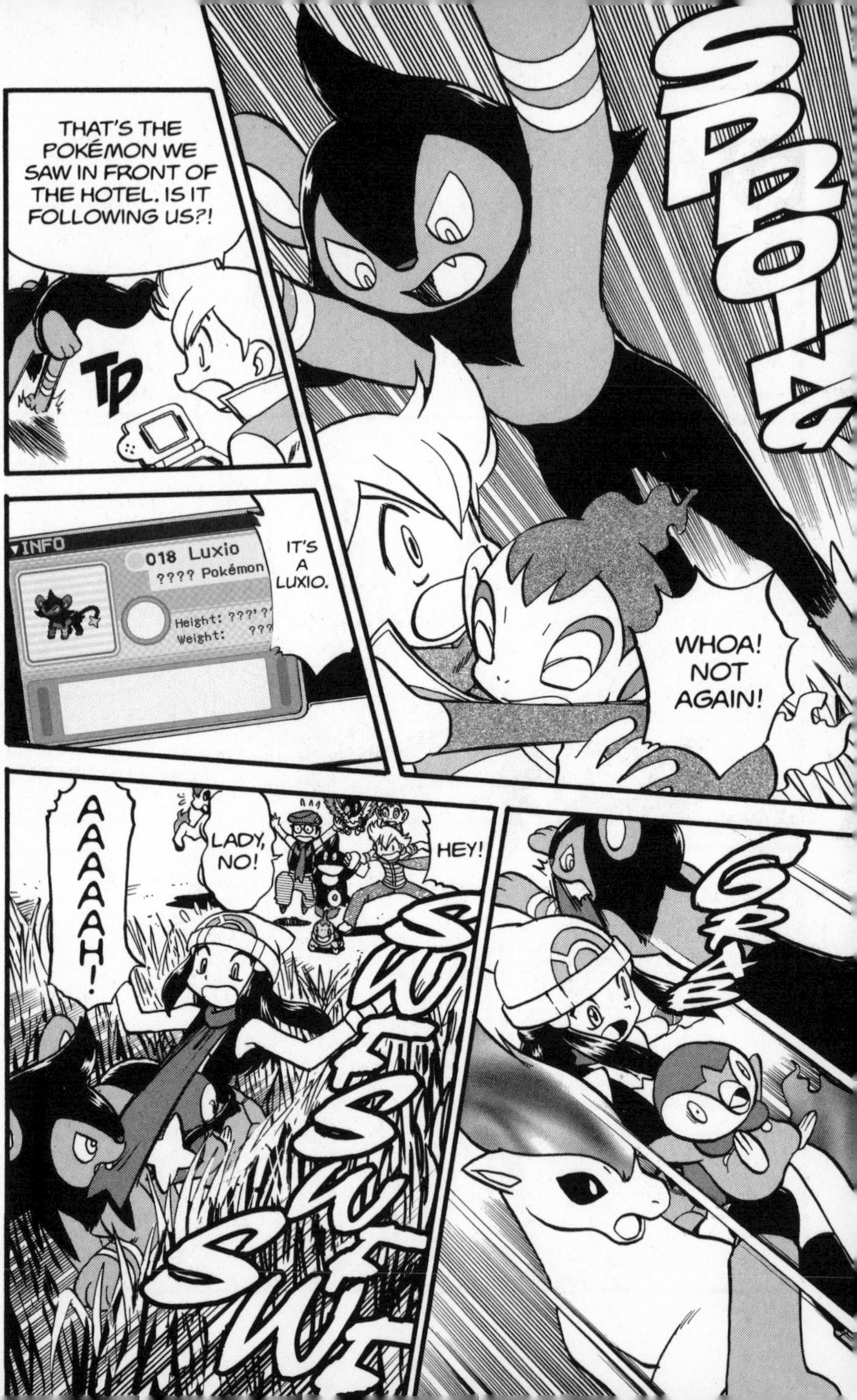
THAT'S THE POKÉMON WE SAW IN FRONT OF THE HOTEL. IS IT FOLLOWING US?!
TP
SPROING
INFO
018 Luxio
???? Pokémon
Height:
Weight:
IT'S A LUXIO.
WHOA! NOT AGAIN!
AAAAAAH!
LADY, NO!
HEY!

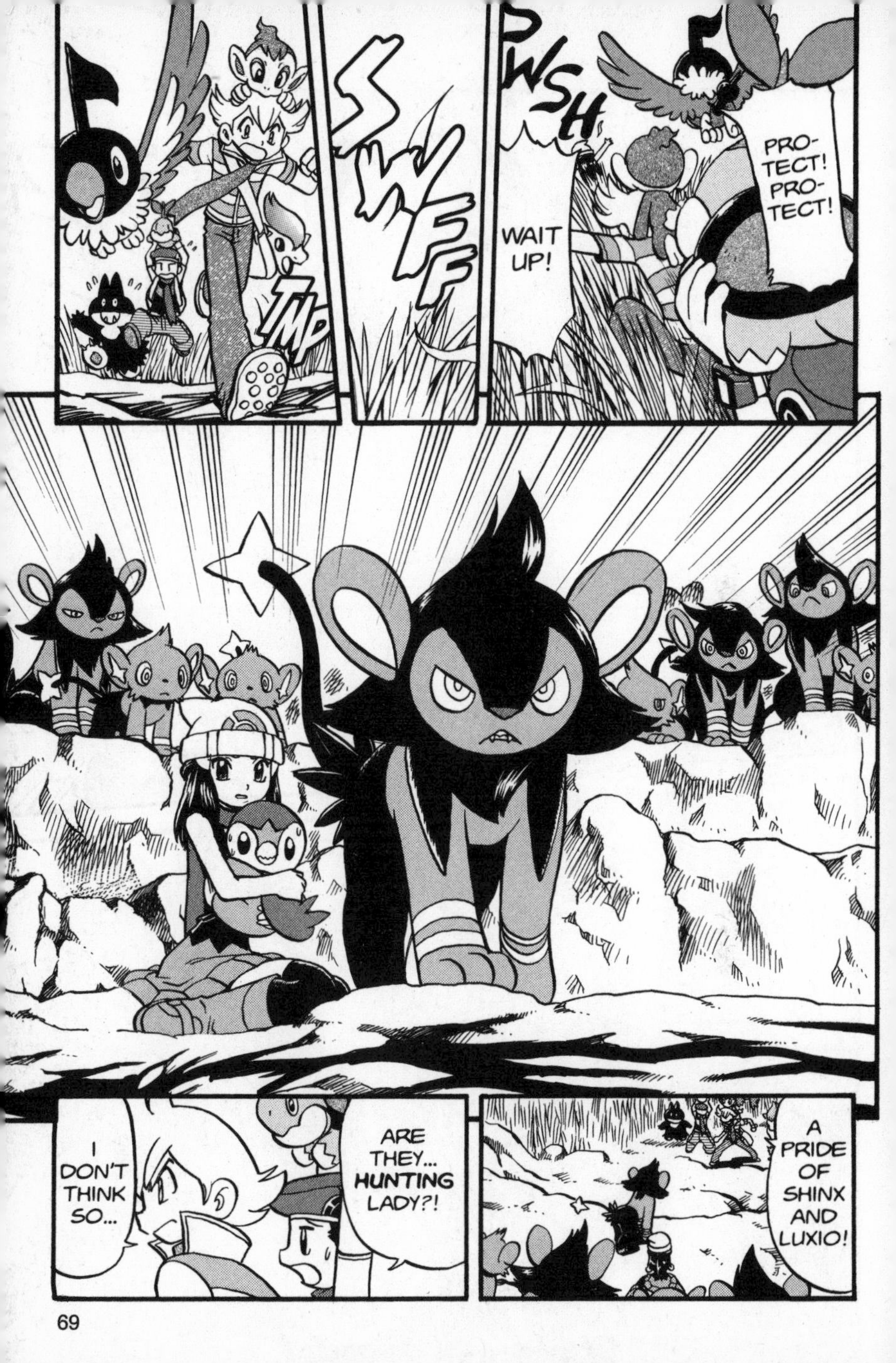
TMP
SWFF
PWSH
WAIT UP!
PROTECT! PROTECT!
A PRIDE OF SHINX AND LUXIO!
ARE THEY... **HUNTING** LADY?!
I DON'T THINK SO...

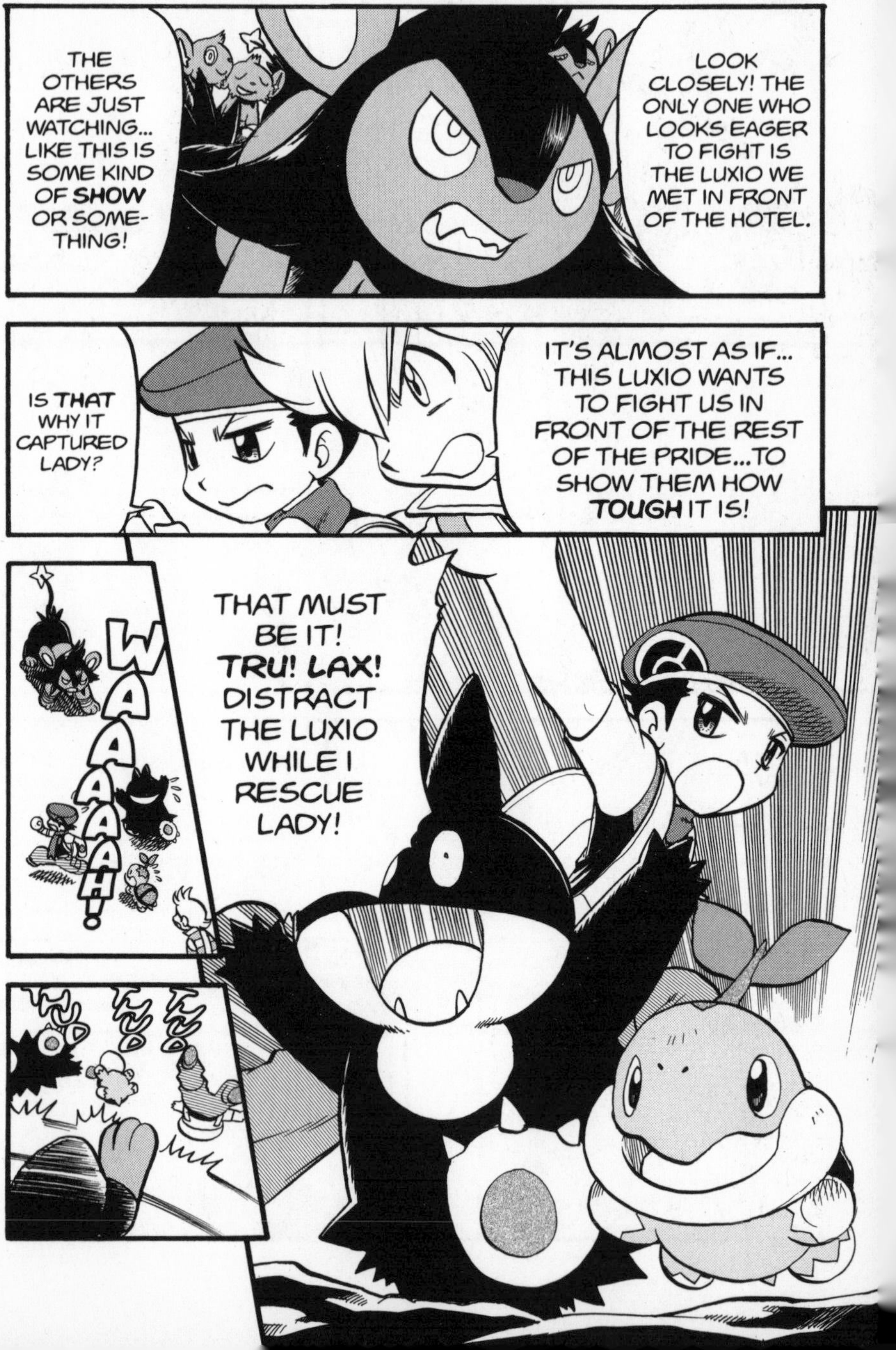

THE OTHERS ARE JUST WATCHING... LIKE THIS IS SOME KIND OF **SHOW** OR SOME- THING!
LOOK CLOSELY! THE ONLY ONE WHO LOOKS EAGER TO FIGHT IS THE LUXIO WE MET IN FRONT OF THE HOTEL.
IS **THAT** WHY IT CAPTURED LADY?
IT'S ALMOST AS IF... THIS LUXIO WANTS TO FIGHT US IN FRONT OF THE REST OF THE PRIDE...TO SHOW THEM HOW **TOUGH** IT IS!
THAT MUST BE IT! **TRU! LAX!** DISTRACT THE LUXIO WHILE I RESCUE LADY!
WAAAAAAAH!

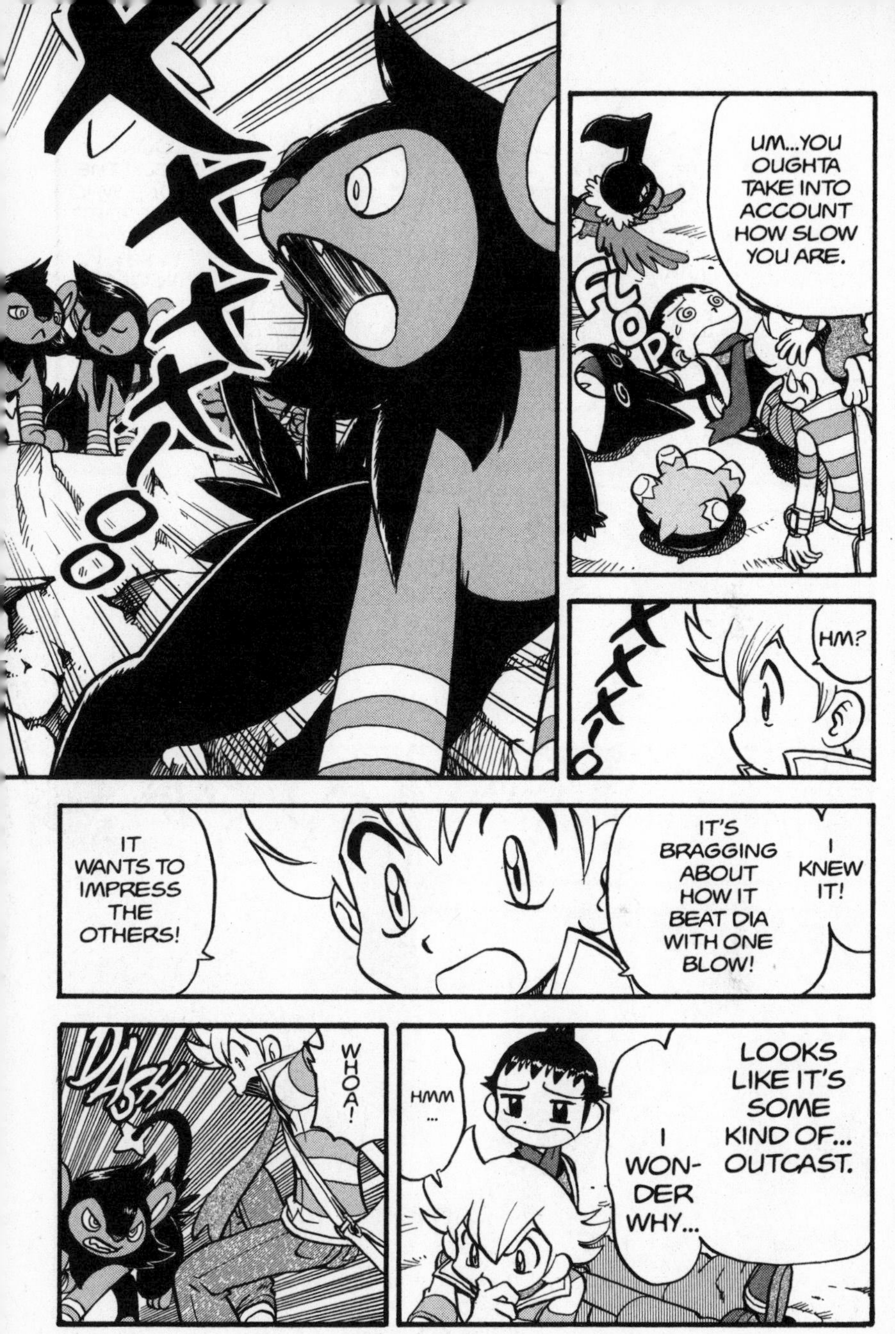
UM...YOU OUGHTA TAKE INTO ACCOUNT HOW SLOW YOU ARE.
FLOP
HM?
I KNEW IT!
IT'S BRAGGING ABOUT HOW IT BEAT DIA WITH ONE BLOW!
IT WANTS TO IMPRESS THE OTHERS!
LOOKS LIKE IT'S SOME KIND OF... OUTCAST.
I WONDER WHY...
HMM ...
WHOA!
DASH

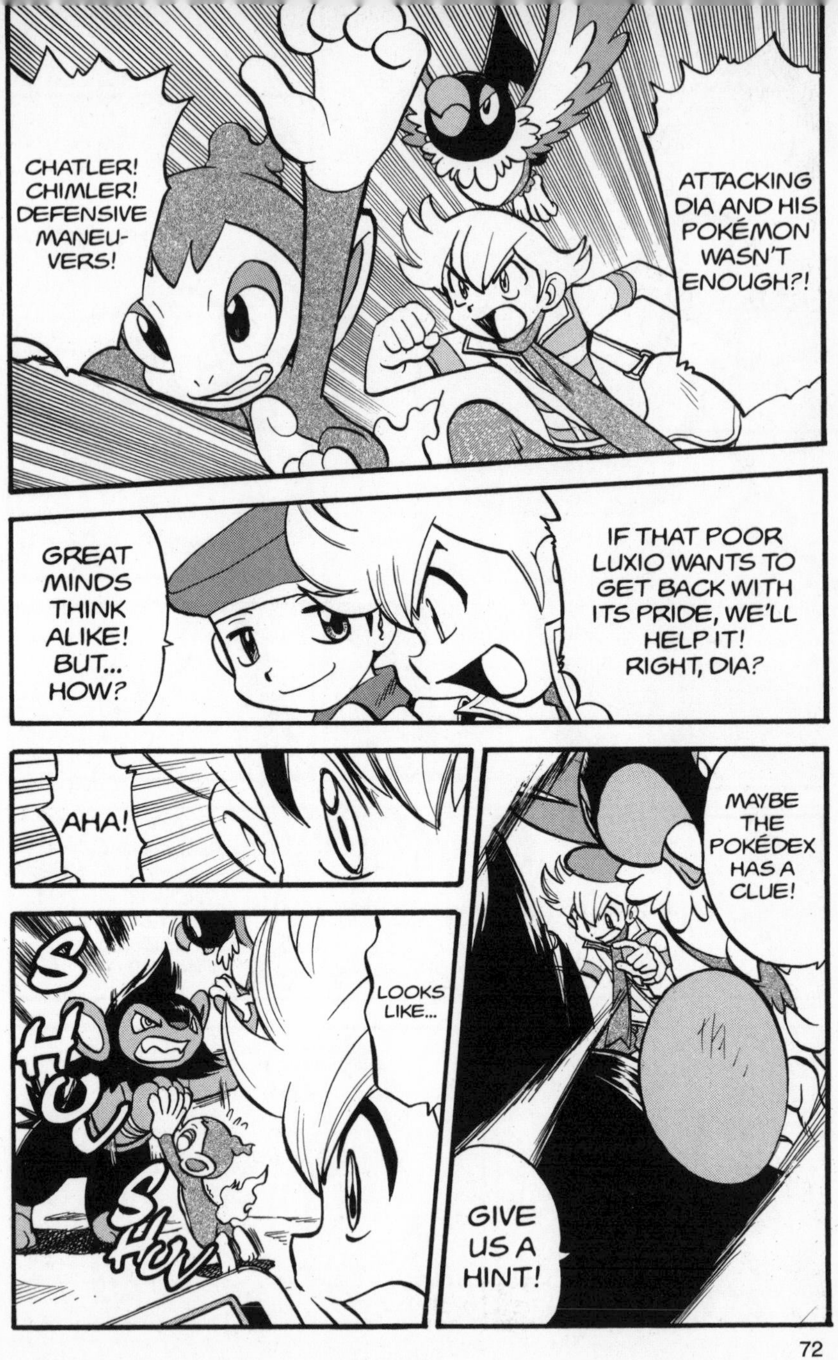
ATTACKING DIA AND HIS POKÉMON WASN'T ENOUGH?!
CHATLER! CHIMLER! DEFENSIVE MANEU-VERS!
IF THAT POOR LUXIO WANTS TO GET BACK WITH ITS PRIDE, WE'LL HELP IT! RIGHT, DIA?
GREAT MINDS THINK ALIKE! BUT... HOW?
MAYBE THE POKÉDEX HAS A CLUE!
AHA!
LOOKS LIKE...
SHOU
SHOU
GIVE US A HINT!

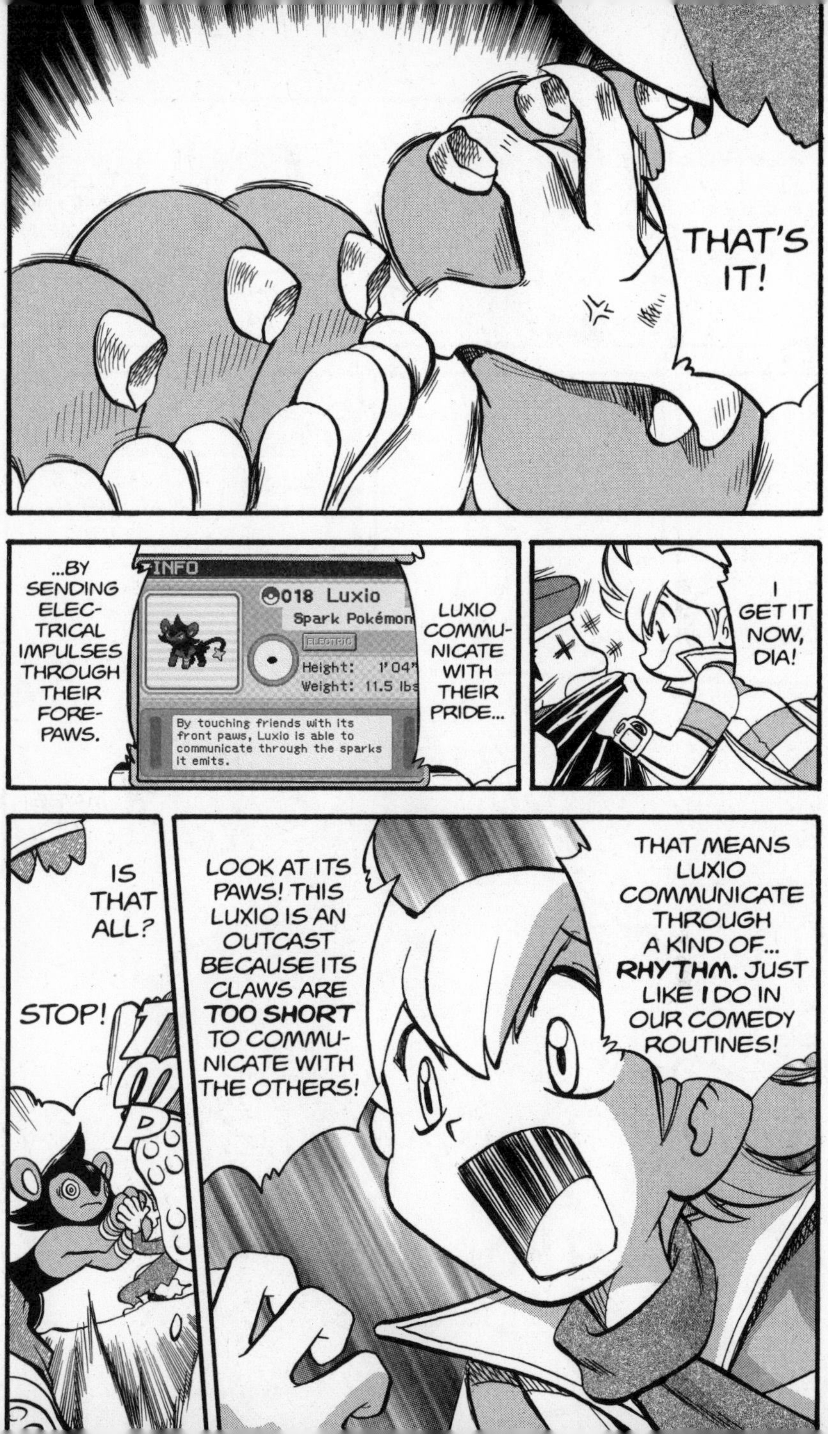
THAT'S IT!
I GET IT NOW, DIA!
LUXIO COMMUNICATE WITH THEIR PRIDE...
...BY SENDING ELECTRICAL IMPULSES THROUGH THEIR FOREPAWS.
INFO
018 Luxio
Spark Pokémon
ELECTRIC
Height: 1'04"
Weight: 11.5 lbs
By touching friends with its front paws, Luxio is able to communicate through the sparks it emits.
THAT MEANS LUXIO COMMUNICATE THROUGH A KIND OF... **RHYTHM.** JUST LIKE I DO IN OUR COMEDY ROUTINES!
LOOK AT ITS PAWS! THIS LUXIO IS AN OUTCAST BECAUSE ITS CLAWS ARE **TOO SHORT** TO COMMUNICATE WITH THE OTHERS!
IS THAT ALL?
STOP!

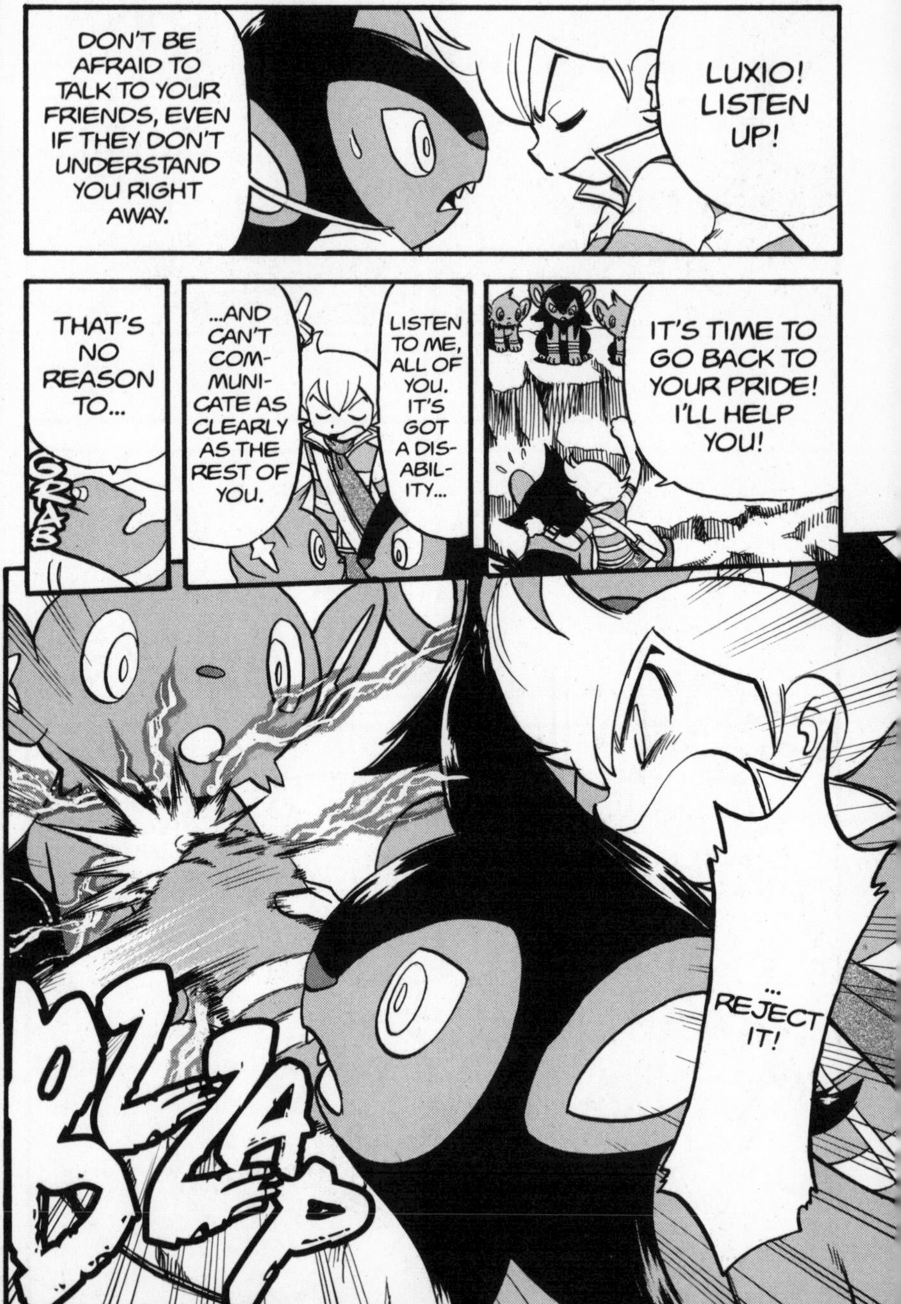
LUXIO! LISTEN UP!
DON'T BE AFRAID TO TALK TO YOUR FRIENDS, EVEN IF THEY DON'T UNDERSTAND YOU RIGHT AWAY.
IT'S TIME TO GO BACK TO YOUR PRIDE! I'LL HELP YOU!
LISTEN TO ME, ALL OF YOU. IT'S GOT A DIS-ABIL-ITY...
...AND CAN'T COM-MUNI-CATE AS CLEARLY AS THE REST OF YOU.
THAT'S NO REASON TO...
GRAB
...REJECT IT!
BZZAP

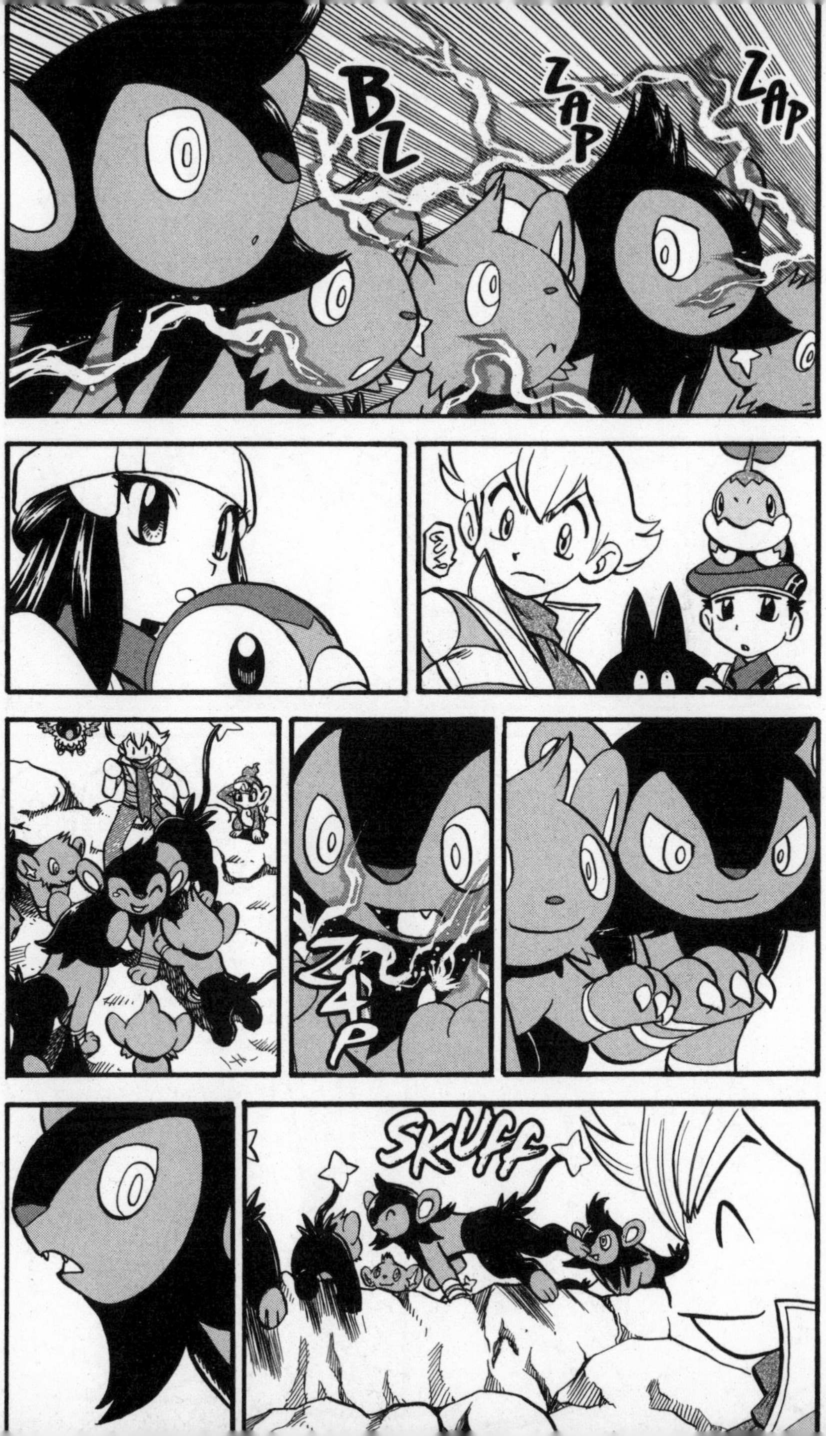
ZAP
ZAP
BZZ
ZAP
SKUFF

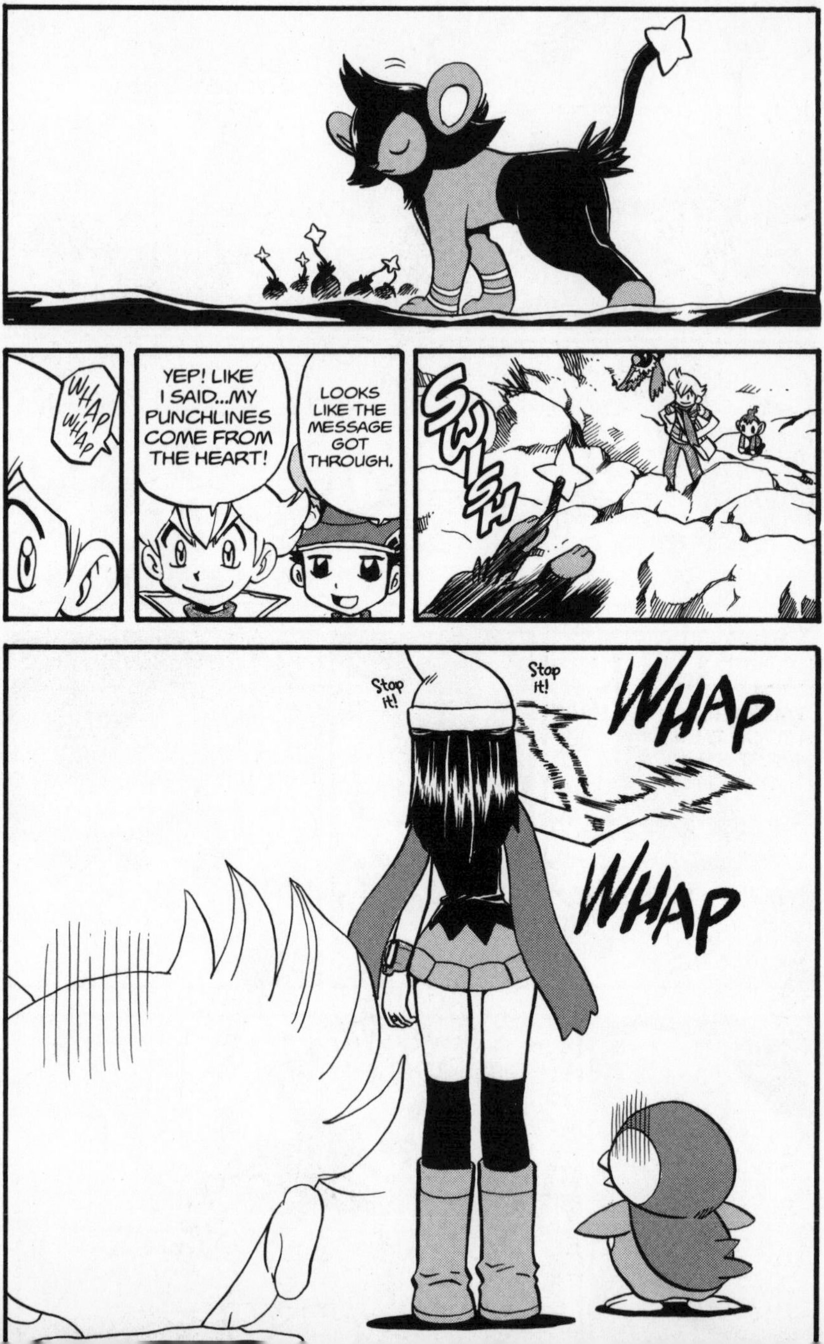
SWISH
LOOKS LIKE THE MESSAGE GOT THROUGH.
YEP! LIKE I SAID...MY PUNCHLINES COME FROM THE HEART!
WHAP WHAP
WHAP
WHAP
Stop it!
Stop it!

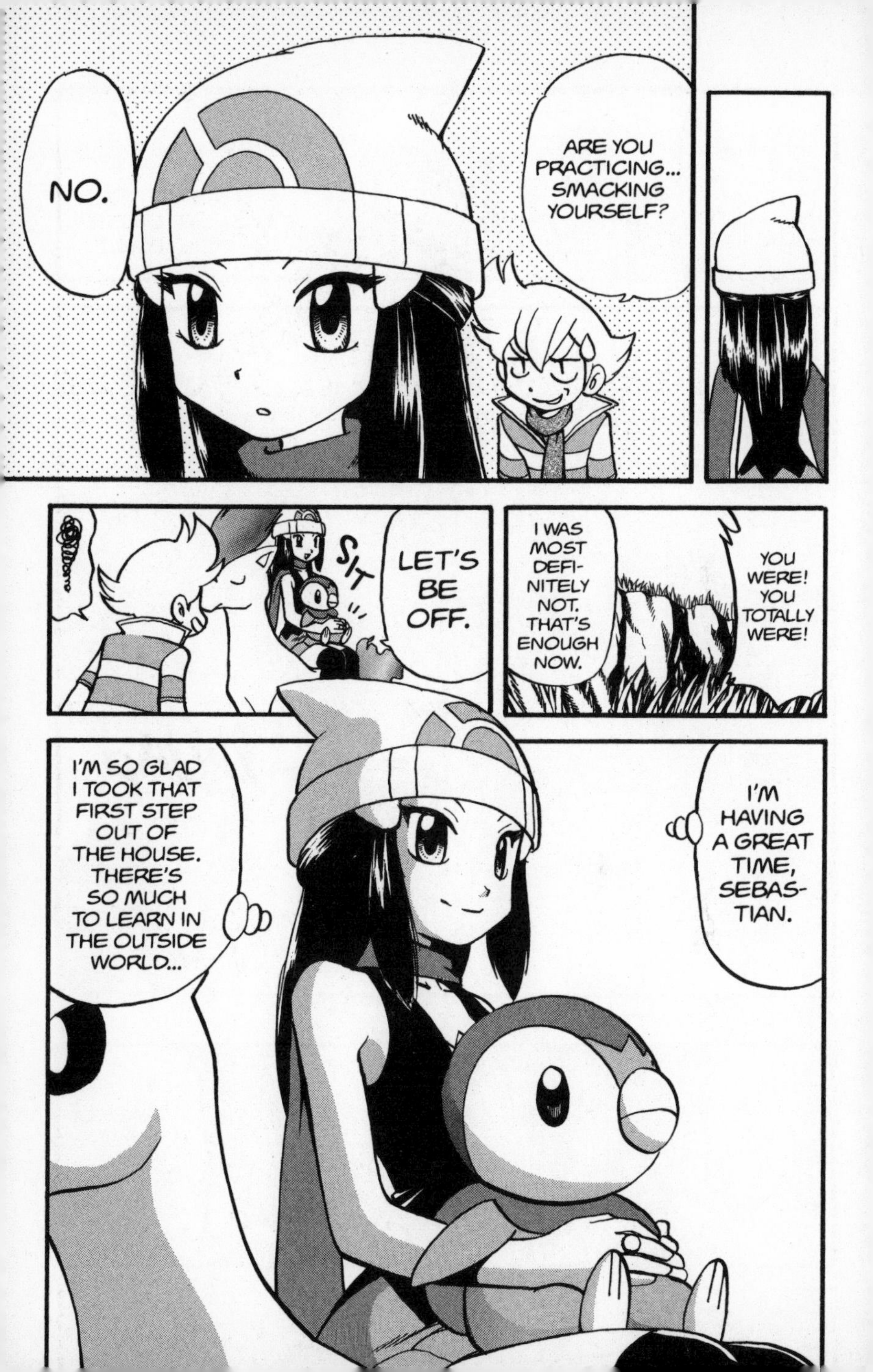
ARE YOU PRACTICING... SMACKING YOURSELF?
NO.
YOU WERE! YOU TOTALLY WERE!
I WAS MOST DEFI- NITELY NOT. THAT'S ENOUGH NOW.
LET'S BE OFF.
SIT
I'M HAVING A GREAT TIME, SEBAS- TIAN.
I'M SO GLAD I TOOK THAT FIRST STEP OUT OF THE HOUSE. THERE'S SO MUCH TO LEARN IN THE OUTSIDE WORLD...

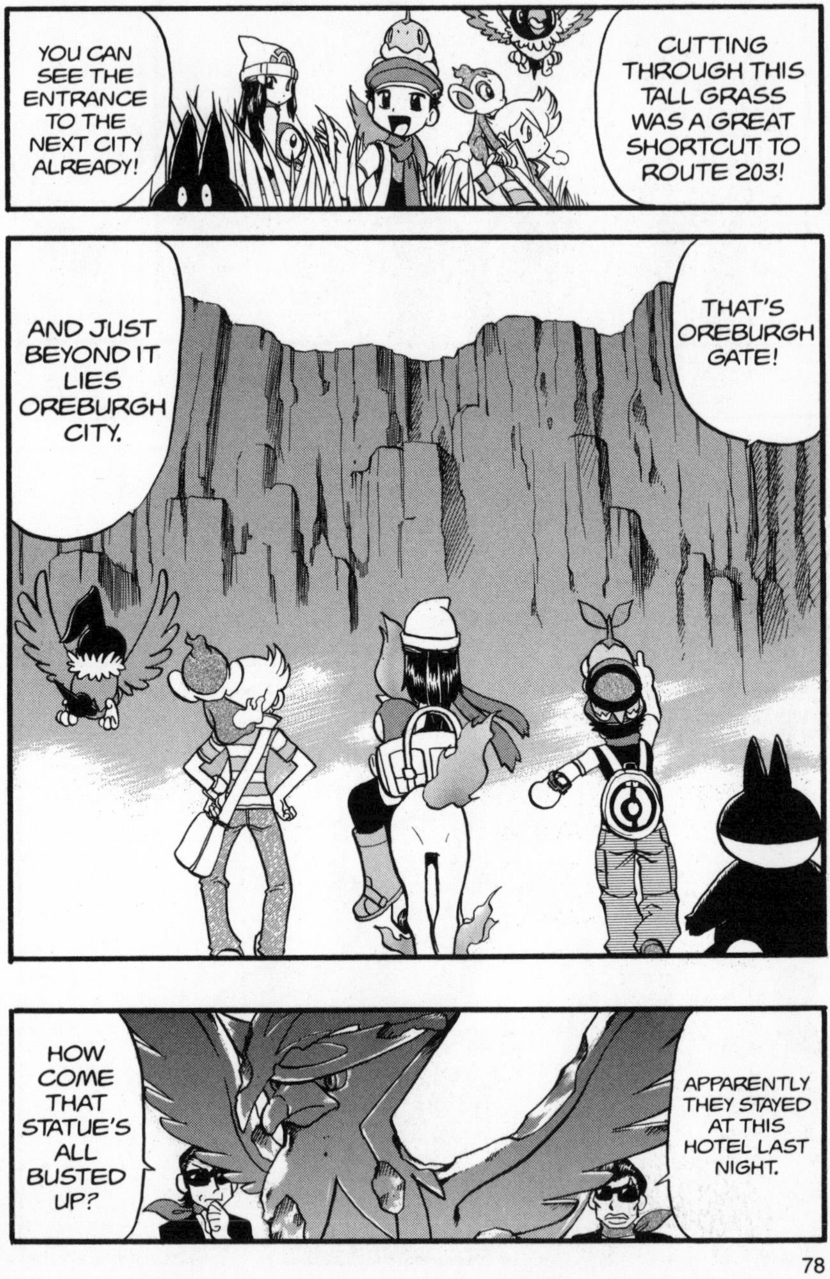
CUTTING THROUGH THIS TALL GRASS WAS A GREAT SHORTCUT TO ROUTE 203!
YOU CAN SEE THE ENTRANCE TO THE NEXT CITY ALREADY!
THAT'S OREBURGH GATE!
AND JUST BEYOND IT LIES OREBURGH CITY.
APPARENTLY THEY STAYED AT THIS HOTEL LAST NIGHT.
HOW COME THAT STATUE'S ALL BUSTED UP?

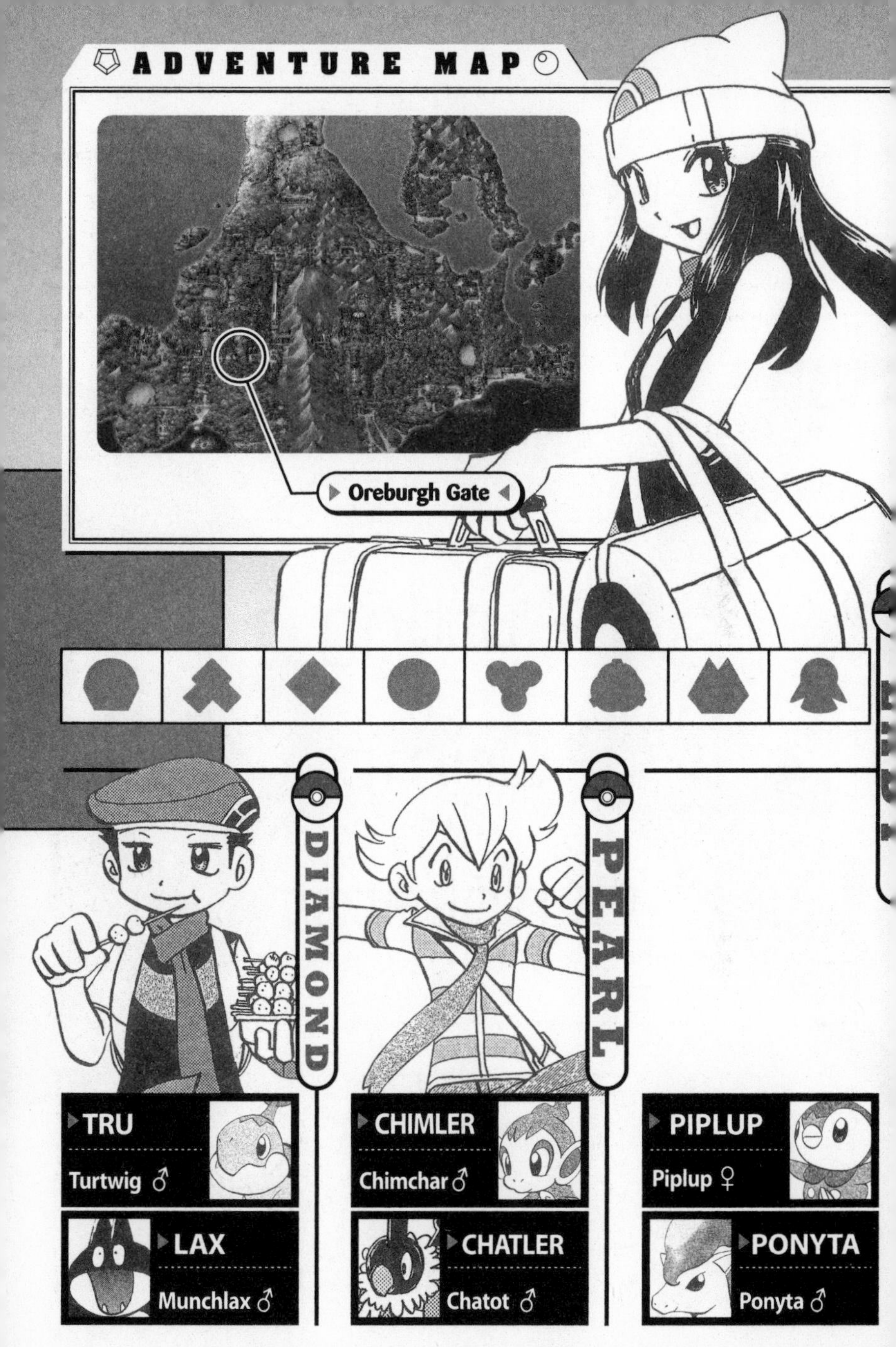
ADVENTURE MAP
Oreburgh Gate
DIAMOND
PEARL
TRU
Turtwig ♂
LAX
Munchlax ♂
CHIMLER
Chimchar ♂
CHATLER
Chatot ♂
PIPLUP
Piplup ♀
PONYTA
Ponyta ♂

4

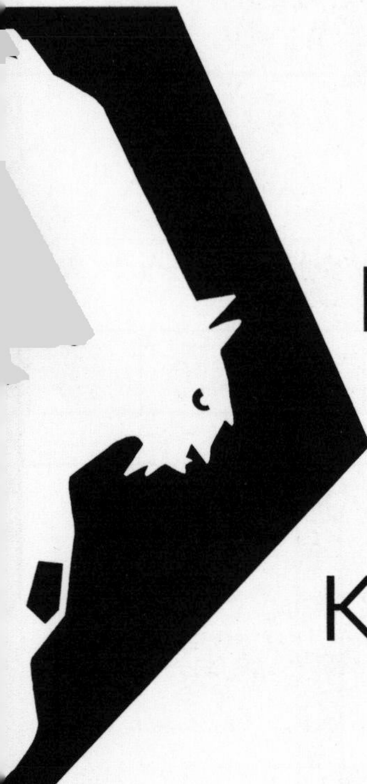

Putting a Crimp in Kricketot

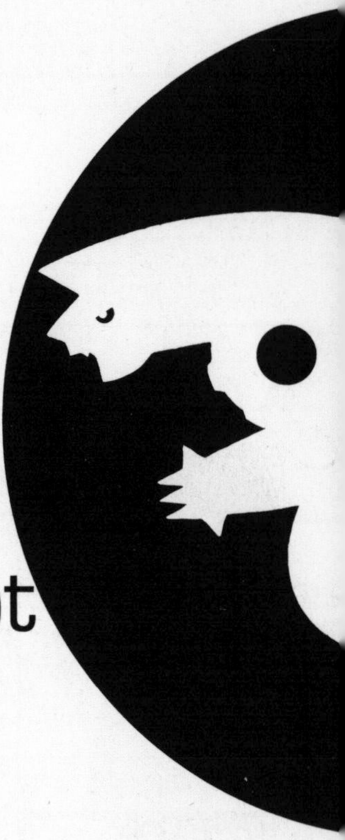

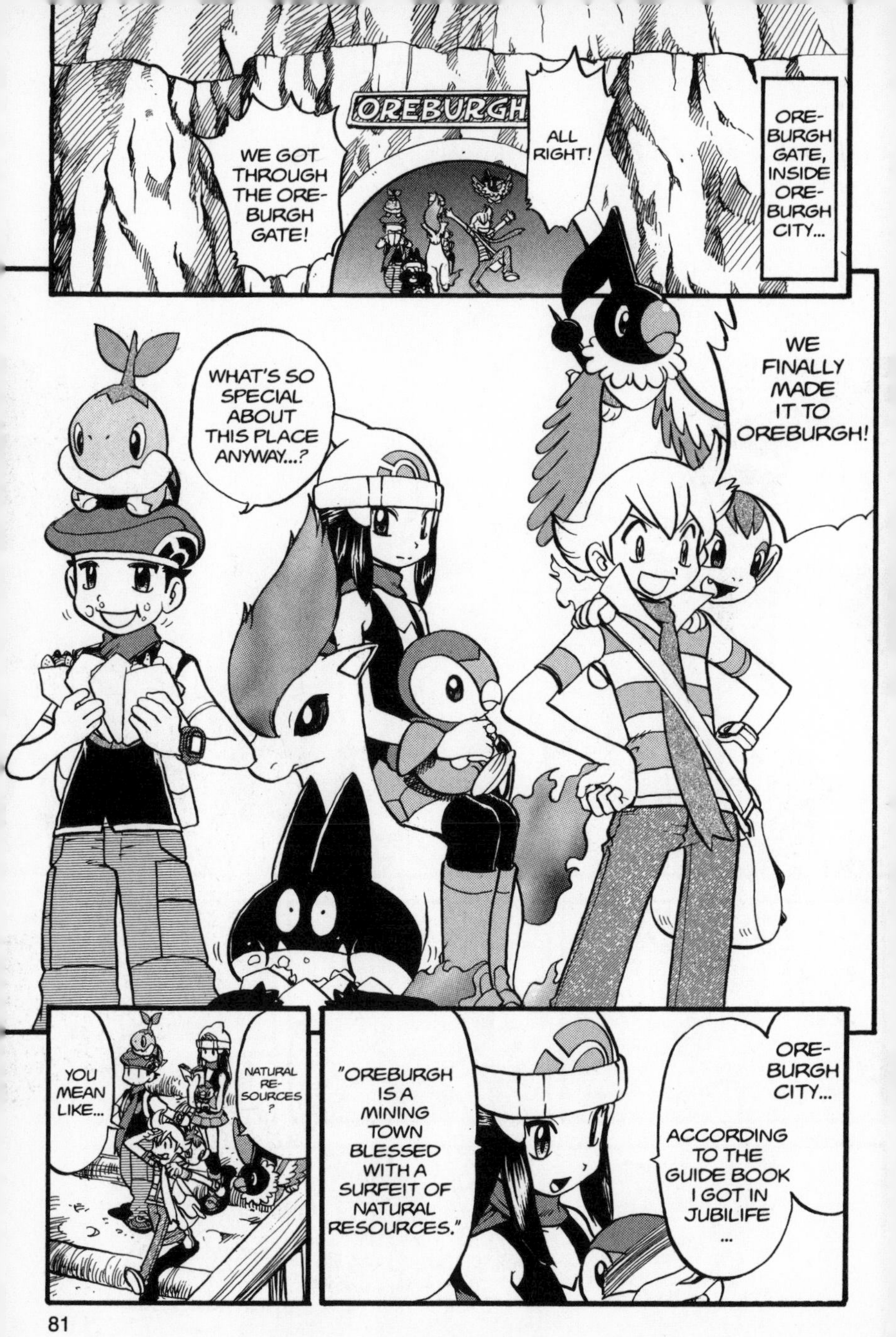
OREBURGH GATE, INSIDE OREBURGH CITY...
OREBURGH
ALL RIGHT!
WE GOT THROUGH THE OREBURGH GATE!
WE FINALLY MADE IT TO OREBURGH!
WHAT'S SO SPECIAL ABOUT THIS PLACE ANYWAY...?
OREBURGH CITY...
ACCORDING TO THE GUIDE BOOK I GOT IN JUBILIFE...
"OREBURGH IS A MINING TOWN BLESSED WITH A SURFEIT OF NATURAL RESOURCES."
NATURAL RESOURCES?
YOU MEAN LIKE...

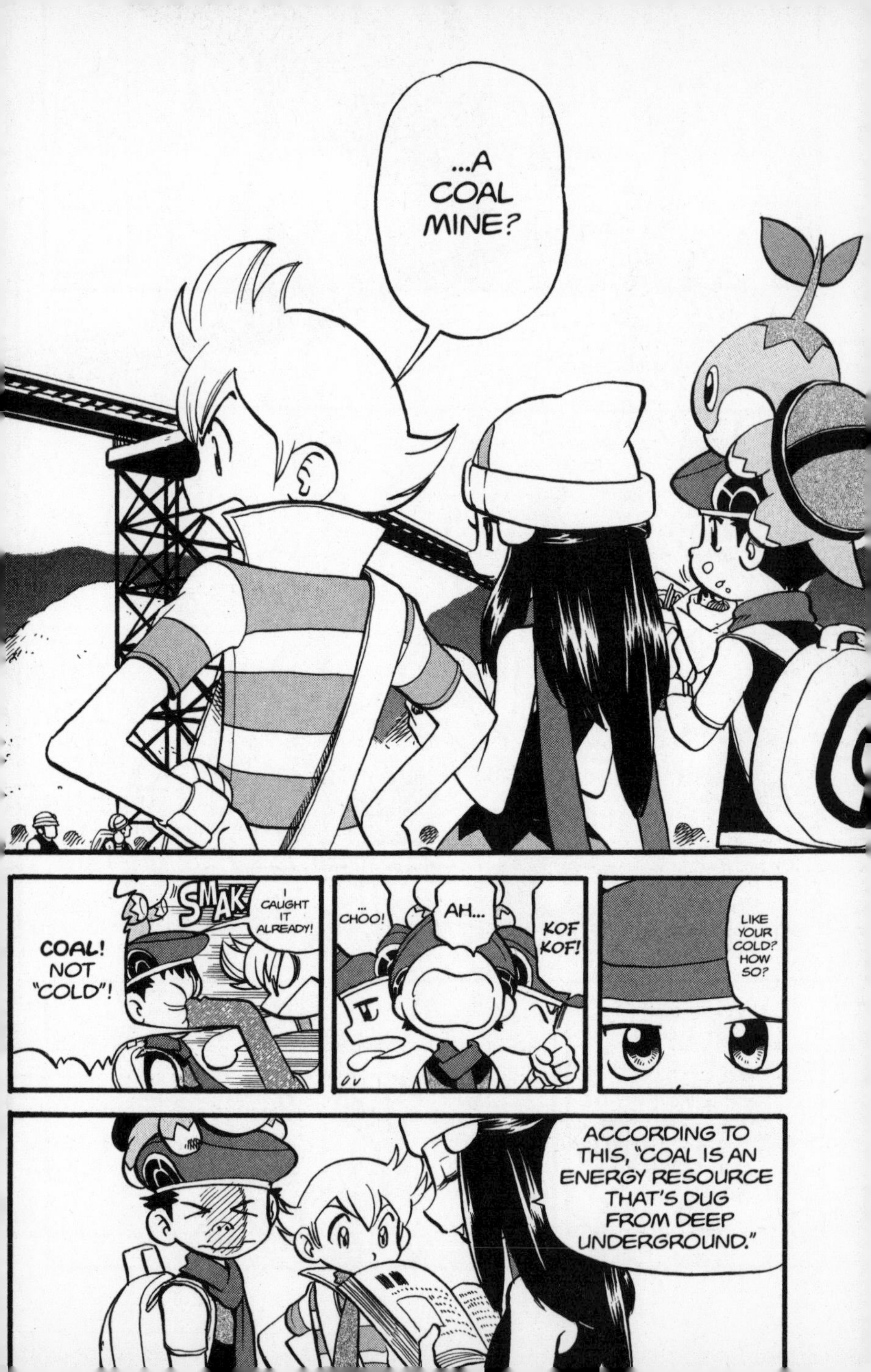
...A COAL MINE?
LIKE YOUR COLD? HOW SO?
KOF KOF!
AH...
...CHOO!
I CAUGHT IT ALREADY!
SMAK
COAL! NOT "COLD"!
ACCORDING TO THIS, "COAL IS AN ENERGY RESOURCE THAT'S DUG FROM DEEP UNDERGROUND."

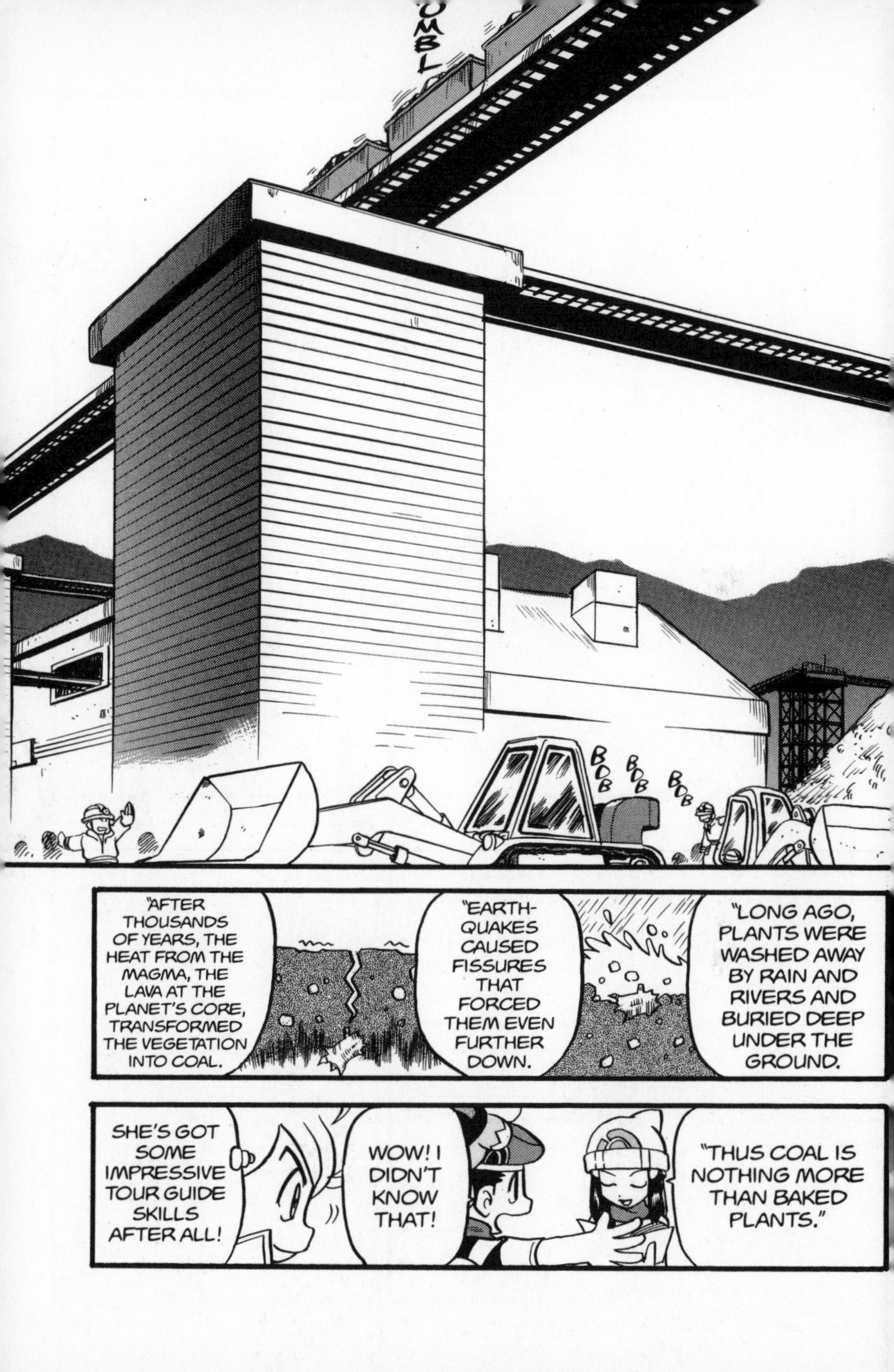
UMBL
BOB
BOB
BOB
"LONG AGO, PLANTS WERE WASHED AWAY BY RAIN AND RIVERS AND BURIED DEEP UNDER THE GROUND.
"EARTH-QUAKES CAUSED FISSURES THAT FORCED THEM EVEN FURTHER DOWN.
"AFTER THOUSANDS OF YEARS, THE HEAT FROM THE MAGMA, THE LAVA AT THE PLANET'S CORE, TRANSFORMED THE VEGETATION INTO COAL.
"THUS COAL IS NOTHING MORE THAN BAKED PLANTS."
WOW! I DIDN'T KNOW THAT!
SHE'S GOT SOME IMPRESSIVE TOUR GUIDE SKILLS AFTER ALL!

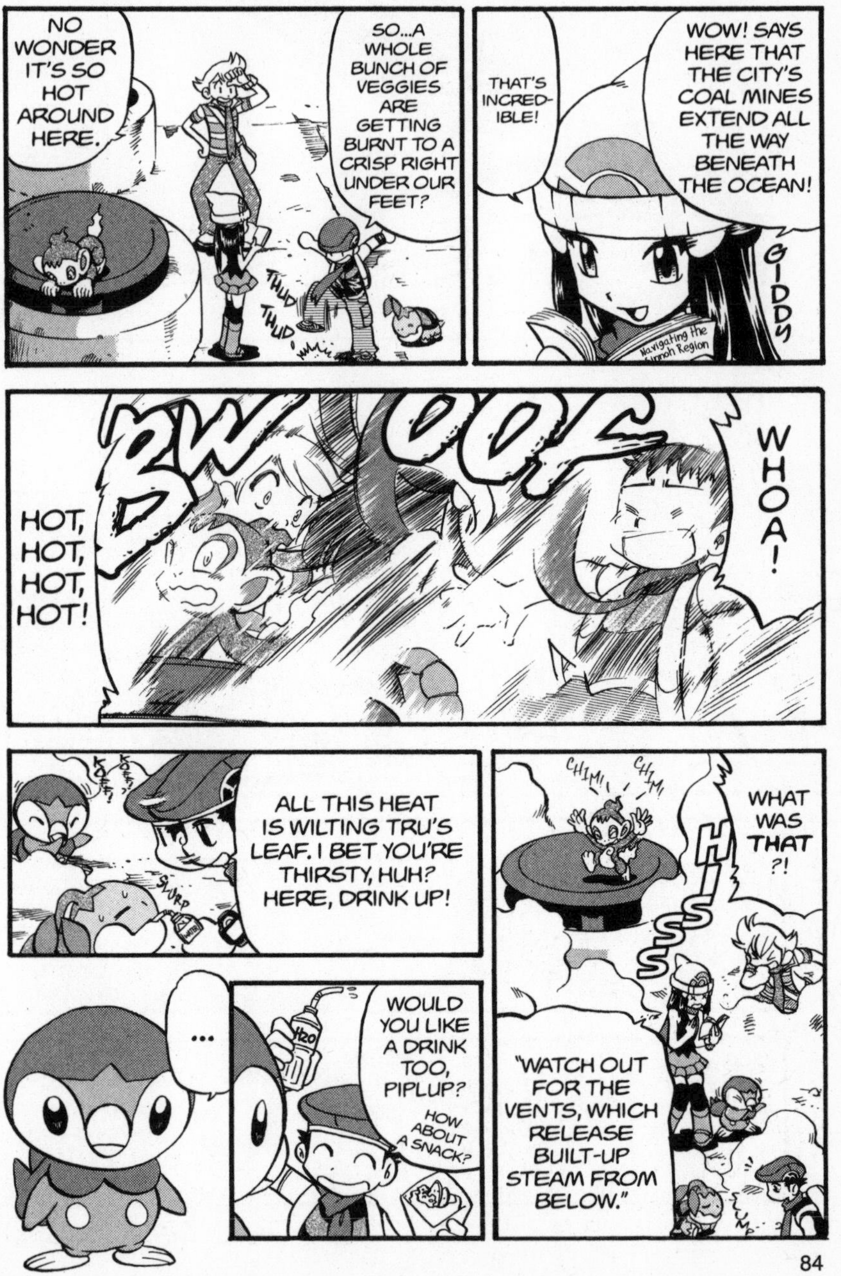
NO WONDER IT'S SO HOT AROUND HERE.
SO...A WHOLE BUNCH OF VEGGIES ARE GETTING BURNT TO A CRISP RIGHT UNDER OUR FEET?
THUD THUD
THAT'S INCREDIBLE!
WOW! SAYS HERE THAT THE CITY'S COAL MINES EXTEND ALL THE WAY BENEATH THE OCEAN!
GIDDY
Navigating the Sinnoh Region
WHOA!
HOT, HOT, HOT, HOT!
ALL THIS HEAT IS WILTING TRU'S LEAF. I BET YOU'RE THIRSTY, HUH? HERE, DRINK UP!
SLURP
CHIM! CHIM
WHAT WAS THAT?!
HISSS
"WATCH OUT FOR THE VENTS, WHICH RELEASE BUILT-UP STEAM FROM BELOW."
...
WOULD YOU LIKE A DRINK TOO, PIPLUP?
HOW ABOUT A SNACK?
H2O

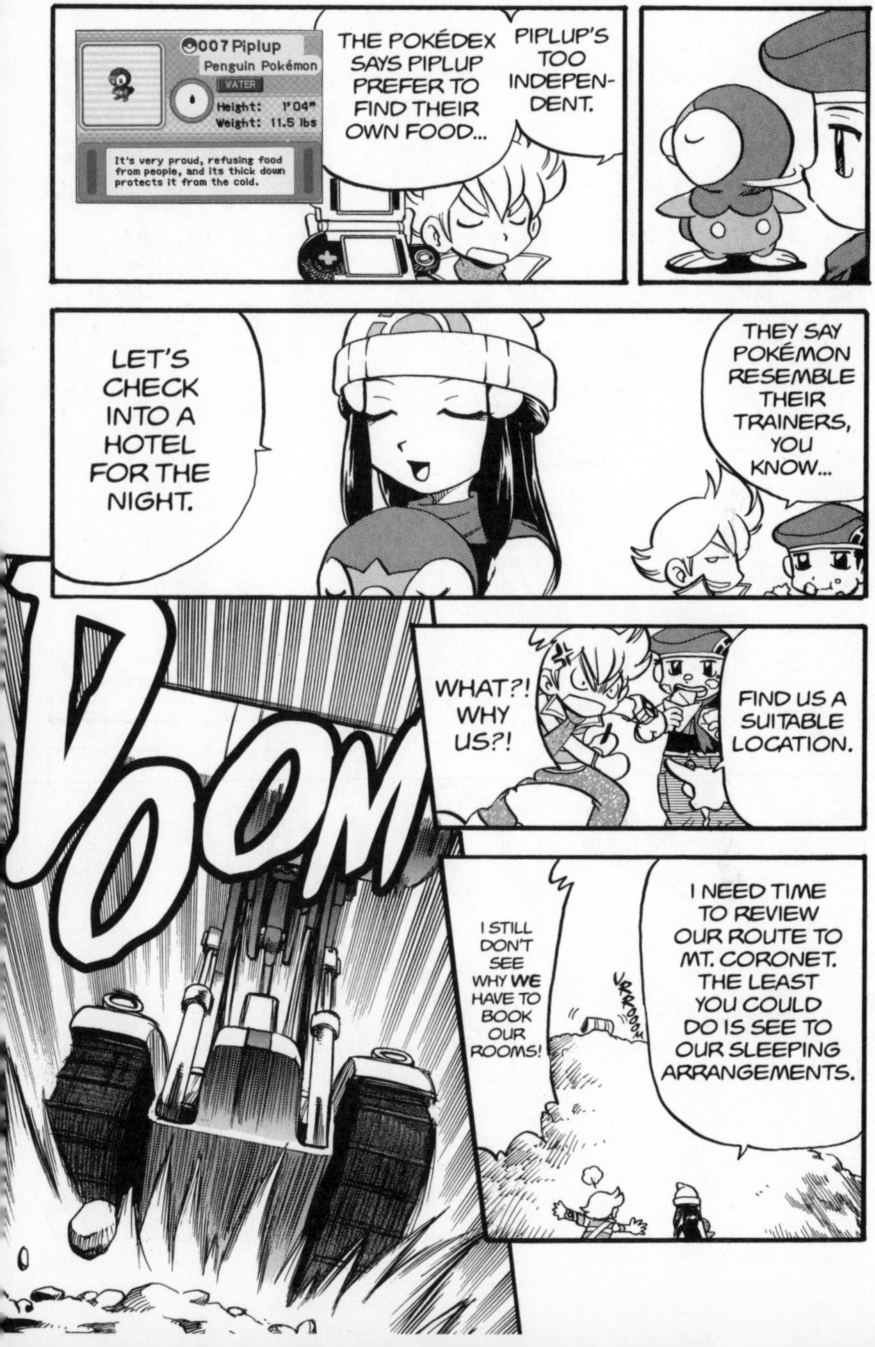

007 Piplup
Penguin Pokémon
WATER
Height: 1'04"
Weight: 11.5 lbs
It's very proud, refusing food from people, and its thick down protects it from the cold.
THE POKÉDEX SAYS PIPLUP PREFER TO FIND THEIR OWN FOOD...
PIPLUP'S TOO INDEPEN-DENT.
LET'S CHECK INTO A HOTEL FOR THE NIGHT.
THEY SAY POKÉMON RESEMBLE THEIR TRAINERS, YOU KNOW...
FIND US A SUITABLE LOCATION.
WHAT?! WHY US?!
I NEED TIME TO REVIEW OUR ROUTE TO MT. CORONET. THE LEAST YOU COULD DO IS SEE TO OUR SLEEPING ARRANGEMENTS.
I STILL DON'T SEE WHY WE HAVE TO BOOK OUR ROOMS!
VRROOOM

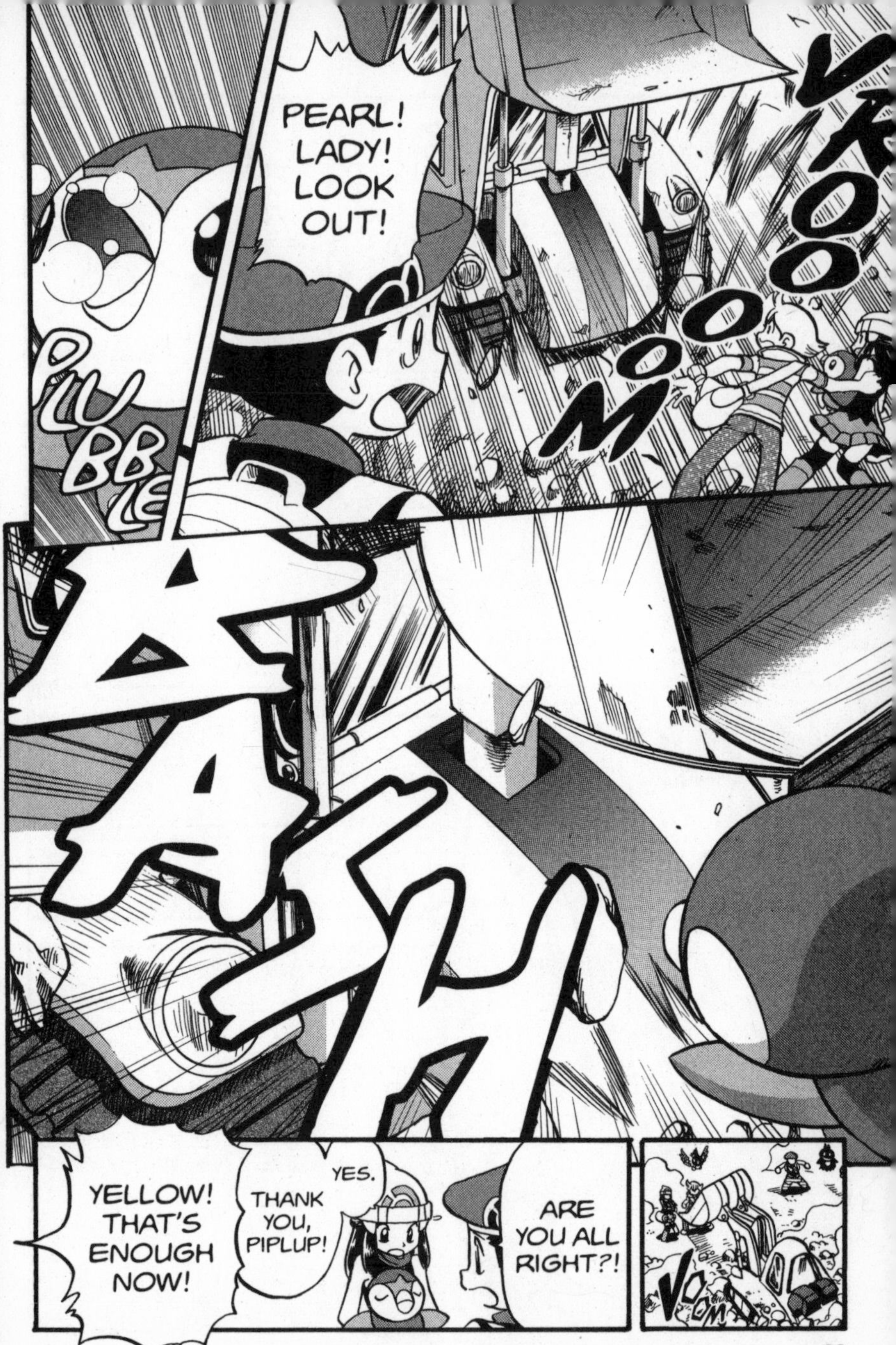
PEARL! LADY! LOOK OUT!
VROOOOOM
YELLOW! THAT'S ENOUGH NOW!
YES.
THANK YOU, PIPLUP!
ARE YOU ALL RIGHT?!

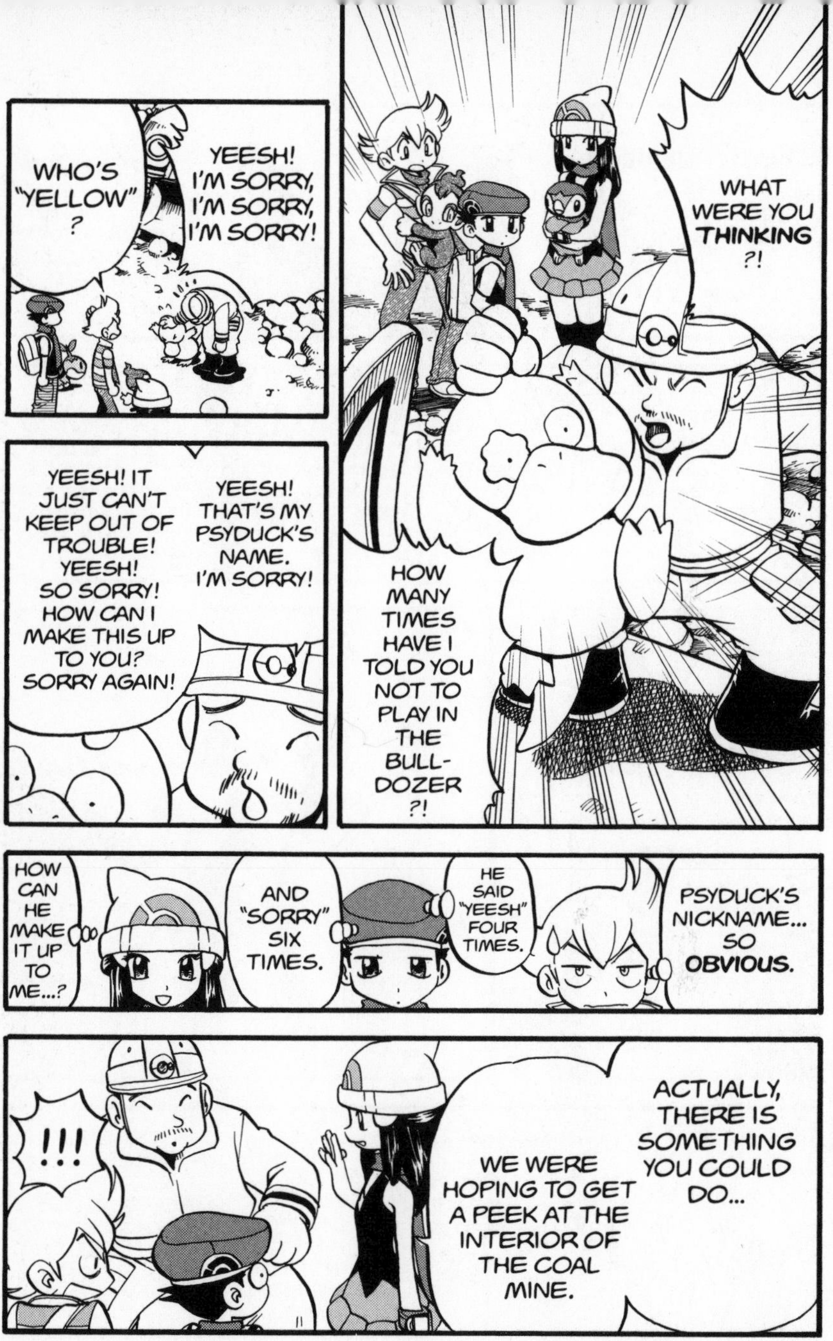
WHAT WERE YOU **THINKING** ?!
HOW MANY TIMES HAVE I TOLD YOU NOT TO PLAY IN THE BULL-DOZER ?!
YEESH! I'M SORRY, I'M SORRY, I'M SORRY!
WHO'S "YELLOW" ?
YEESH! THAT'S MY PSYDUCK'S NAME. I'M SORRY!
YEESH! IT JUST CAN'T KEEP OUT OF TROUBLE! YEESH! SO SORRY! HOW CAN I MAKE THIS UP TO YOU? SORRY AGAIN!
PSYDUCK'S NICKNAME... SO **OBVIOUS.**
HE SAID "YEESH" FOUR TIMES.
AND "SORRY" SIX TIMES.
HOW CAN HE MAKE IT UP TO ME...?
ACTUALLY, THERE IS SOMETHING YOU COULD DO...
WE WERE HOPING TO GET A PEEK AT THE INTERIOR OF THE COAL MINE.
!!!

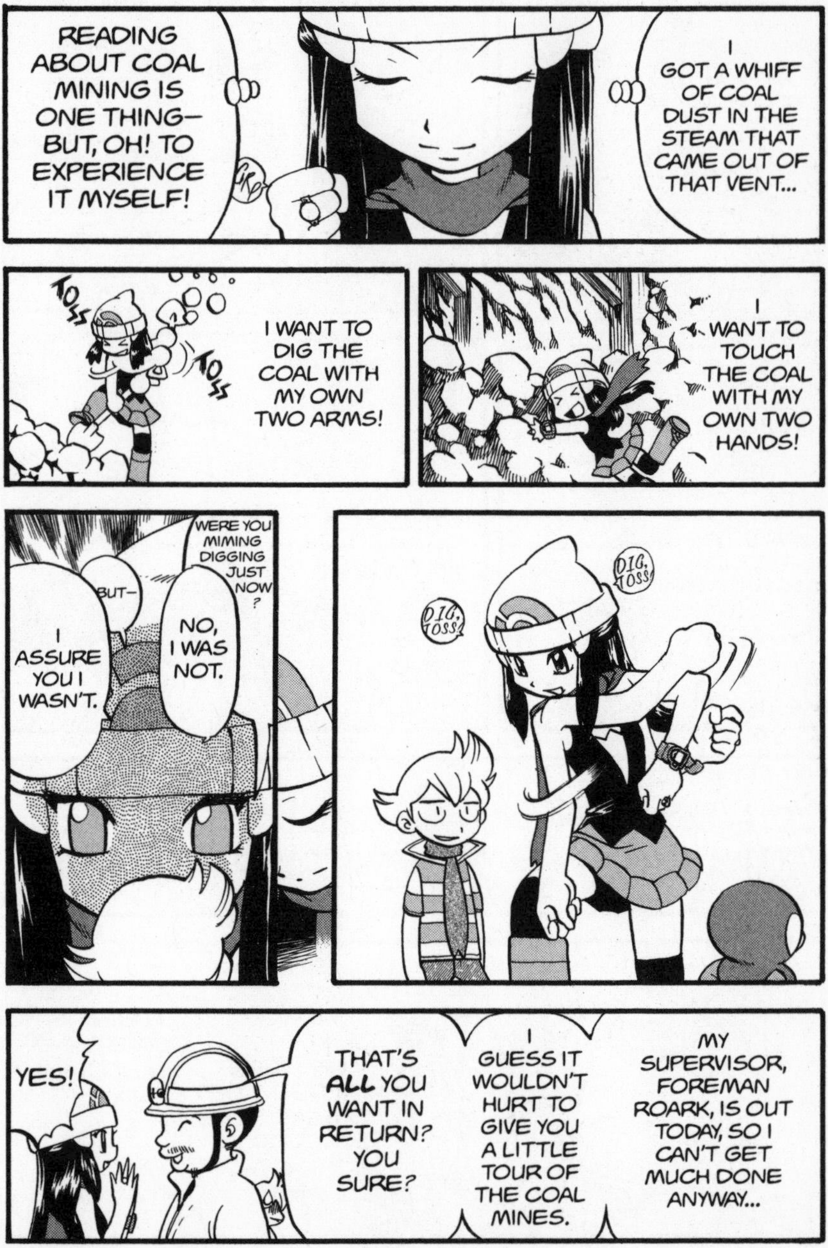
I GOT A WHIFF OF COAL DUST IN THE STEAM THAT CAME OUT OF THAT VENT...
READING ABOUT COAL MINING IS ONE THING—BUT, OH! TO EXPERIENCE IT MYSELF!
I WANT TO TOUCH THE COAL WITH MY OWN TWO HANDS!
I WANT TO DIG THE COAL WITH MY OWN TWO ARMS!
TOSS
TOSS
DIG, TOSS!
DIG, TOSS!
WERE YOU MIMING DIGGING JUST NOW?
NO, I WAS NOT.
BUT—
I ASSURE YOU I WASN'T.
MY SUPERVISOR, FOREMAN ROARK, IS OUT TODAY, SO I CAN'T GET MUCH DONE ANYWAY...
I GUESS IT WOULDN'T HURT TO GIVE YOU A LITTLE TOUR OF THE COAL MINES.
THAT'S **ALL** YOU WANT IN RETURN? YOU SURE?
YES!

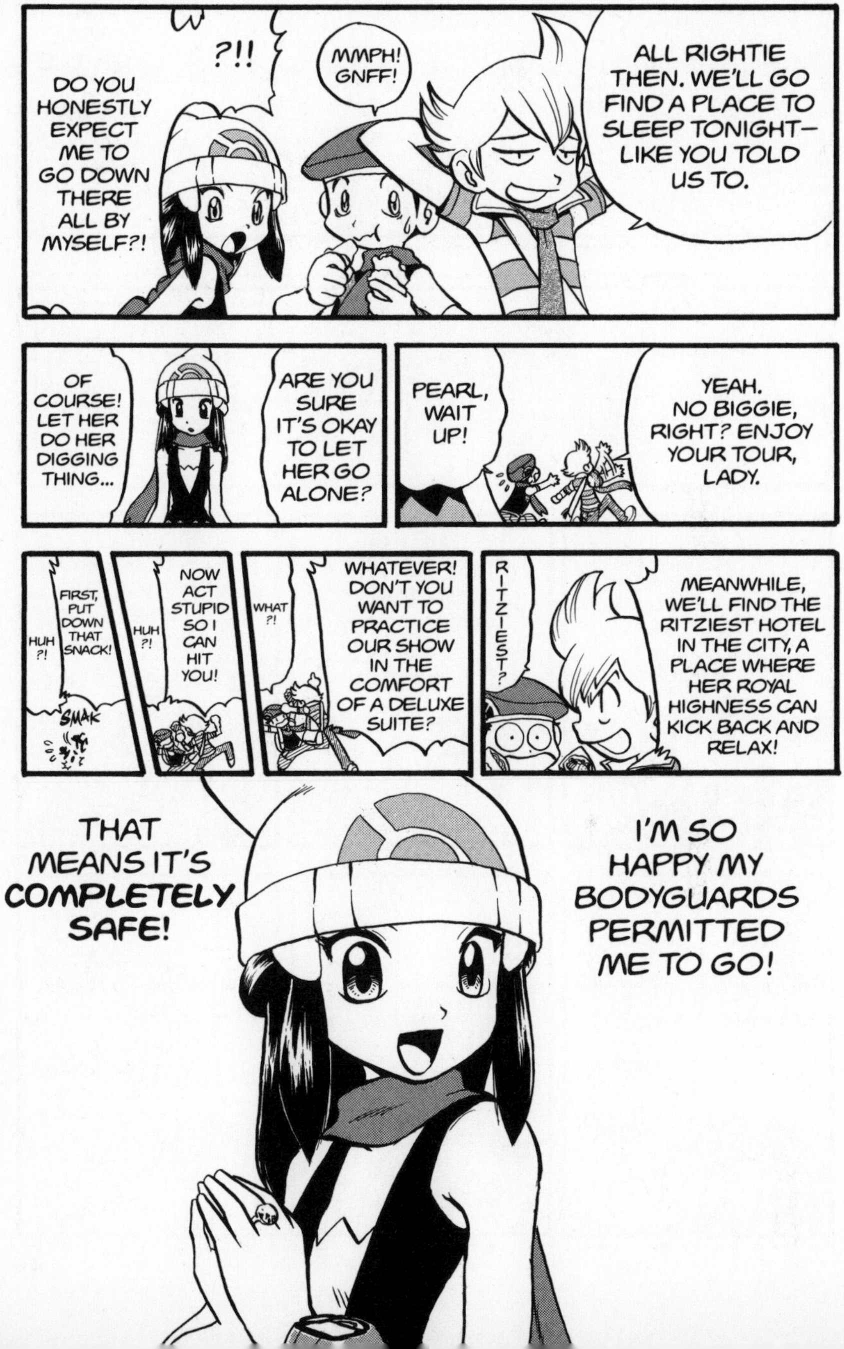
ALL RIGHTIE THEN. WE'LL GO FIND A PLACE TO SLEEP TONIGHT—LIKE YOU TOLD US TO.
MMPH! GNFF!
?!!
DO YOU HONESTLY EXPECT ME TO GO DOWN THERE ALL BY MYSELF?!
YEAH. NO BIGGIE, RIGHT? ENJOY YOUR TOUR, LADY.
PEARL, WAIT UP!
ARE YOU SURE IT'S OKAY TO LET HER GO ALONE?
OF COURSE! LET HER DO HER DIGGING THING...
MEANWHILE, WE'LL FIND THE RITZIEST HOTEL IN THE CITY, A PLACE WHERE HER ROYAL HIGHNESS CAN KICK BACK AND RELAX!
RITZIEST?
WHATEVER! DON'T YOU WANT TO PRACTICE OUR SHOW IN THE COMFORT OF A DELUXE SUITE?
WHAT ?!
NOW ACT STUPID SO I CAN HIT YOU!
HUH ?!
FIRST, PUT DOWN THAT SNACK!
HUH ?!
SMAK
I'M SO HAPPY MY BODYGUARDS PERMITTED ME TO GO!
THAT MEANS IT'S COMPLETELY SAFE!

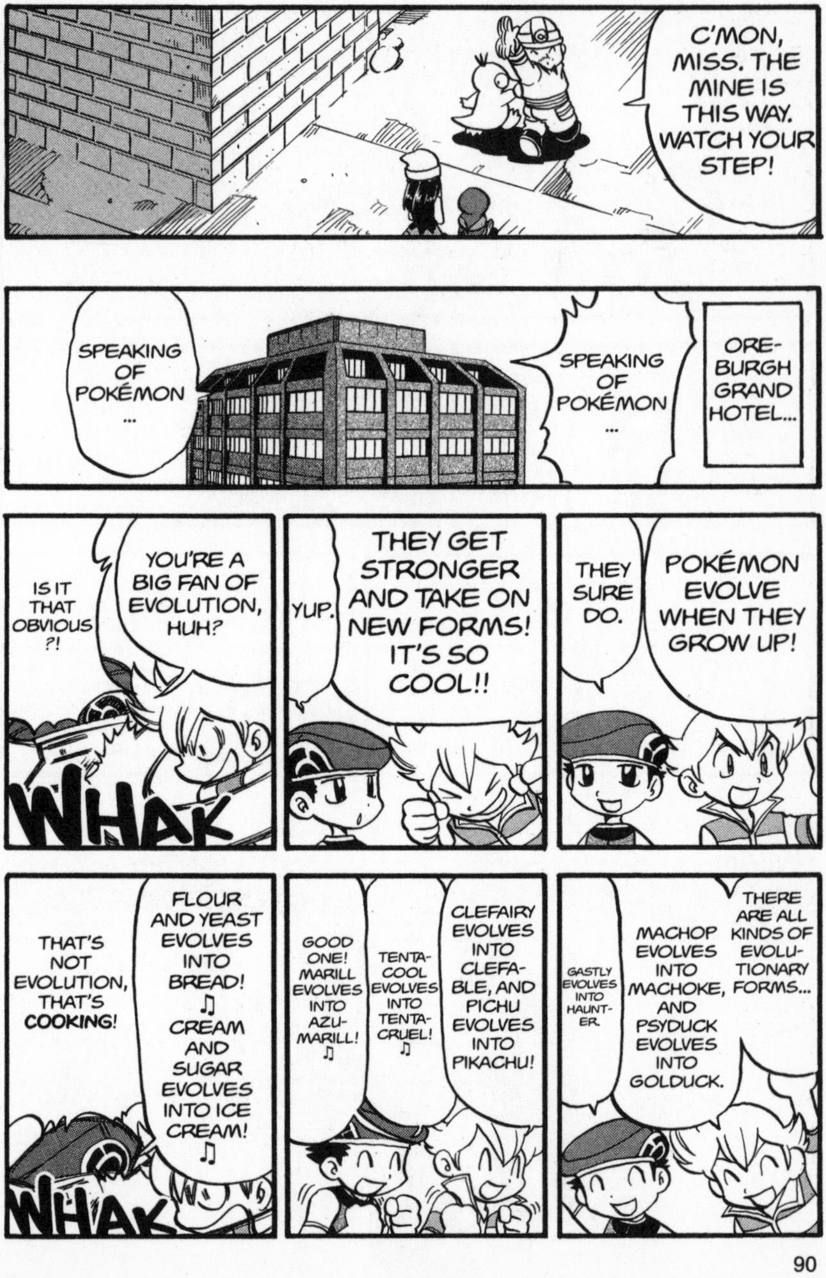
C'MON, MISS. THE MINE IS THIS WAY. WATCH YOUR STEP!
ORE-BURGH GRAND HOTEL...
SPEAKING OF POKÉMON ...
SPEAKING OF POKÉMON ...
POKÉMON EVOLVE WHEN THEY GROW UP!
THEY SURE DO.
THEY GET STRONGER AND TAKE ON NEW FORMS! IT'S SO COOL!!
YUP.
YOU'RE A BIG FAN OF EVOLUTION, HUH?
IS IT THAT OBVIOUS ?!
WHAK
THERE ARE ALL KINDS OF EVOLUTIONARY FORMS...
MACHOP EVOLVES INTO MACHOKE, AND PSYDUCK EVOLVES INTO GOLDUCK.
GASTLY EVOLVES INTO HAUNTER.
CLEFAIRY EVOLVES INTO CLEFABLE, AND PICHU EVOLVES INTO PIKACHU!
TENTACOOL EVOLVES INTO TENTACRUEL! ♫
GOOD ONE! MARILL EVOLVES INTO AZUMARILL! ♫
FLOUR AND YEAST EVOLVES INTO BREAD! ♫ CREAM AND SUGAR EVOLVES INTO ICE CREAM! ♫
THAT'S NOT EVOLUTION, THAT'S **COOKING**!
WHAK

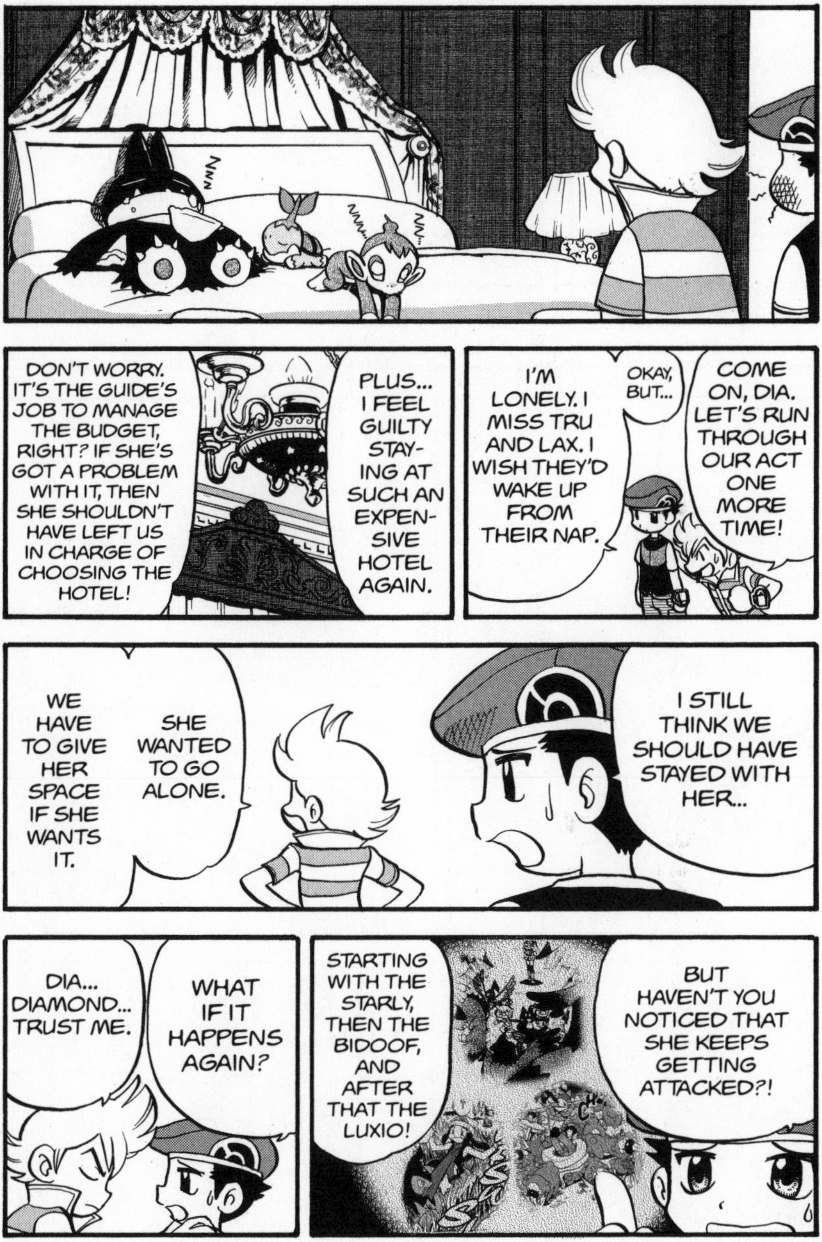
COME ON, DIA. LET'S RUN THROUGH OUR ACT ONE MORE TIME!
OKAY, BUT...
I'M LONELY. I MISS TRU AND LAX. I WISH THEY'D WAKE UP FROM THEIR NAP.
PLUS... I FEEL GUILTY STAYING AT SUCH AN EXPENSIVE HOTEL AGAIN.
DON'T WORRY. IT'S THE GUIDE'S JOB TO MANAGE THE BUDGET, RIGHT? IF SHE'S GOT A PROBLEM WITH IT, THEN SHE SHOULDN'T HAVE LEFT US IN CHARGE OF CHOOSING THE HOTEL!
I STILL THINK WE SHOULD HAVE STAYED WITH HER...
SHE WANTED TO GO ALONE.
WE HAVE TO GIVE HER SPACE IF SHE WANTS IT.
BUT HAVEN'T YOU NOTICED THAT SHE KEEPS GETTING ATTACKED?!
STARTING WITH THE STARLY, THEN THE BIDOOF, AND AFTER THAT THE LUXIO!
WHAT IF IT HAPPENS AGAIN?
DIA... DIAMOND... TRUST ME.

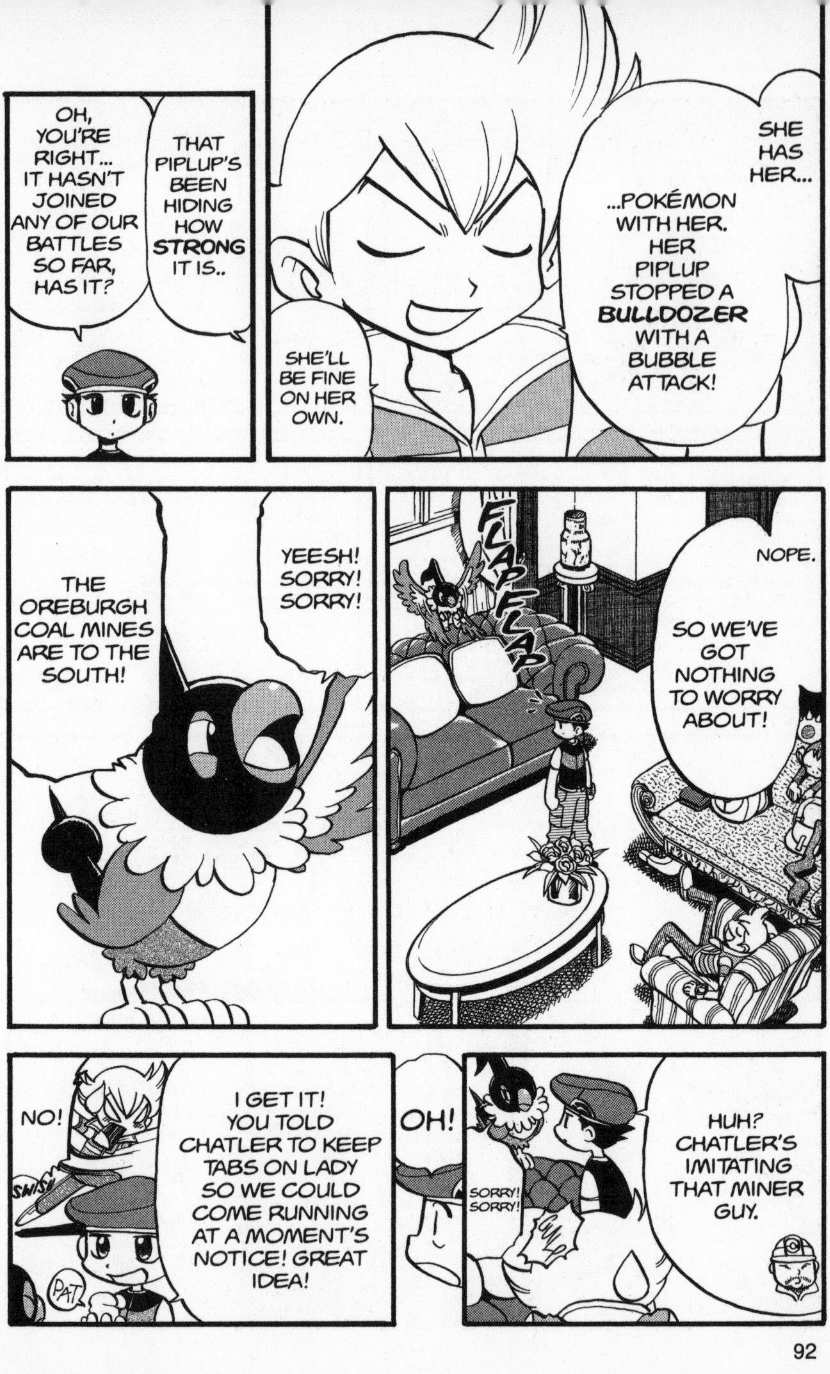
SHE HAS HER...
...POKÉMON WITH HER. HER PIPLUP STOPPED A BULLDOZER WITH A BUBBLE ATTACK!
SHE'LL BE FINE ON HER OWN.
THAT PIPLUP'S BEEN HIDING HOW STRONG IT IS..
OH, YOU'RE RIGHT... IT HASN'T JOINED ANY OF OUR BATTLES SO FAR, HAS IT?
NOPE.
SO WE'VE GOT NOTHING TO WORRY ABOUT!
FLAP FLAP
YEESH! SORRY! SORRY!
THE OREBURGH COAL MINES ARE TO THE SOUTH!
HUH? CHATLER'S IMITATING THAT MINER GUY.
SORRY! SORRY!
GULP
OH!
I GET IT! YOU TOLD CHATLER TO KEEP TABS ON LADY SO WE COULD COME RUNNING AT A MOMENT'S NOTICE! GREAT IDEA!
NO!
SWISH
PAT

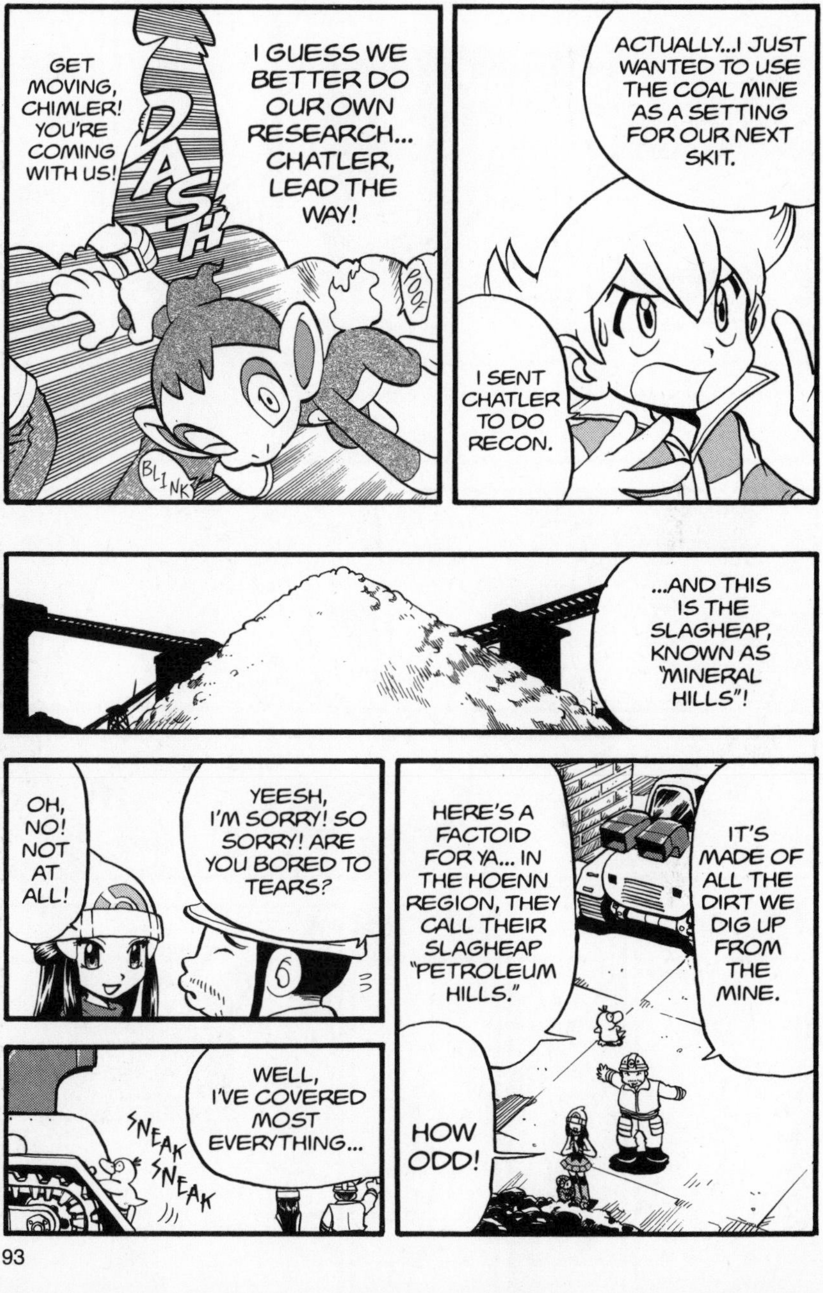

GET MOVING, CHIMLER! YOU'RE COMING WITH US!
I GUESS WE BETTER DO OUR OWN RESEARCH... CHATLER, LEAD THE WAY!
DASH
POOF
BLINK
ACTUALLY...I JUST WANTED TO USE THE COAL MINE AS A SETTING FOR OUR NEXT SKIT.
I SENT CHATLER TO DO RECON.
...AND THIS IS THE SLAGHEAP, KNOWN AS "MINERAL HILLS"!
OH, NO! NOT AT ALL!
YEESH, I'M SORRY! SO SORRY! ARE YOU BORED TO TEARS?
HERE'S A FACTOID FOR YA... IN THE HOENN REGION, THEY CALL THEIR SLAGHEAP "PETROLEUM HILLS."
IT'S MADE OF ALL THE DIRT WE DIG UP FROM THE MINE.
HOW ODD!
WELL, I'VE COVERED MOST EVERYTHING...
SNEAK
SNEAK

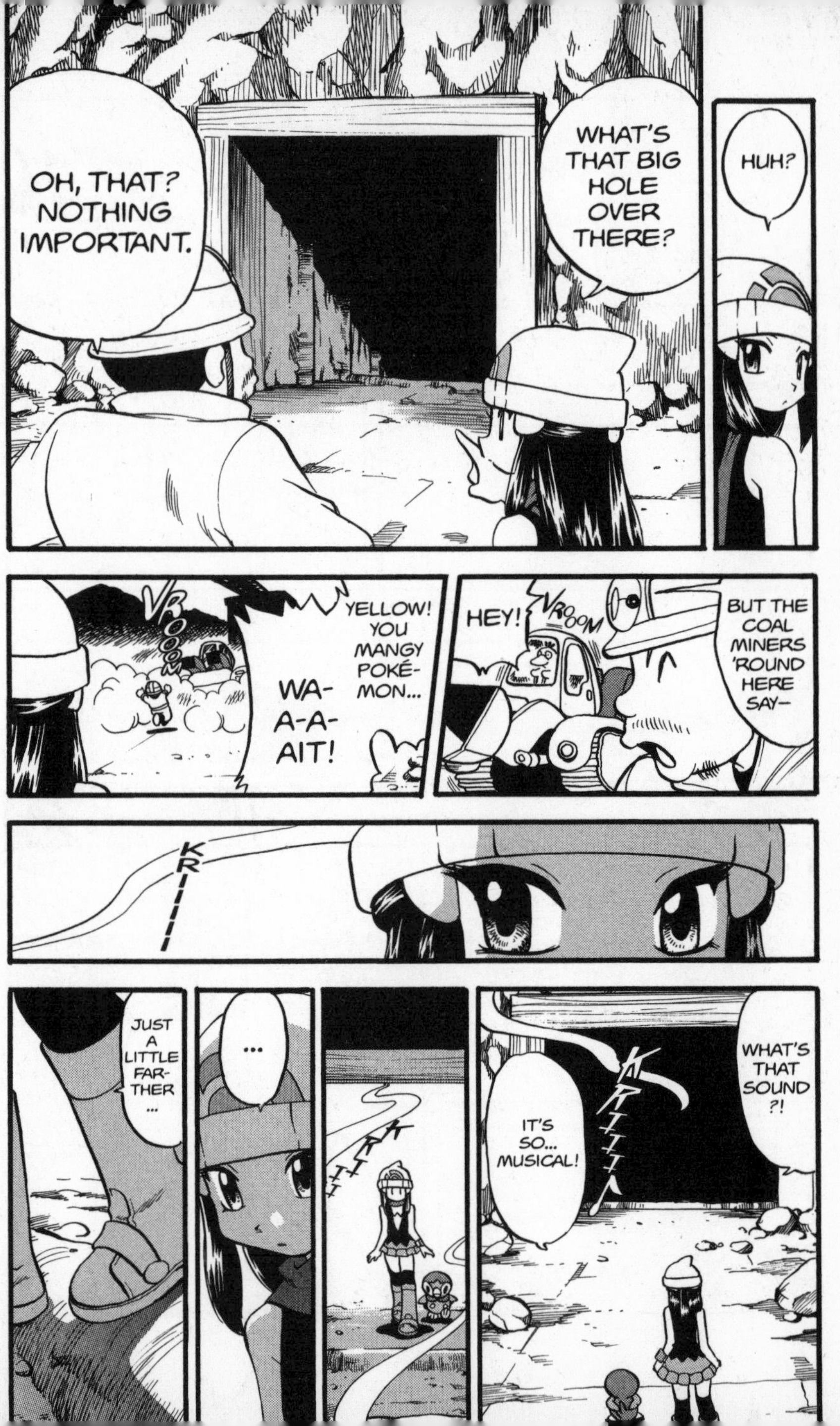
WHAT'S THAT BIG HOLE OVER THERE?
OH, THAT? NOTHING IMPORTANT.
HUH?
BUT THE COAL MINERS 'ROUND HERE SAY—
HEY!
VROOOM
YELLOW! YOU MANGY POKÉ-MON...
WA-A-A-AIT!
VROOOOOM
KRIIIII
WHAT'S THAT SOUND ?!
IT'S SO... MUSICAL!
KRIIIII
KRIIII
...
JUST A LITTLE FAR-THER ...

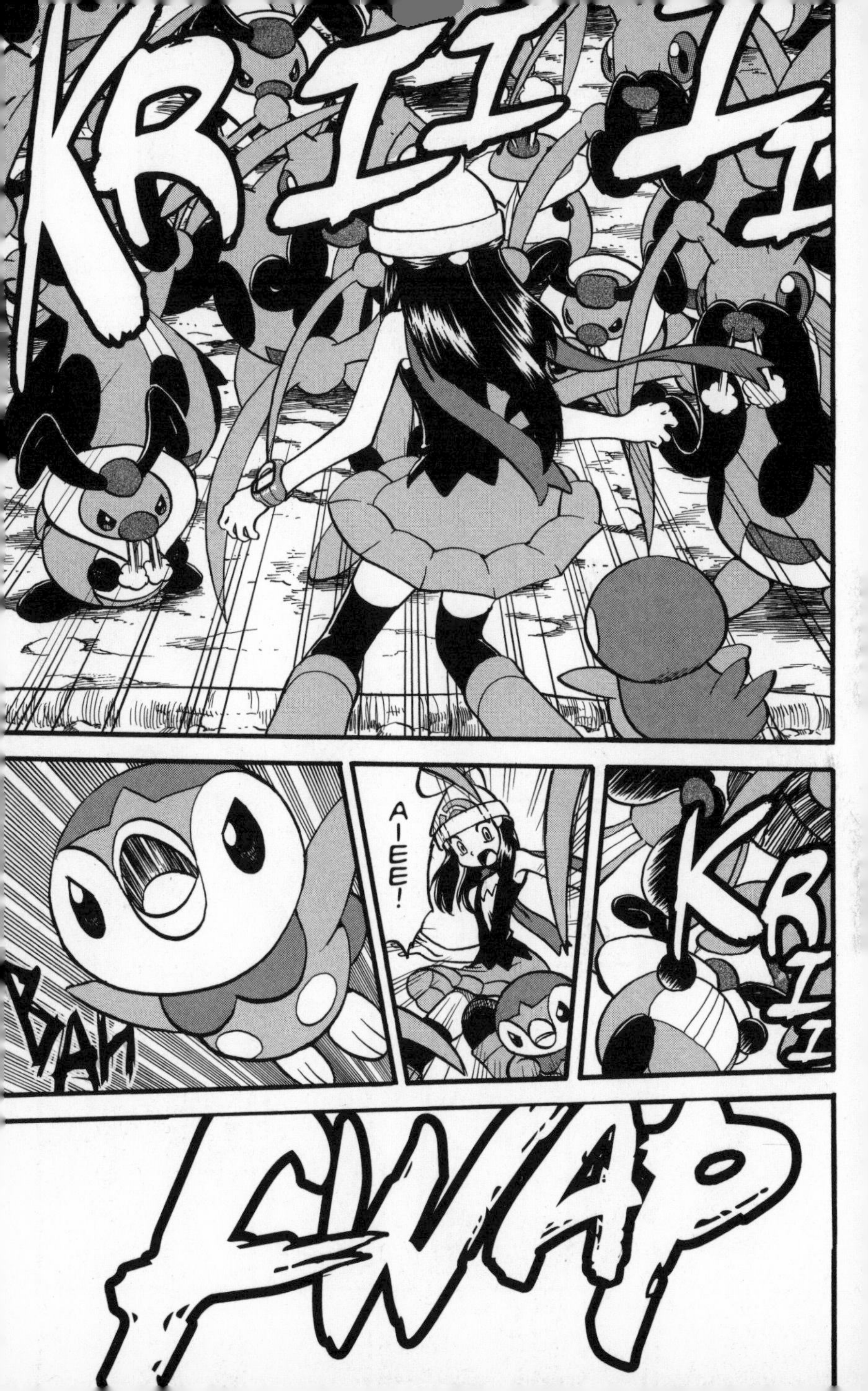
KRIIII
BAH
AIEE!
KRII
FWAP

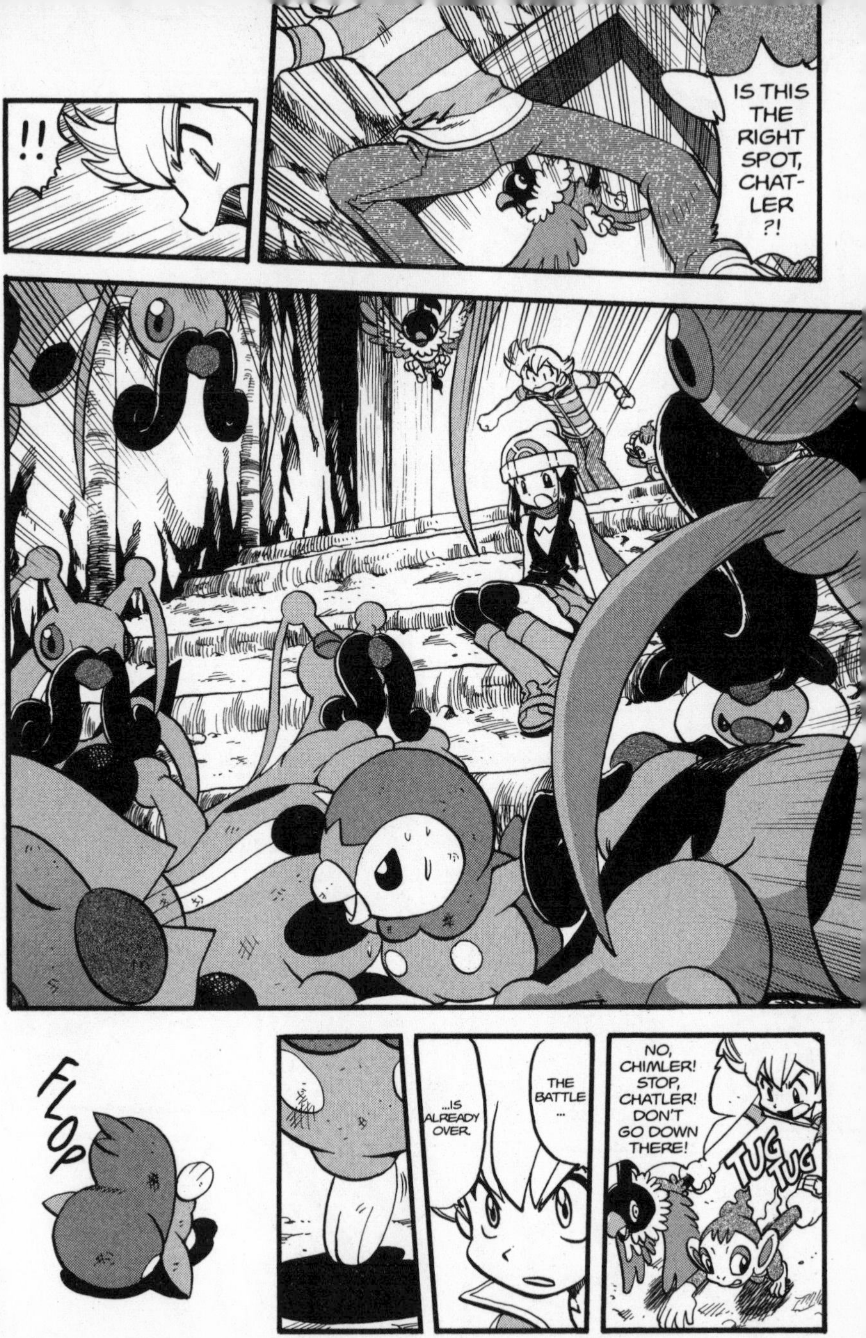
!!
IS THIS THE RIGHT SPOT, CHATLER ?!
FLOP
THE BATTLE ...
...IS ALREADY OVER.
NO, CHIMLER! STOP, CHATLER! DON'T GO DOWN THERE!
TUG TUG

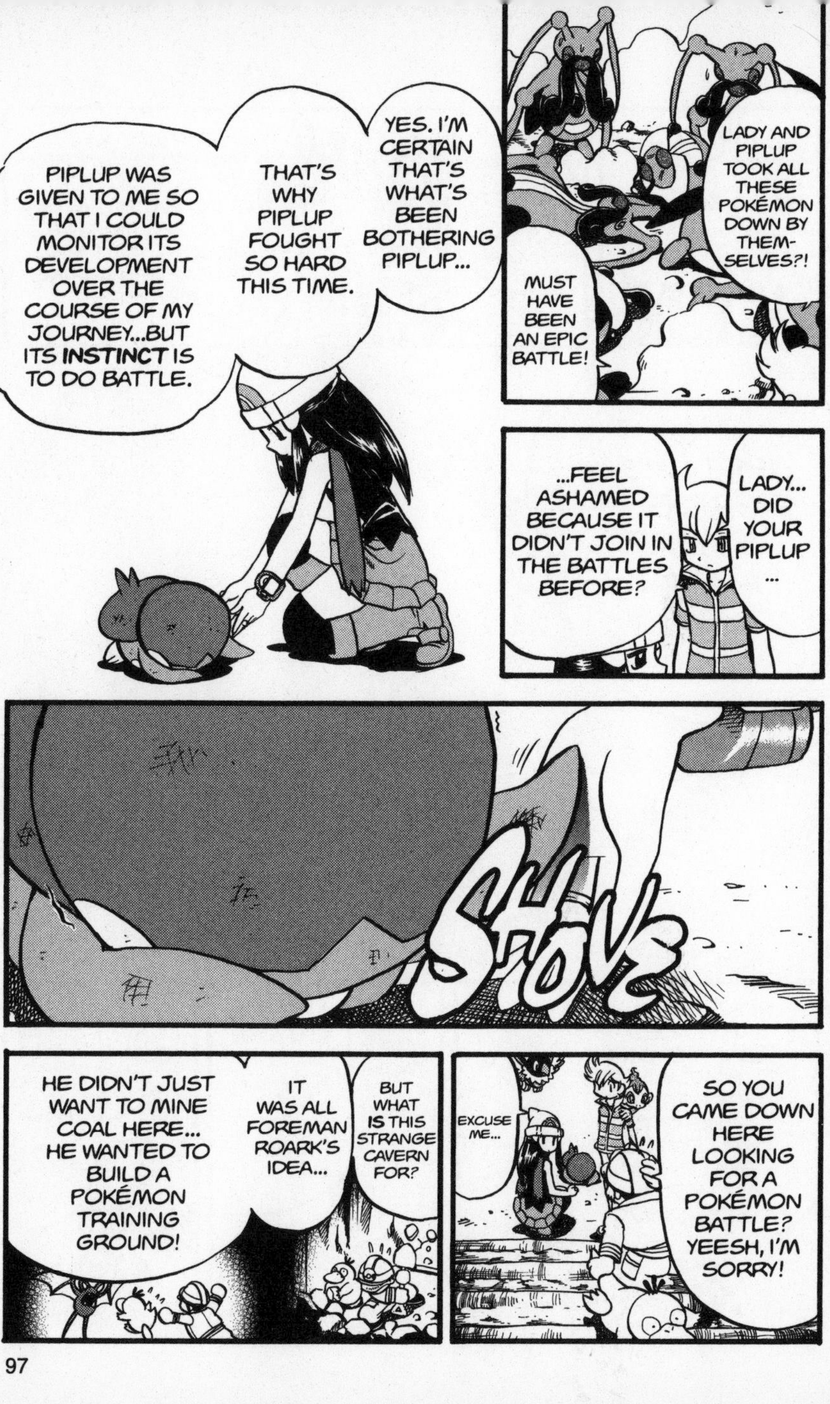
LADY AND PIPLUP TOOK ALL THESE POKÉMON DOWN BY THEM-SELVES?!
MUST HAVE BEEN AN EPIC BATTLE!
YES. I'M CERTAIN THAT'S WHAT'S BEEN BOTHERING PIPLUP...
THAT'S WHY PIPLUP FOUGHT SO HARD THIS TIME.
PIPLUP WAS GIVEN TO ME SO THAT I COULD MONITOR ITS DEVELOPMENT OVER THE COURSE OF MY JOURNEY...BUT ITS **INSTINCT** IS TO DO BATTLE.
LADY... DID YOUR PIPLUP ...
...FEEL ASHAMED BECAUSE IT DIDN'T JOIN IN THE BATTLES BEFORE?
SHOVE
SO YOU CAME DOWN HERE LOOKING FOR A POKÉMON BATTLE? YEESH, I'M SORRY!
EXCUSE ME...
BUT WHAT **IS** THIS STRANGE CAVERN FOR?
IT WAS ALL FOREMAN ROARK'S IDEA...
HE DIDN'T JUST WANT TO MINE COAL HERE... HE WANTED TO BUILD A POKÉMON TRAINING GROUND!

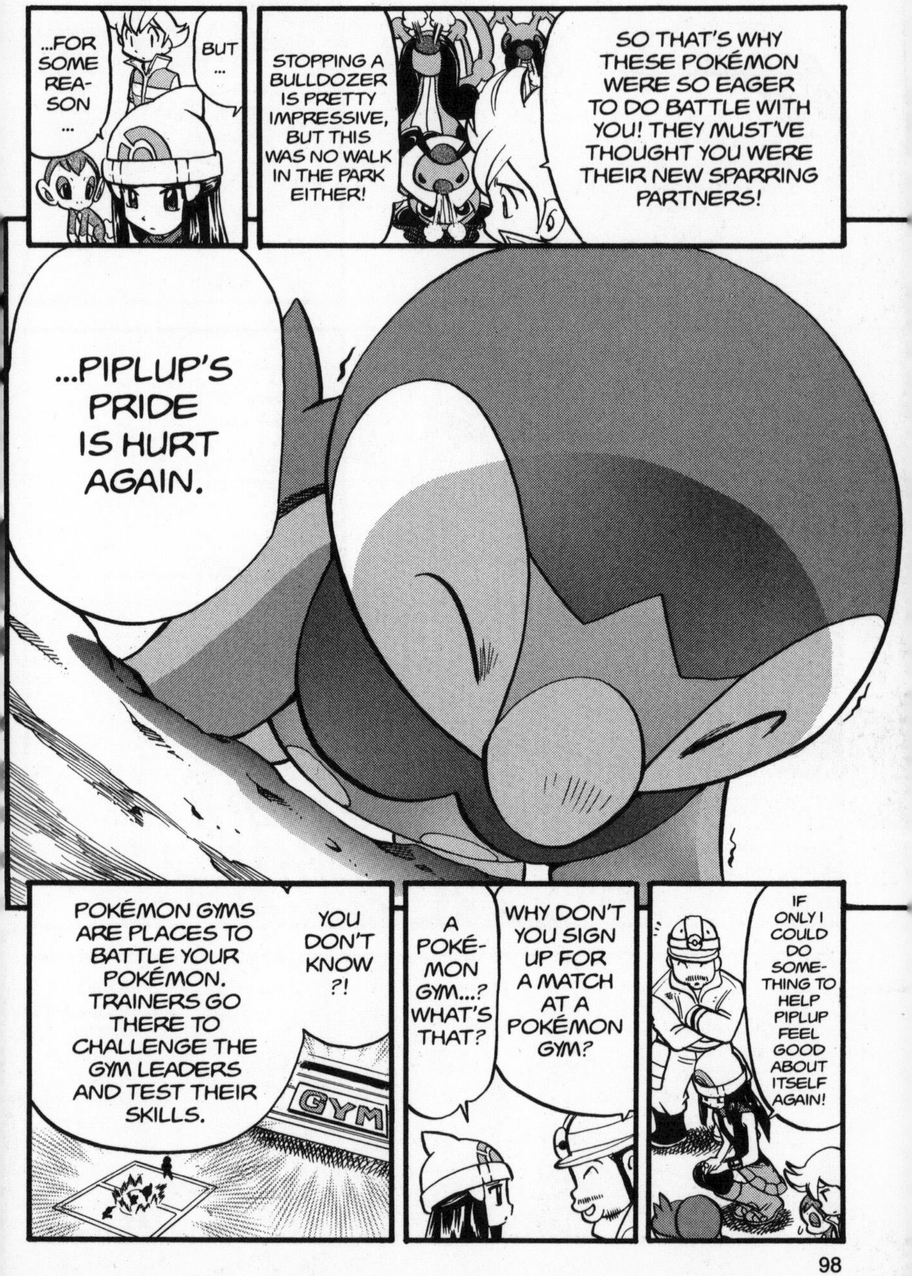
...FOR SOME REA-SON ...
BUT ...
STOPPING A BULLDOZER IS PRETTY IMPRESSIVE, BUT THIS WAS NO WALK IN THE PARK EITHER!
SO THAT'S WHY THESE POKÉMON WERE SO EAGER TO DO BATTLE WITH YOU! THEY MUST'VE THOUGHT YOU WERE THEIR NEW SPARRING PARTNERS!
...PIPLUP'S PRIDE IS HURT AGAIN.
IF ONLY I COULD DO SOME-THING TO HELP PIPLUP FEEL GOOD ABOUT ITSELF AGAIN!
WHY DON'T YOU SIGN UP FOR A MATCH AT A POKÉMON GYM?
A POKÉ-MON GYM...? WHAT'S THAT?
YOU DON'T KNOW ?!
POKÉMON GYMS ARE PLACES TO BATTLE YOUR POKÉMON. TRAINERS GO THERE TO CHALLENGE THE GYM LEADERS AND TEST THEIR SKILLS.
GYM

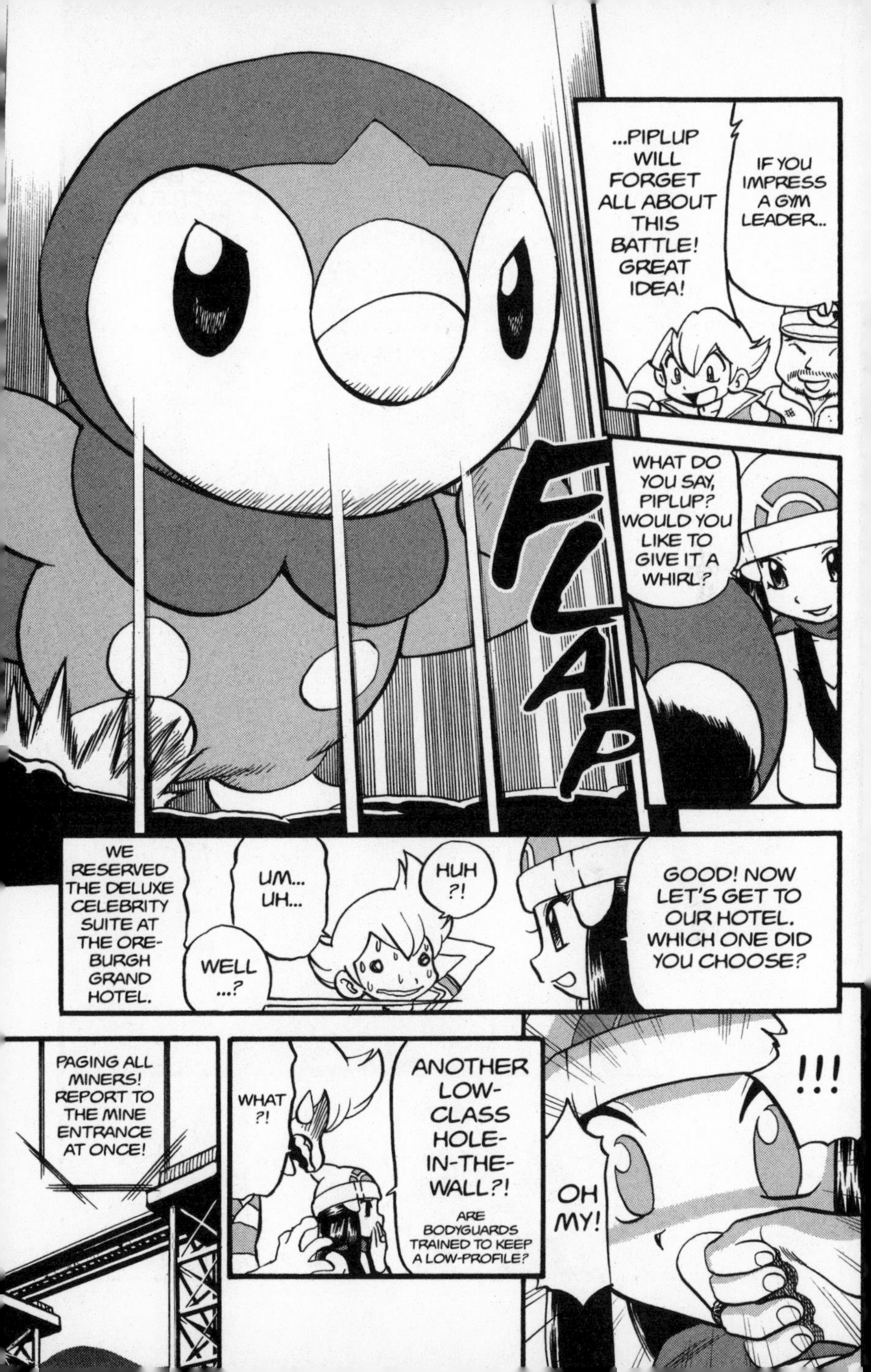
IF YOU IMPRESS A GYM LEADER...
...PIPLUP WILL FORGET ALL ABOUT THIS BATTLE! GREAT IDEA!
WHAT DO YOU SAY, PIPLUP? WOULD YOU LIKE TO GIVE IT A WHIRL?
FLAP
GOOD! NOW LET'S GET TO OUR HOTEL. WHICH ONE DID YOU CHOOSE?
HUH ?!
UM... UH...
WELL ...?
WE RESERVED THE DELUXE CELEBRITY SUITE AT THE ORE-BURGH GRAND HOTEL.
!!!
OH MY!
ANOTHER LOW-CLASS HOLE-IN-THE-WALL?!
ARE BODYGUARDS TRAINED TO KEEP A LOW-PROFILE?
WHAT ?!
PAGING ALL MINERS! REPORT TO THE MINE ENTRANCE AT ONCE!

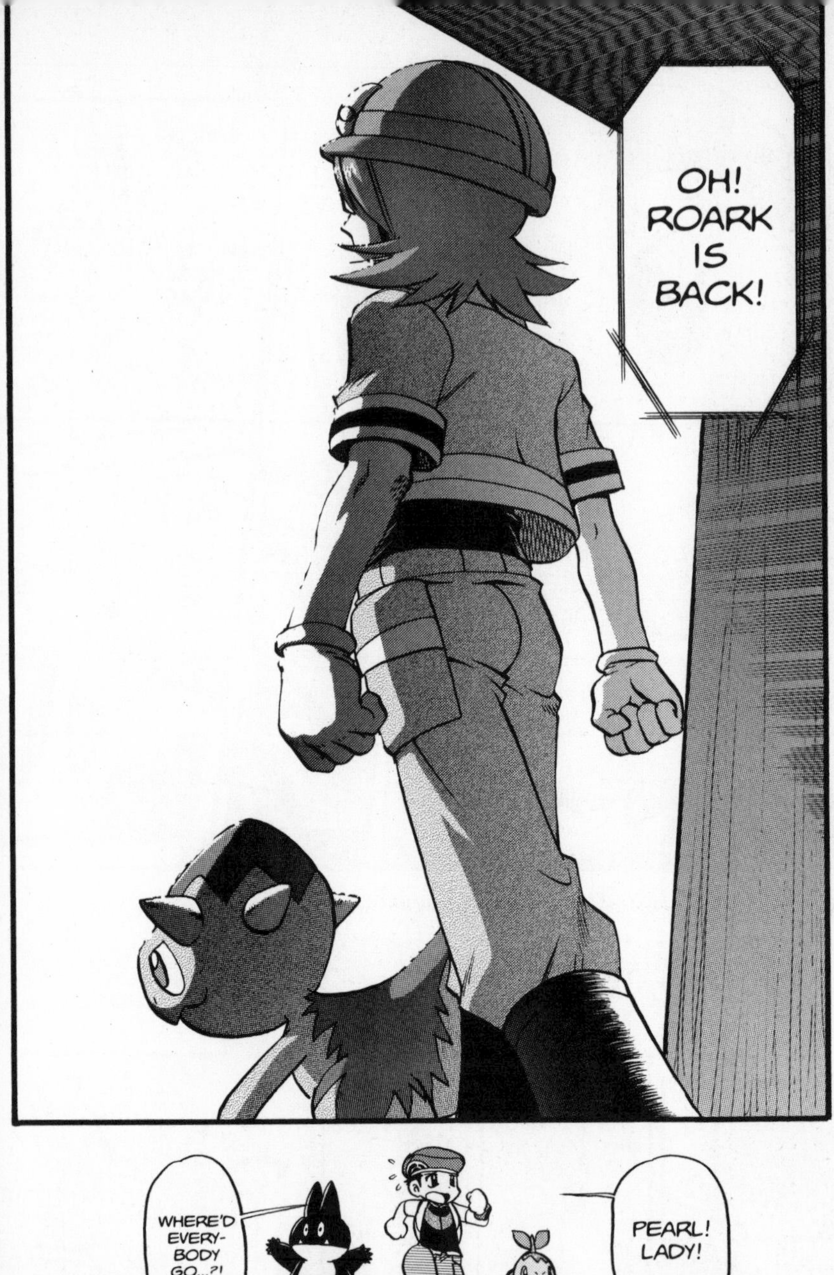
OH! ROARK IS BACK!
WHERE'D EVERY-BODY GO...?!
PEARL! LADY!

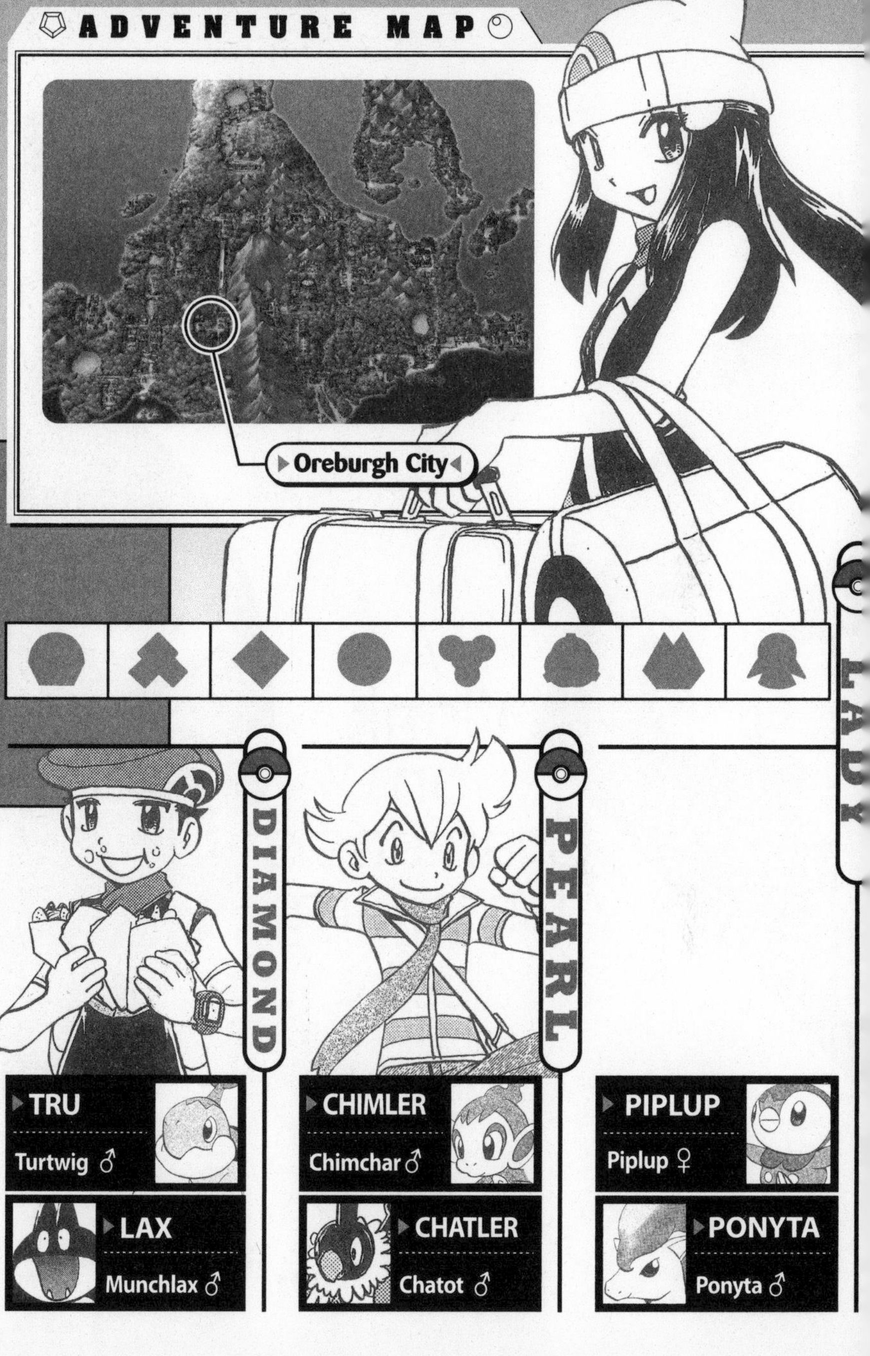
ADVENTURE MAP
Oreburgh City
LADY
DIAMOND
PEARL
TRU
Turtwig ♂
LAX
Munchlax ♂
CHIMLER
Chimchar ♂
CHATLER
Chatot ♂
PIPLUP
Piplup ♀
PONYTA
Ponyta ♂

5

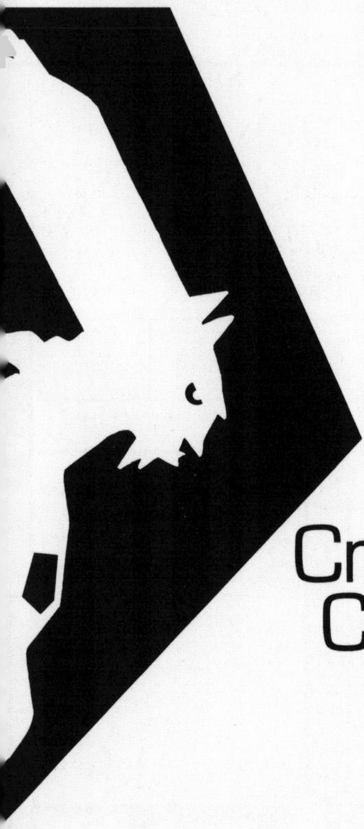

A Conk on Cranidos's Cranium

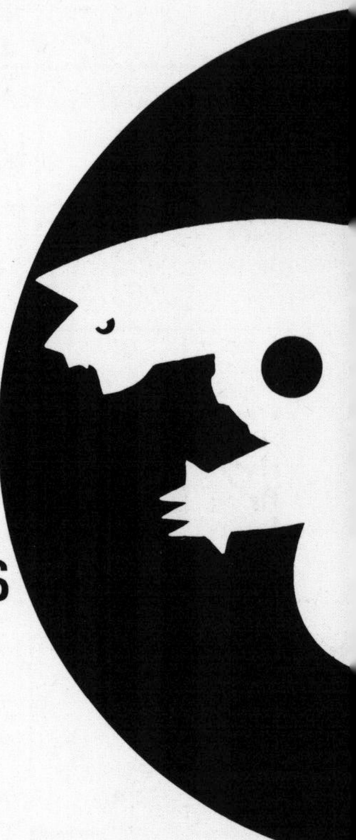

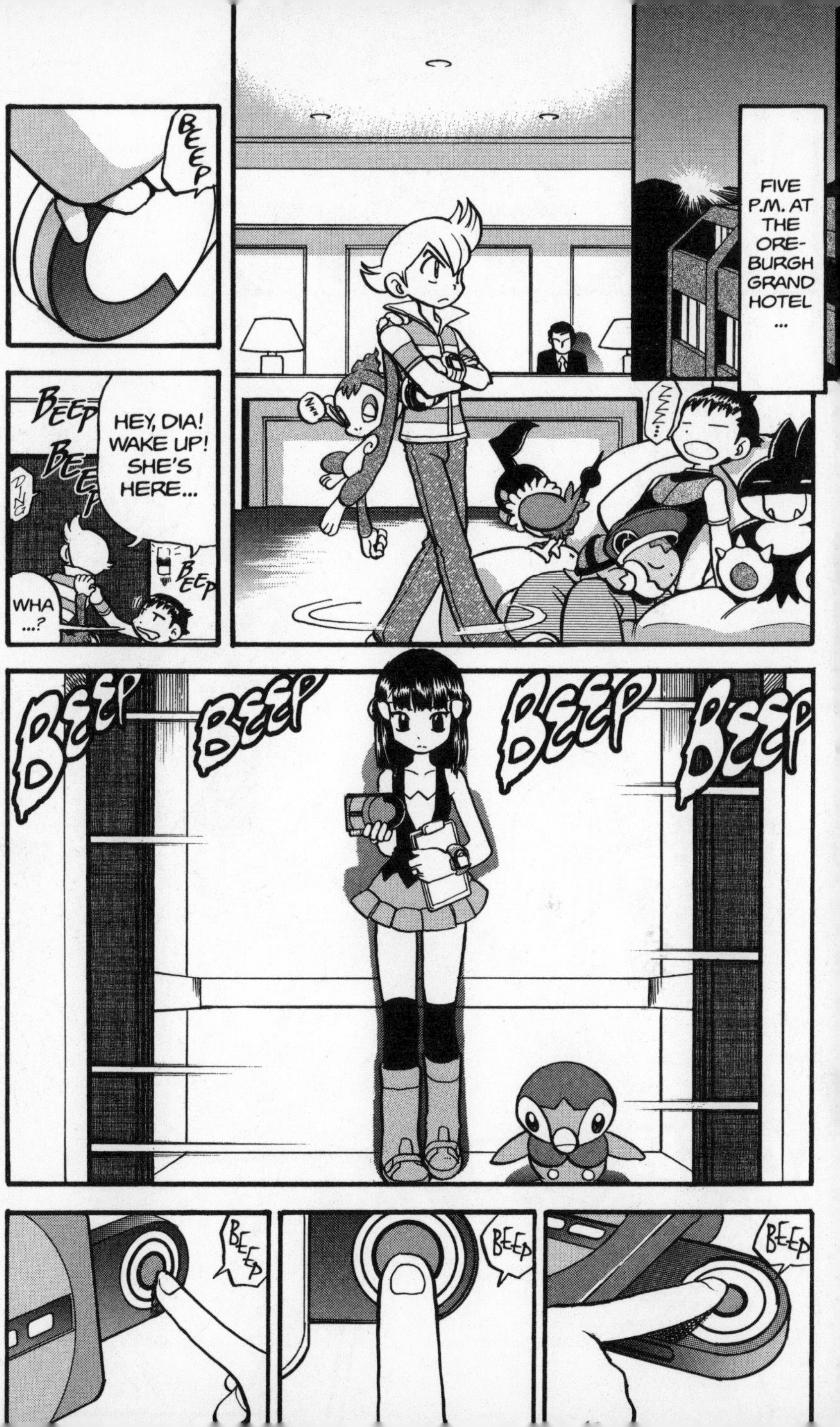
FIVE P.M. AT THE ORE-BURGH GRAND HOTEL ...
BEEP
ZZZ...
HEY, DIA! WAKE UP! SHE'S HERE...
BEEP
BEEP
DING
BEEP
WHA ...?
BEEP
BEEP
BEEP
BEEP
BEEP
BEEP
BEEP

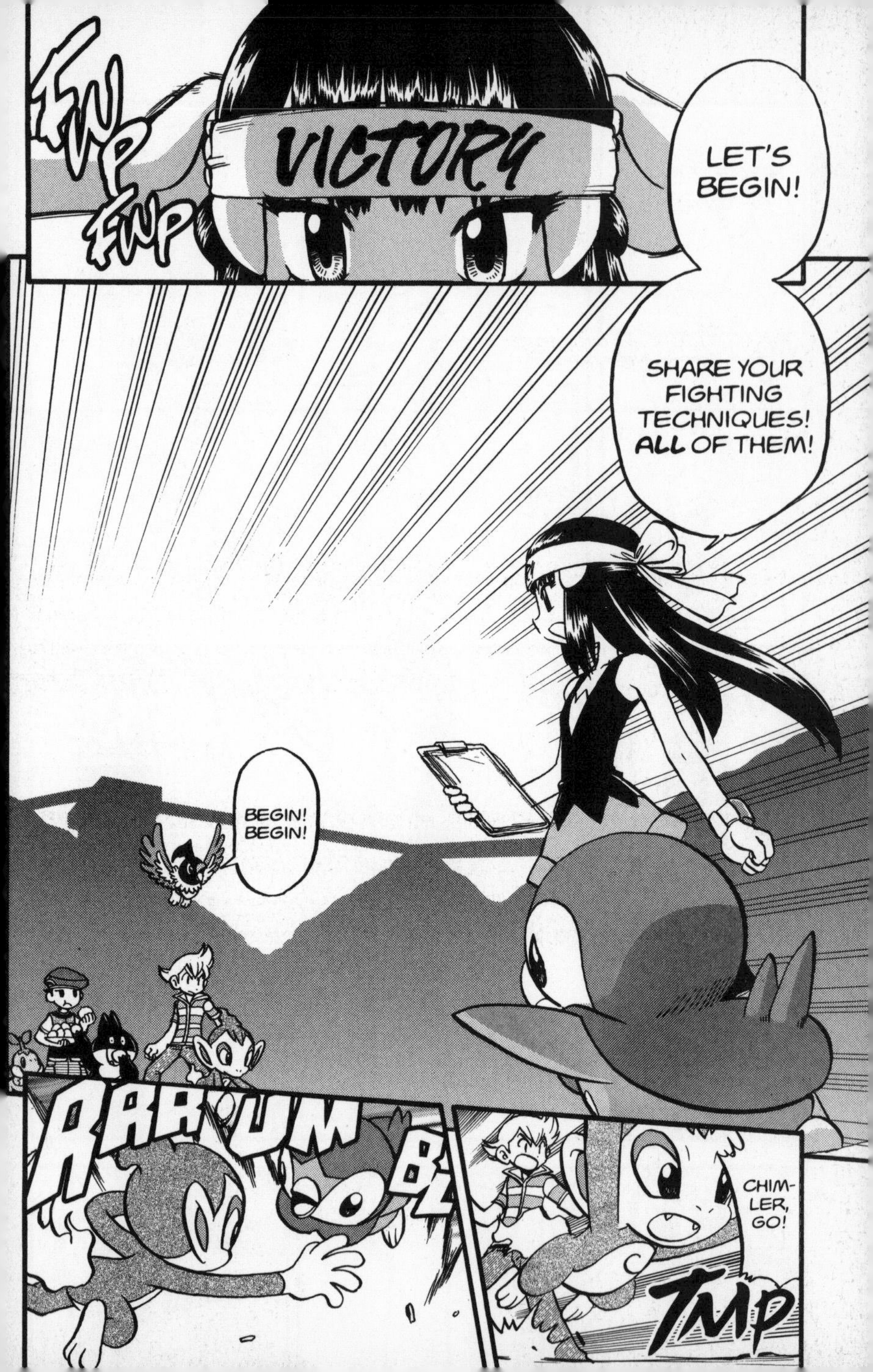
FWP FWP FWP
VICTORY
LET'S BEGIN!
SHARE YOUR FIGHTING TECHNIQUES! ALL OF THEM!
BEGIN! BEGIN!
ARRRUM
CHIM-LER, GO!
TMP

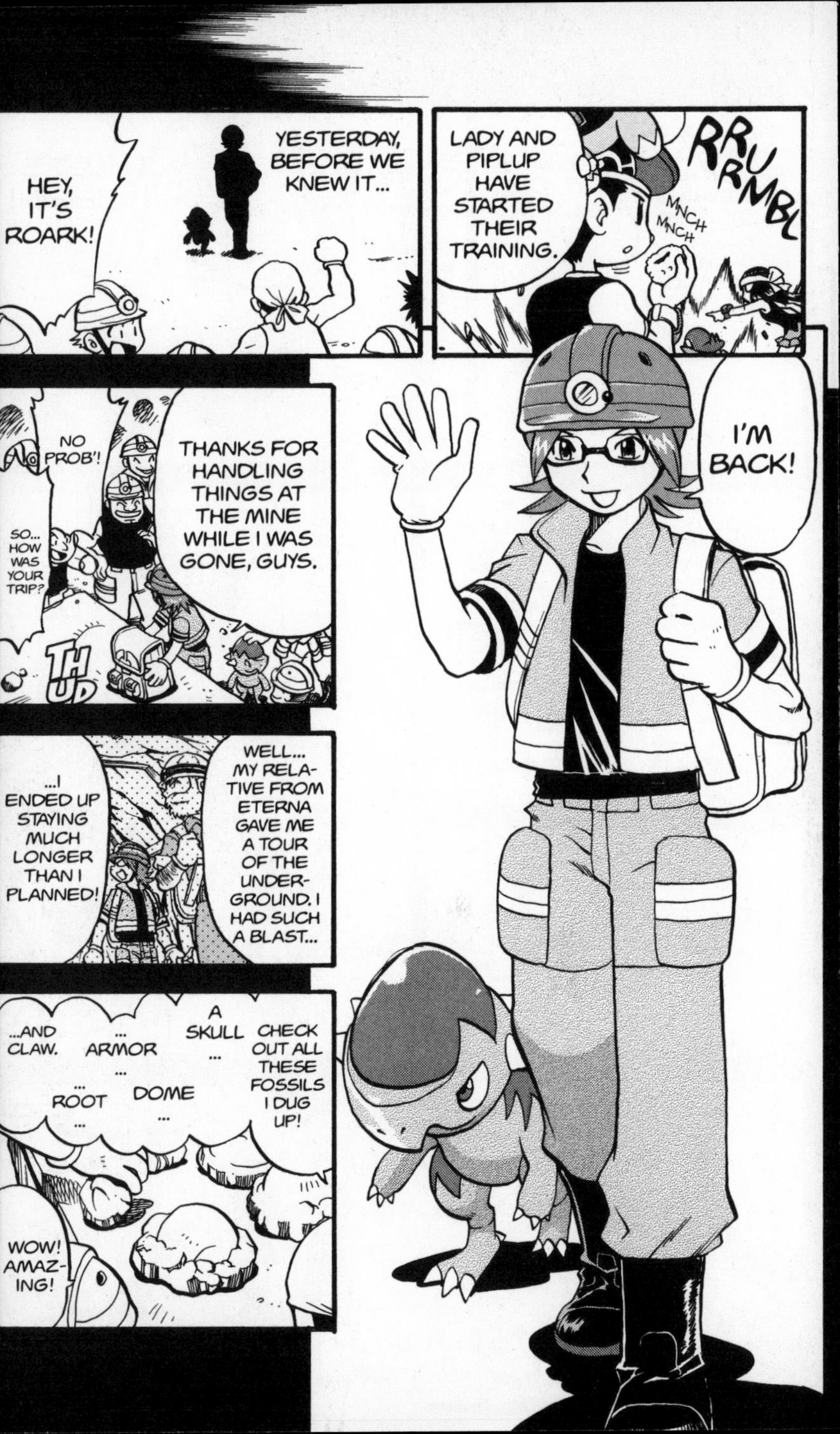
HEY, IT'S ROARK!
YESTERDAY, BEFORE WE KNEW IT...
LADY AND PIPLUP HAVE STARTED THEIR TRAINING.
RRURMBL
MNCH MNCH
NO PROB'!
SO... HOW WAS YOUR TRIP?
THANKS FOR HANDLING THINGS AT THE MINE WHILE I WAS GONE, GUYS.
THUD
I'M BACK!
...I ENDED UP STAYING MUCH LONGER THAN I PLANNED!
WELL... MY RELATIVE FROM ETERNA GAVE ME A TOUR OF THE UNDERGROUND. I HAD SUCH A BLAST...
...AND CLAW.
... ARMOR ...
... ROOT ...
DOME ...
A SKULL ...
CHECK OUT ALL THESE FOSSILS I DUG UP!
WOW! AMAZING!

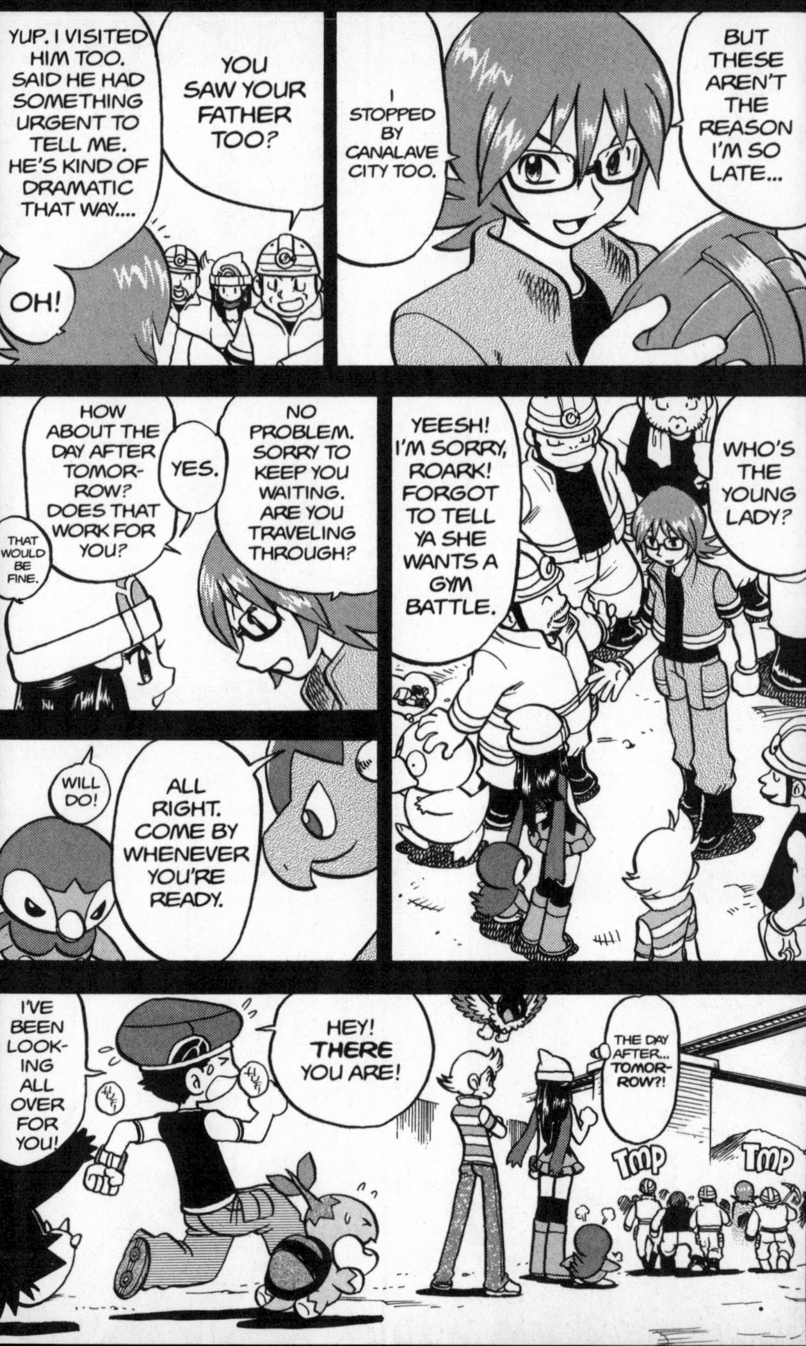
OH!
YOU SAW YOUR FATHER TOO?
YUP. I VISITED HIM TOO. SAID HE HAD SOMETHING URGENT TO TELL ME. HE'S KIND OF DRAMATIC THAT WAY....
I STOPPED BY CANALAVE CITY TOO.
BUT THESE AREN'T THE REASON I'M SO LATE...
WHO'S THE YOUNG LADY?
YEESH! I'M SORRY, ROARK! FORGOT TO TELL YA SHE WANTS A GYM BATTLE.
NO PROBLEM. SORRY TO KEEP YOU WAITING. ARE YOU TRAVELING THROUGH?
YES.
HOW ABOUT THE DAY AFTER TOMOR-ROW? DOES THAT WORK FOR YOU?
THAT WOULD BE FINE.
ALL RIGHT. COME BY WHENEVER YOU'RE READY.
WILL DO!
THE DAY AFTER... TOMOR-ROW?!
TMP
TMP
HEY! THERE YOU ARE!
I'VE BEEN LOOKING ALL OVER FOR YOU!

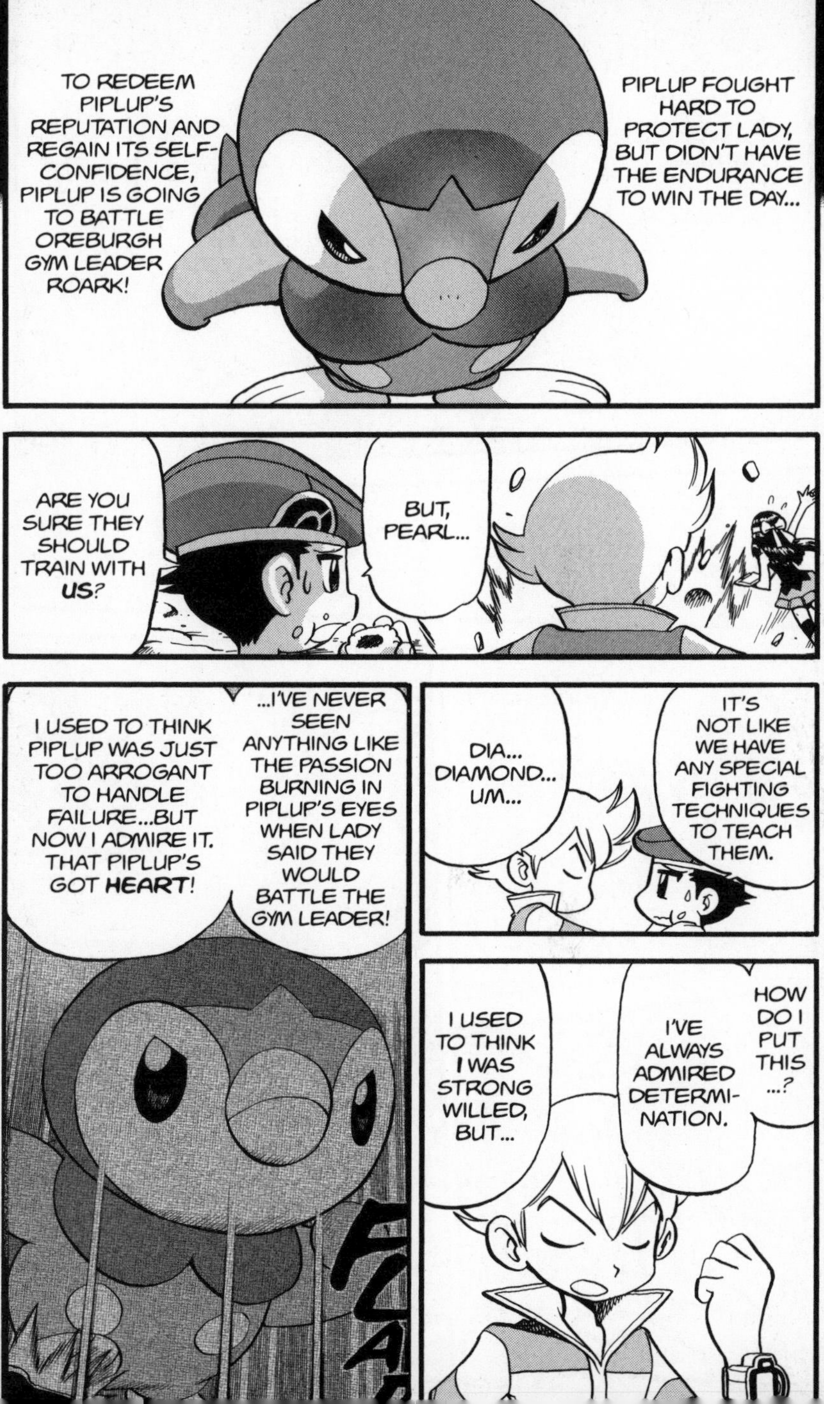
PIPLUP FOUGHT HARD TO PROTECT LADY, BUT DIDN'T HAVE THE ENDURANCE TO WIN THE DAY...
TO REDEEM PIPLUP'S REPUTATION AND REGAIN ITS SELF-CONFIDENCE, PIPLUP IS GOING TO BATTLE OREBURGH GYM LEADER ROARK!
BUT, PEARL...
ARE YOU SURE THEY SHOULD TRAIN WITH **US**?
IT'S NOT LIKE WE HAVE ANY SPECIAL FIGHTING TECHNIQUES TO TEACH THEM.
DIA... DIAMOND... UM...
HOW DO I PUT THIS ...?
I'VE ALWAYS ADMIRED DETERMINATION.
I USED TO THINK **I** WAS STRONG WILLED, BUT...
...I'VE NEVER SEEN ANYTHING LIKE THE PASSION BURNING IN PIPLUP'S EYES WHEN LADY SAID THEY WOULD BATTLE THE GYM LEADER!
I USED TO THINK PIPLUP WAS JUST TOO ARROGANT TO HANDLE FAILURE...BUT NOW I ADMIRE IT. THAT PIPLUP'S GOT **HEART**!

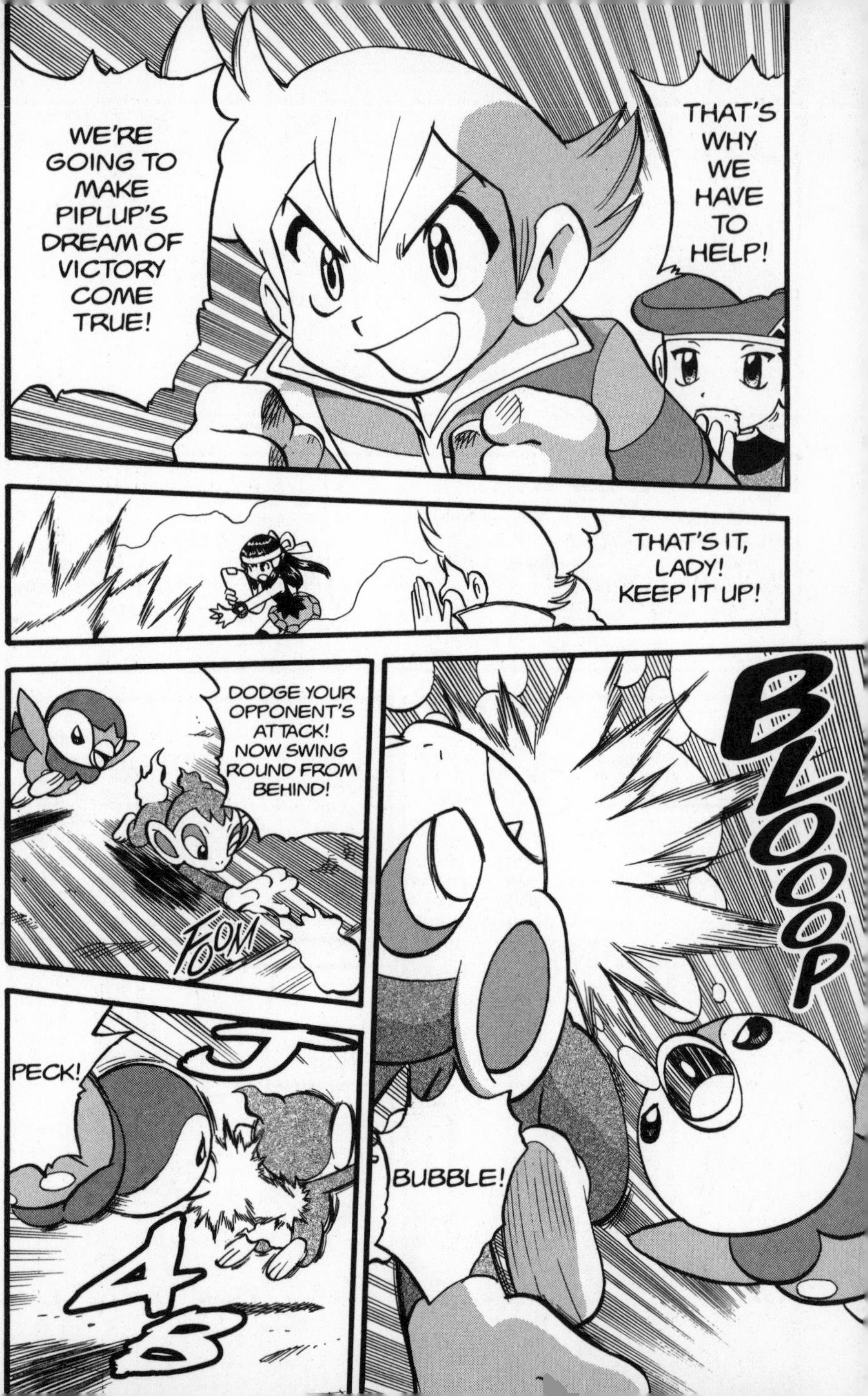
WE'RE GOING TO MAKE PIPLUP'S DREAM OF VICTORY COME TRUE!
THAT'S WHY WE HAVE TO HELP!
THAT'S IT, LADY! KEEP IT UP!
DODGE YOUR OPPONENT'S ATTACK! NOW SWING ROUND FROM BEHIND!
FOOM
BLOOOP
BUBBLE!
PECK!

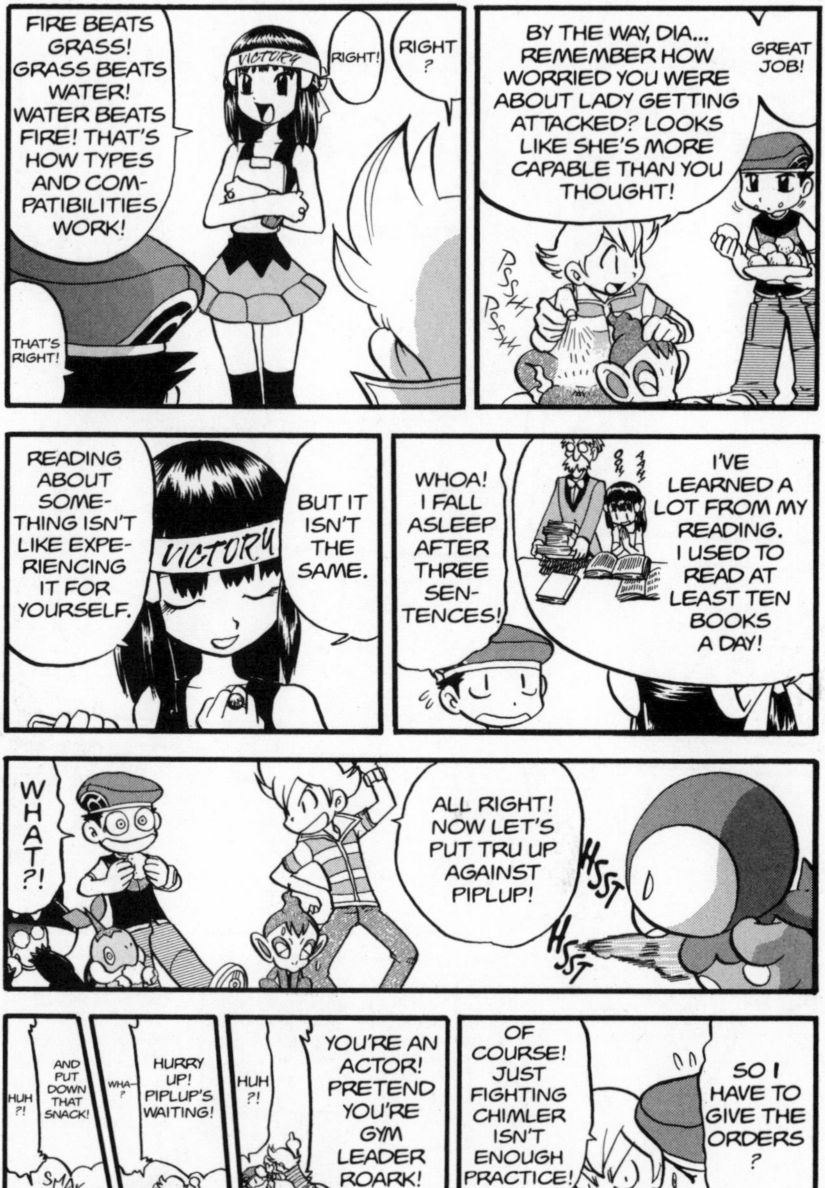
FIRE BEATS GRASS! GRASS BEATS WATER! WATER BEATS FIRE! THAT'S HOW TYPES AND COM-PATIBILITIES WORK!
VICTORY
RIGHT!
RIGHT?
THAT'S RIGHT!
BY THE WAY, DIA... REMEMBER HOW WORRIED YOU WERE ABOUT LADY GETTING ATTACKED? LOOKS LIKE SHE'S MORE CAPABLE THAN YOU THOUGHT!
GREAT JOB!
PSSHH PSSHH
READING ABOUT SOME-THING ISN'T LIKE EXPE-RIENCING IT FOR YOURSELF.
VICTORY
BUT IT ISN'T THE SAME.
WHOA! I FALL ASLEEP AFTER THREE SEN-TENCES!
I'VE LEARNED A LOT FROM MY READING. I USED TO READ AT LEAST TEN BOOKS A DAY!
WHAT?!
ALL RIGHT! NOW LET'S PUT TRU UP AGAINST PIPLUP!
HSST
HSST
HUH?!
AND PUT DOWN THAT SNACK!
SMAK
SMAK
WHA-?
HURRY UP! PIPLUP'S WAITING!
HUH?!
YOU'RE AN ACTOR! PRETEND YOU'RE GYM LEADER ROARK!
OF COURSE! JUST FIGHTING CHIMLER ISN'T ENOUGH PRACTICE!
SO I HAVE TO GIVE THE ORDERS?

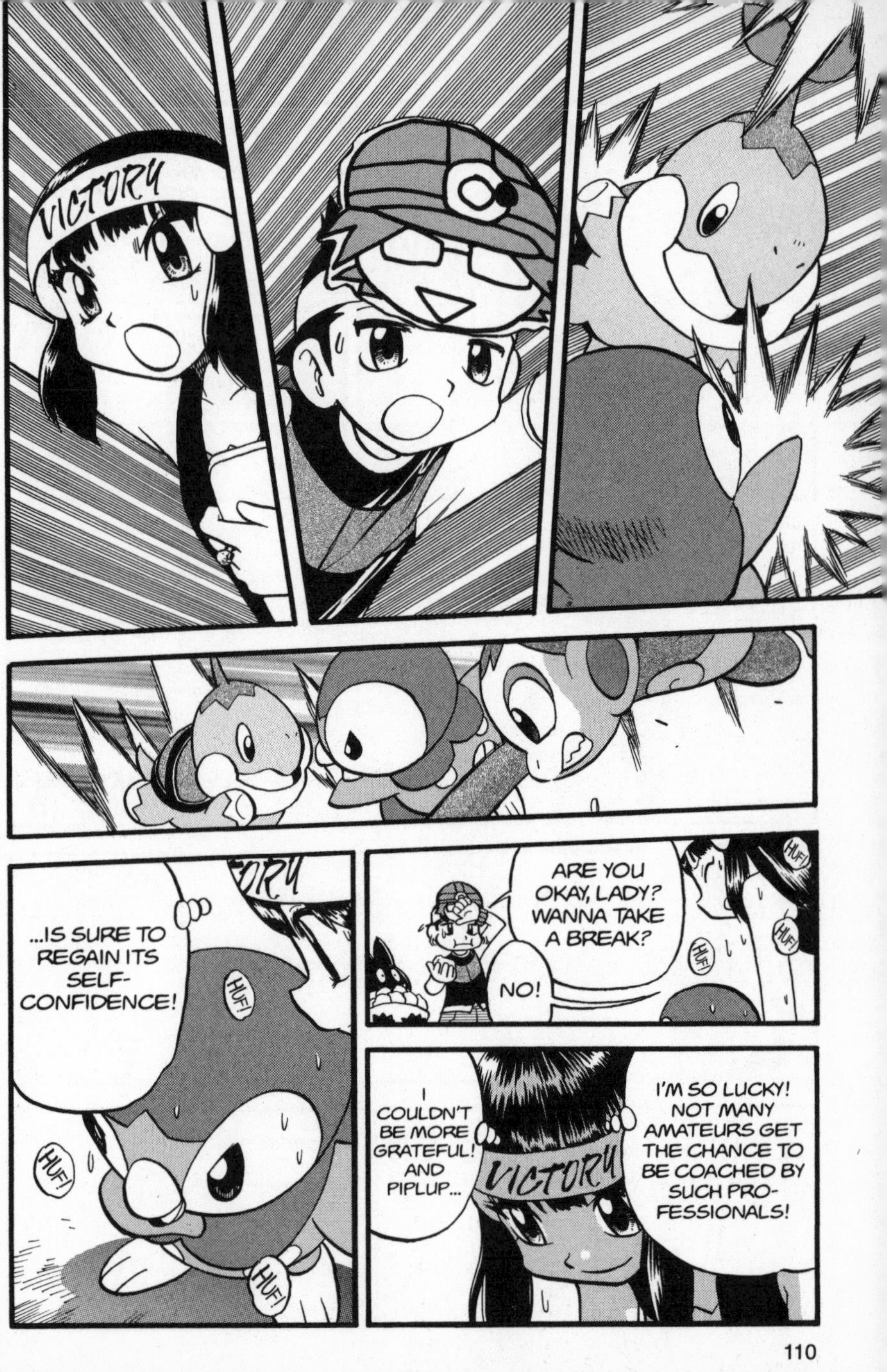
VICTORY
...IS SURE TO REGAIN ITS SELF-CONFIDENCE!
HUF!
HUF!
HUF!
ARE YOU OKAY, LADY? WANNA TAKE A BREAK?
NO!
HUF!
HUF!
HUF!
I'M SO LUCKY! NOT MANY AMATEURS GET THE CHANCE TO BE COACHED BY SUCH PRO-FESSIONALS!
I COULDN'T BE MORE GRATEFUL! AND PIPLUP...
VICTORY

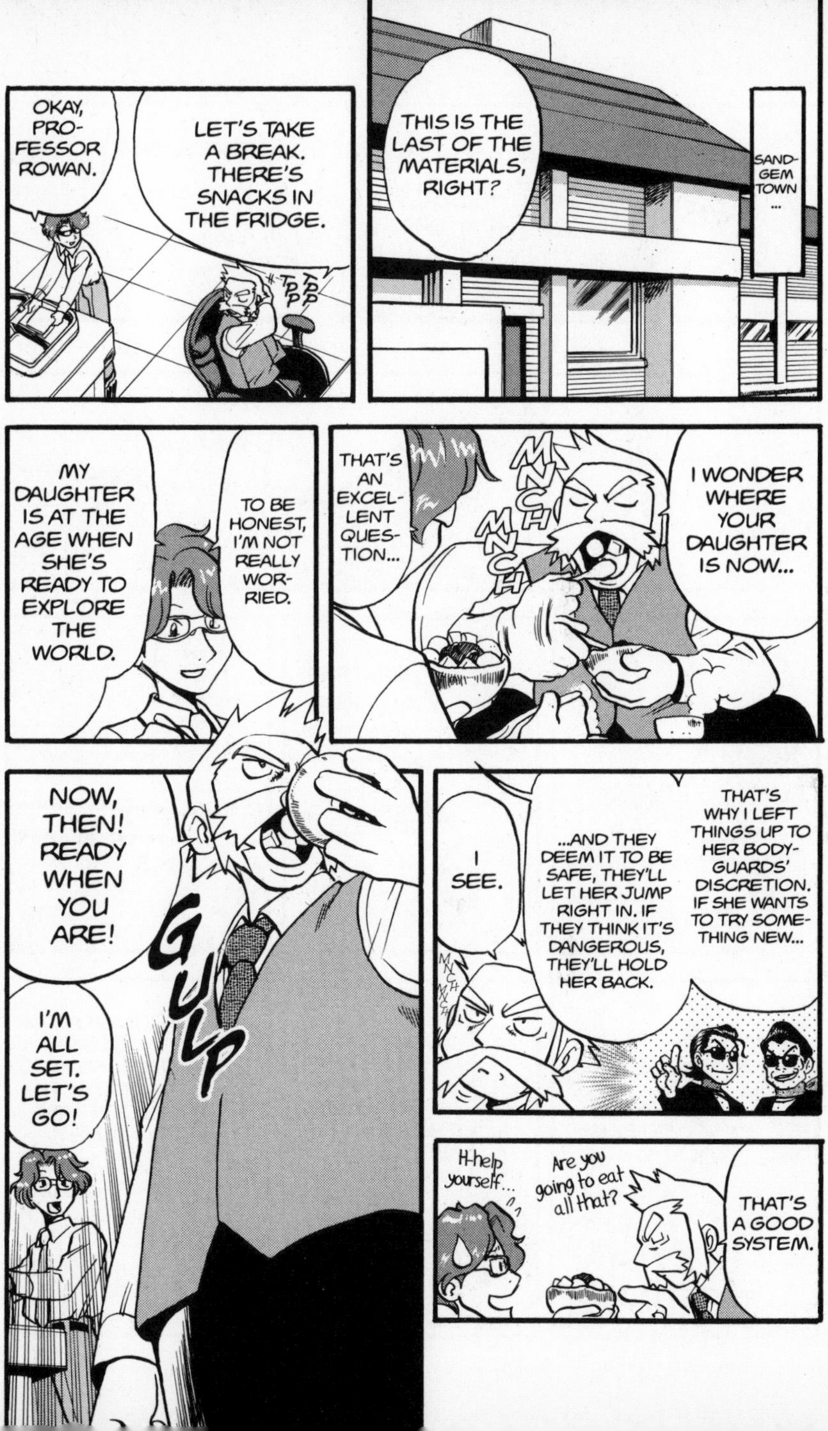
SANDGEM TOWN...
THIS IS THE LAST OF THE MATERIALS, RIGHT?
LET'S TAKE A BREAK. THERE'S SNACKS IN THE FRIDGE.
OKAY, PROFESSOR ROWAN.
I WONDER WHERE YOUR DAUGHTER IS NOW...
MNCH MNCH
THAT'S AN EXCELLENT QUESTION...
TO BE HONEST, I'M NOT REALLY WORRIED.
MY DAUGHTER IS AT THE AGE WHEN SHE'S READY TO EXPLORE THE WORLD.
THAT'S WHY I LEFT THINGS UP TO HER BODYGUARDS' DISCRETION. IF SHE WANTS TO TRY SOMETHING NEW...
...AND THEY DEEM IT TO BE SAFE, THEY'LL LET HER JUMP RIGHT IN. IF THEY THINK IT'S DANGEROUS, THEY'LL HOLD HER BACK.
I SEE.
THAT'S A GOOD SYSTEM.
Are you going to eat all that?
H-help yourself...
NOW, THEN! READY WHEN YOU ARE!
GULP
I'M ALL SET. LET'S GO!

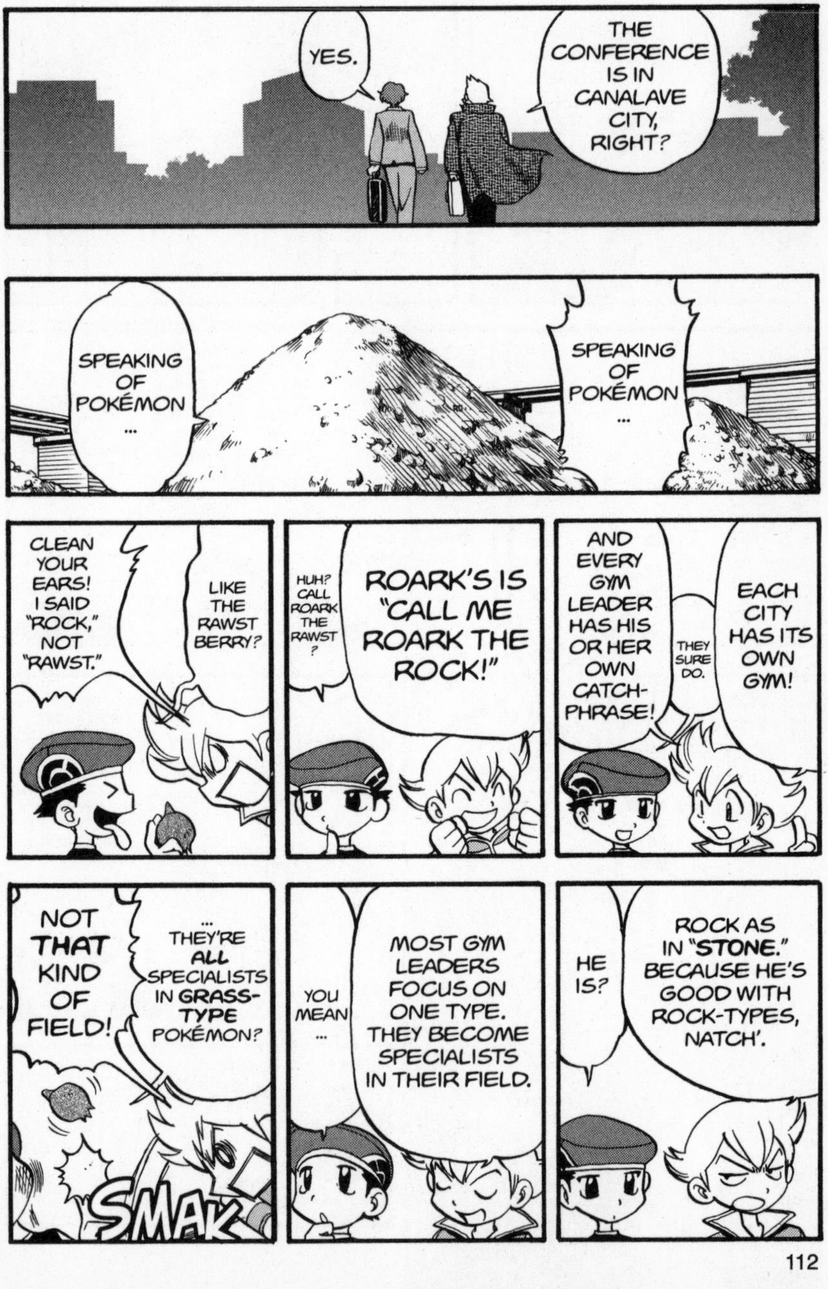
THE CONFERENCE IS IN CANALAVE CITY, RIGHT?
YES.
SPEAKING OF POKÉMON ...
SPEAKING OF POKÉMON ...
EACH CITY HAS ITS OWN GYM!
THEY SURE DO.
AND EVERY GYM LEADER HAS HIS OR HER OWN CATCH-PHRASE!
ROARK'S IS "CALL ME ROARK THE ROCK!"
HUH? CALL ROARK THE RAWST?
LIKE THE RAWST BERRY?
CLEAN YOUR EARS! I SAID "ROCK," NOT "RAWST."
ROCK AS IN "STONE." BECAUSE HE'S GOOD WITH ROCK-TYPES, NATCH'.
HE IS?
MOST GYM LEADERS FOCUS ON ONE TYPE. THEY BECOME SPECIALISTS IN THEIR FIELD.
YOU MEAN ...
... THEY'RE ALL SPECIALISTS IN GRASS-TYPE POKÉMON?
NOT THAT KIND OF FIELD!
SMAK

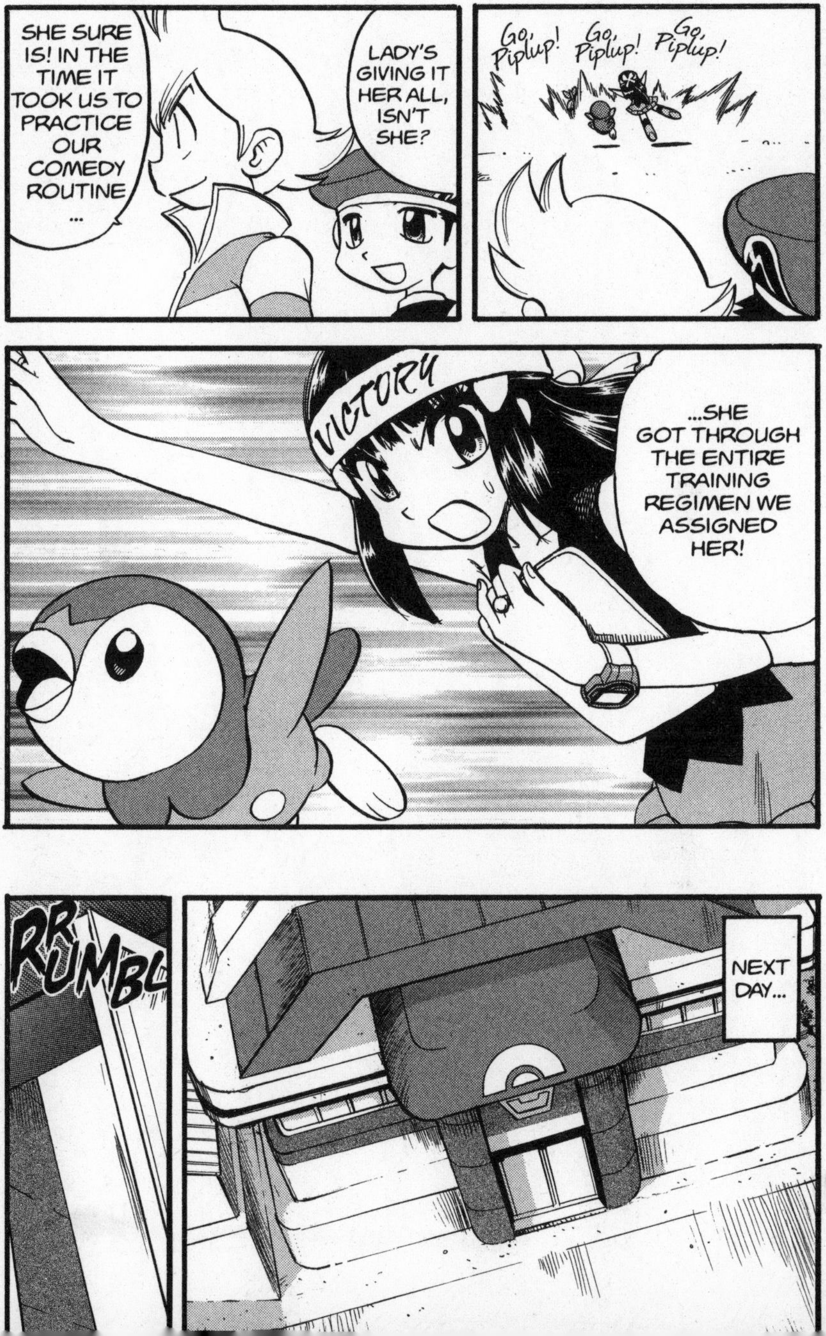
LADY'S GIVING IT HER ALL, ISN'T SHE?
SHE SURE IS! IN THE TIME IT TOOK US TO PRACTICE OUR COMEDY ROUTINE ...
Go, Piplup! Go, Piplup! Go, Piplup!
VICTORY
...SHE GOT THROUGH THE ENTIRE TRAINING REGIMEN WE ASSIGNED HER!
NEXT DAY...
RRUMBL

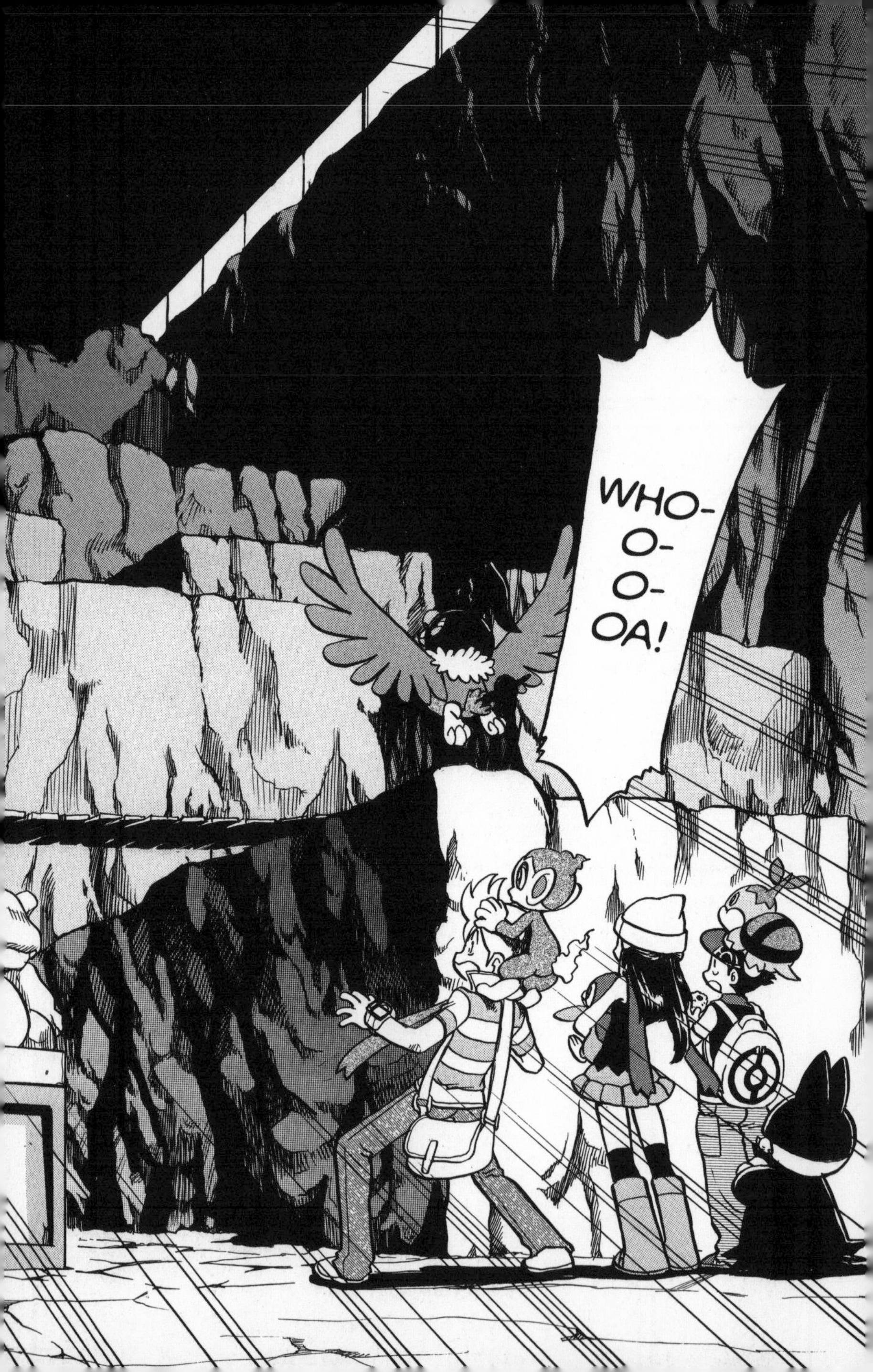
WHO-
O-
O-
OA!

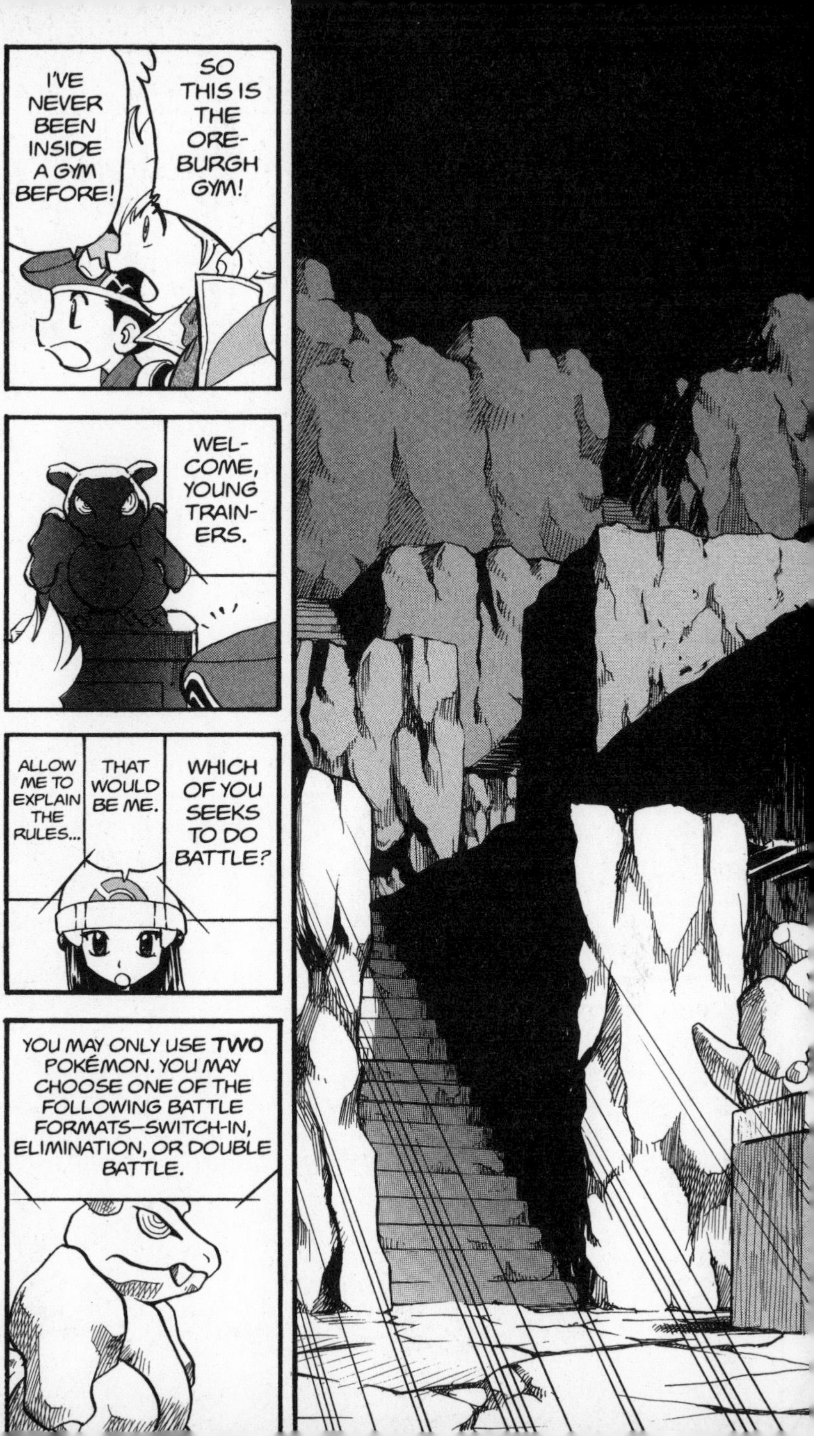
SO THIS IS THE ORE-BURGH GYM!
I'VE NEVER BEEN INSIDE A GYM BEFORE!
WEL-COME, YOUNG TRAIN-ERS.
WHICH OF YOU SEEKS TO DO BATTLE?
THAT WOULD BE ME.
ALLOW ME TO EXPLAIN THE RULES...
YOU MAY ONLY USE TWO POKÉMON. YOU MAY CHOOSE ONE OF THE FOLLOWING BATTLE FORMATS—SWITCH-IN, ELIMINATION, OR DOUBLE BATTLE.

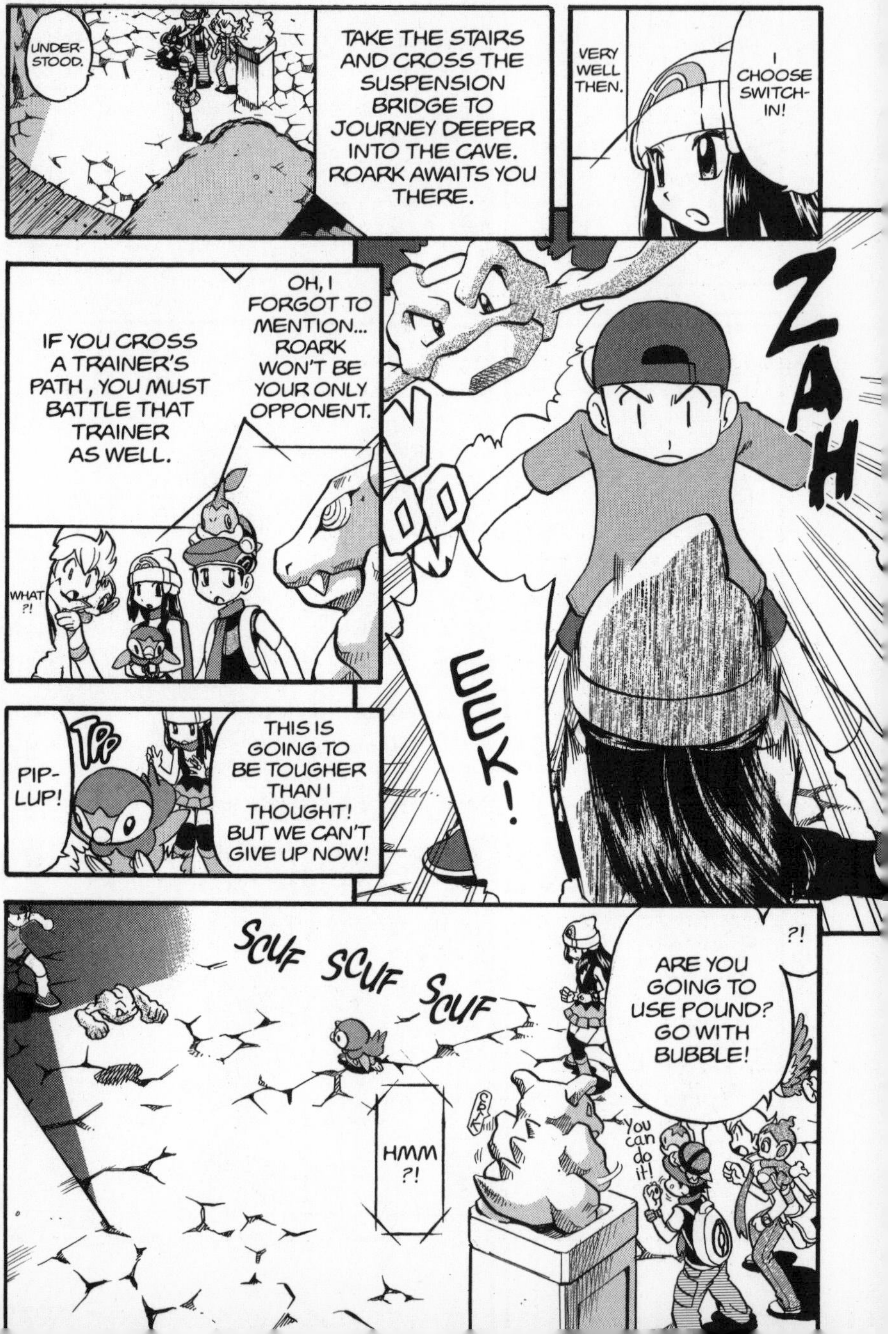
TAKE THE STAIRS AND CROSS THE SUSPENSION BRIDGE TO JOURNEY DEEPER INTO THE CAVE. ROARK AWAITS YOU THERE.
UNDER-STOOD.
OH, I FORGOT TO MENTION... ROARK WON'T BE YOUR ONLY OPPONENT.
IF YOU CROSS A TRAINER'S PATH, YOU MUST BATTLE THAT TRAINER AS WELL.
WHAT ?!
TPP
PIP-LUP!
THIS IS GOING TO BE TOUGHER THAN I THOUGHT! BUT WE CAN'T GIVE UP NOW!
VERY WELL THEN.
I CHOOSE SWITCH-IN!
ZAH
EEK!
SCUF SCUF SCUF
HMM ?!
?!
ARE YOU GOING TO USE POUND? GO WITH BUBBLE!
CRK
You can do it!

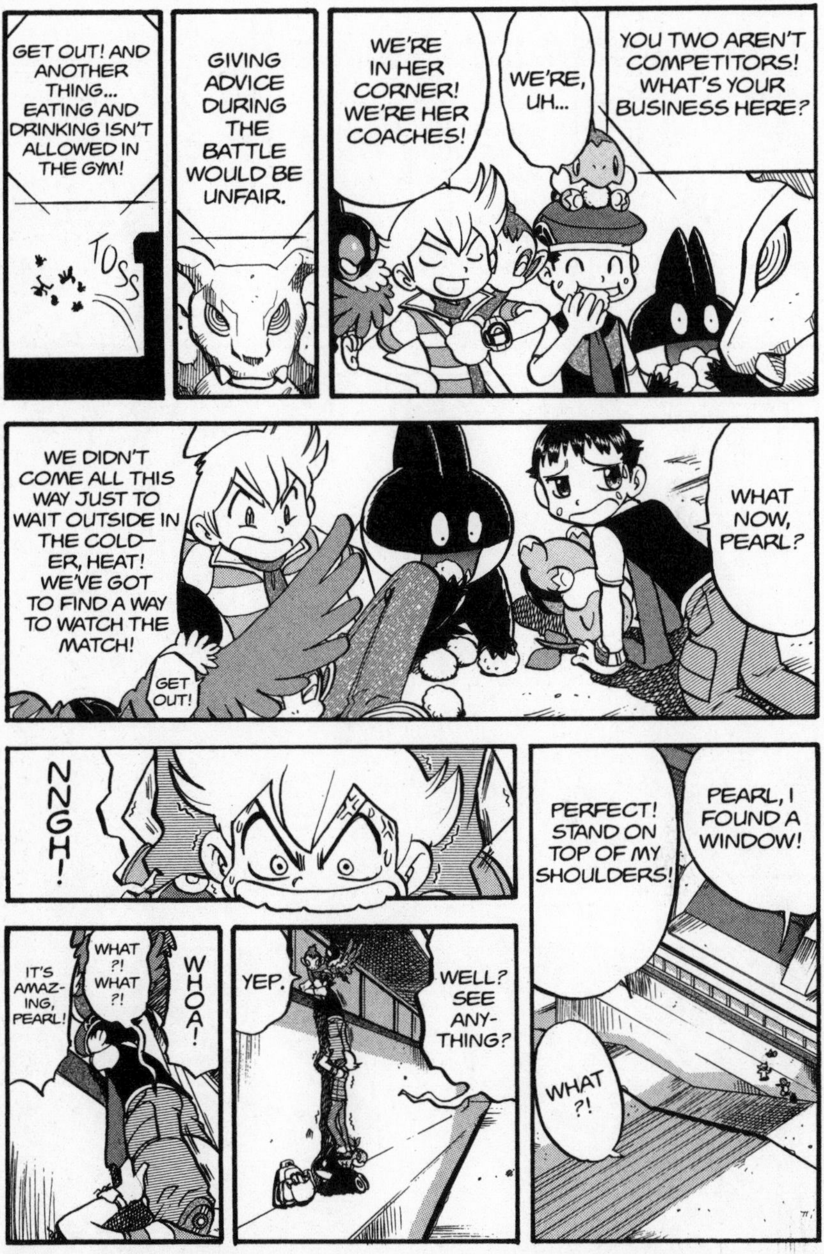
YOU TWO AREN'T COMPETITORS! WHAT'S YOUR BUSINESS HERE?
WE'RE, UH...
WE'RE IN HER CORNER! WE'RE HER COACHES!
GIVING ADVICE DURING THE BATTLE WOULD BE UNFAIR.
GET OUT! AND ANOTHER THING... EATING AND DRINKING ISN'T ALLOWED IN THE GYM!
TOSS
GET OUT!
WE DIDN'T COME ALL THIS WAY JUST TO WAIT OUTSIDE IN THE COLD— ER, HEAT! WE'VE GOT TO FIND A WAY TO WATCH THE MATCH!
WHAT NOW, PEARL?
PEARL, I FOUND A WINDOW!
PERFECT! STAND ON TOP OF MY SHOULDERS!
WHAT ?!
NNGH!
WELL? SEE ANYTHING?
YEP.
WHOA!
WHAT ?! WHAT ?!
IT'S AMAZING, PEARL!

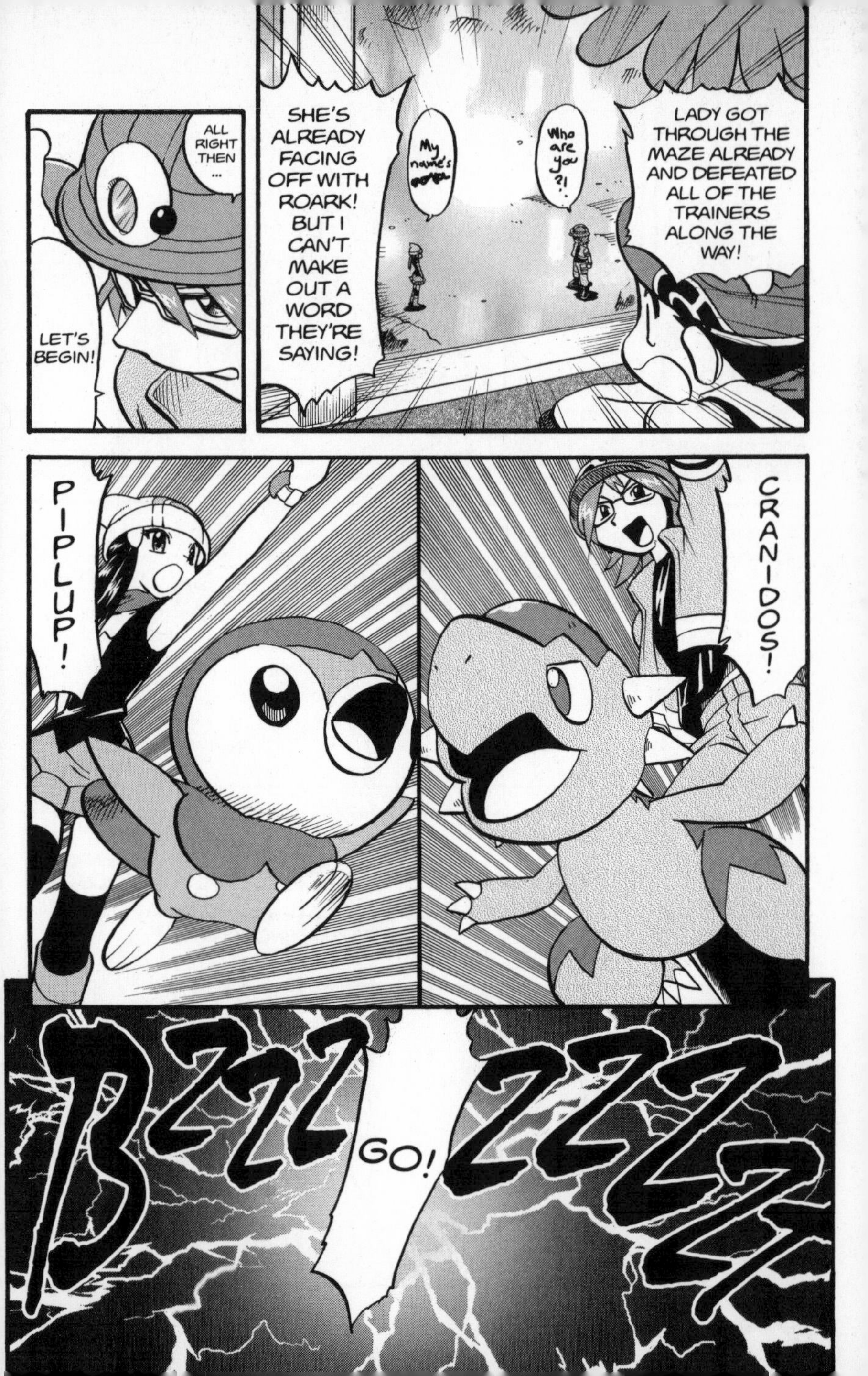
LADY GOT THROUGH THE MAZE ALREADY AND DEFEATED ALL OF THE TRAINERS ALONG THE WAY!
Who are you?!
My name's
SHE'S ALREADY FACING OFF WITH ROARK! BUT I CAN'T MAKE OUT A WORD THEY'RE SAYING!
ALL RIGHT THEN...
LET'S BEGIN!
CRANIDOS!
PIPLUP!
BZZZ ZZZZ
GO!

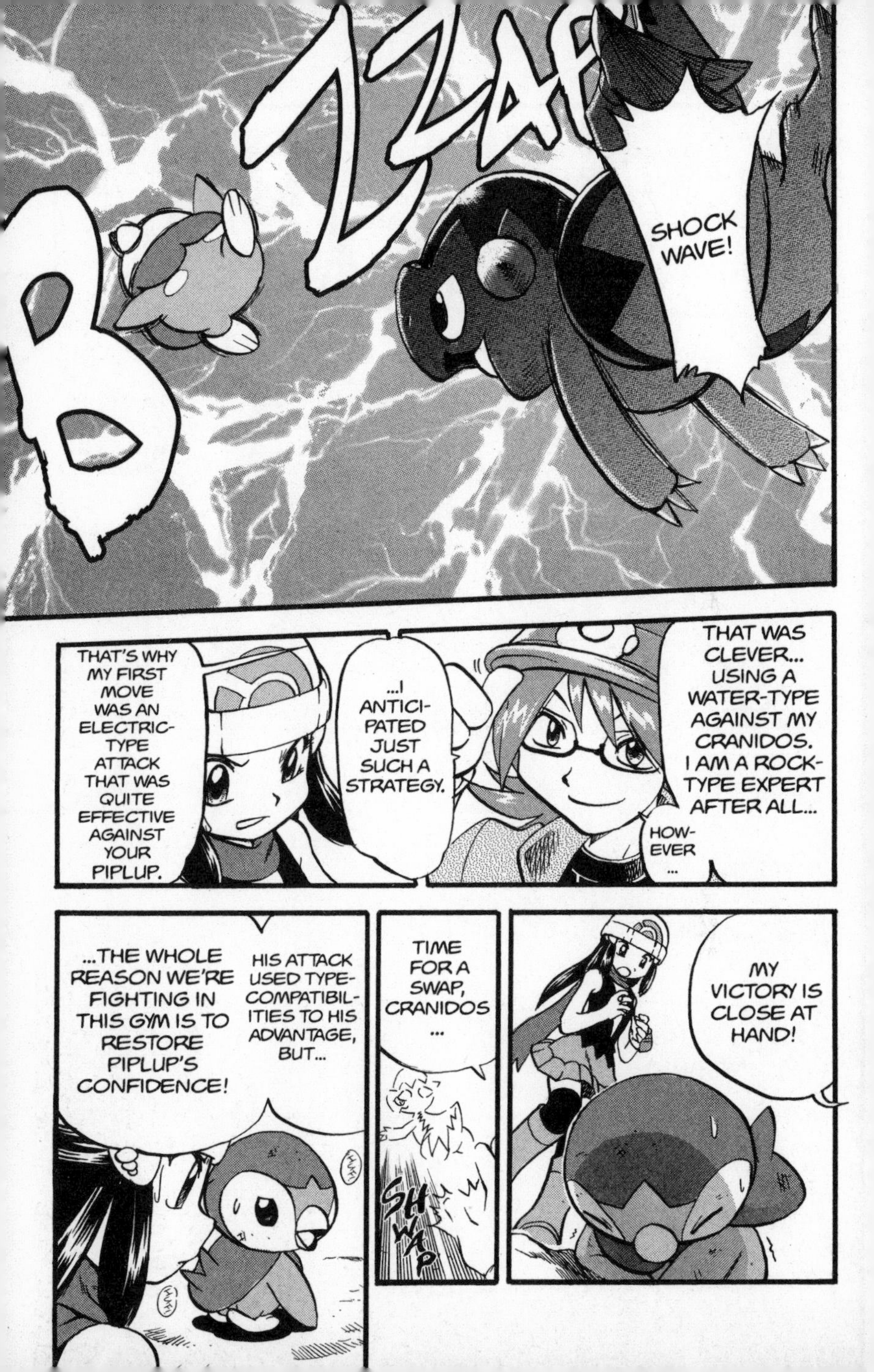
ZZAP
SHOCK WAVE!
THAT WAS CLEVER... USING A WATER-TYPE AGAINST MY CRANIDOS. I AM A ROCK-TYPE EXPERT AFTER ALL...
HOWEVER...
...I ANTICIPATED JUST SUCH A STRATEGY.
THAT'S WHY MY FIRST MOVE WAS AN ELECTRIC-TYPE ATTACK THAT WAS QUITE EFFECTIVE AGAINST YOUR PIPLUP.
MY VICTORY IS CLOSE AT HAND!
TIME FOR A SWAP, CRANIDOS...
SHWAP
HIS ATTACK USED TYPE-COMPATIBILITIES TO HIS ADVANTAGE, BUT...
...THE WHOLE REASON WE'RE FIGHTING IN THIS GYM IS TO RESTORE PIPLUP'S CONFIDENCE!

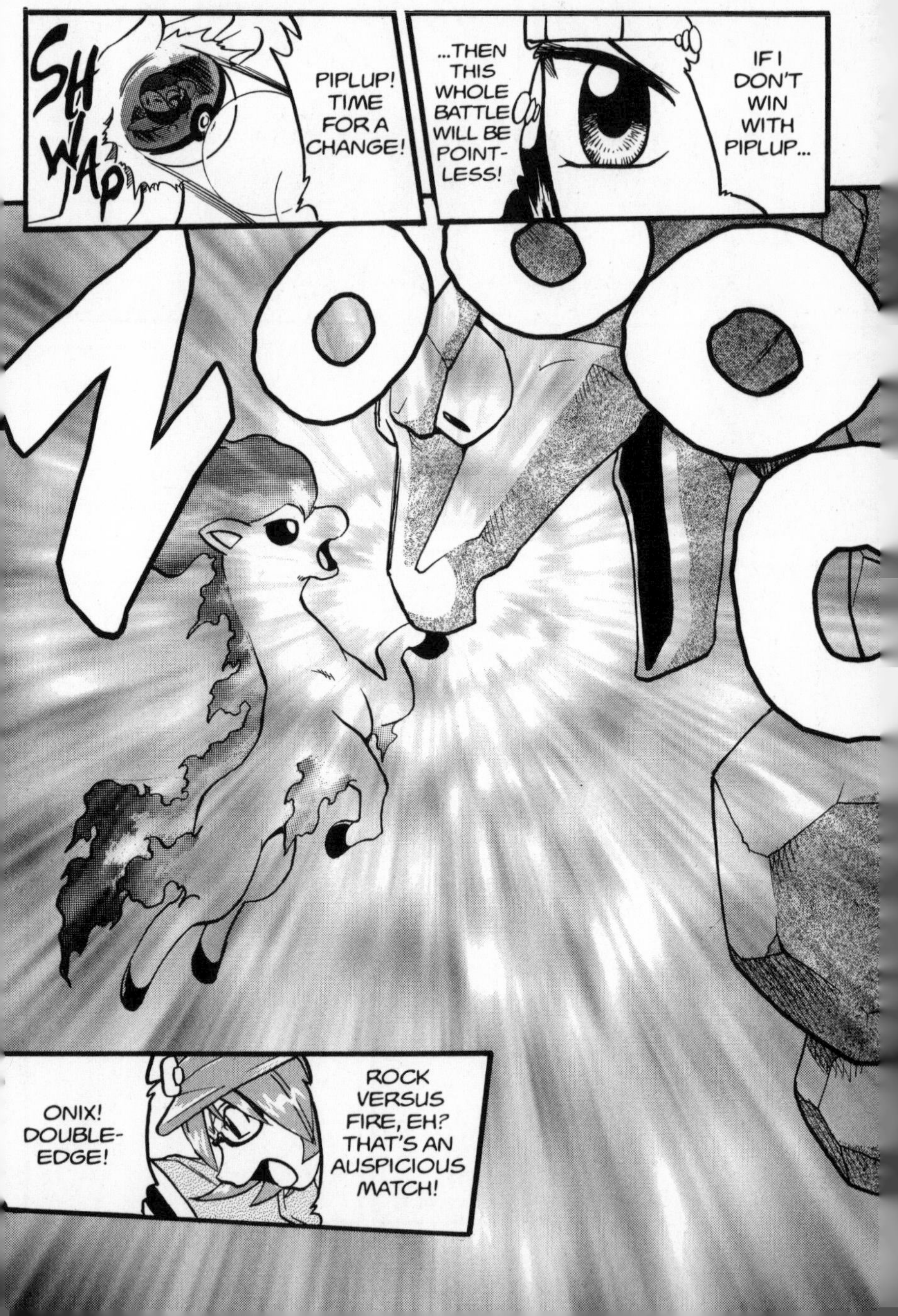
SHWAP
PIPLUP! TIME FOR A CHANGE!
IF I DON'T WIN WITH PIPLUP...
...THEN THIS WHOLE BATTLE WILL BE POINT-LESS!
ZOOOO
ONIX! DOUBLE-EDGE!
ROCK VERSUS FIRE, EH? THAT'S AN AUSPICIOUS MATCH!

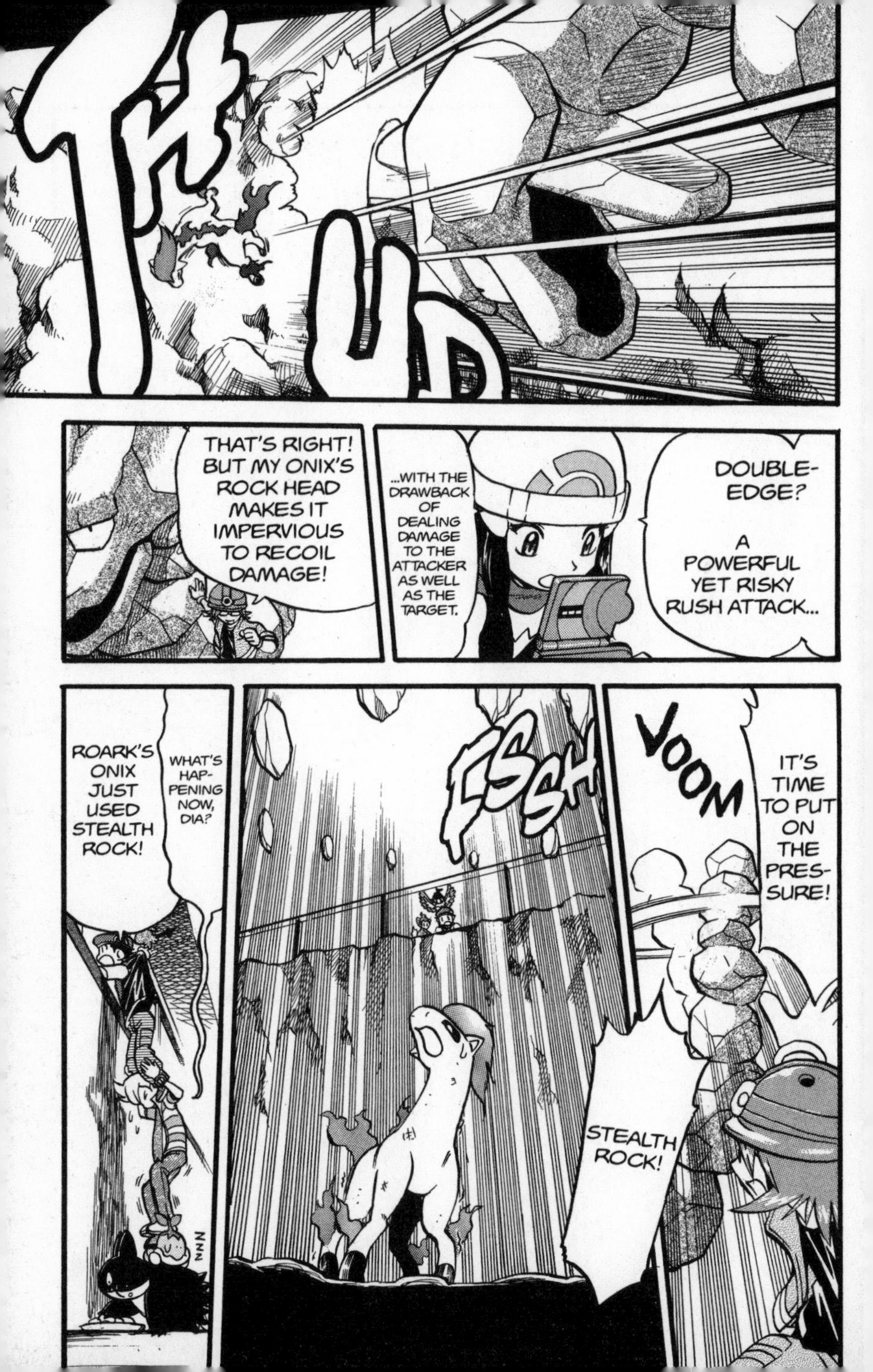
THUD
DOUBLE-EDGE?
A POWERFUL YET RISKY RUSH ATTACK...
...WITH THE DRAWBACK OF DEALING DAMAGE TO THE ATTACKER AS WELL AS THE TARGET.
THAT'S RIGHT! BUT MY ONIX'S ROCK HEAD MAKES IT IMPERVIOUS TO RECOIL DAMAGE!
IT'S TIME TO PUT ON THE PRESSURE!
STEALTH ROCK!
VOOM
FSSH
WHAT'S HAP-PENING NOW, DIA?
ROARK'S ONIX JUST USED STEALTH ROCK!

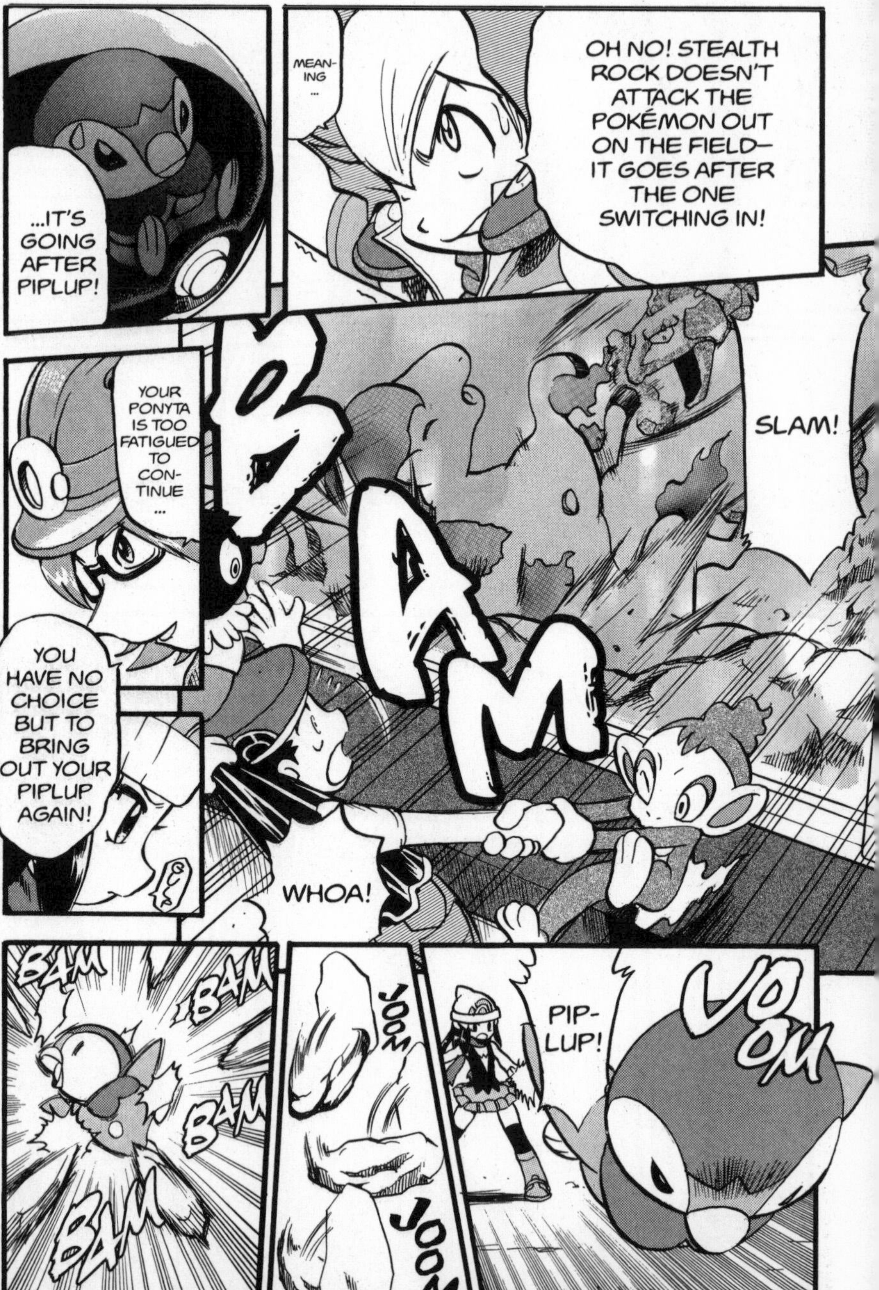

OH NO! STEALTH ROCK DOESN'T ATTACK THE POKÉMON OUT ON THE FIELD—IT GOES AFTER THE ONE SWITCHING IN!
MEAN-ING...
...IT'S GOING AFTER PIPLUP!
SLAM!
BAM
YOUR PONYTA IS TOO FATIGUED TO CON-TINUE...
YOU HAVE NO CHOICE BUT TO BRING OUT YOUR PIPLUP AGAIN!
WHOA!
VOOM
PIP-LUP!
JOOM
JOOM
BAM
BAM
BAM
BAM

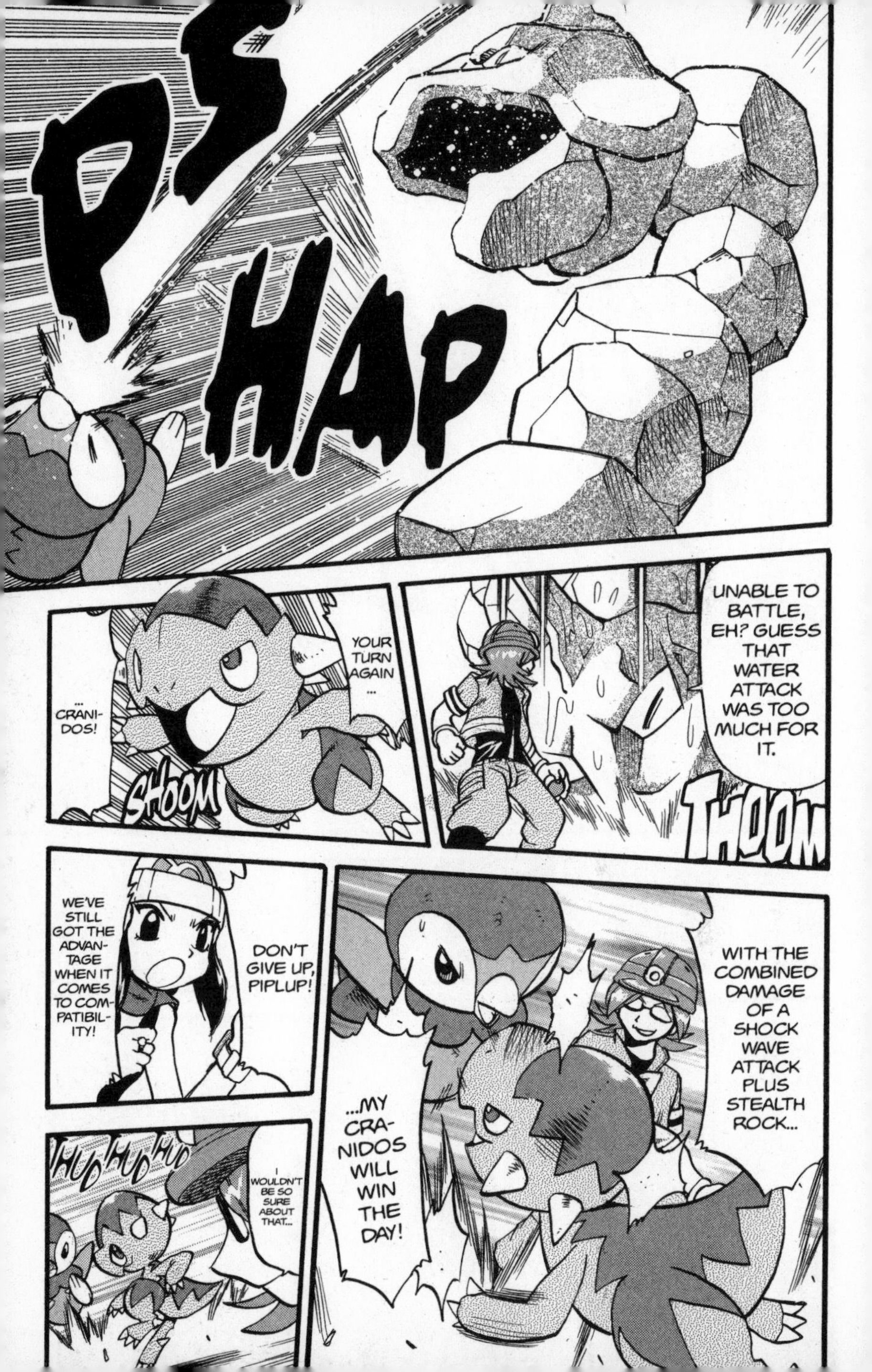
HAP
UNABLE TO BATTLE, EH? GUESS THAT WATER ATTACK WAS TOO MUCH FOR IT.
THOOM
YOUR TURN AGAIN ...
... CRANIDOS!
SHOOM
WE'VE STILL GOT THE ADVANTAGE WHEN IT COMES TO COMPATIBILITY!
DON'T GIVE UP, PIPLUP!
WITH THE COMBINED DAMAGE OF A SHOCK WAVE ATTACK PLUS STEALTH ROCK...
...MY CRANIDOS WILL WIN THE DAY!
I WOULDN'T BE SO SURE ABOUT THAT...

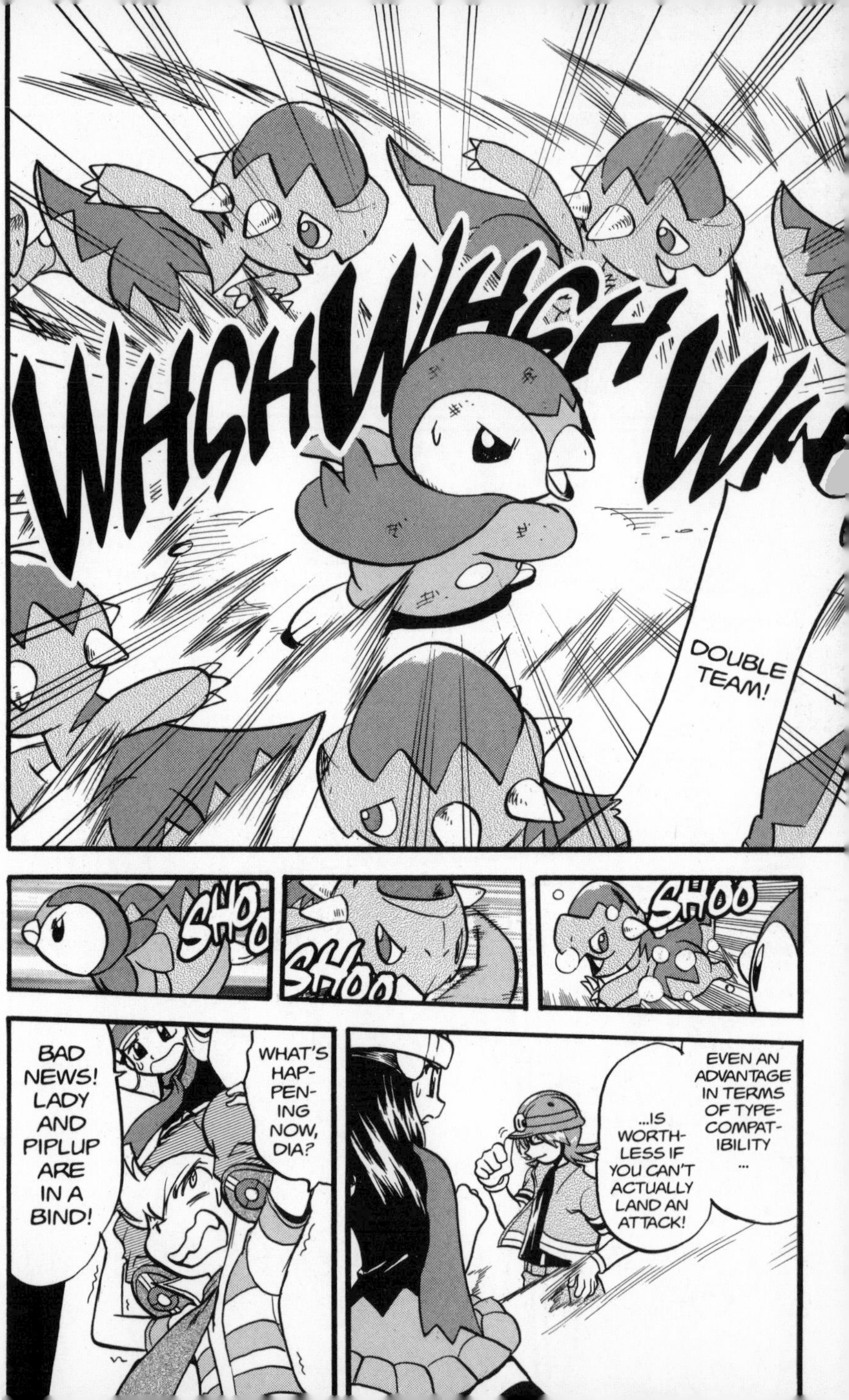
WHSH WHSH WHSH
DOUBLE TEAM!
SHOO
SHOO
SHOO
EVEN AN ADVANTAGE IN TERMS OF TYPE-COMPATIBILITY...
...IS WORTHLESS IF YOU CAN'T ACTUALLY LAND AN ATTACK!
WHAT'S HAPPENING NOW, DIA?
BAD NEWS! LADY AND PIPLUP ARE IN A BIND!

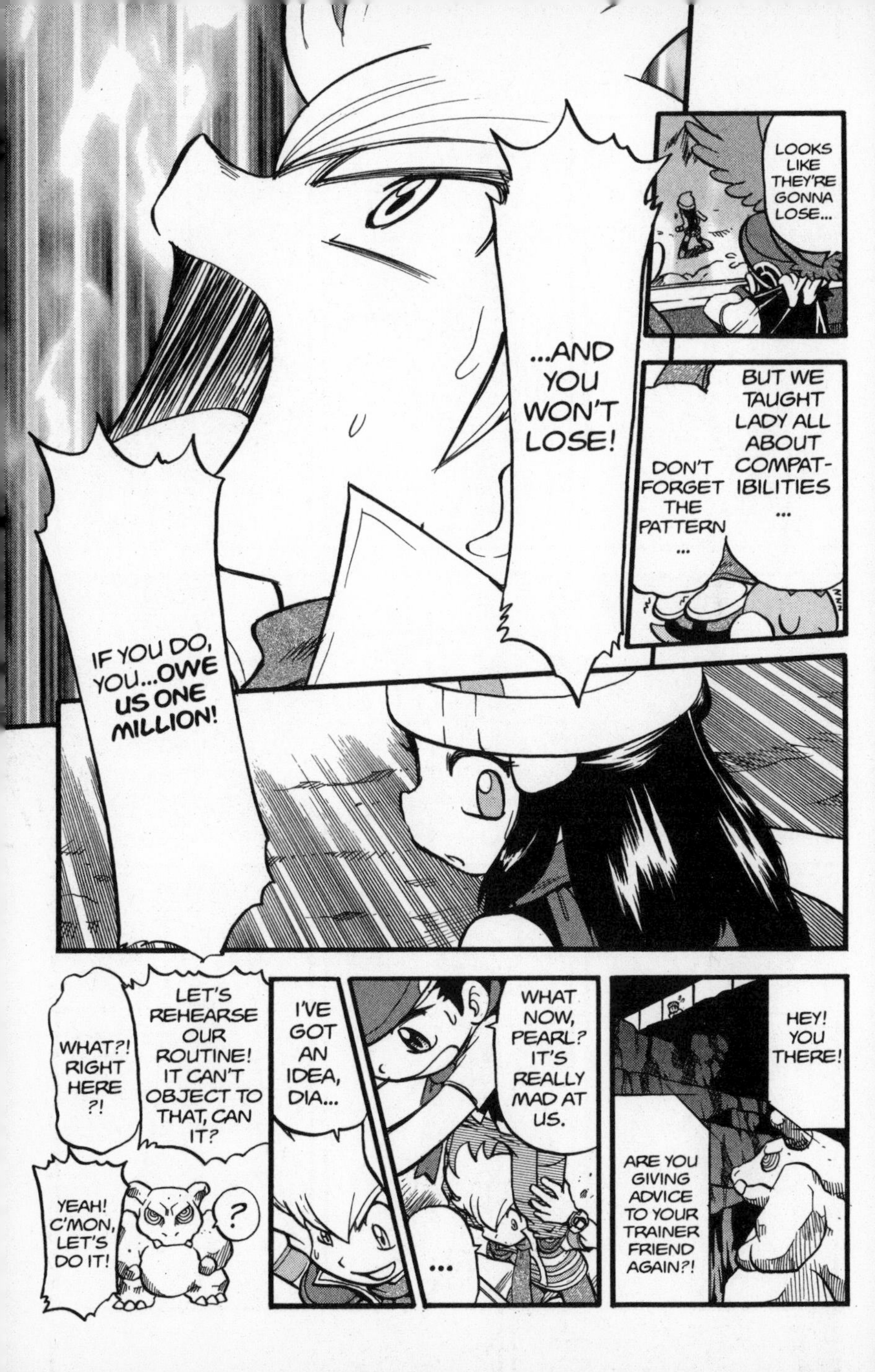
LOOKS LIKE THEY'RE GONNA LOSE...
BUT WE TAUGHT LADY ALL ABOUT COMPAT-IBILITIES...
DON'T FORGET THE PATTERN...
...AND YOU WON'T LOSE!
IF YOU DO, YOU...OWE US ONE MILLION!
HEY! YOU THERE!
ARE YOU GIVING ADVICE TO YOUR TRAINER FRIEND AGAIN?!
WHAT NOW, PEARL? IT'S REALLY MAD AT US.
...
I'VE GOT AN IDEA, DIA...
LET'S REHEARSE OUR ROUTINE! IT CAN'T OBJECT TO THAT, CAN IT?
WHAT?! RIGHT HERE?!
YEAH! C'MON, LET'S DO IT!
?

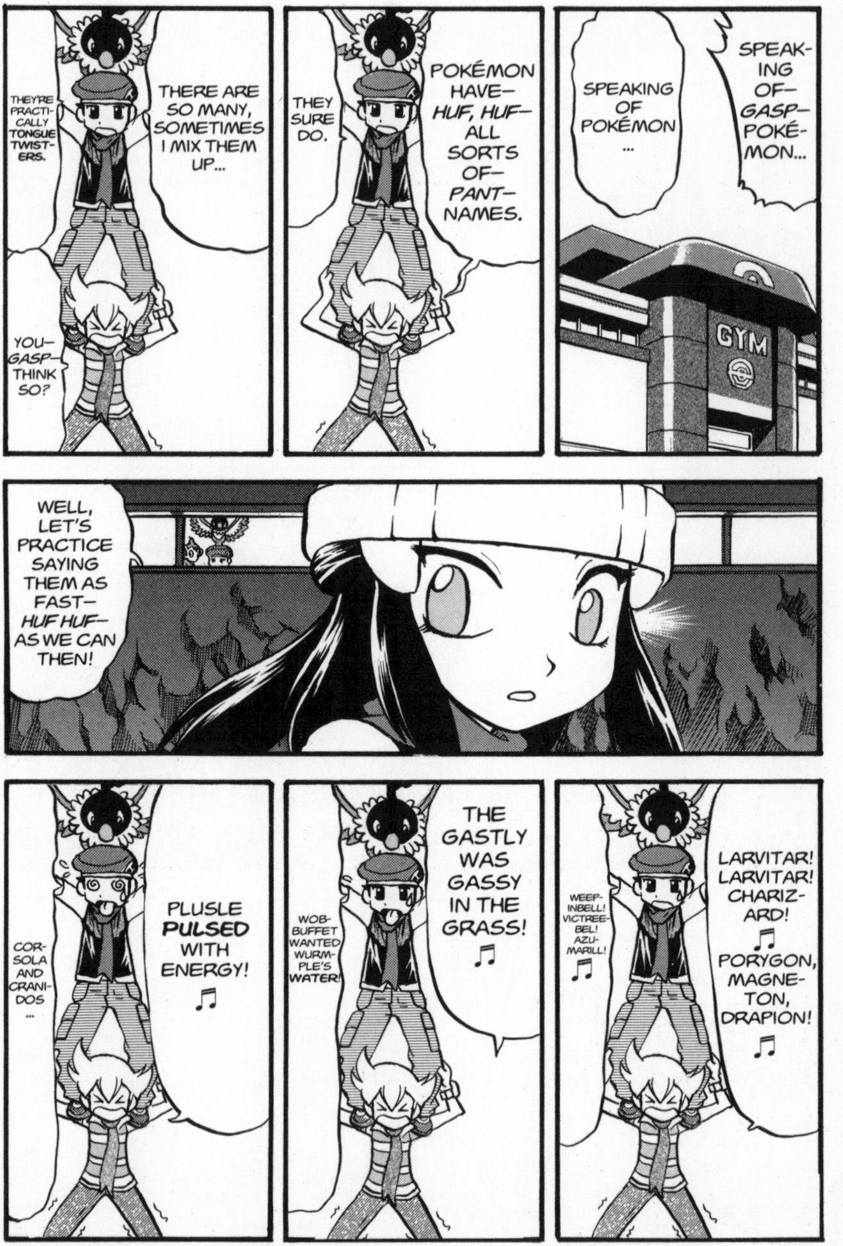
THEY'RE PRACTICALLY TONGUE TWISTERS.
THERE ARE SO MANY, SOMETIMES I MIX THEM UP...
YOU—GASP—THINK SO?
THEY SURE DO.
POKÉMON HAVE—HUF, HUF—ALL SORTS OF—PANT—NAMES.
SPEAKING OF POKÉMON ...
SPEAKING OF—GASP—POKÉMON...
GYM
WELL, LET'S PRACTICE SAYING THEM AS FAST—HUF HUF—AS WE CAN THEN!
CORSOLA AND CRANIDOS ...
PLUSLE PULSED WITH ENERGY! ♫
WOBBUFFET WANTED WURMPLE'S WATER!
THE GASTLY WAS GASSY IN THE GRASS! ♫
WEEPINBELL! VICTREEBEL! AZUMARILL! ♫
LARVITAR! LARVITAR! CHARIZARD! ♫
PORYGON, MAGNETON, DRAPION! ♫

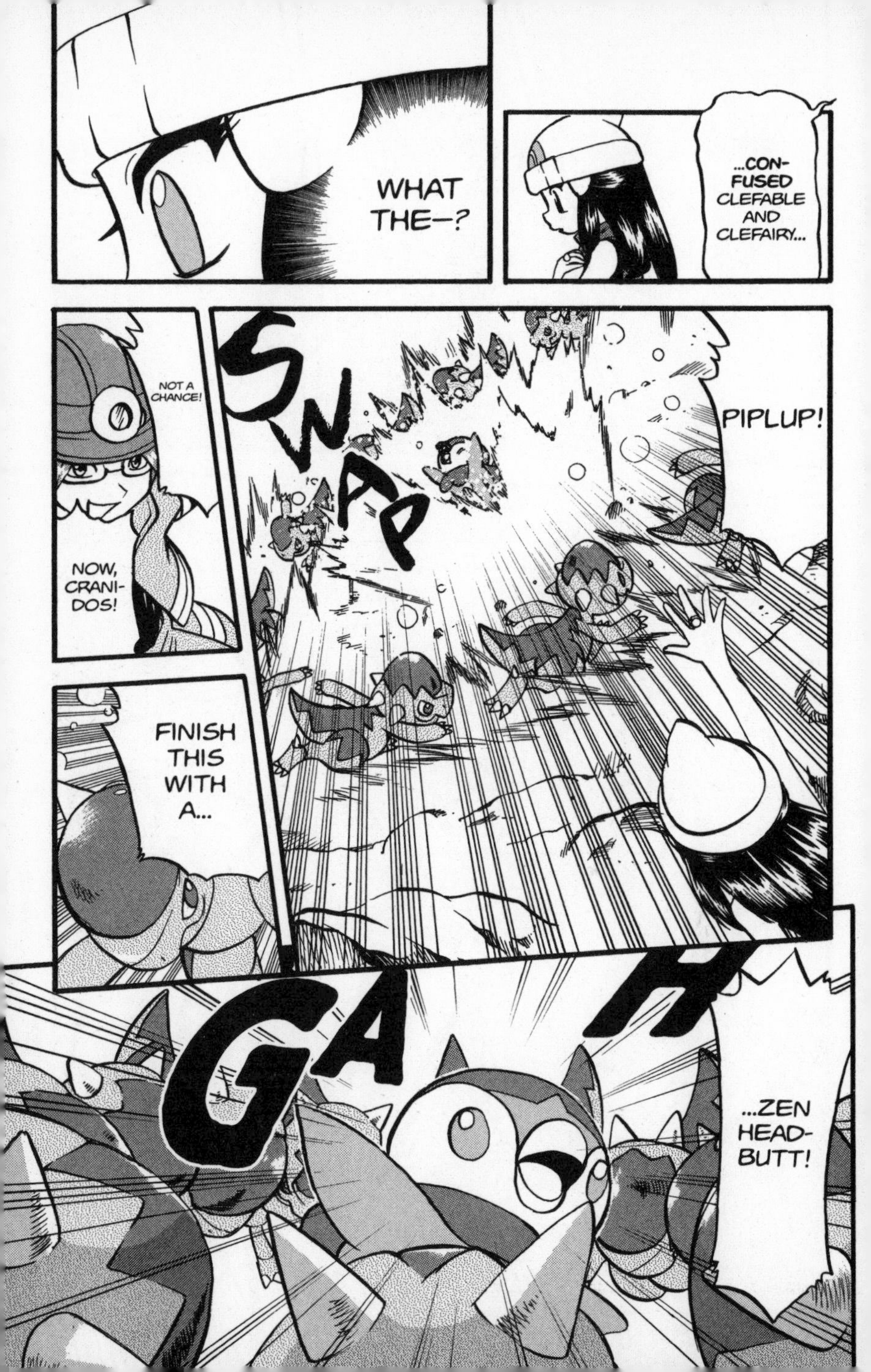
WHAT THE--?
...CON-FUSED CLEFABLE AND CLEFAIRY...
NOT A CHANCE!
NOW, CRANI-DOS!
SWAPP
PIPLUP!
FINISH THIS WITH A...
GAH
...ZEN HEAD-BUTT!

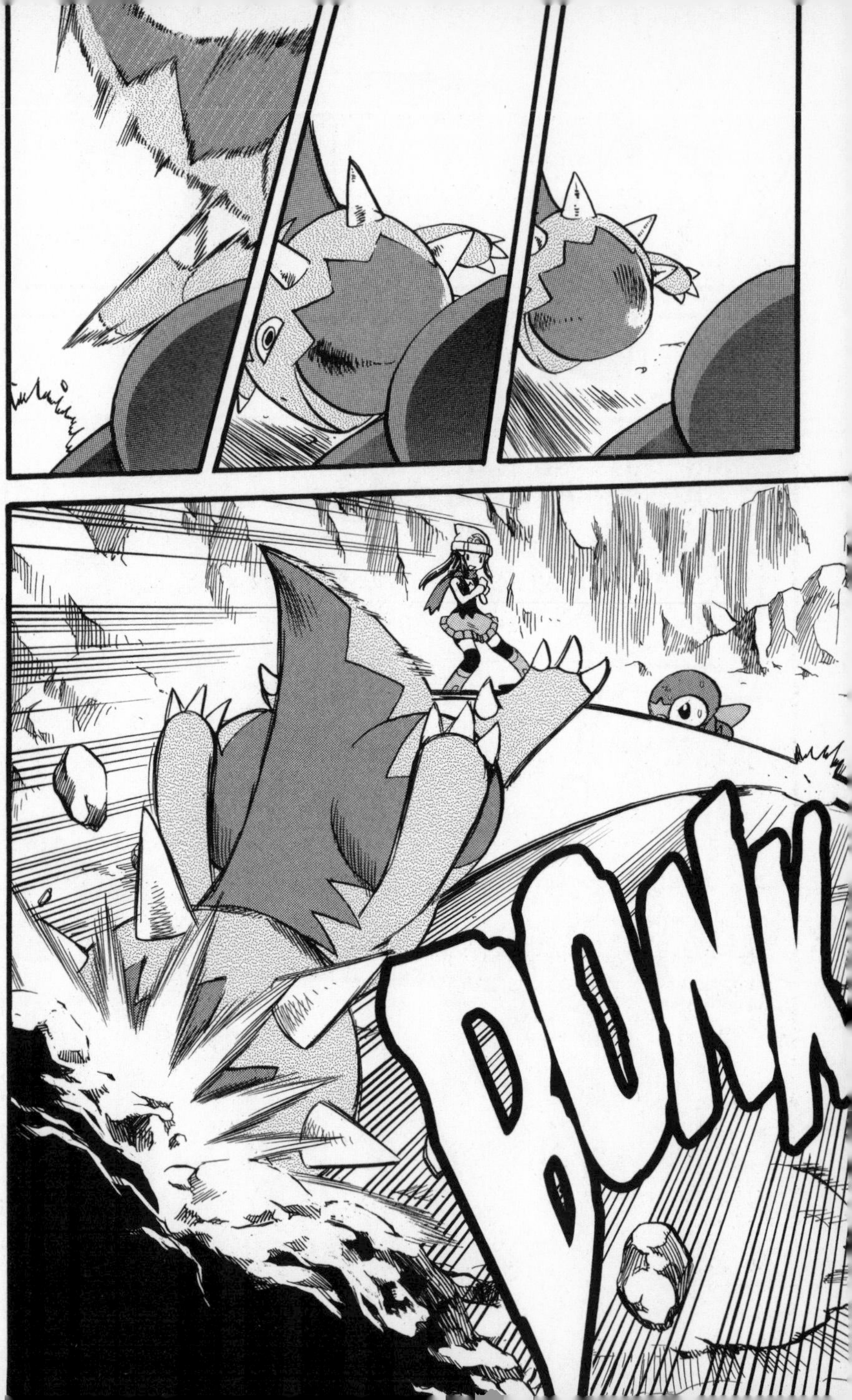
BONK

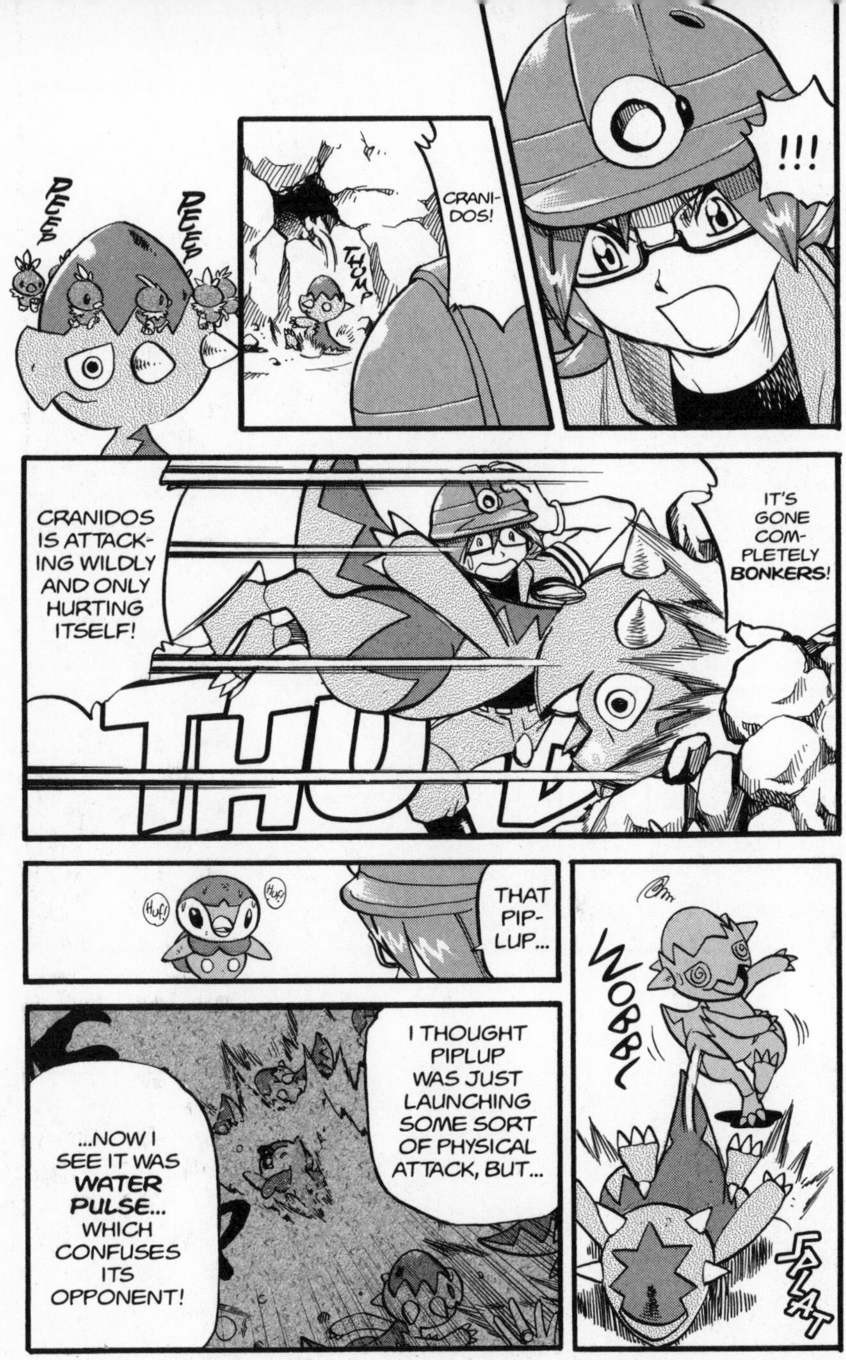
PECCA
PECCA
THOMP
CRANI-
DOS!
!!!
CRANIDOS IS ATTACKING WILDLY AND ONLY HURTING ITSELF!
IT'S GONE COMPLETELY BONKERS!
Huf!
Huf!
THAT PIP-
LUP...
WOBBL
I THOUGHT PIPLUP WAS JUST LAUNCHING SOME SORT OF PHYSICAL ATTACK, BUT...
...NOW I SEE IT WAS WATER PULSE... WHICH CONFUSES ITS OPPONENT!
SPLAT

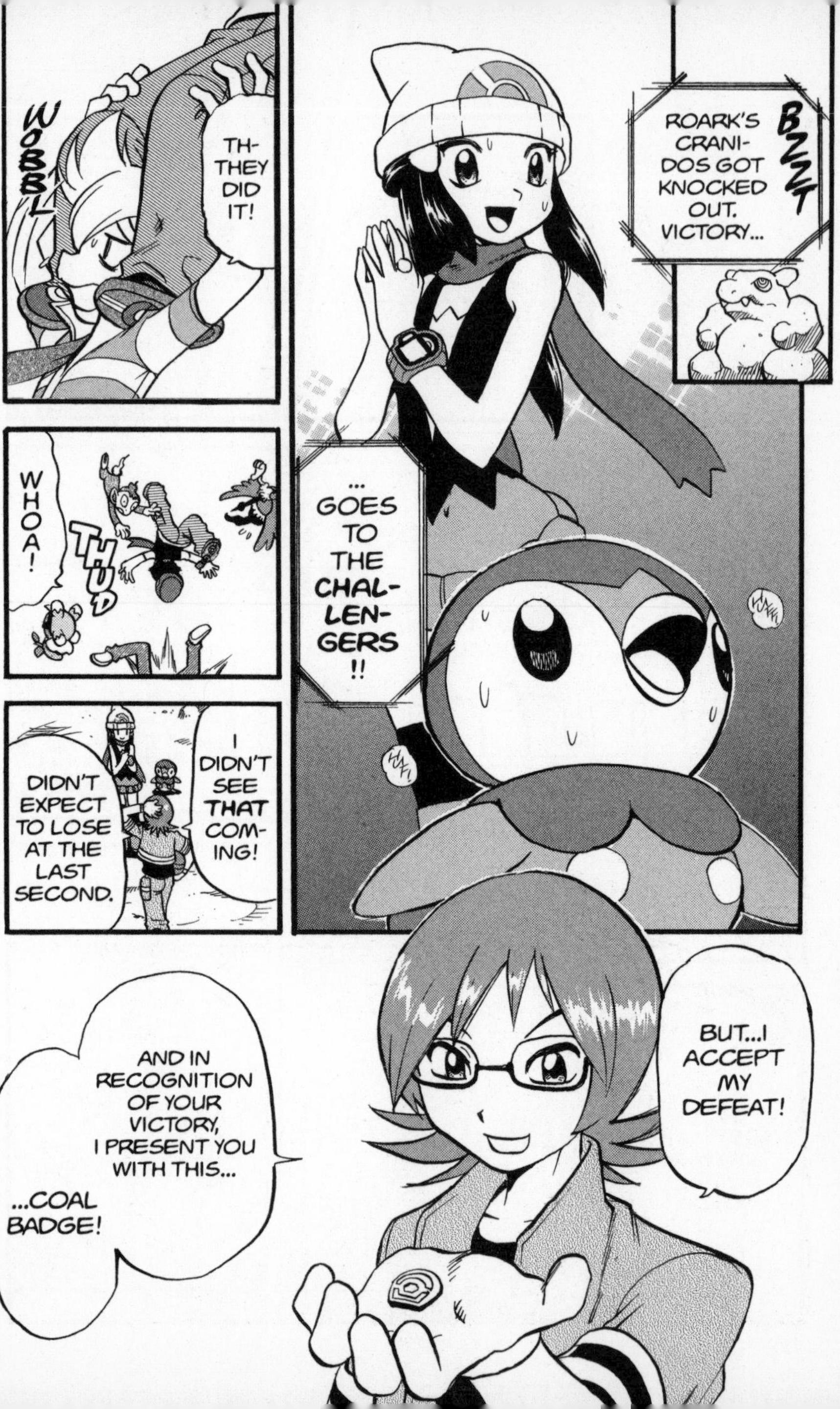
ROARK'S CRANIDOS GOT KNOCKED OUT. VICTORY...
BZZT
...GOES TO THE CHALLENGERS!!
TH-THEY DID IT!
WOBBL
WHOA!
THUD
I DIDN'T SEE THAT COMING!
DIDN'T EXPECT TO LOSE AT THE LAST SECOND.
BUT...I ACCEPT MY DEFEAT!
AND IN RECOGNITION OF YOUR VICTORY, I PRESENT YOU WITH THIS...
...COAL BADGE!

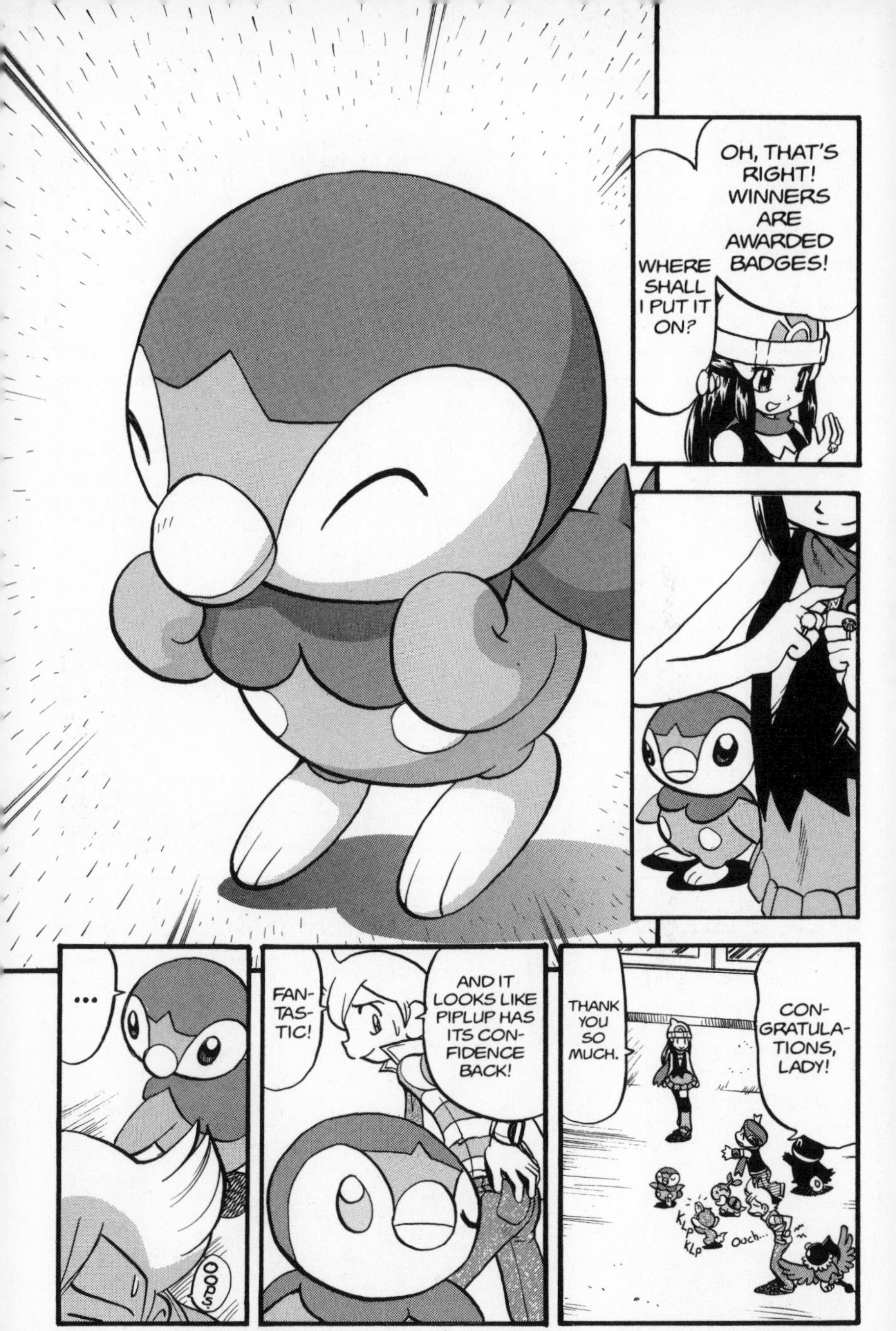
OH, THAT'S RIGHT! WINNERS ARE AWARDED BADGES!
WHERE SHALL I PUT IT ON?
CON-GRATULA-TIONS, LADY!
THANK YOU SO MUCH.
KLP KLP
OUCH...
AND IT LOOKS LIKE PIPLUP HAS ITS CON-FIDENCE BACK!
FAN-TAS-TIC!
...
OOPS.

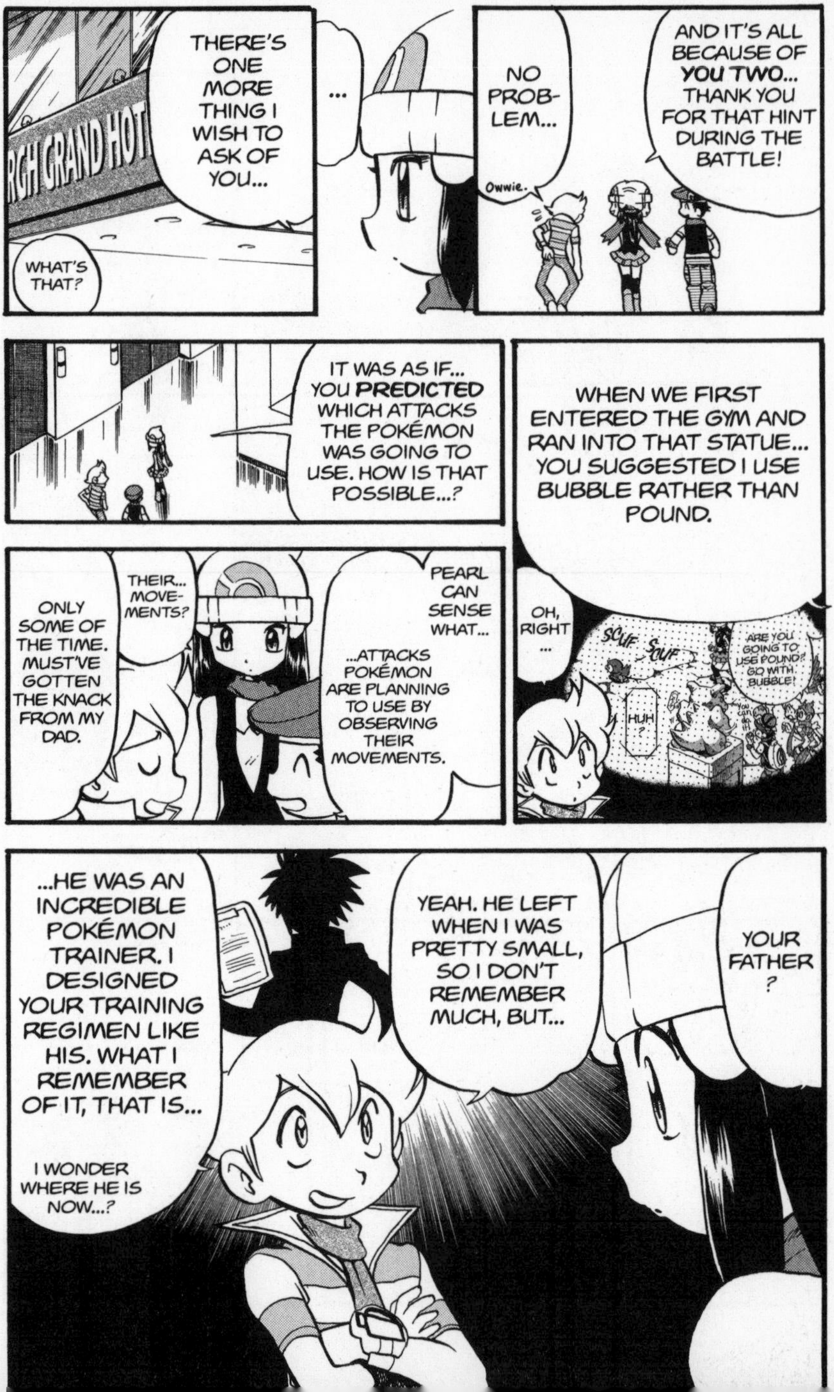
THERE'S ONE MORE THING I WISH TO ASK OF YOU...
...
WHAT'S THAT?
AND IT'S ALL BECAUSE OF YOU TWO... THANK YOU FOR THAT HINT DURING THE BATTLE!
NO PROBLEM...
Owwie.
IT WAS AS IF... YOU PREDICTED WHICH ATTACKS THE POKÉMON WAS GOING TO USE. HOW IS THAT POSSIBLE...?
WHEN WE FIRST ENTERED THE GYM AND RAN INTO THAT STATUE... YOU SUGGESTED I USE BUBBLE RATHER THAN POUND.
OH, RIGHT...
SCUF
SCUF
ARE YOU GOING TO USE POUND?! GO WITH BUBBLE!
HUH?
PEARL CAN SENSE WHAT...
...ATTACKS POKÉMON ARE PLANNING TO USE BY OBSERVING THEIR MOVEMENTS.
THEIR... MOVEMENTS?
ONLY SOME OF THE TIME. MUST'VE GOTTEN THE KNACK FROM MY DAD.
YOUR FATHER?
YEAH. HE LEFT WHEN I WAS PRETTY SMALL, SO I DON'T REMEMBER MUCH, BUT...
...HE WAS AN INCREDIBLE POKÉMON TRAINER. I DESIGNED YOUR TRAINING REGIMEN LIKE HIS. WHAT I REMEMBER OF IT, THAT IS...
I WONDER WHERE HE IS NOW...?

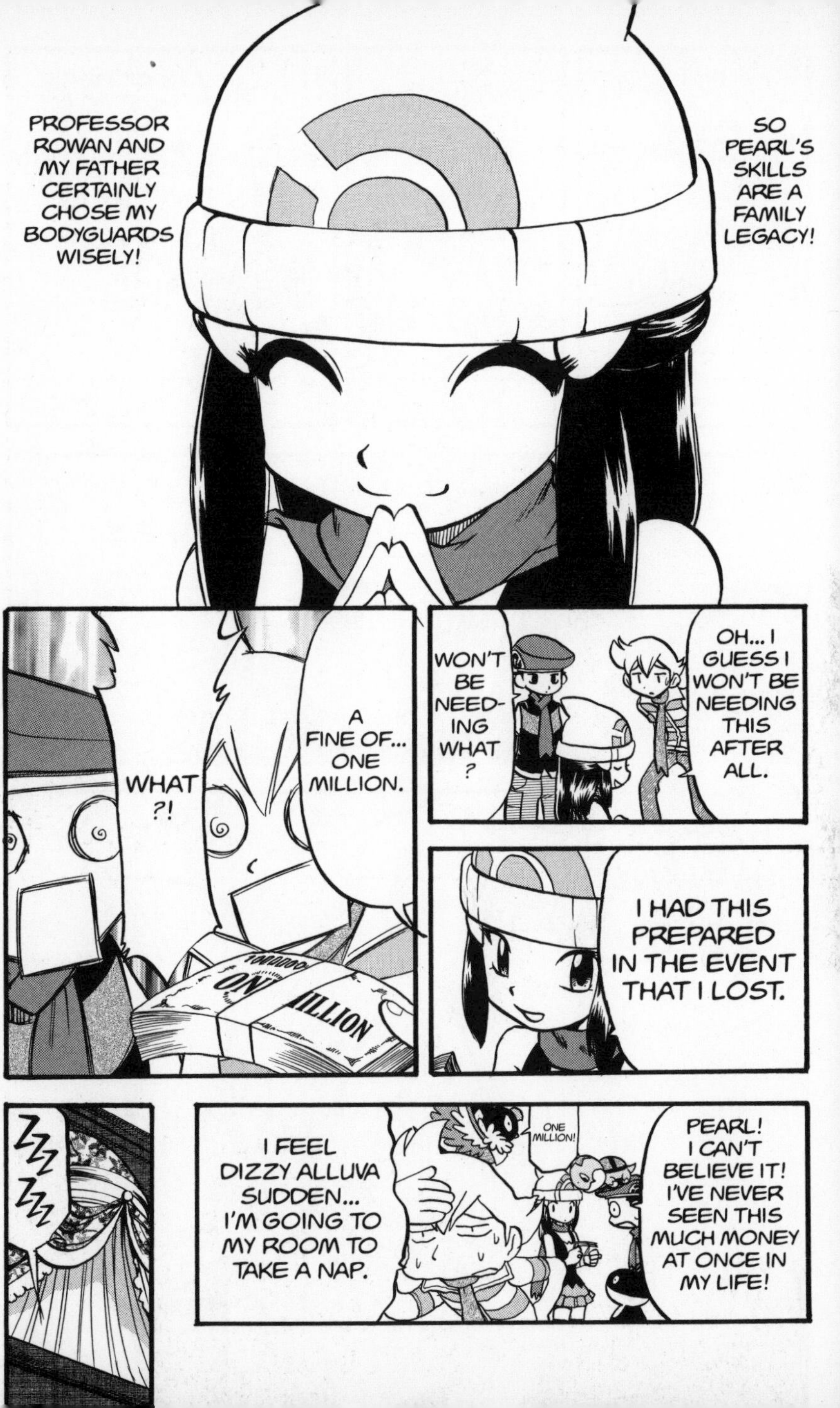
SO PEARL'S SKILLS ARE A FAMILY LEGACY!
PROFESSOR ROWAN AND MY FATHER CERTAINLY CHOSE MY BODYGUARDS WISELY!
OH... I GUESS I WON'T BE NEEDING THIS AFTER ALL.
WON'T BE NEEDING WHAT?
I HAD THIS PREPARED IN THE EVENT THAT I LOST.
A FINE OF... ONE MILLION.
WHAT?!
PEARL! I CAN'T BELIEVE IT! I'VE NEVER SEEN THIS MUCH MONEY AT ONCE IN MY LIFE!
ONE MILLION!
I FEEL DIZZY ALLUVA SUDDEN... I'M GOING TO MY ROOM TO TAKE A NAP.
ZZZ
ZZZ

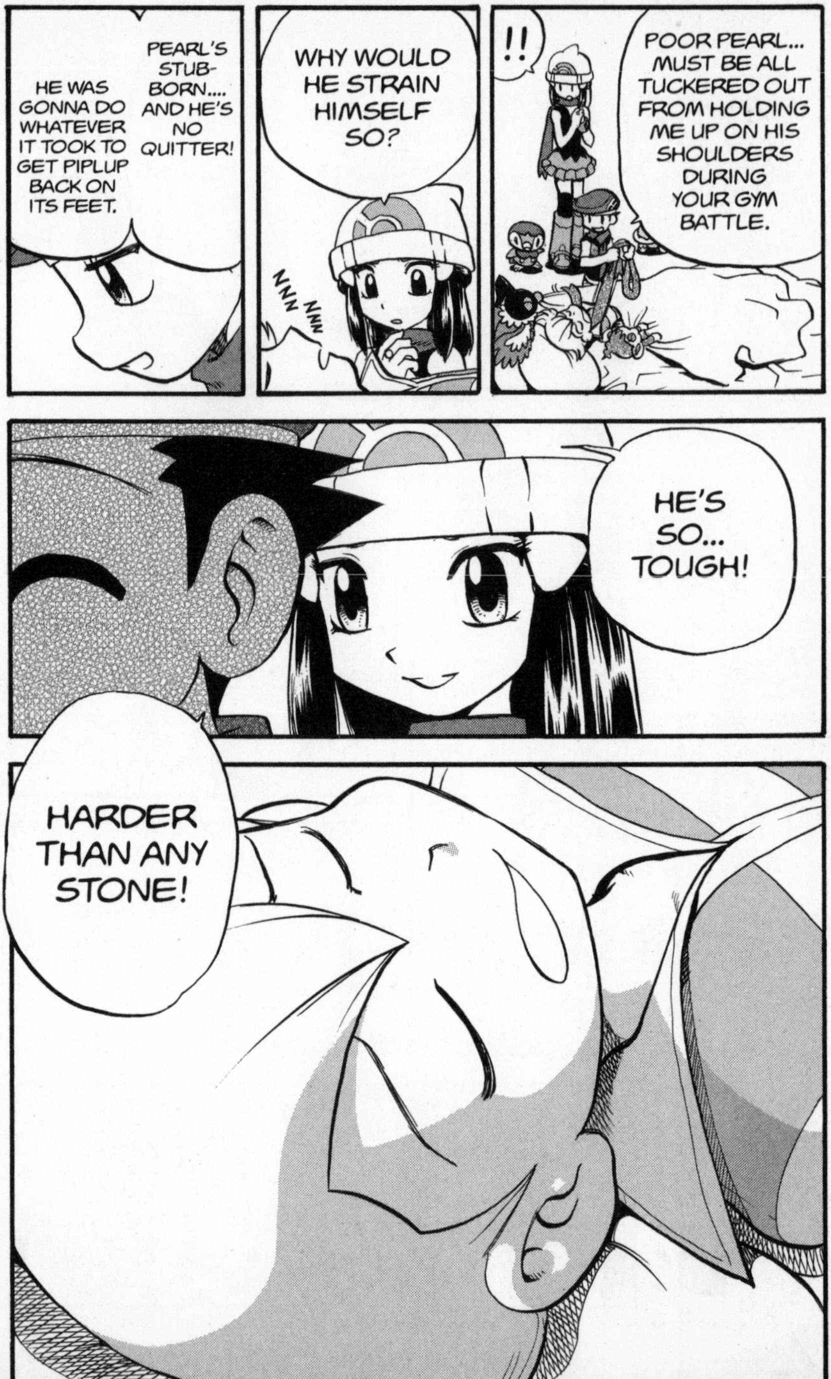
POOR PEARL... MUST BE ALL TUCKERED OUT FROM HOLDING ME UP ON HIS SHOULDERS DURING YOUR GYM BATTLE.
!!
WHY WOULD HE STRAIN HIMSELF SO?
NNN NNN
PEARL'S STUB-BORN.... AND HE'S NO QUITTER!
HE WAS GONNA DO WHATEVER IT TOOK TO GET PIPLUP BACK ON ITS FEET.
HE'S SO... TOUGH!
HARDER THAN ANY STONE!

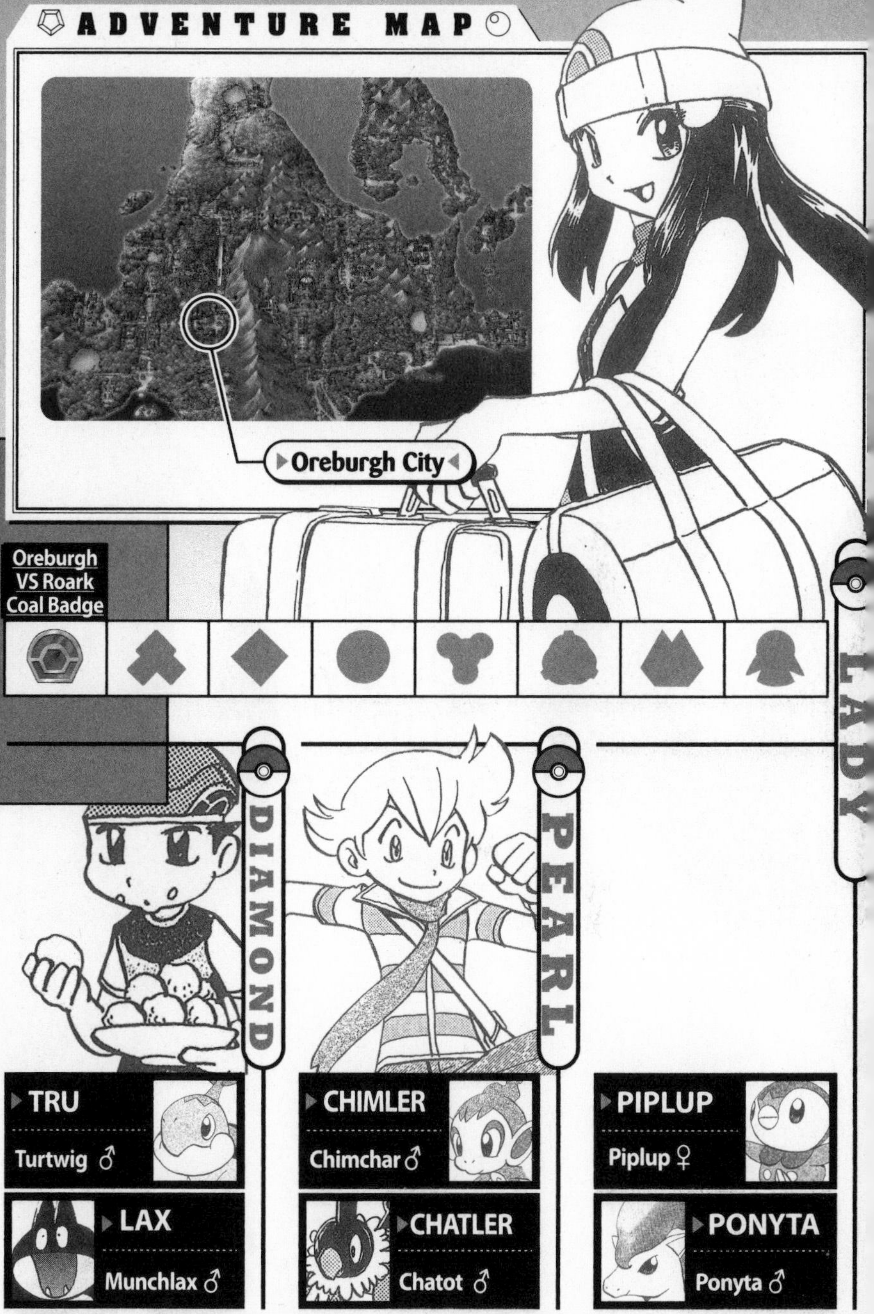
ADVENTURE MAP
Oreburgh City
Oreburgh
VS Roark
Coal Badge
LADY
DIAMOND
PEARL
TRU
Turtwig ♂
CHIMLER
Chimchar ♂
PIPLUP
Piplup ♀
LAX
Munchlax ♂
CHATLER
Chatot ♂
PONYTA
Ponyta ♂

6

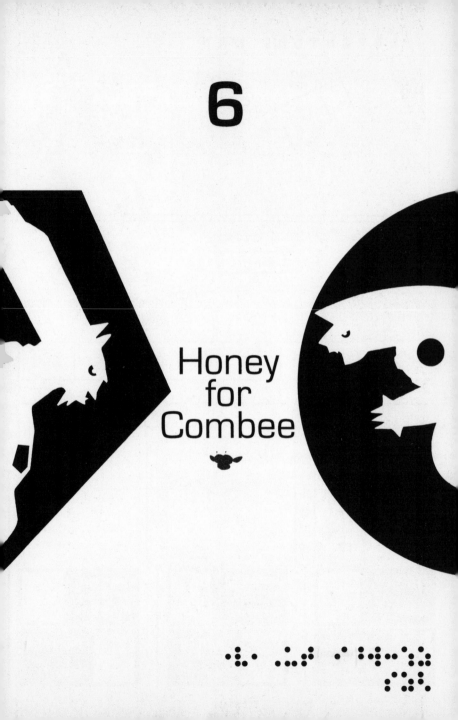

Honey
for
Combee

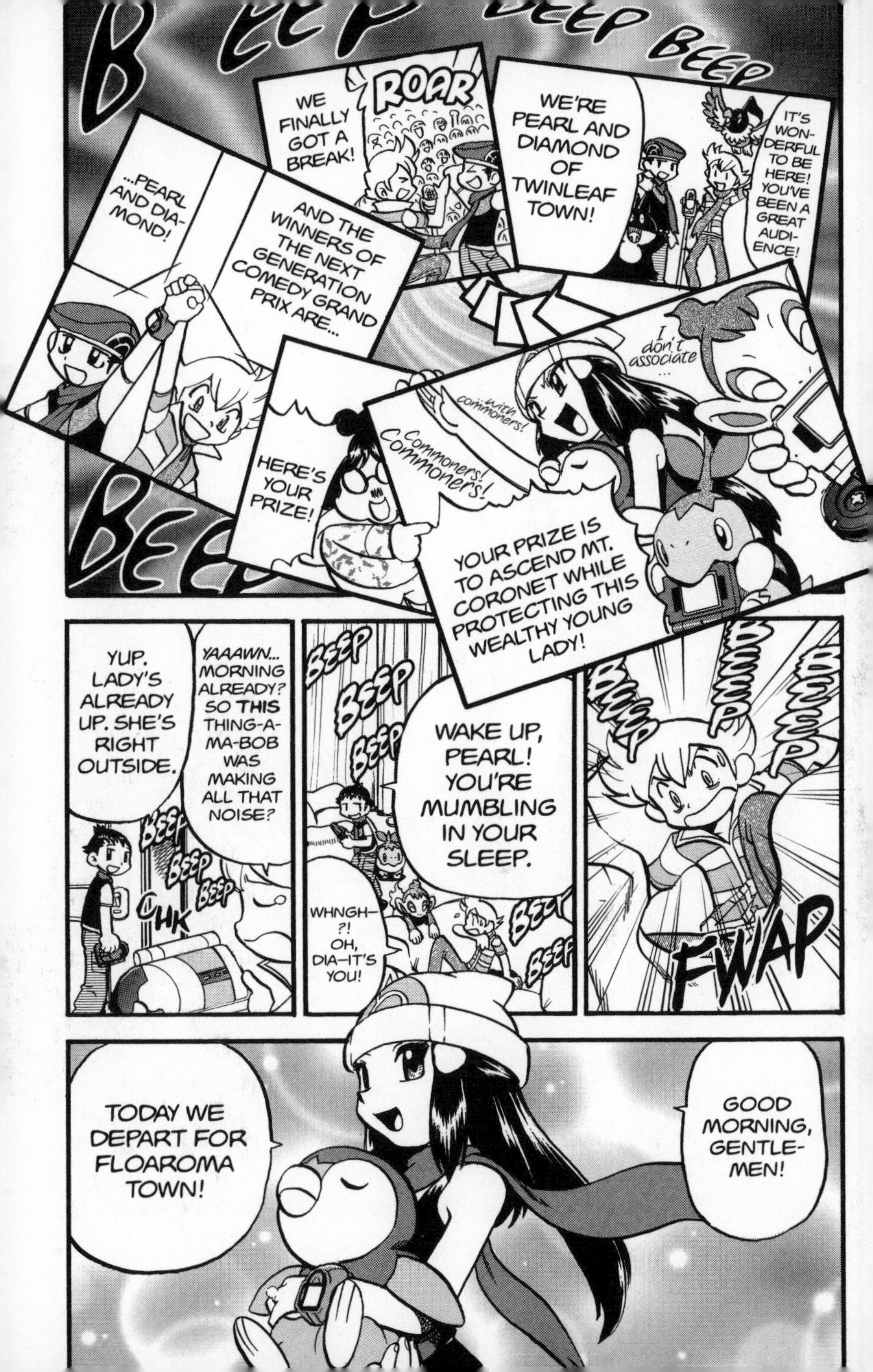
BEEP BEEP BEEP BEEP
ROAR
WE FINALLY GOT A BREAK!
WE'RE PEARL AND DIAMOND OF TWINLEAF TOWN!
IT'S WONDERFUL TO BE HERE! YOU'VE BEEN A GREAT AUDIENCE!
AND THE WINNERS OF THE NEXT GENERATION COMEDY GRAND PRIX ARE...
...PEARL AND DIAMOND!
I don't associate...
...with commoners!
Commoners! Commoners!
HERE'S YOUR PRIZE!
YOUR PRIZE IS TO ASCEND MT. CORONET WHILE PROTECTING THIS WEALTHY YOUNG LADY!
BEEP
WAKE UP, PEARL! YOU'RE MUMBLING IN YOUR SLEEP.
BEEP BEEP BEEP
WHNGH—?! OH, DIA—IT'S YOU!
YAAAWN... MORNING ALREADY? SO THIS THING-A-MA-BOB WAS MAKING ALL THAT NOISE?
YUP. LADY'S ALREADY UP. SHE'S RIGHT OUTSIDE.
BEEP BEEP BEEP
CHK
GOOD MORNING, GENTLEMEN!
TODAY WE DEPART FOR FLOAROMA TOWN!

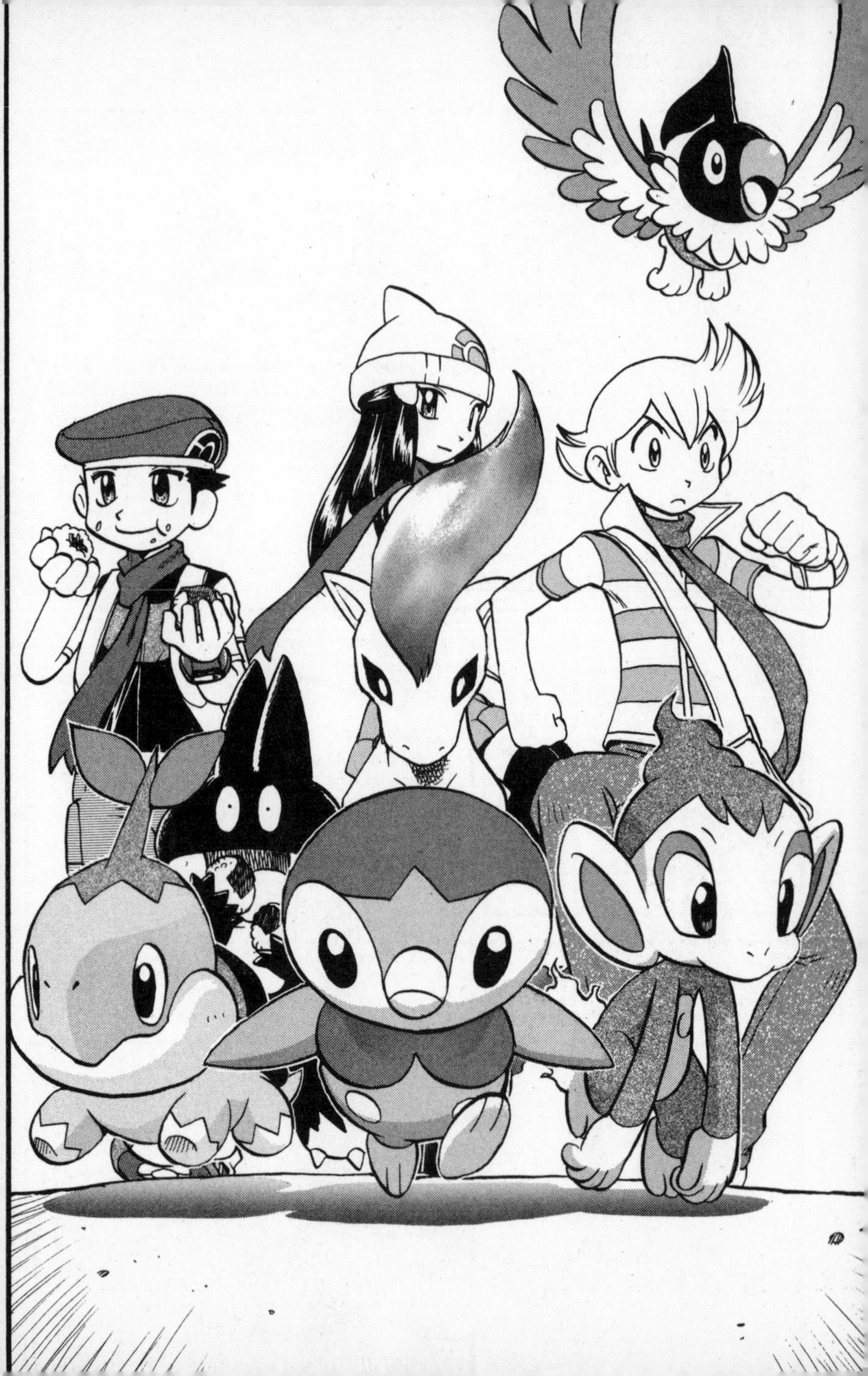

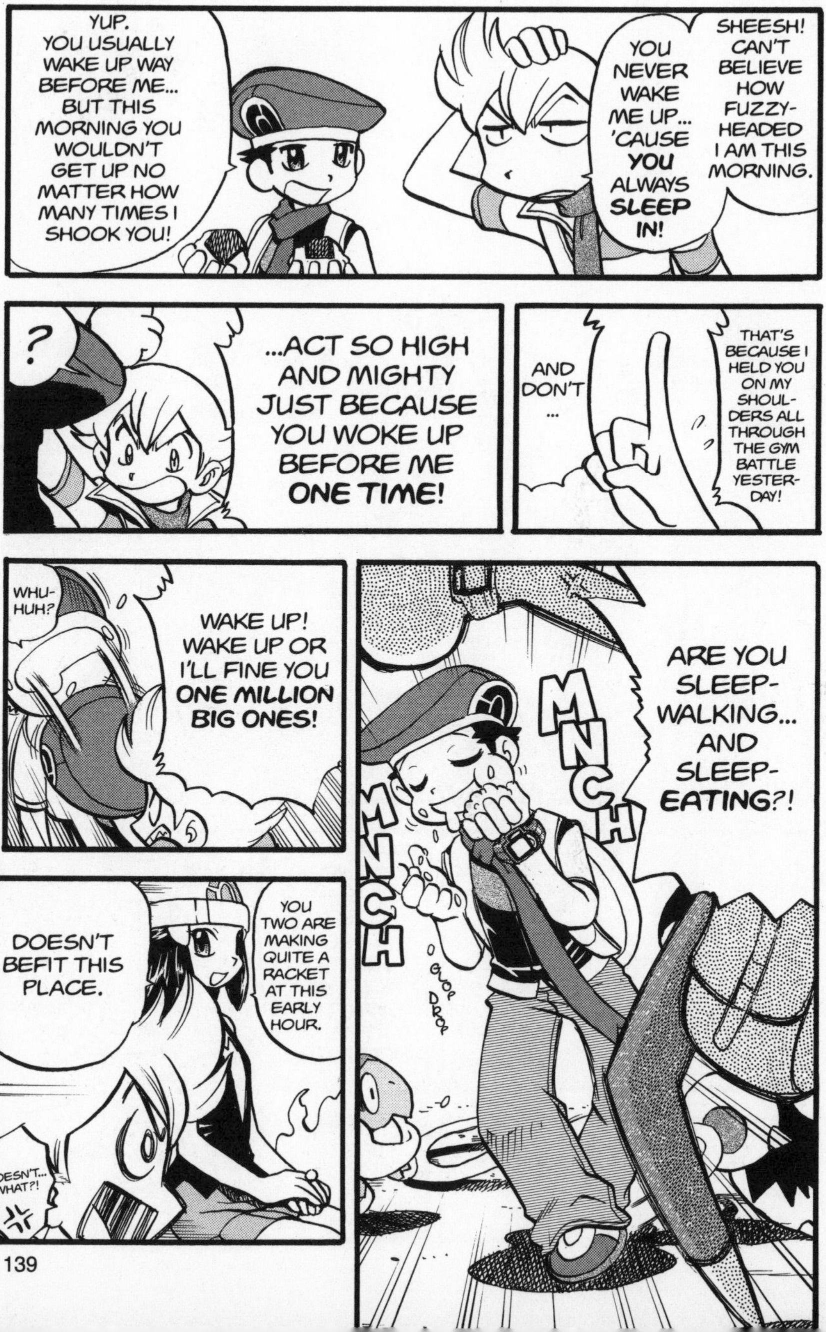
SHEESH! CAN'T BELIEVE HOW FUZZY-HEADED I AM THIS MORNING.
YUP. YOU USUALLY WAKE UP WAY BEFORE ME... BUT THIS MORNING YOU WOULDN'T GET UP NO MATTER HOW MANY TIMES I SHOOK YOU!
YOU NEVER WAKE ME UP... 'CAUSE **YOU** ALWAYS **SLEEP IN!**
THAT'S BECAUSE I HELD YOU ON MY SHOUL-DERS ALL THROUGH THE GYM BATTLE YESTER-DAY!
AND DON'T ...
?
...ACT SO HIGH AND MIGHTY JUST BECAUSE YOU WOKE UP BEFORE ME **ONE TIME!**
ARE YOU SLEEP-WALKING... AND SLEEP-**EATING?!**
MNCH
MNCH
WAKE UP! WAKE UP OR I'LL FINE YOU **ONE MILLION BIG ONES!**
WHU-HUH?
YOU TWO ARE MAKING QUITE A RACKET AT THIS EARLY HOUR.
DOESN'T BEFIT THIS PLACE.
DOESN'T... WHAT?!

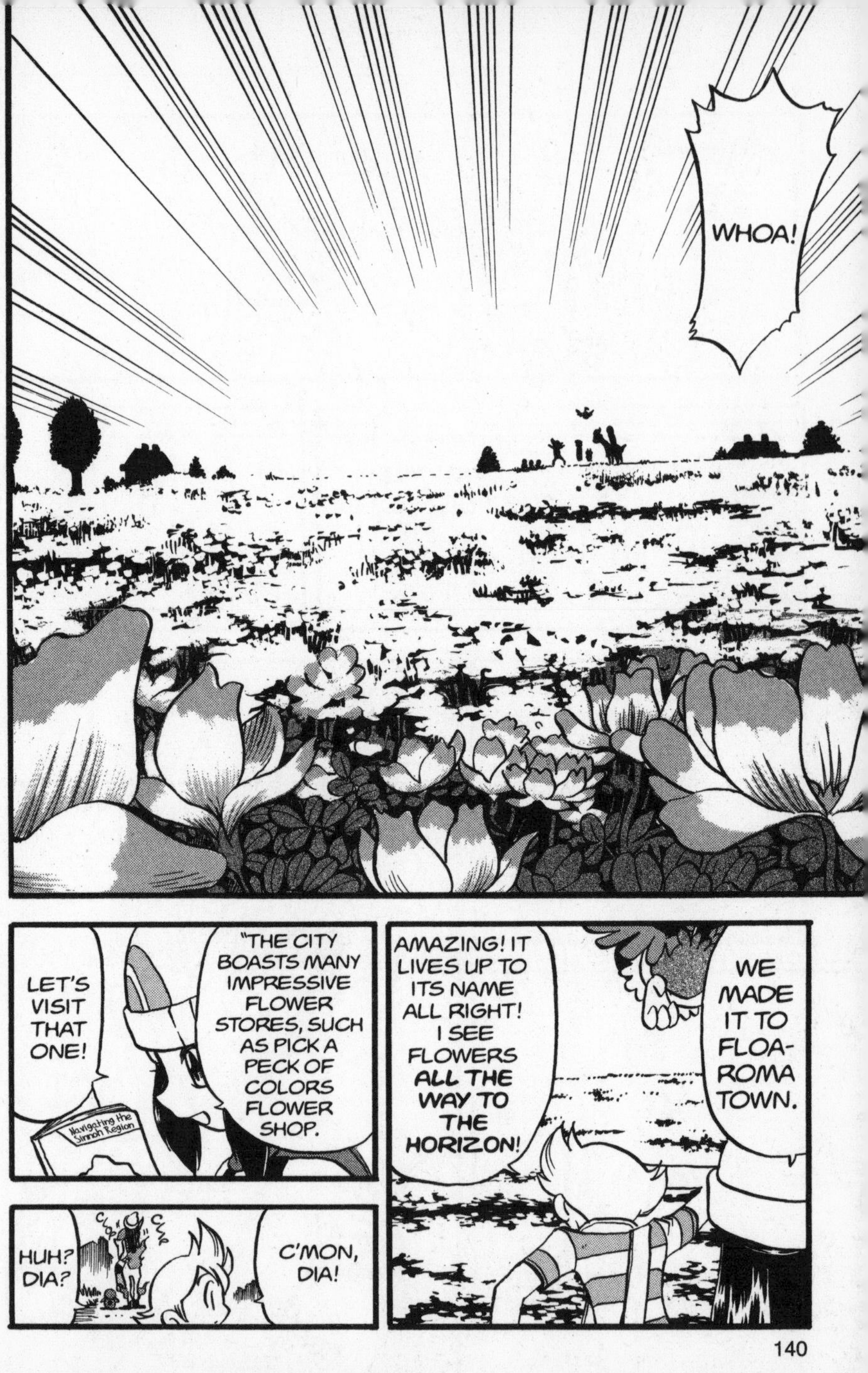
WHOA!
WE MADE IT TO FLOA-ROMA TOWN.
AMAZING! IT LIVES UP TO ITS NAME ALL RIGHT! I SEE FLOWERS ALL THE WAY TO THE HORIZON!
"THE CITY BOASTS MANY IMPRESSIVE FLOWER STORES, SUCH AS PICK A PECK OF COLORS FLOWER SHOP.
LET'S VISIT THAT ONE!
Navigating the Sinnoh Region
C'MON, DIA!
HUH? DIA?

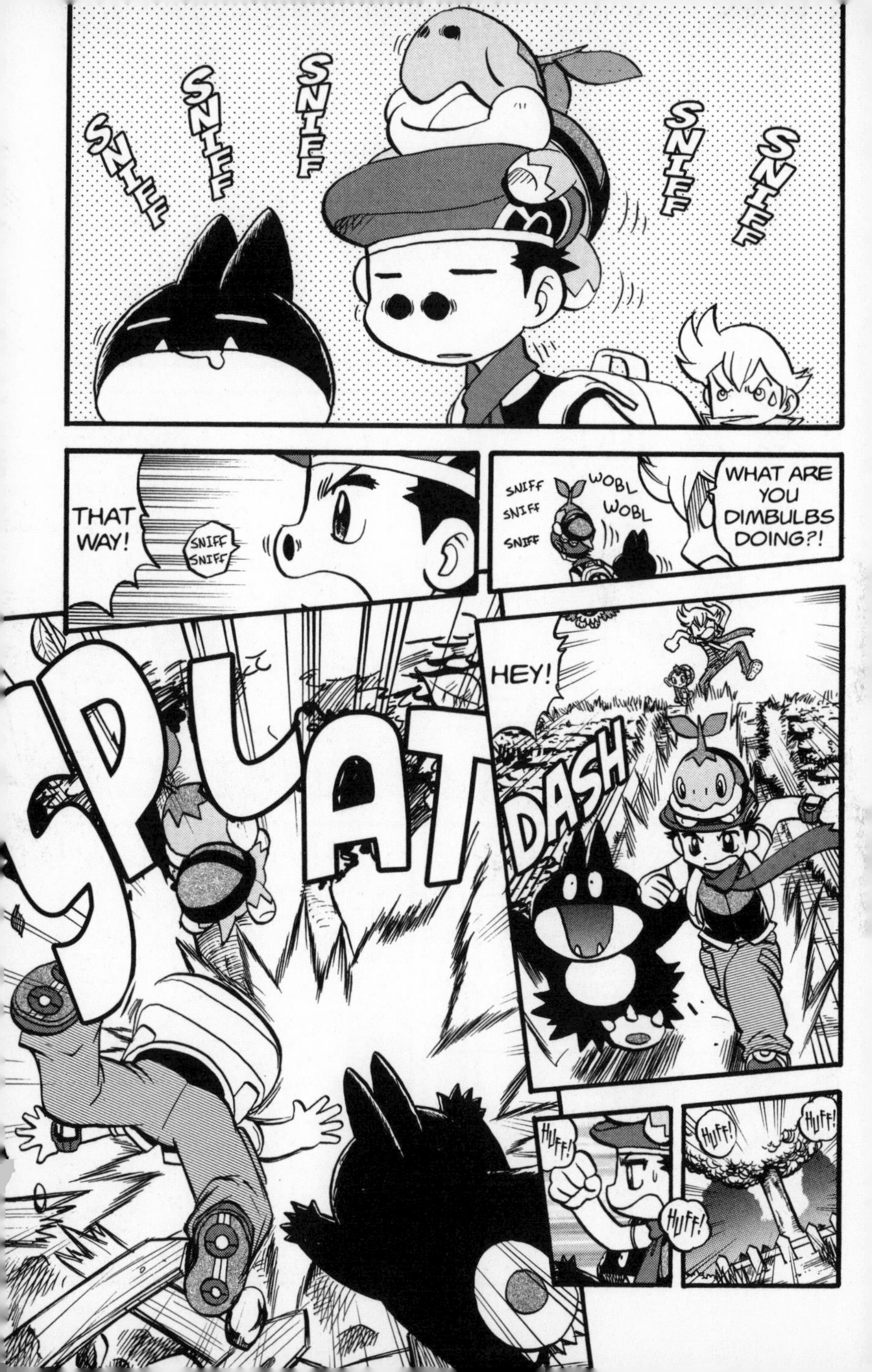

SNIFF
SNIFF
SNIFF
SNIFF
SNIFF
THAT WAY!
SNIFF SNIFF
WHAT ARE YOU DIMBULBS DOING?!
SNIFF SNIFF SNIFF
WOBL WOBL
HEY!
DASH
SPLAT
HUFF!
HUFF!
HUFF!
HUFF!

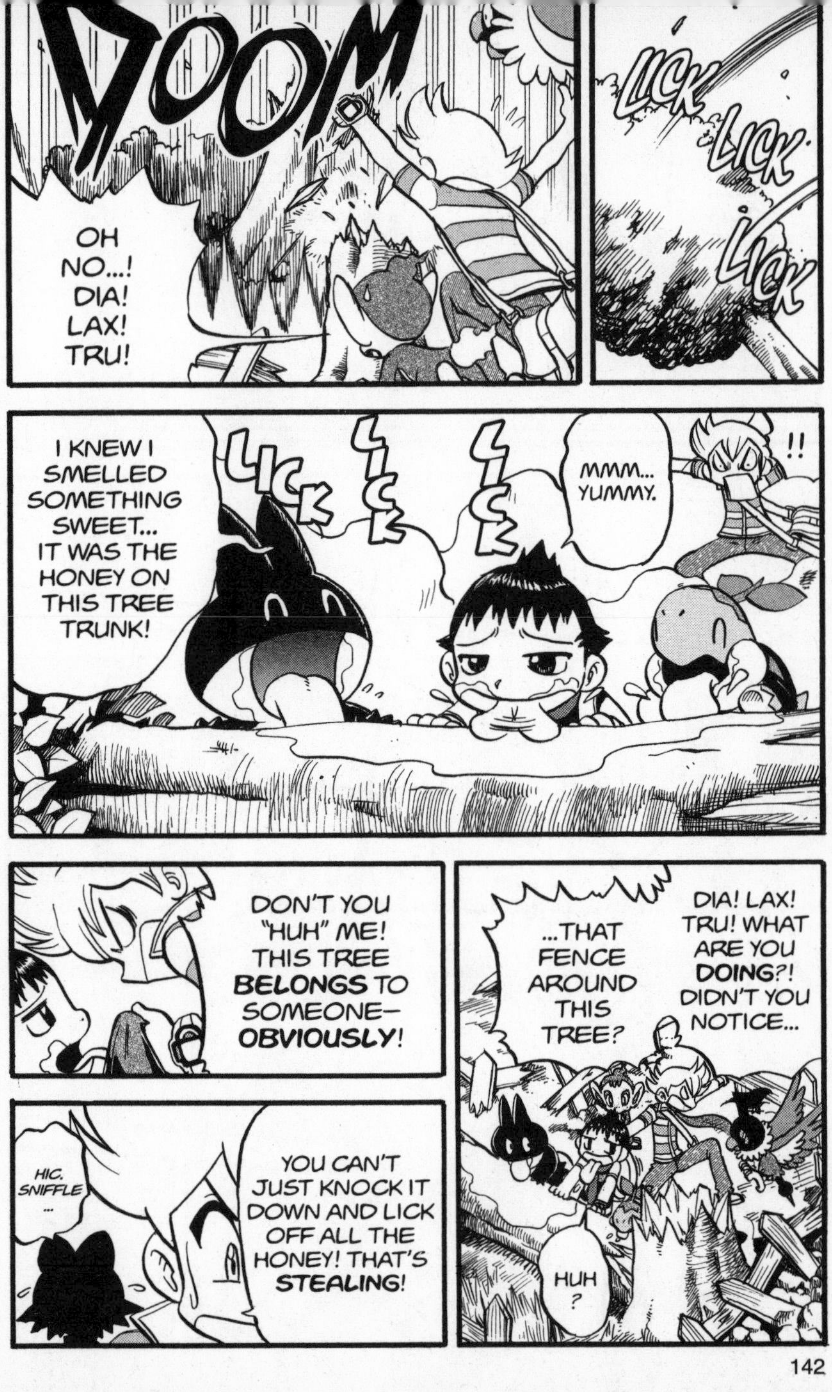

DOOM
OH NO...! DIA! LAX! TRU!
LICK LICK LICK
I KNEW I SMELLED SOMETHING SWEET... IT WAS THE HONEY ON THIS TREE TRUNK!
LICK LICK LICK
MMM... YUMMY.
!!
DIA! LAX! TRU! WHAT ARE YOU **DOING**?! DIDN'T YOU NOTICE...
...THAT FENCE AROUND THIS TREE?
HUH?
DON'T YOU "HUH" ME! THIS TREE **BELONGS** TO SOMEONE—**OBVIOUSLY**!
YOU CAN'T JUST KNOCK IT DOWN AND LICK OFF ALL THE HONEY! THAT'S **STEALING**!
HIC. SNIFFLE...

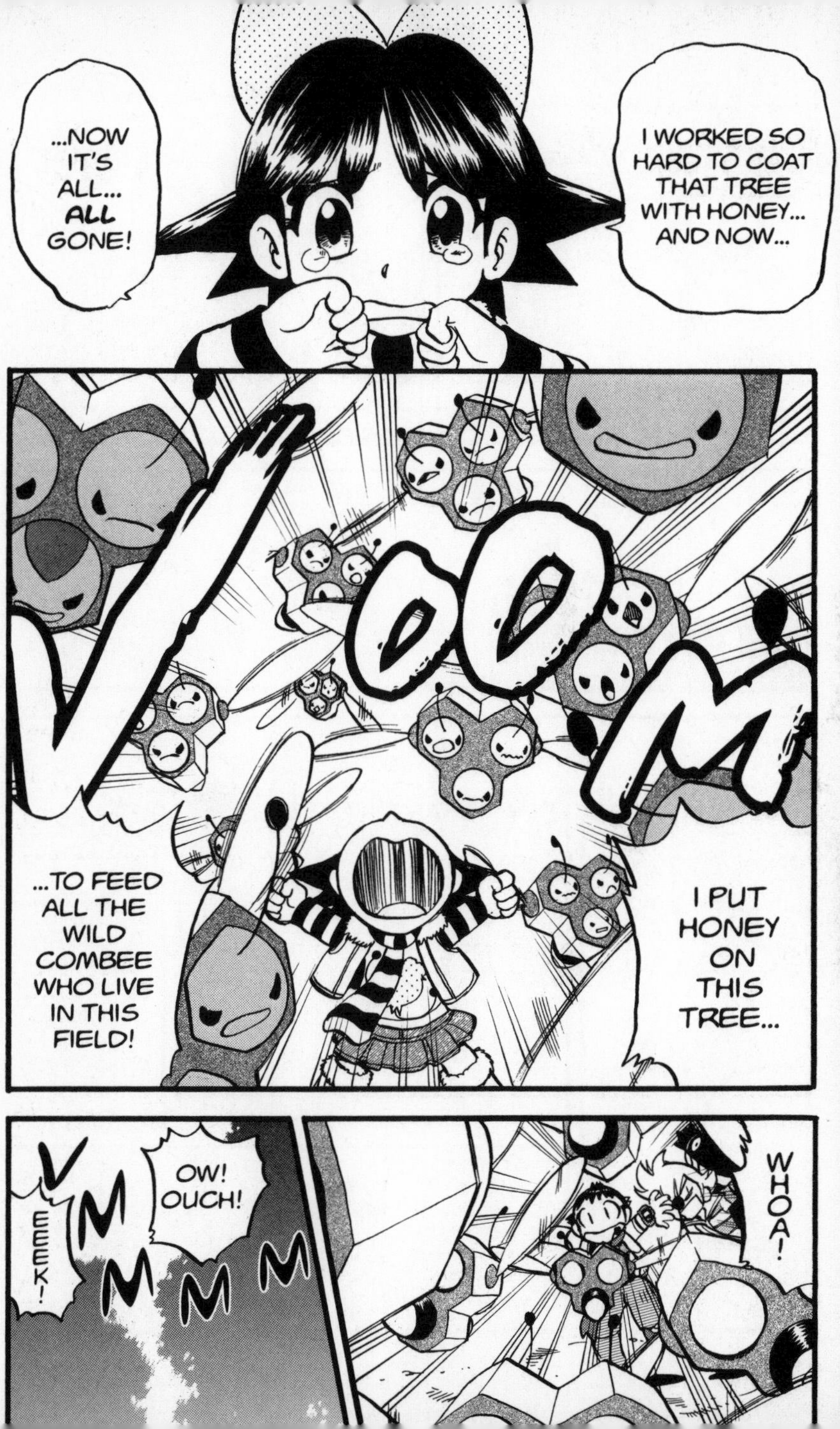
I WORKED SO HARD TO COAT THAT TREE WITH HONEY... AND NOW...
...NOW IT'S ALL... ALL GONE!
VOOM
I PUT HONEY ON THIS TREE...
...TO FEED ALL THE WILD COMBEE WHO LIVE IN THIS FIELD!
WHOA!
OW! OUCH!
EEEK!
VMMMMM

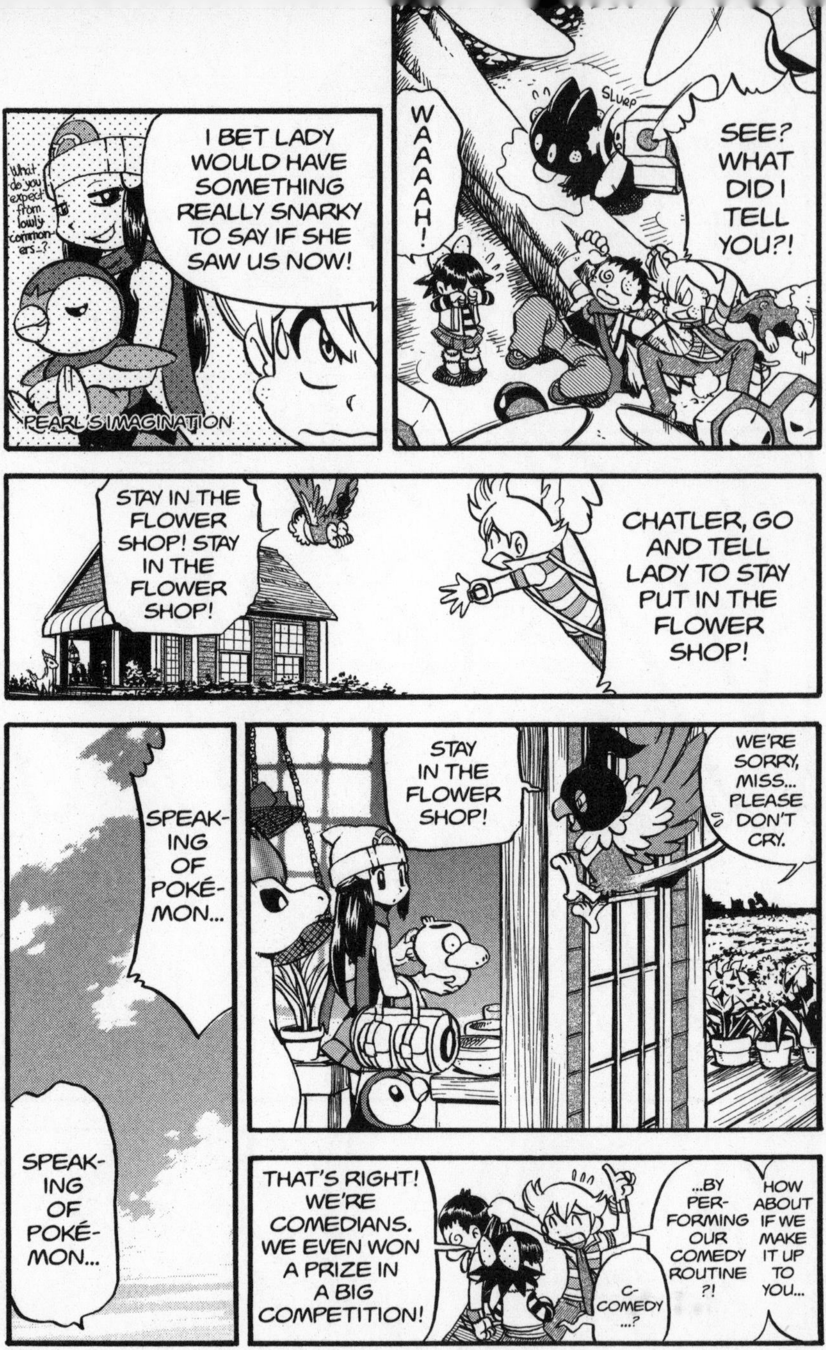
What do you expect from lowly commoners..?
I BET LADY WOULD HAVE SOMETHING REALLY SNARKY TO SAY IF SHE SAW US NOW!
PEARL'S IMAGINATION
WAAAAAH!
SLURP
SEE? WHAT DID I TELL YOU?!
CHATLER, GO AND TELL LADY TO STAY PUT IN THE FLOWER SHOP!
STAY IN THE FLOWER SHOP! STAY IN THE FLOWER SHOP!
SPEAK-ING OF POKÉ-MON...
STAY IN THE FLOWER SHOP!
WE'RE SORRY, MISS... PLEASE DON'T CRY.
HOW ABOUT IF WE MAKE IT UP TO YOU...
...BY PER-FORMING OUR COMEDY ROUTINE?!
C-COMEDY...?
THAT'S RIGHT! WE'RE COMEDIANS. WE EVEN WON A PRIZE IN A BIG COMPETITION!
SPEAK-ING OF POKÉ-MON...

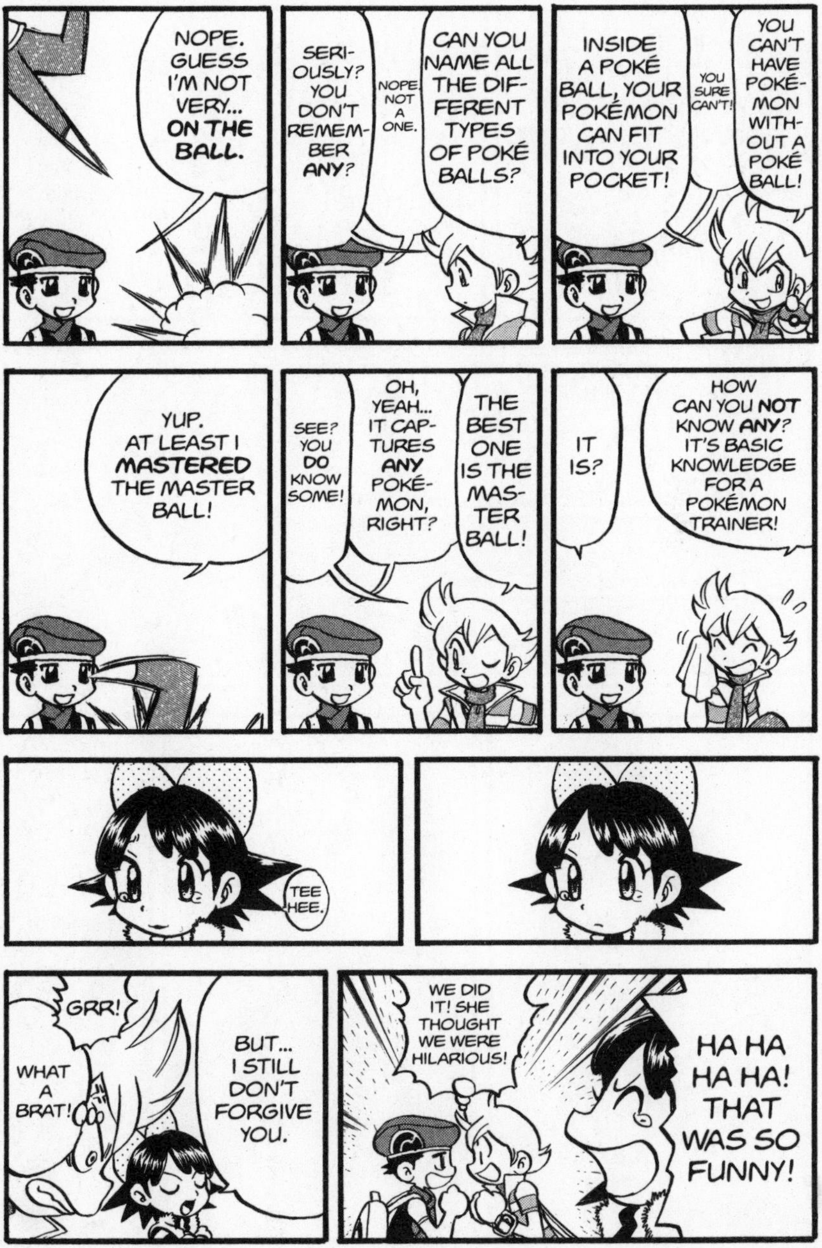
YOU CAN'T HAVE POKÉMON WITHOUT A POKÉ BALL!
YOU SURE CAN'T!
INSIDE A POKÉ BALL, YOUR POKÉMON CAN FIT INTO YOUR POCKET!
CAN YOU NAME ALL THE DIFFERENT TYPES OF POKÉ BALLS?
NOPE, NOT A ONE.
SERIOUSLY? YOU DON'T REMEMBER **ANY**?
NOPE. GUESS I'M NOT VERY... **ON THE BALL.**
HOW CAN YOU **NOT** KNOW **ANY**? IT'S BASIC KNOWLEDGE FOR A POKÉMON TRAINER!
IT IS?
THE BEST ONE IS THE MASTER BALL!
OH, YEAH... IT CAPTURES **ANY** POKÉMON, RIGHT?
SEE? YOU **DO** KNOW SOME!
YUP. AT LEAST I **MASTERED** THE MASTER BALL!
TEE HEE.
HA HA HA HA! THAT WAS SO FUNNY!
WE DID IT! SHE THOUGHT WE WERE HILARIOUS!
BUT... I STILL DON'T FORGIVE YOU.
GRR!
WHAT A BRAT!

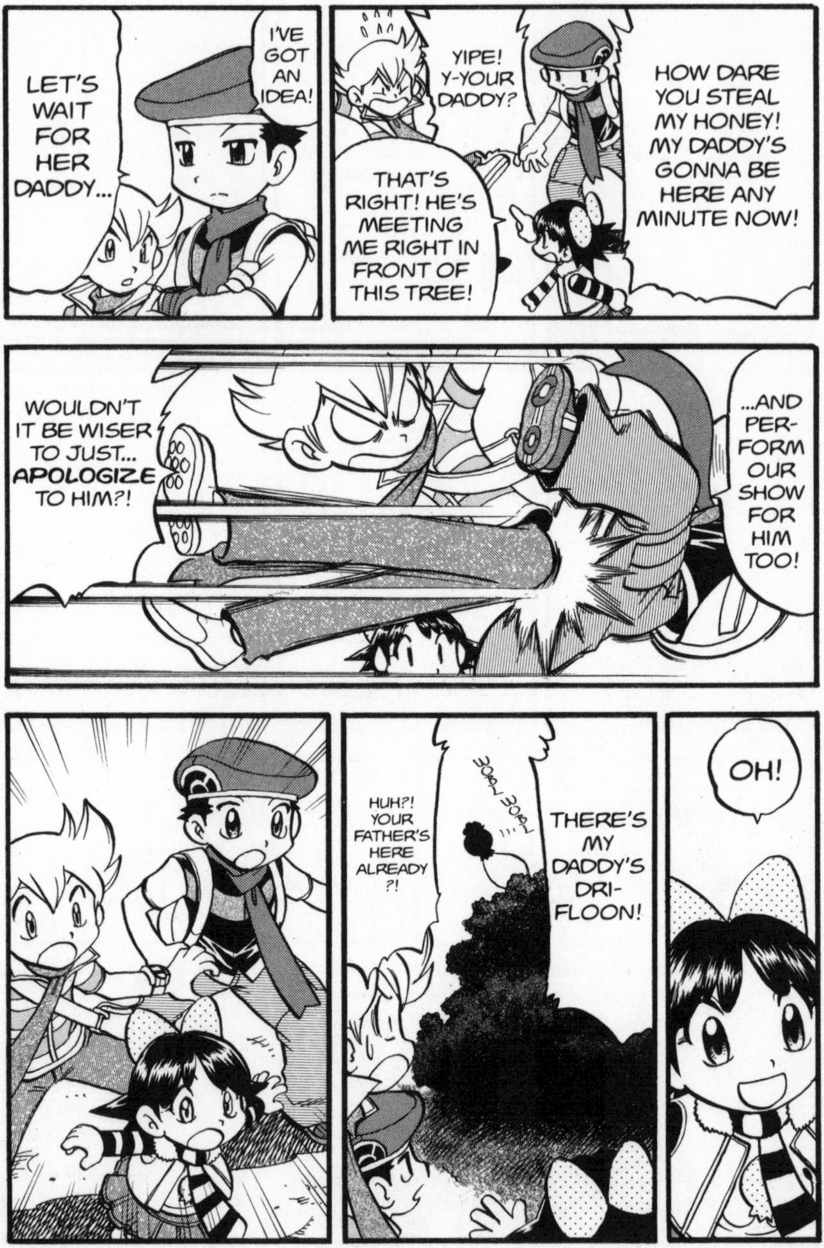
LET'S WAIT FOR HER DADDY...
I'VE GOT AN IDEA!
HOW DARE YOU STEAL MY HONEY! MY DADDY'S GONNA BE HERE ANY MINUTE NOW!
YIPE! Y-YOUR DADDY?
THAT'S RIGHT! HE'S MEETING ME RIGHT IN FRONT OF THIS TREE!
WOULDN'T IT BE WISER TO JUST... APOLOGIZE TO HIM?!
...AND PER-FORM OUR SHOW FOR HIM TOO!
OH!
THERE'S MY DADDY'S DRI-FLOON!
WOBL WOBL
HUH?! YOUR FATHER'S HERE ALREADY?!

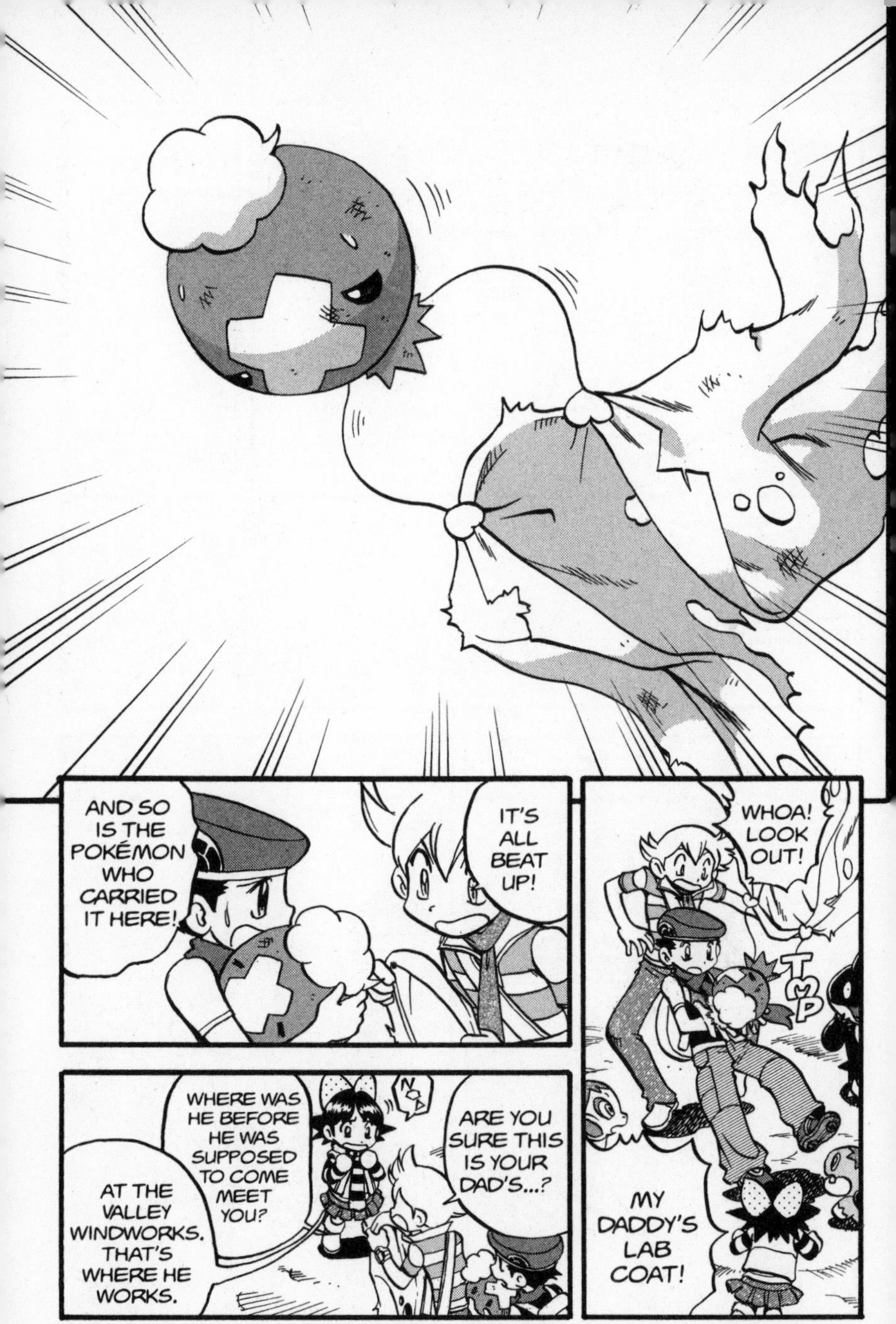
WHOA! LOOK OUT!
TMP
MY DADDY'S LAB COAT!
IT'S ALL BEAT UP!
AND SO IS THE POKÉMON WHO CARRIED IT HERE!
ARE YOU SURE THIS IS YOUR DAD'S...?
NOD
WHERE WAS HE BEFORE HE WAS SUPPOSED TO COME MEET YOU?
AT THE VALLEY WINDWORKS. THAT'S WHERE HE WORKS.

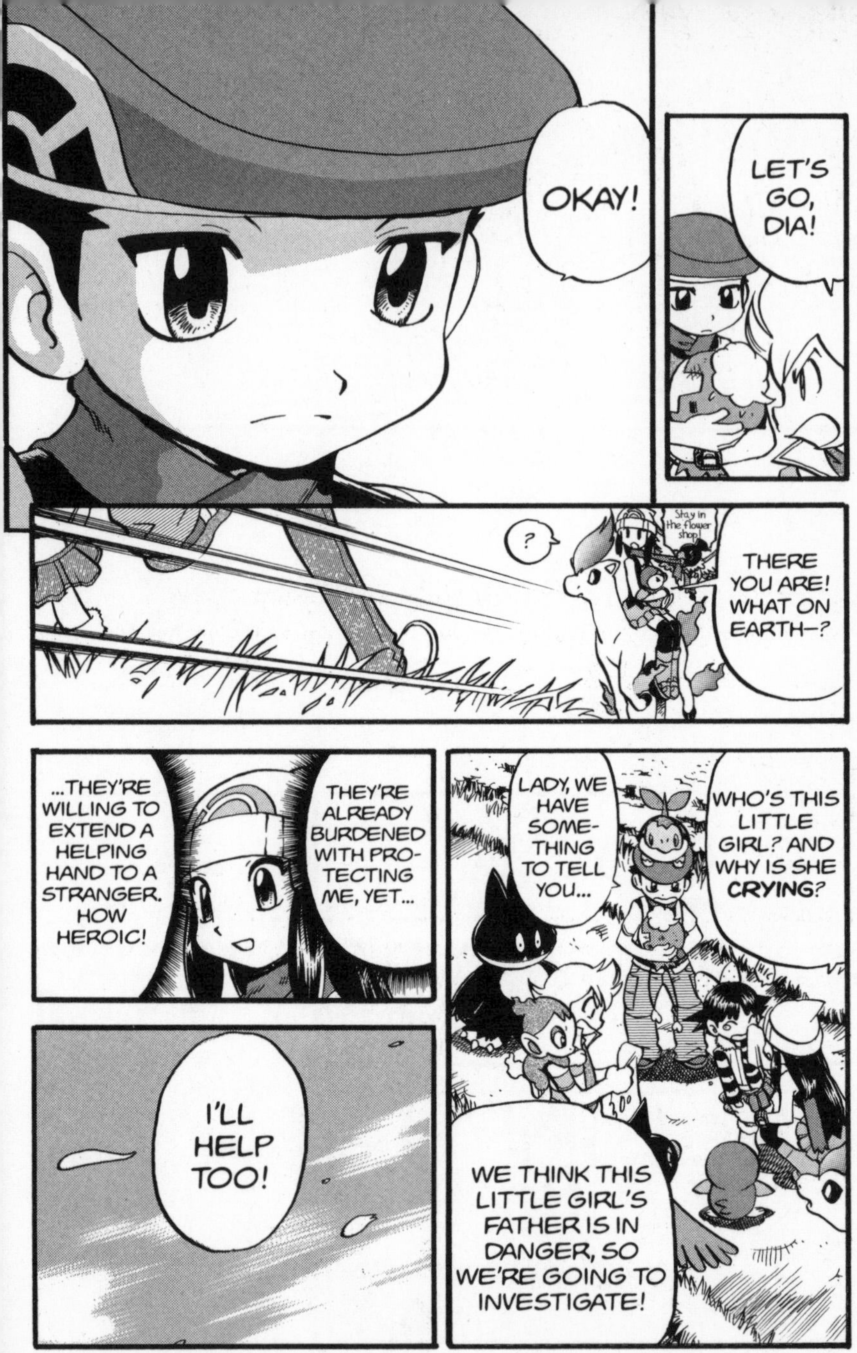
LET'S GO, DIA!
OKAY!
THERE YOU ARE! WHAT ON EARTH—?
Stay in the flower shop
?
WHO'S THIS LITTLE GIRL? AND WHY IS SHE **CRYING**?
LADY, WE HAVE SOME-THING TO TELL YOU...
HIC
WE THINK THIS LITTLE GIRL'S FATHER IS IN DANGER, SO WE'RE GOING TO INVESTIGATE!
THEY'RE ALREADY BURDENED WITH PRO-TECTING ME, YET...
...THEY'RE WILLING TO EXTEND A HELPING HAND TO A STRANGER. HOW HEROIC!
I'LL HELP TOO!

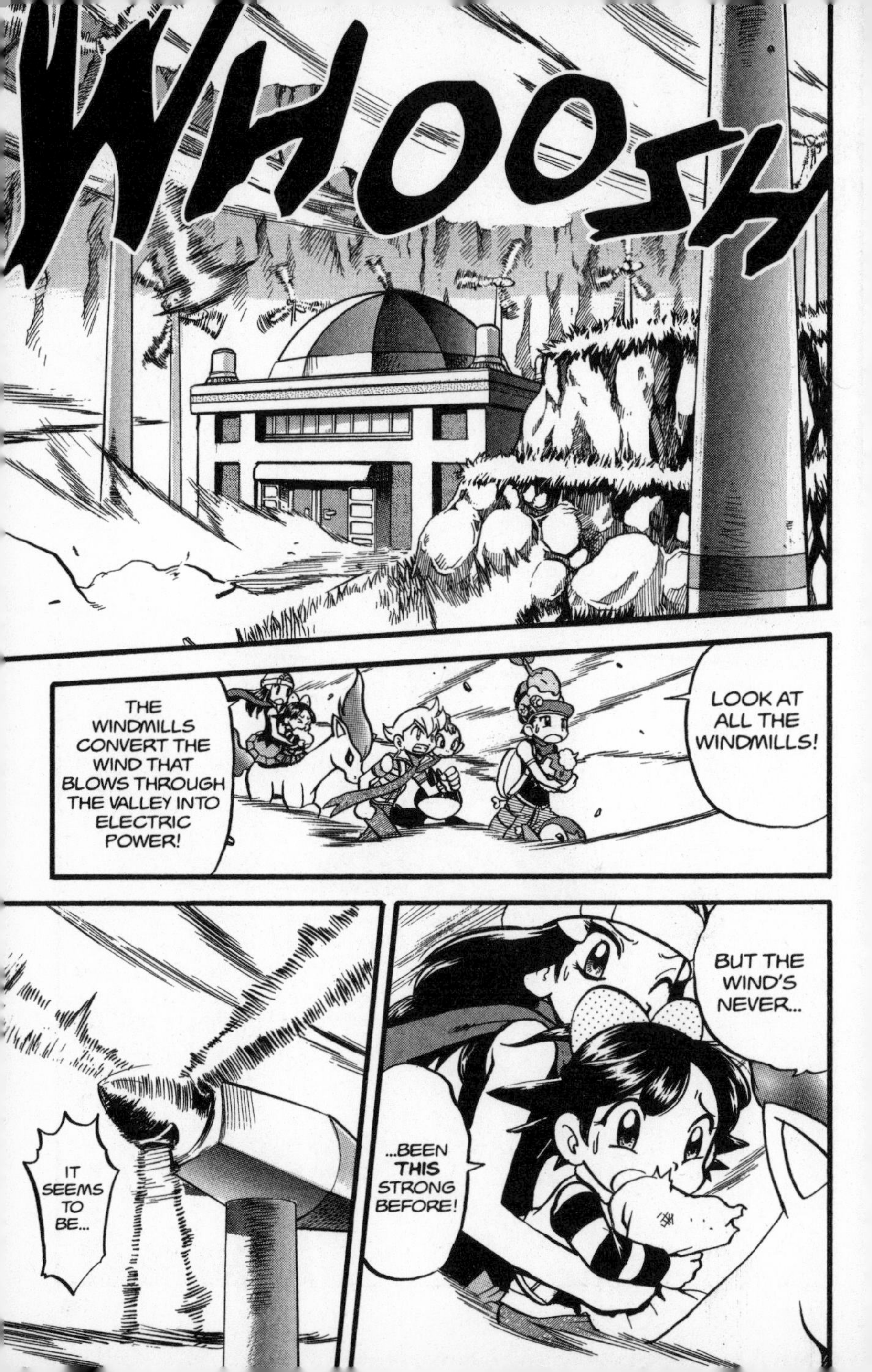
WHOOSH
LOOK AT ALL THE WINDMILLS!
THE WINDMILLS CONVERT THE WIND THAT BLOWS THROUGH THE VALLEY INTO ELECTRIC POWER!
IT SEEMS TO BE...
BUT THE WIND'S NEVER...
...BEEN THIS STRONG BEFORE!

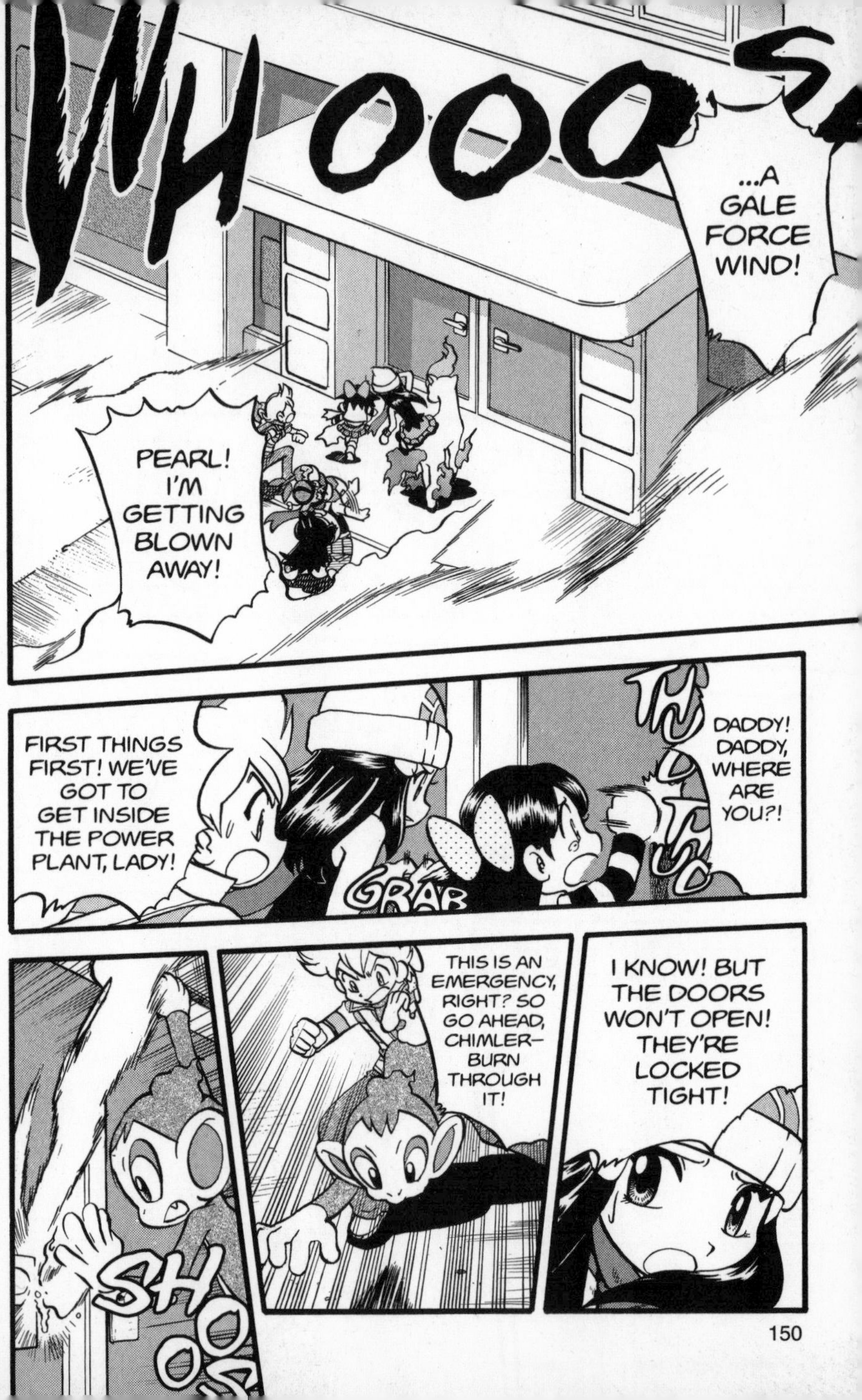
WHOOOS
...A GALE FORCE WIND!
PEARL! I'M GETTING BLOWN AWAY!
THUD THUD
DADDY! DADDY, WHERE ARE YOU?!
FIRST THINGS FIRST! WE'VE GOT TO GET INSIDE THE POWER PLANT, LADY!
GRAB
I KNOW! BUT THE DOORS WON'T OPEN! THEY'RE LOCKED TIGHT!
THIS IS AN EMERGENCY, RIGHT? SO GO AHEAD, CHIMLER-BURN THROUGH IT!
SHOOOS

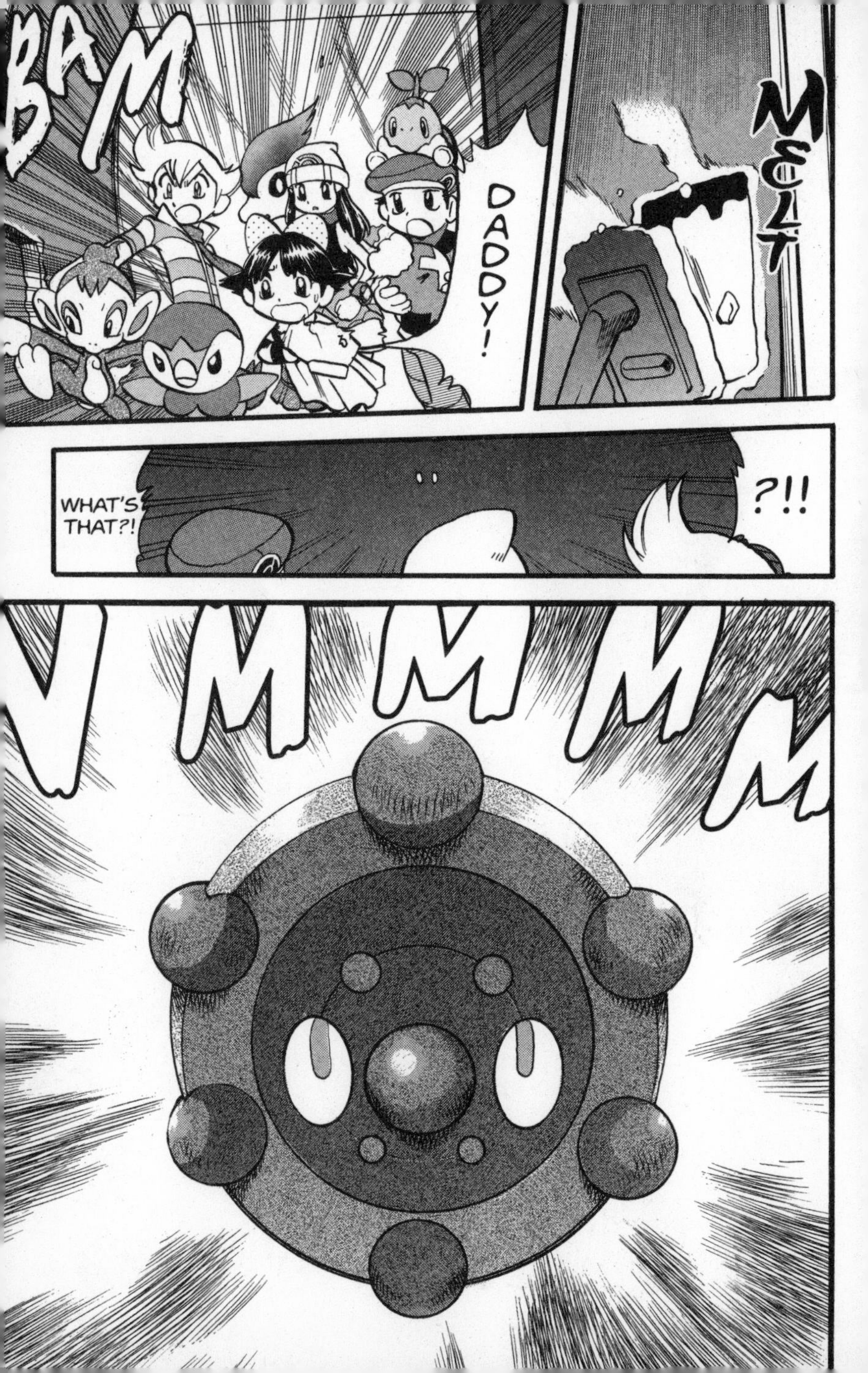
MELT
BAM
DADDY!
?!!
WHAT'S THAT?!
VMMMMM

7

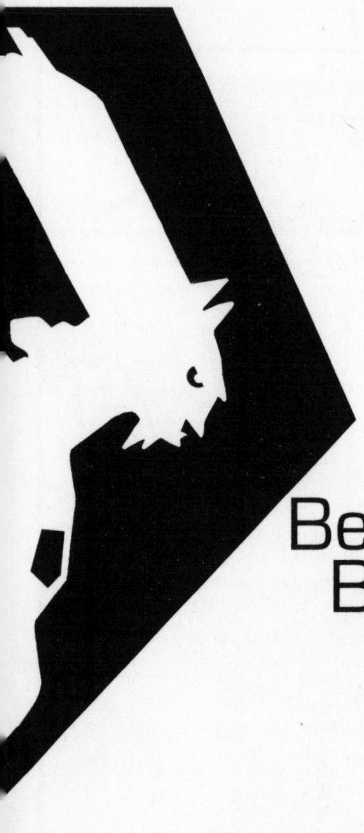

Belligerent Bronzor

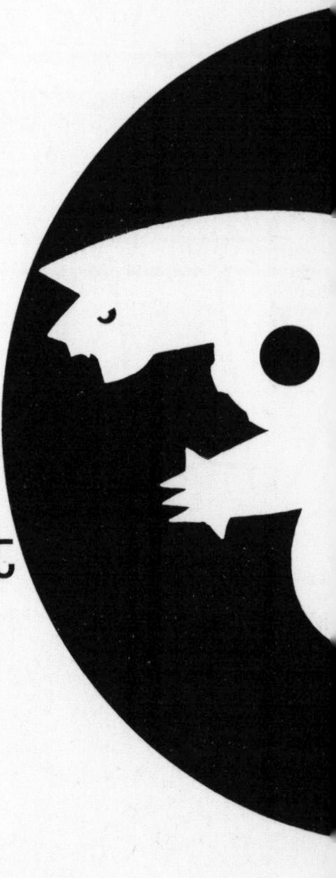

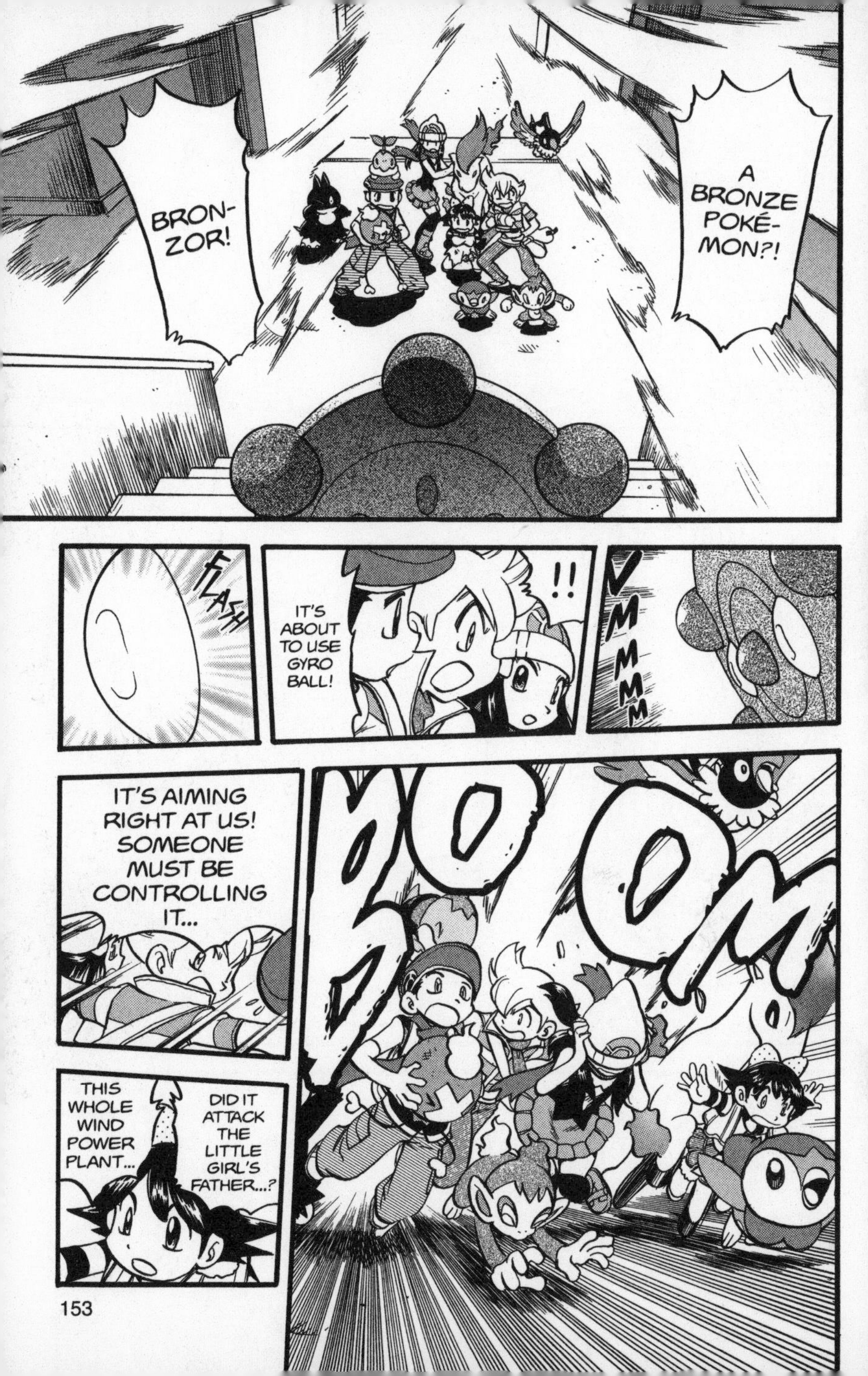
A BRONZE POKÉ-MON?!
BRON-ZOR!
FLASH
!!
IT'S ABOUT TO USE GYRO BALL!
VMMMMM
BOOM
IT'S AIMING RIGHT AT US! SOMEONE MUST BE CONTROLLING IT...
DID IT ATTACK THE LITTLE GIRL'S FATHER...?
THIS WHOLE WIND POWER PLANT...

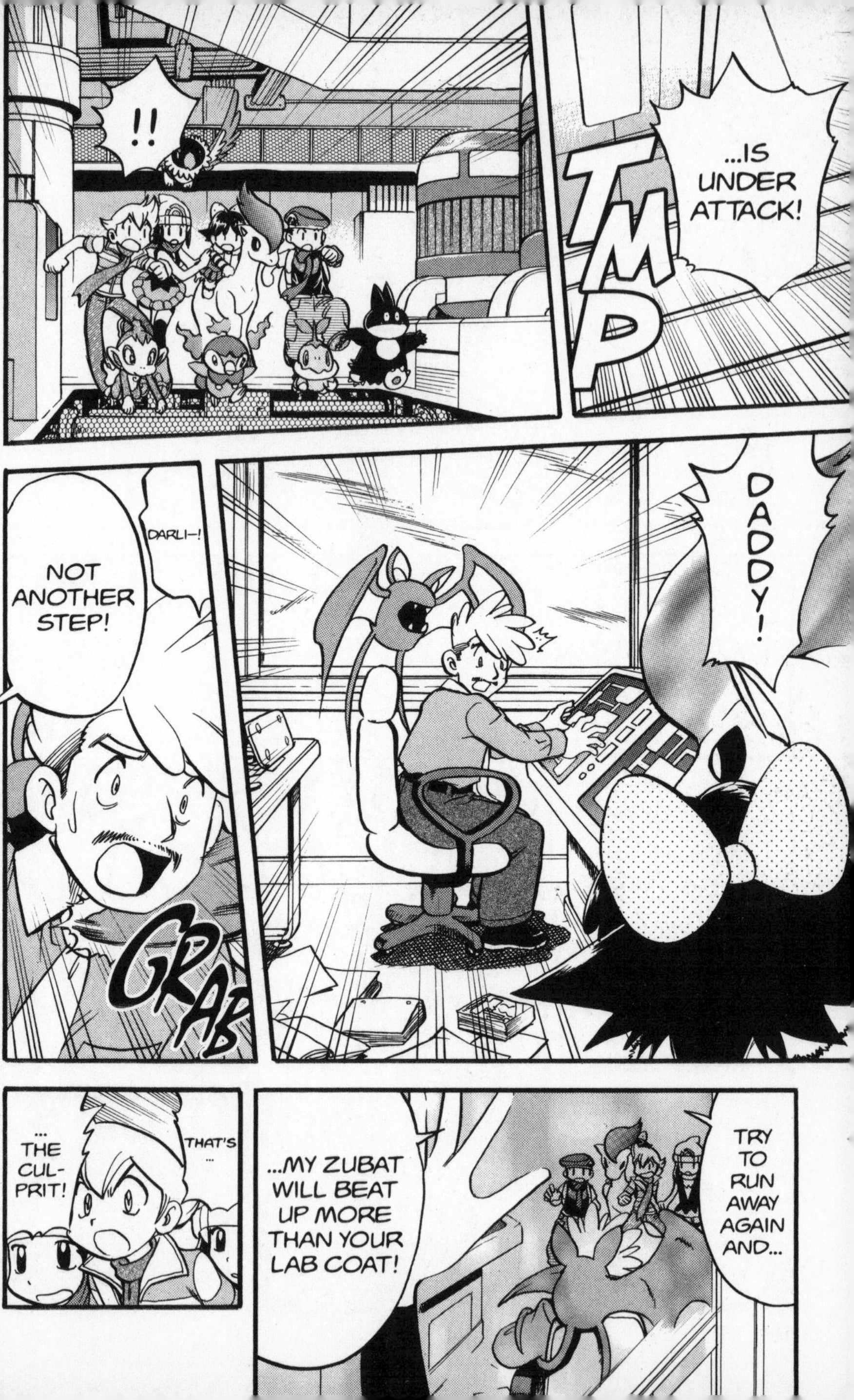
...IS UNDER ATTACK!
TMP
!!
DADDY!
DARLI-!
NOT ANOTHER STEP!
GRAB
TRY TO RUN AWAY AGAIN AND...
...MY ZUBAT WILL BEAT UP MORE THAN YOUR LAB COAT!
THAT'S ...
... THE CUL-PRIT!

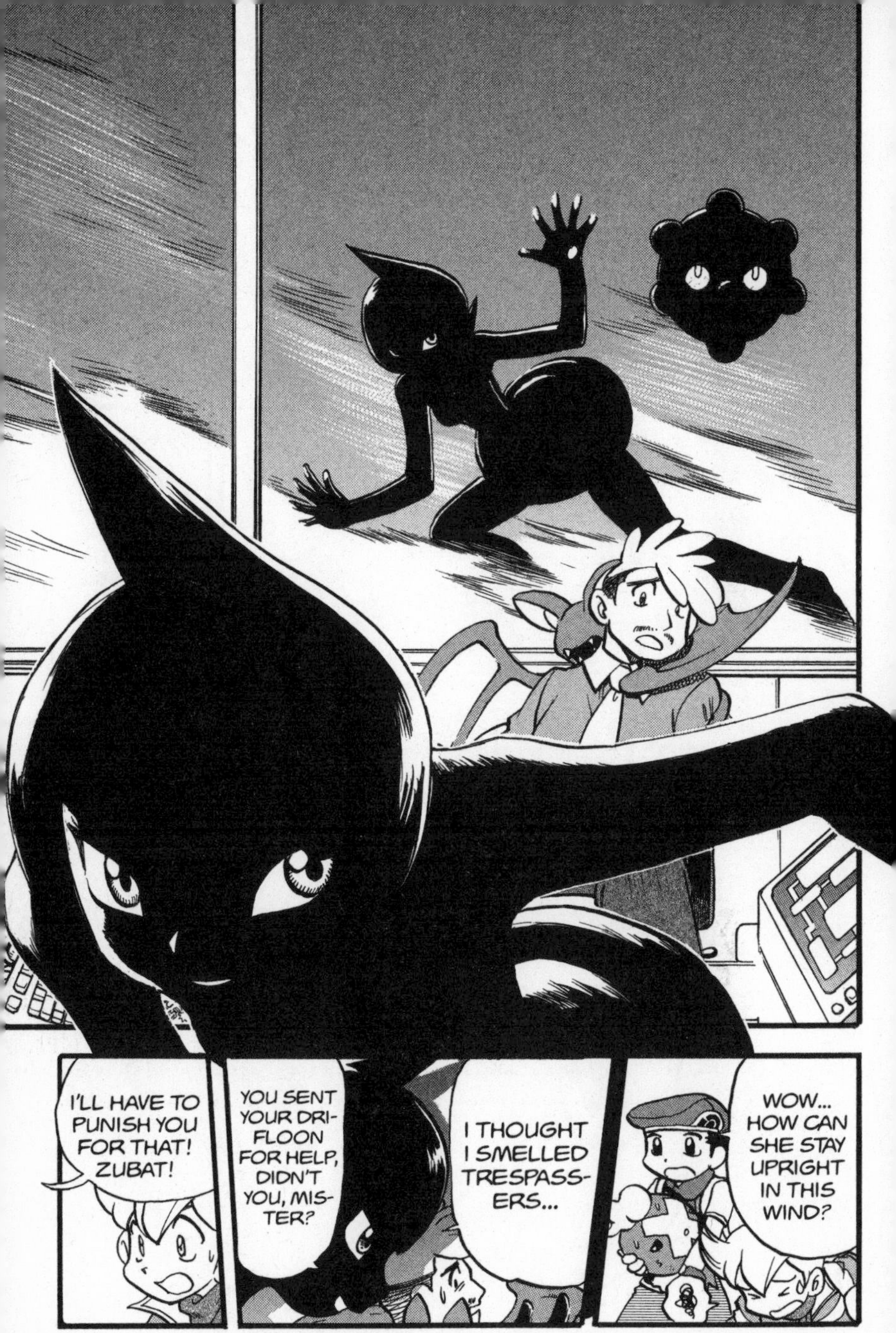
WOW... HOW CAN SHE STAY UPRIGHT IN THIS WIND?
I THOUGHT I SMELLED TRESPASS-ERS...
YOU SENT YOUR DRI-FLOON FOR HELP, DIDN'T YOU, MIS-TER?
I'LL HAVE TO PUNISH YOU FOR THAT! ZUBAT!

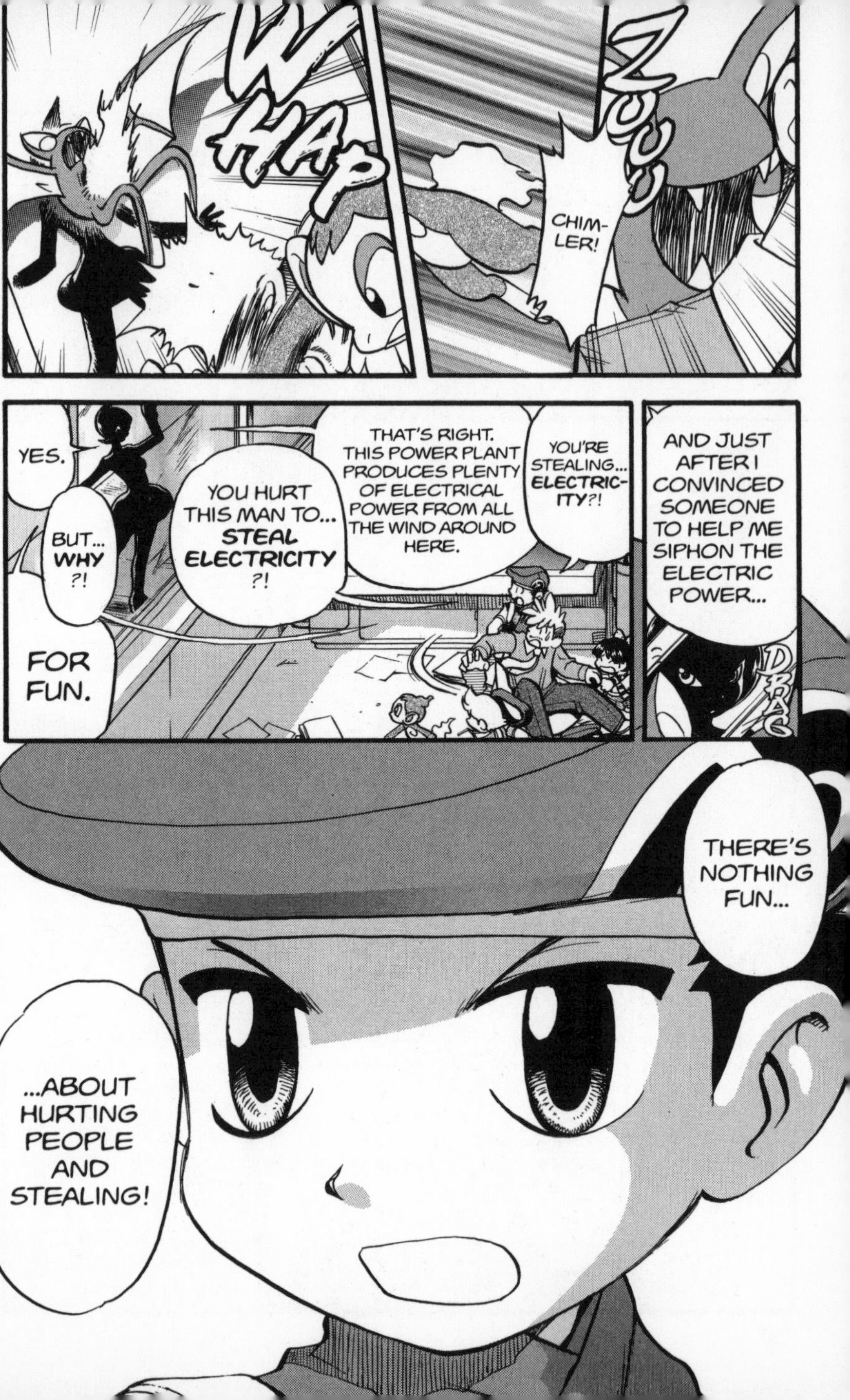
ZOOOOO
CHIMLER!
WHAP
AND JUST AFTER I CONVINCED SOMEONE TO HELP ME SIPHON THE ELECTRIC POWER...
DRAG
YOU'RE STEALING... ELECTRICITY?!
THAT'S RIGHT. THIS POWER PLANT PRODUCES PLENTY OF ELECTRICAL POWER FROM ALL THE WIND AROUND HERE.
YOU HURT THIS MAN TO... STEAL ELECTRICITY?!
YES.
BUT... WHY?!
FOR FUN.
THERE'S NOTHING FUN...
...ABOUT HURTING PEOPLE AND STEALING!

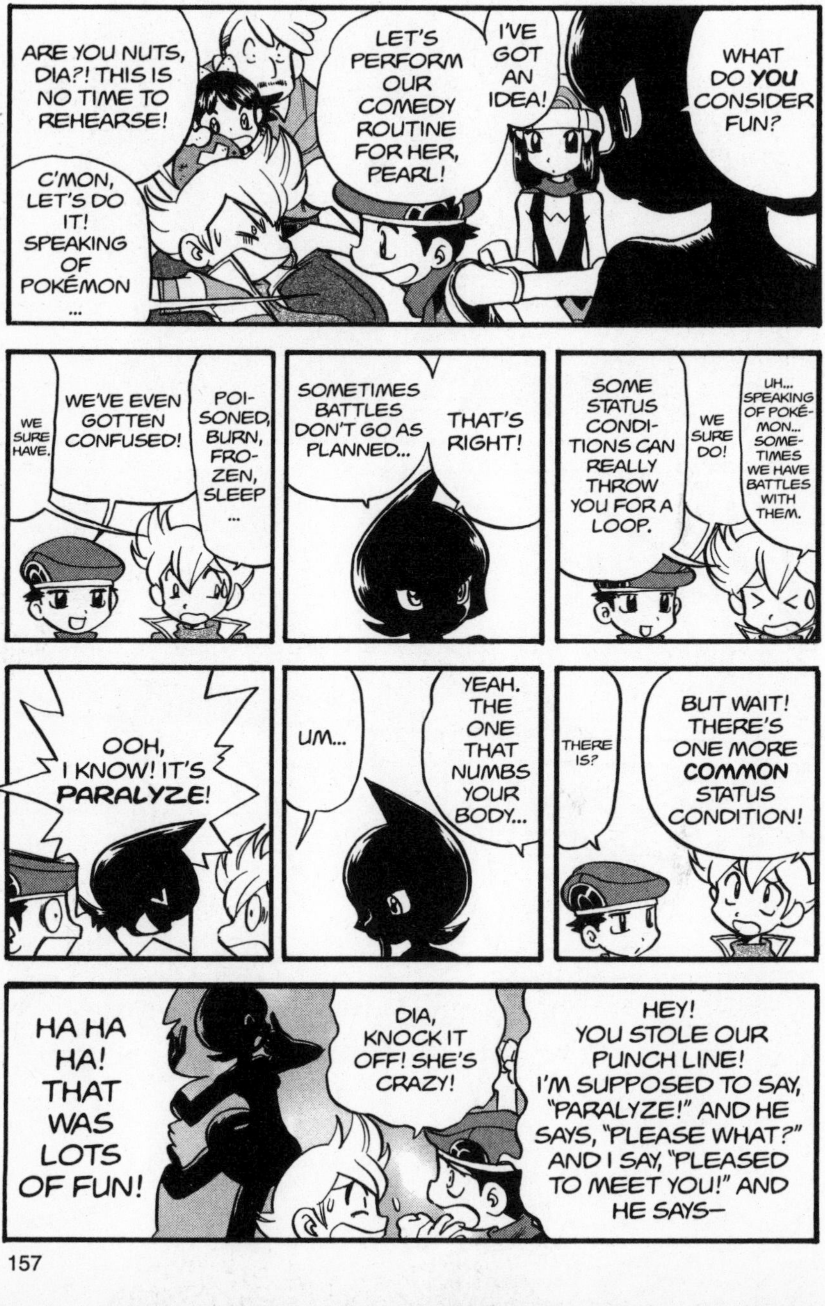
WHAT DO **YOU** CONSIDER FUN?
I'VE GOT AN IDEA!
LET'S PERFORM OUR COMEDY ROUTINE FOR HER, PEARL!
ARE YOU NUTS, DIA?! THIS IS NO TIME TO REHEARSE!
C'MON, LET'S DO IT! SPEAKING OF POKÉMON ...
UH... SPEAKING OF POKÉMON... SOMETIMES WE HAVE BATTLES WITH THEM.
WE SURE DO!
SOME STATUS CONDITIONS CAN REALLY THROW YOU FOR A LOOP.
THAT'S RIGHT!
SOMETIMES BATTLES DON'T GO AS PLANNED...
POISONED, BURN, FROZEN, SLEEP ...
WE'VE EVEN GOTTEN CONFUSED!
WE SURE HAVE.
BUT WAIT! THERE'S ONE MORE **COMMON** STATUS CONDITION!
THERE IS?
YEAH. THE ONE THAT NUMBS YOUR BODY...
UM...
OOH, I KNOW! IT'S **PARALYZE**!
HEY! YOU STOLE OUR PUNCH LINE! I'M SUPPOSED TO SAY, "PARALYZE!" AND HE SAYS, "PLEASE WHAT?" AND I SAY, "PLEASED TO MEET YOU!" AND HE SAYS—
DIA, KNOCK IT OFF! SHE'S CRAZY!
HA HA HA! THAT WAS LOTS OF FUN!

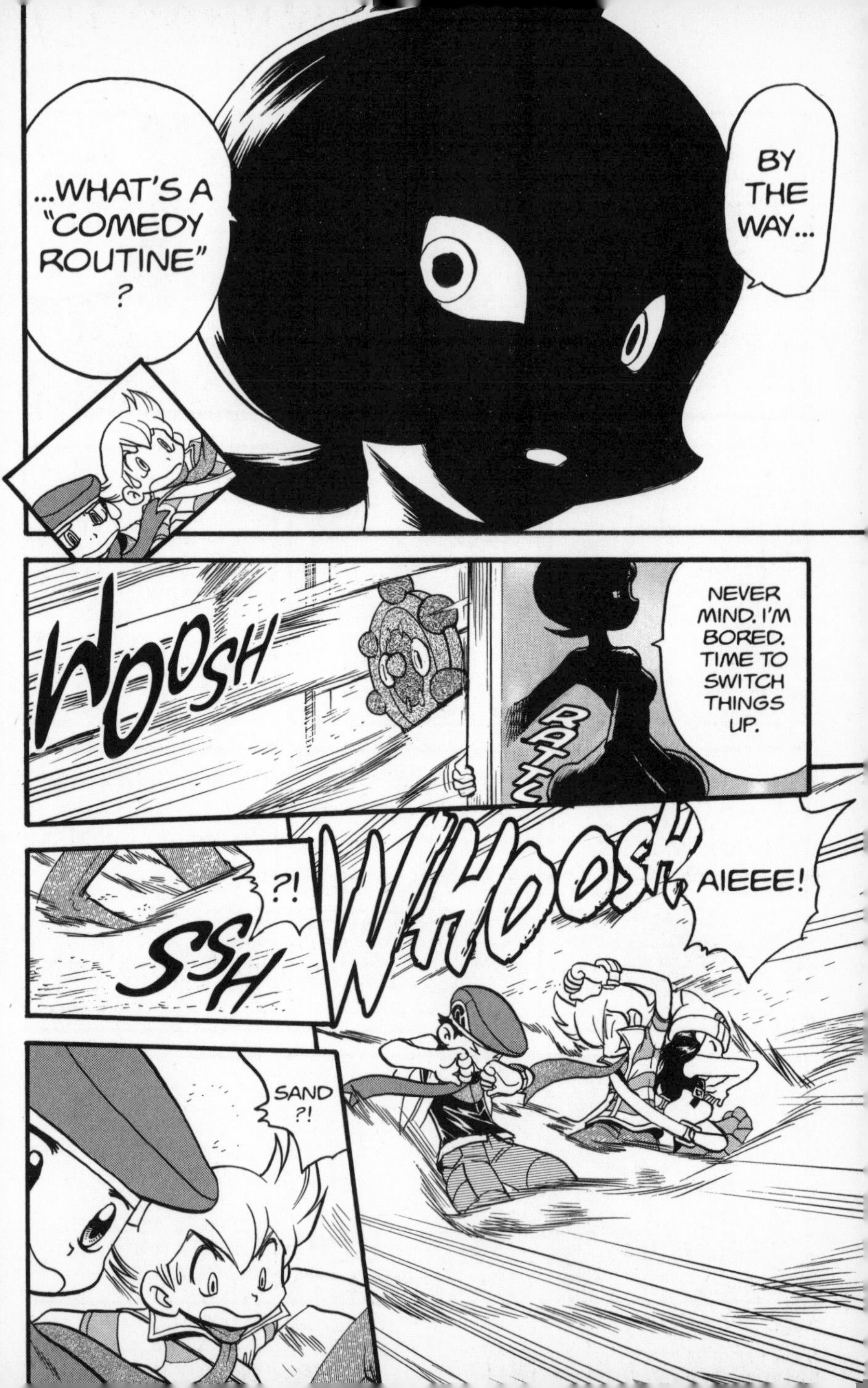
BY THE WAY...
...WHAT'S A "COMEDY ROUTINE" ?
RATTL
NEVER MIND. I'M BORED. TIME TO SWITCH THINGS UP.
WOOSH
WHOOSH
AIEEE!
?!
SSH
SAND ?!

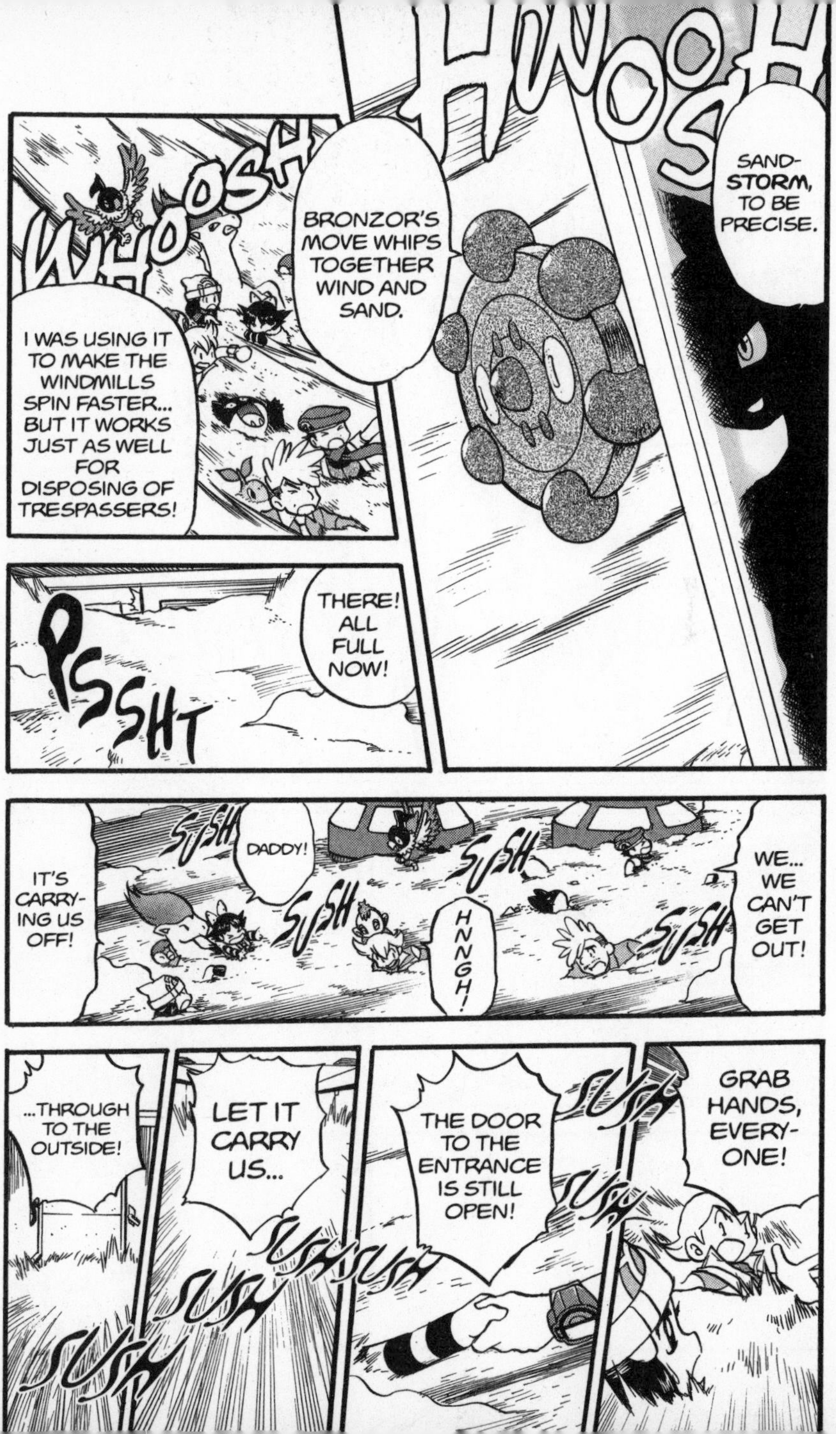
WHOOSH
WHOOSH
BRONZOR'S MOVE WHIPS TOGETHER WIND AND SAND.
SAND-STORM, TO BE PRECISE.
I WAS USING IT TO MAKE THE WINDMILLS SPIN FASTER... BUT IT WORKS JUST AS WELL FOR DISPOSING OF TRESPASSERS!
WHOOSH
PSSHT
THERE! ALL FULL NOW!
IT'S CARRY-ING US OFF!
SUSH
DADDY!
SUSH
SUSH
HNNGH!
SUSH
WE... WE CAN'T GET OUT!
...THROUGH TO THE OUTSIDE!
LET IT CARRY US...
THE DOOR TO THE ENTRANCE IS STILL OPEN!
GRAB HANDS, EVERY-ONE!
SUSH SUSH SUSH SUSH
SUSH SUSH

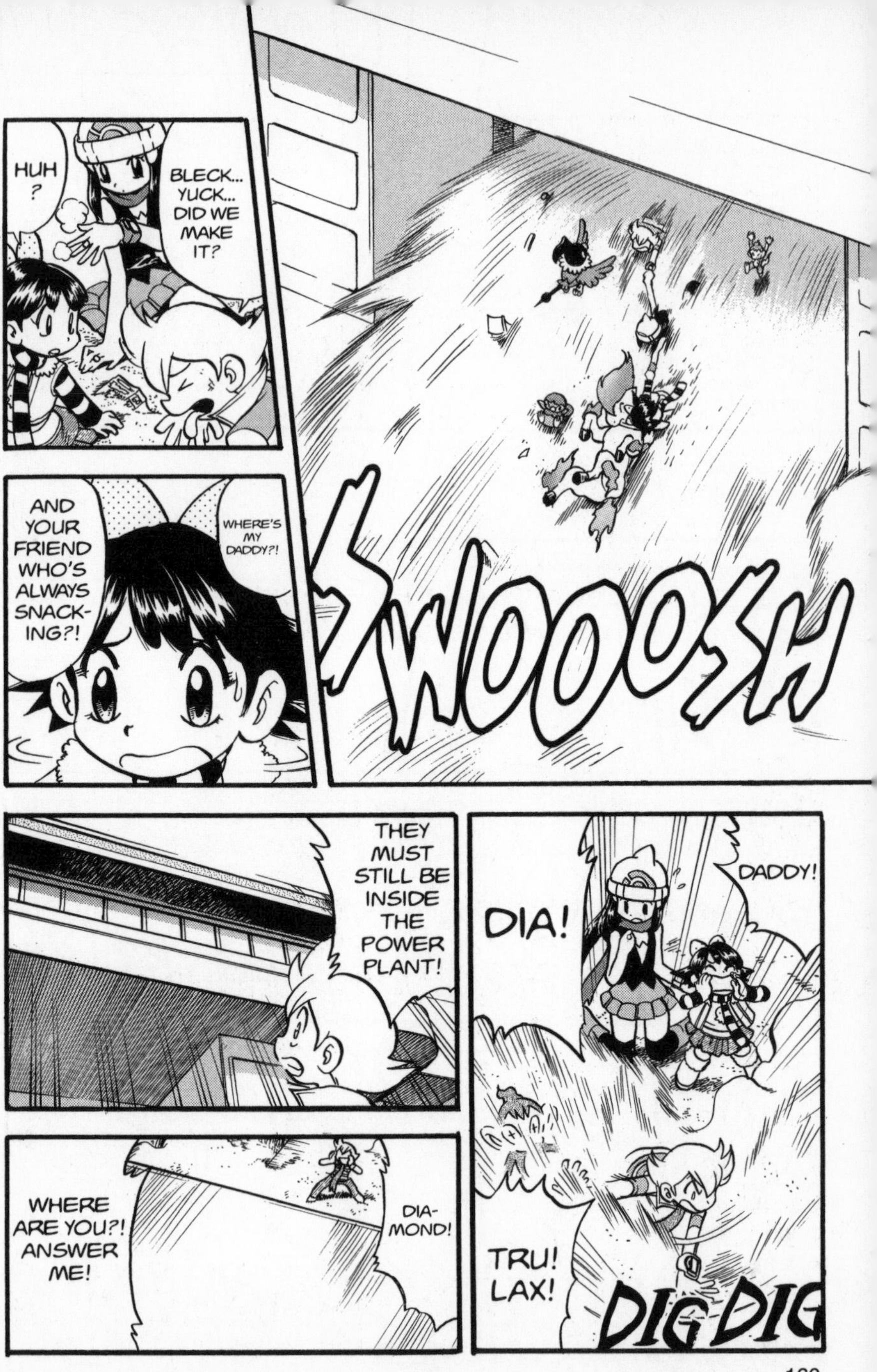

SWOOOSH
HUH?
BLECK... YUCK... DID WE MAKE IT?
AND YOUR FRIEND WHO'S ALWAYS SNACK-ING?!
WHERE'S MY DADDY?!
THEY MUST STILL BE INSIDE THE POWER PLANT!
WHERE ARE YOU?! ANSWER ME!
DIA-MOND!
DIA!
DADDY!
TRU! LAX!
DIG DIG

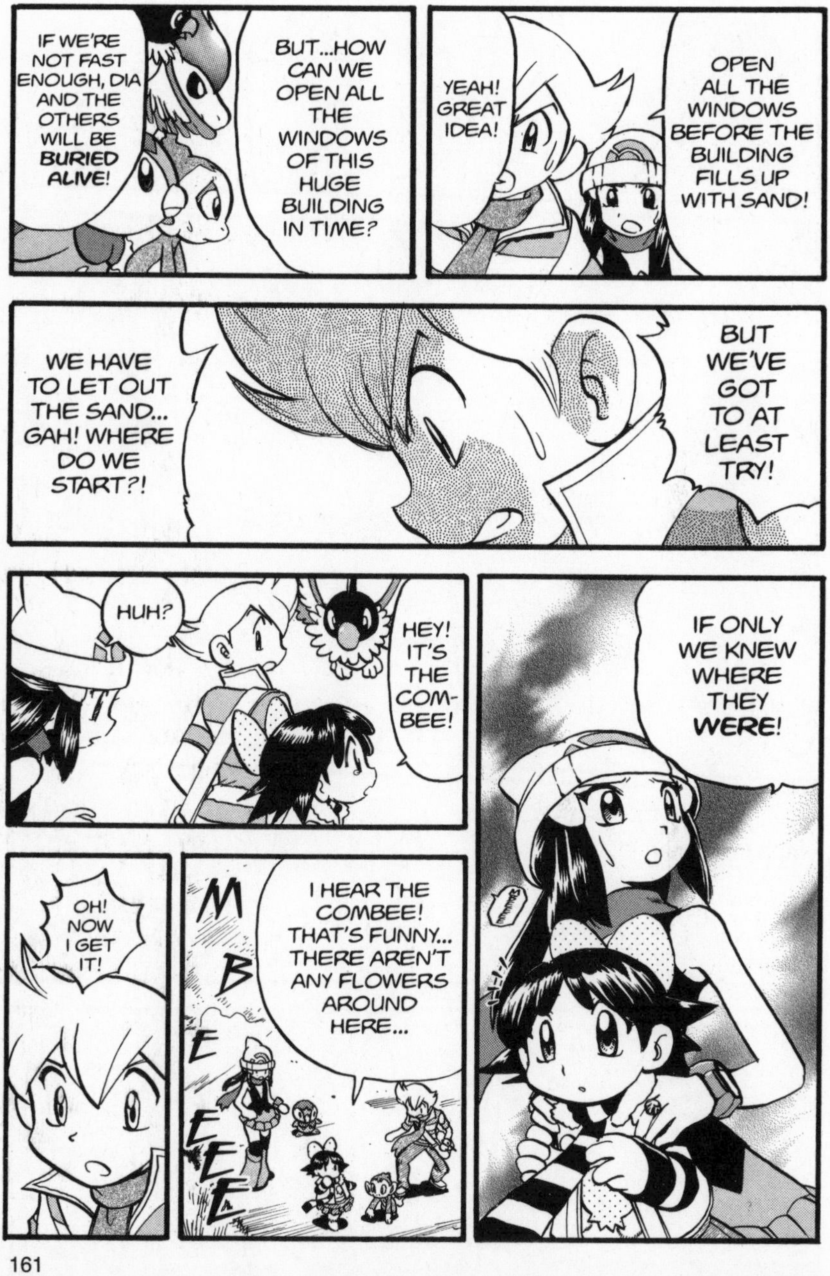
OPEN ALL THE WINDOWS BEFORE THE BUILDING FILLS UP WITH SAND!
YEAH! GREAT IDEA!
BUT...HOW CAN WE OPEN ALL THE WINDOWS OF THIS HUGE BUILDING IN TIME?
IF WE'RE NOT FAST ENOUGH, DIA AND THE OTHERS WILL BE **BURIED ALIVE**!
BUT WE'VE GOT TO AT LEAST TRY!
WE HAVE TO LET OUT THE SAND... GAH! WHERE DO WE START?!
IF ONLY WE KNEW WHERE THEY **WERE**!
HEY! IT'S THE COM-BEE!
HUH?
I HEAR THE COMBEE! THAT'S FUNNY... THERE AREN'T ANY FLOWERS AROUND HERE...
MMBEEEE
OH! NOW I GET IT!

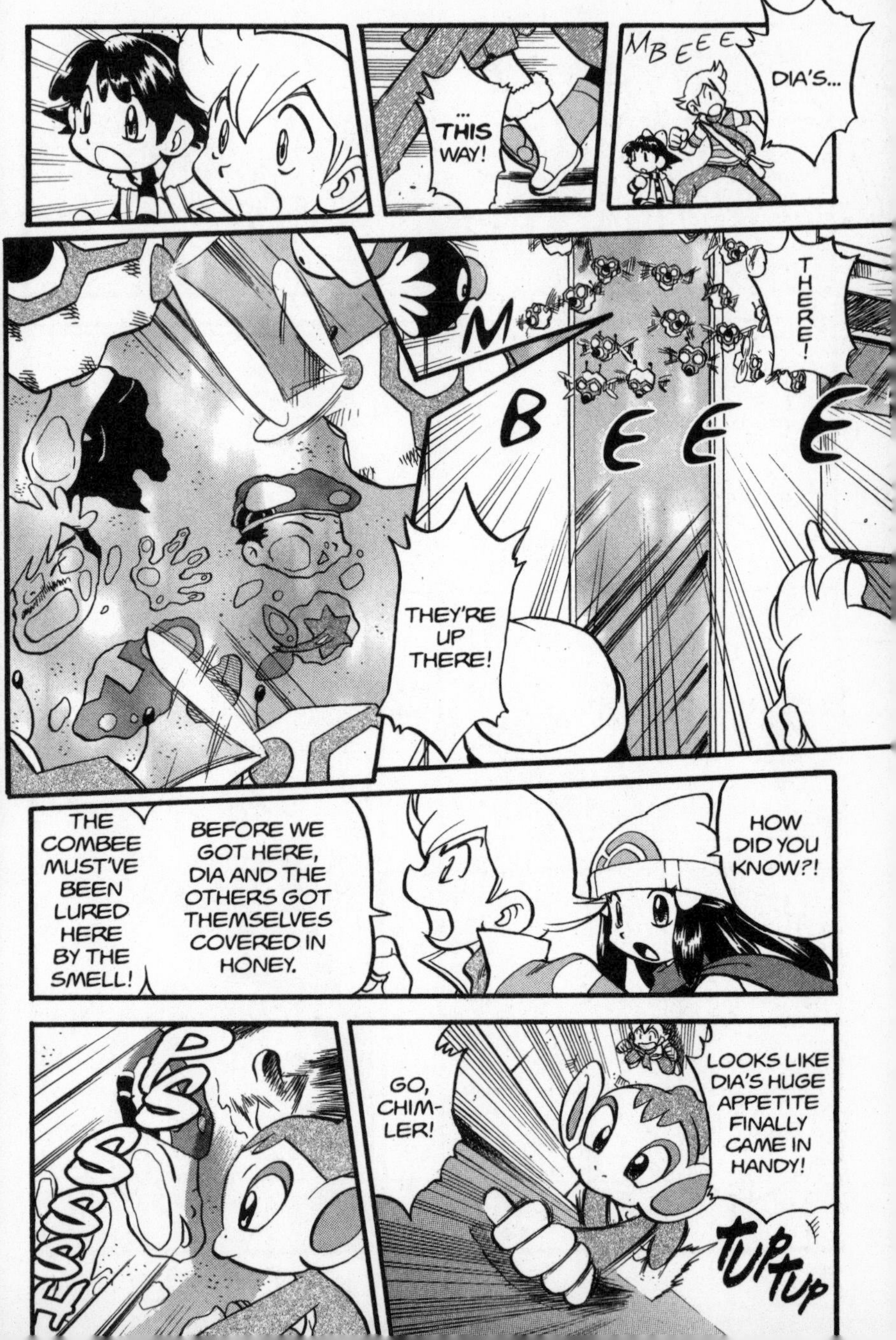
MBEEEE
DIA'S...
...THIS WAY!
THERE!
MBEEE
THEY'RE UP THERE!
HOW DID YOU KNOW?!
BEFORE WE GOT HERE, DIA AND THE OTHERS GOT THEMSELVES COVERED IN HONEY.
THE COMBEE MUST'VE BEEN LURED HERE BY THE SMELL!
LOOKS LIKE DIA'S HUGE APPETITE FINALLY CAME IN HANDY!
GO, CHIMLER!
TUP TUP
PSSSSSSH

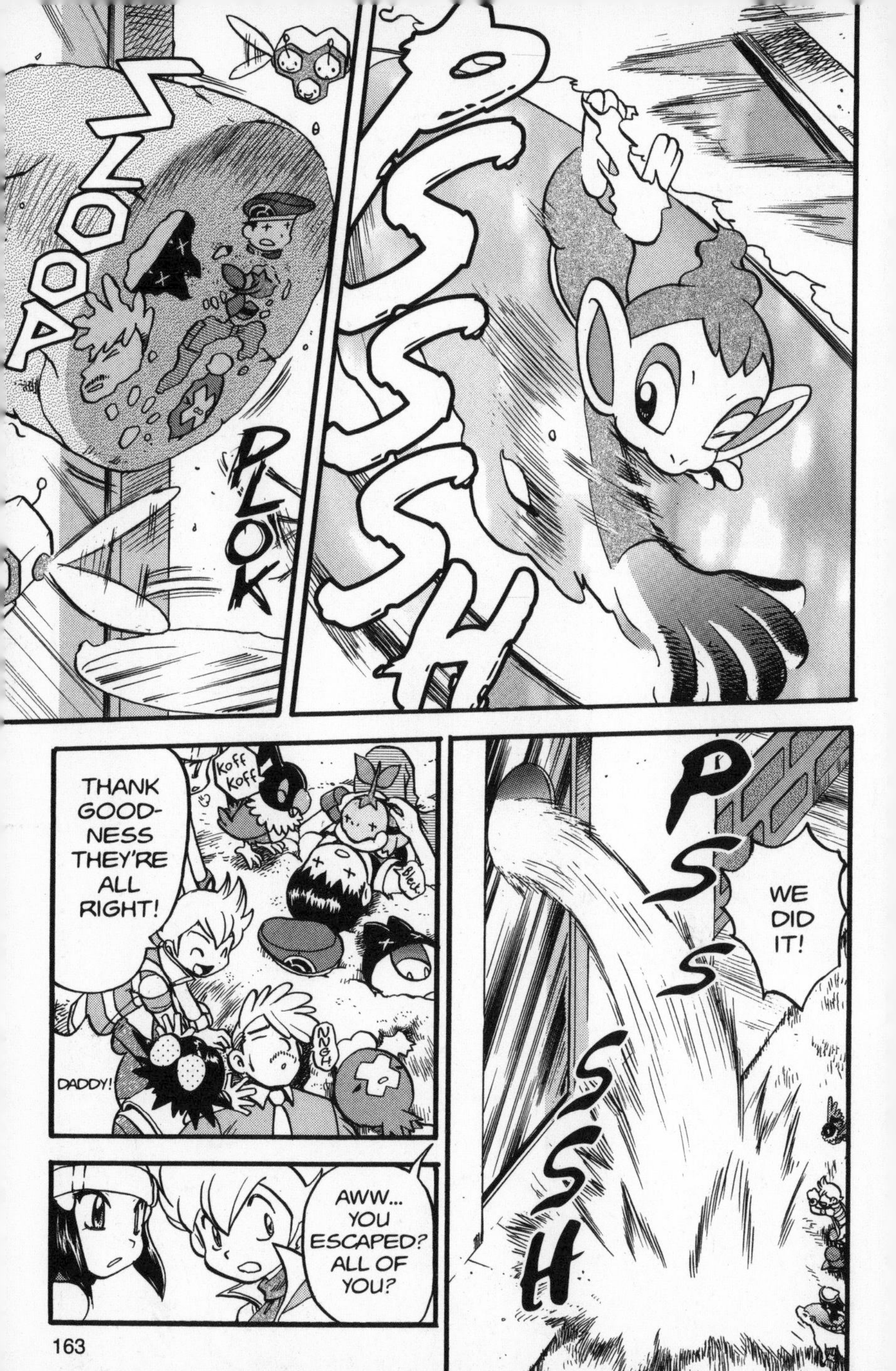
SPLOOSH
SPLOOSH
PLOK
PSSSSH
WE DID IT!
THANK GOODNESS THEY'RE ALL RIGHT!
KOFF KOFF
BLECK
NNGH
DADDY!
AWW... YOU ESCAPED? ALL OF YOU?

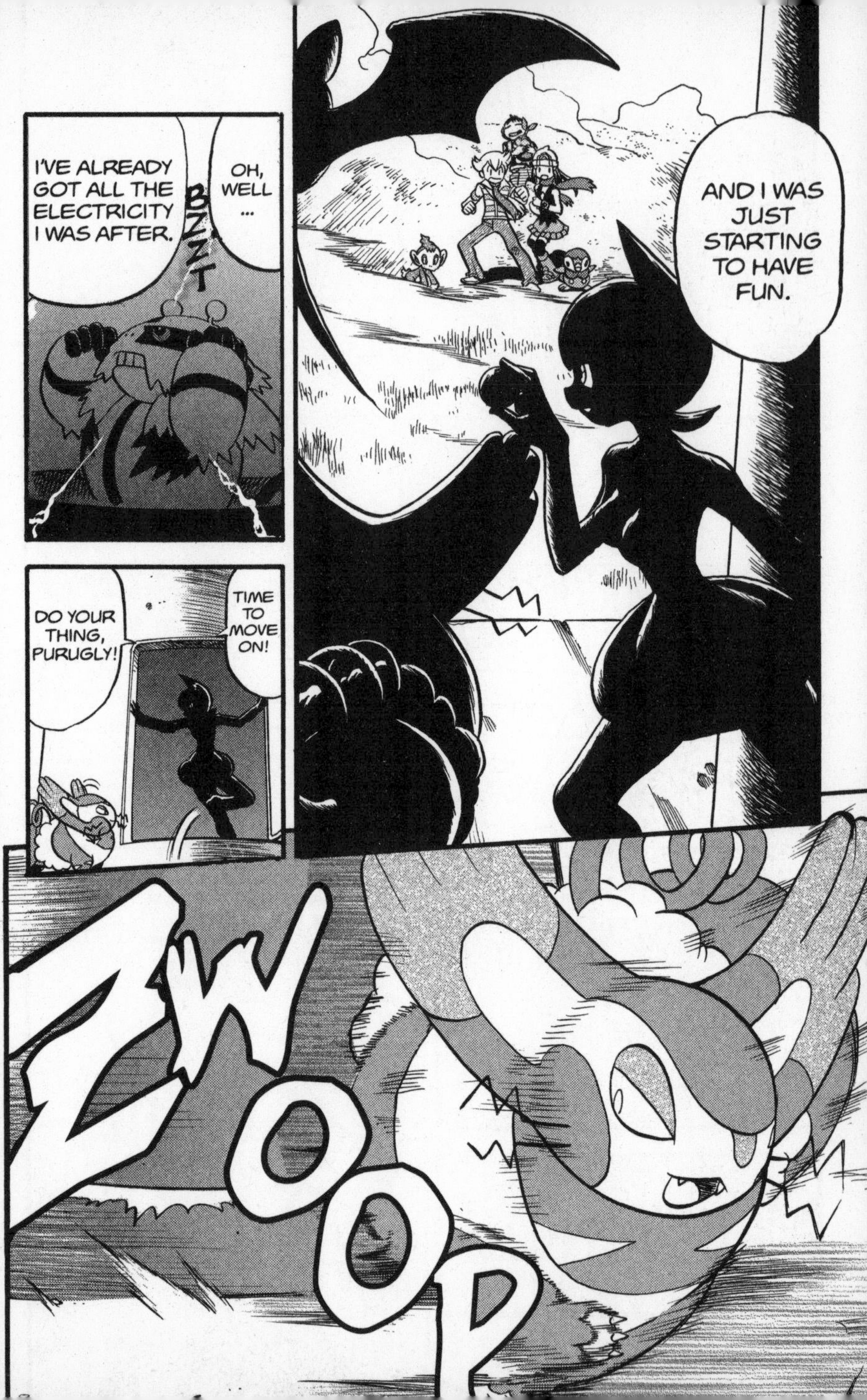
AND I WAS JUST STARTING TO HAVE FUN.
OH, WELL ...
I'VE ALREADY GOT ALL THE ELECTRICITY I WAS AFTER.
BZZZT
...
TIME TO MOVE ON!
DO YOUR THING, PURUGLY!
ZWOOOP

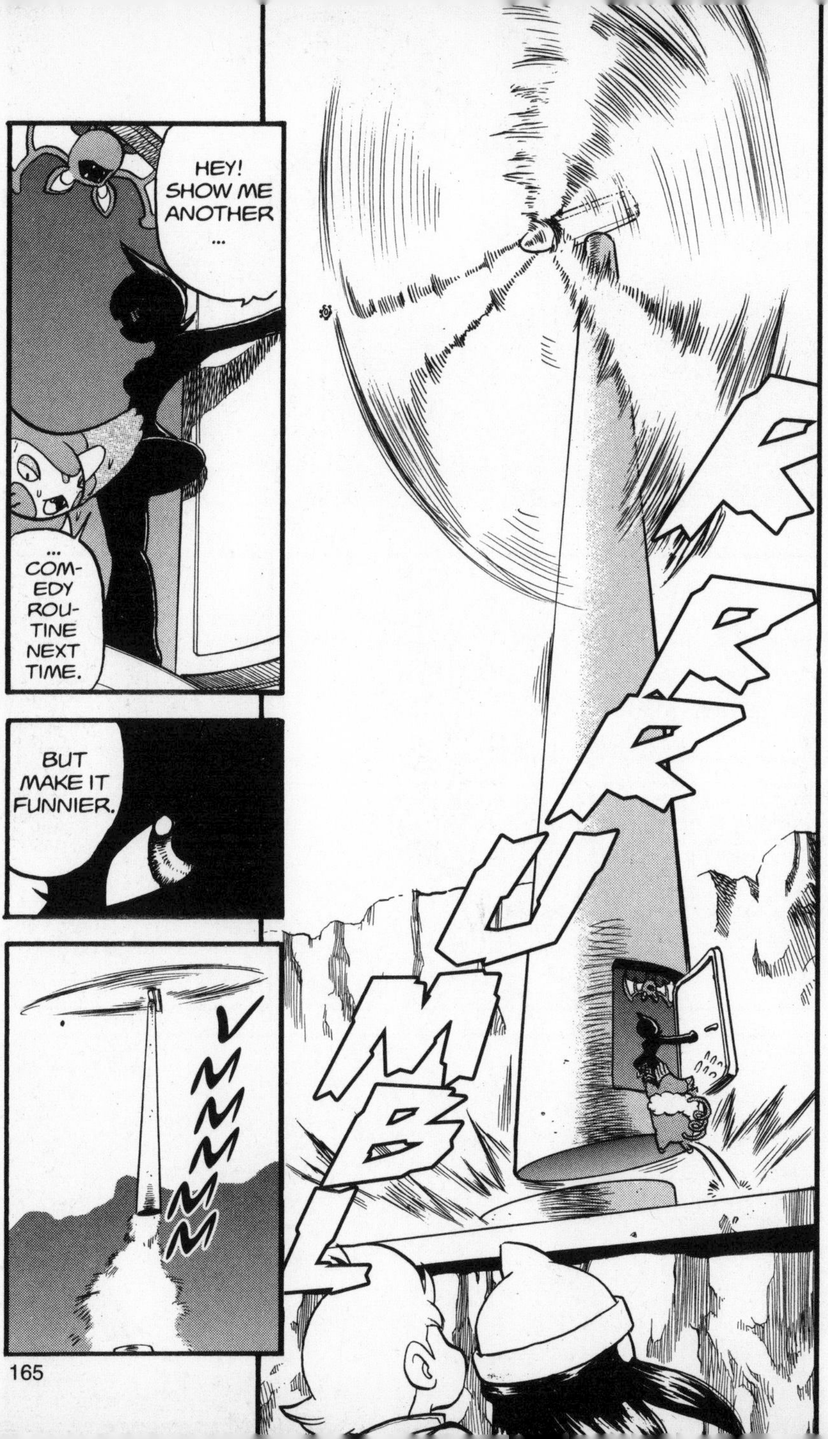
HEY! SHOW ME ANOTHER ...
... COMEDY ROUTINE NEXT TIME.
BUT MAKE IT FUNNIER.
VMMMMMM
RRRUMBL

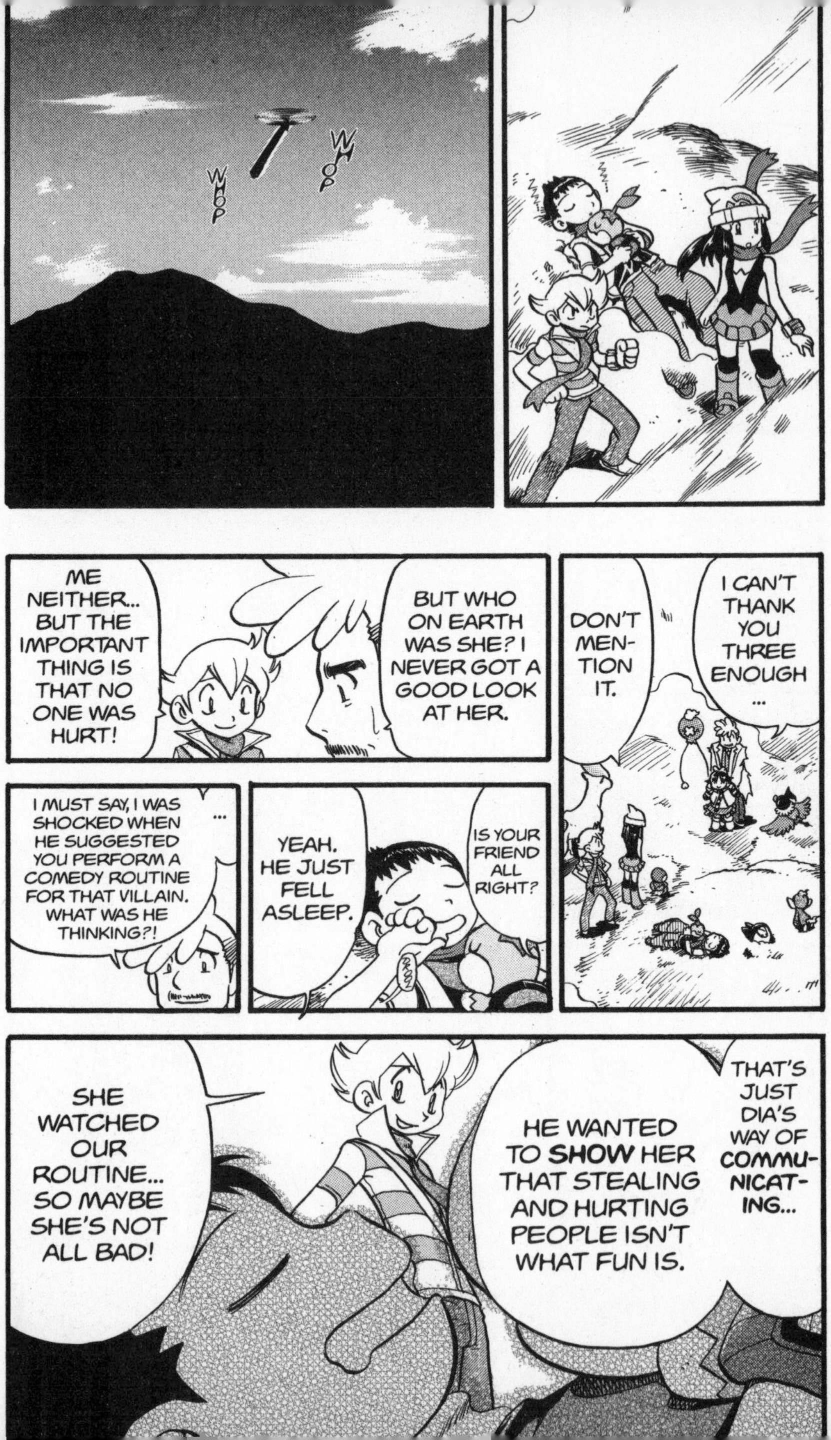
WHOP
WHOP
I CAN'T THANK YOU THREE ENOUGH...
DON'T MEN-TION IT.
BUT WHO ON EARTH WAS SHE? I NEVER GOT A GOOD LOOK AT HER.
ME NEITHER... BUT THE IMPORTANT THING IS THAT NO ONE WAS HURT!
IS YOUR FRIEND ALL RIGHT?
YEAH. HE JUST FELL ASLEEP.
...
I MUST SAY, I WAS SHOCKED WHEN HE SUGGESTED YOU PERFORM A COMEDY ROUTINE FOR THAT VILLAIN. WHAT WAS HE THINKING?!
THAT'S JUST DIA'S WAY OF **COMMU-NICAT-ING...**
HE WANTED TO **SHOW** HER THAT STEALING AND HURTING PEOPLE ISN'T WHAT FUN IS.
SHE WATCHED OUR ROUTINE... SO MAYBE SHE'S NOT ALL BAD!

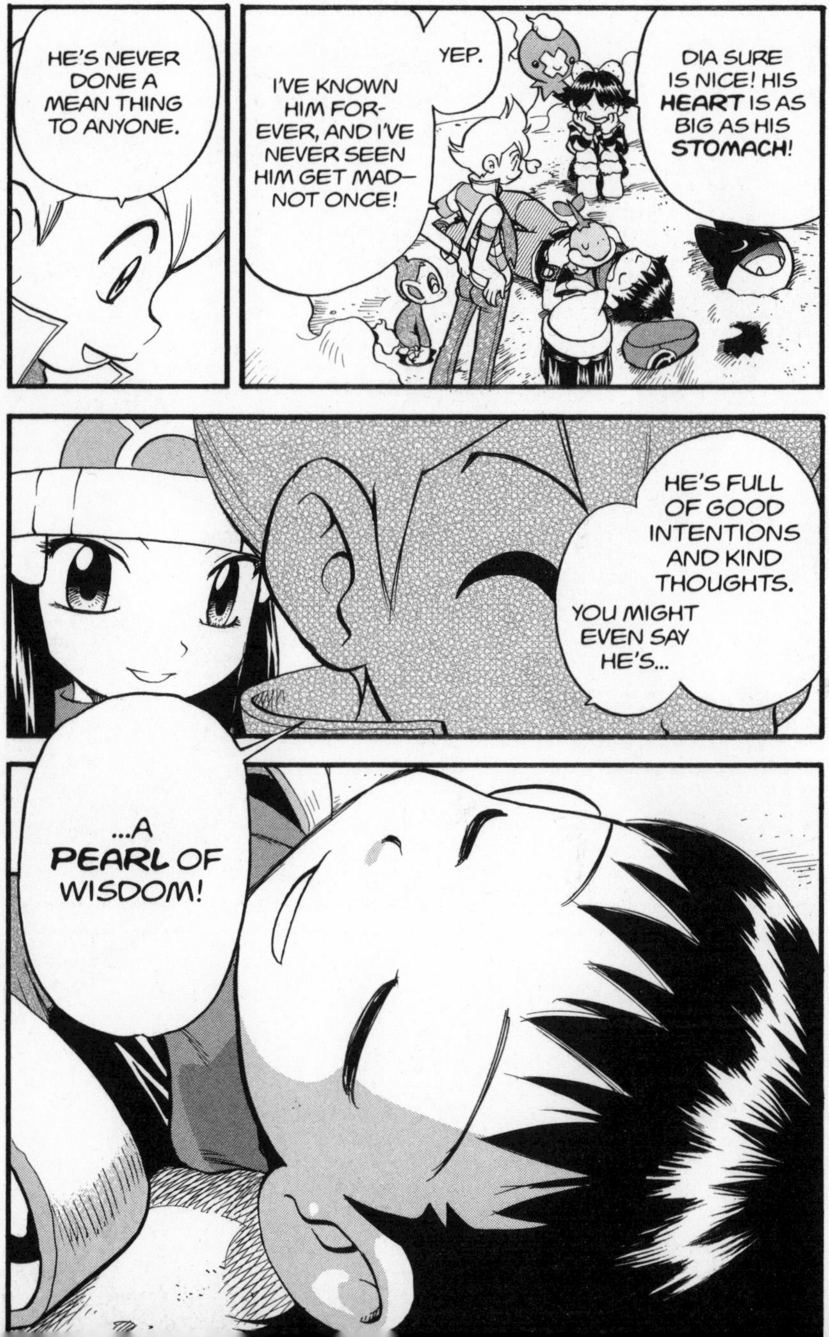

DIA SURE IS NICE! HIS **HEART** IS AS BIG AS HIS **STOMACH**!
YEP.
I'VE KNOWN HIM FOR-EVER, AND I'VE NEVER SEEN HIM GET MAD—NOT ONCE!
HE'S NEVER DONE A MEAN THING TO ANYONE.
HE'S FULL OF GOOD INTENTIONS AND KIND THOUGHTS.
YOU MIGHT EVEN SAY HE'S...
...A **PEARL** OF WISDOM!

8

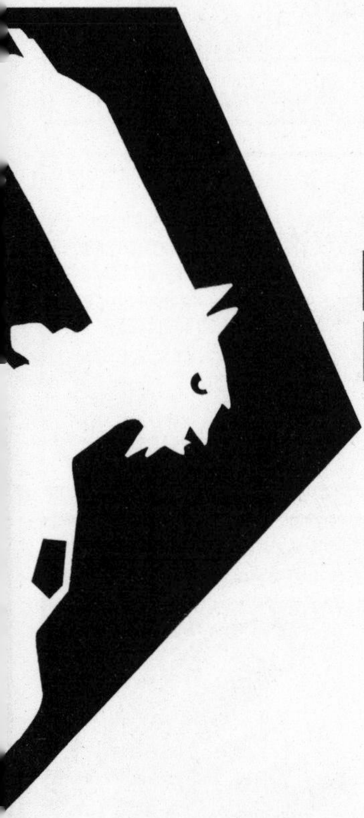

Robust Rotom

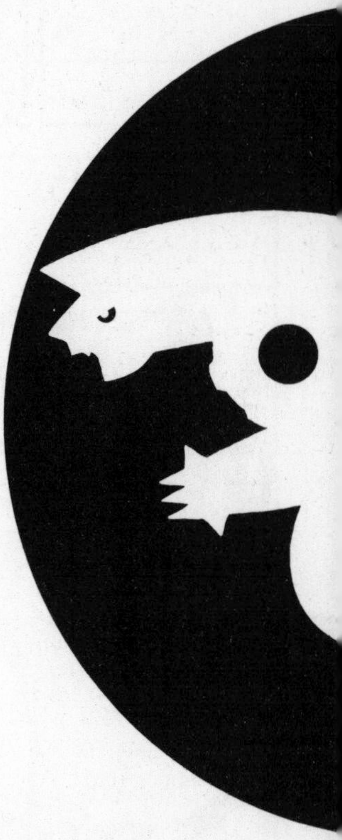

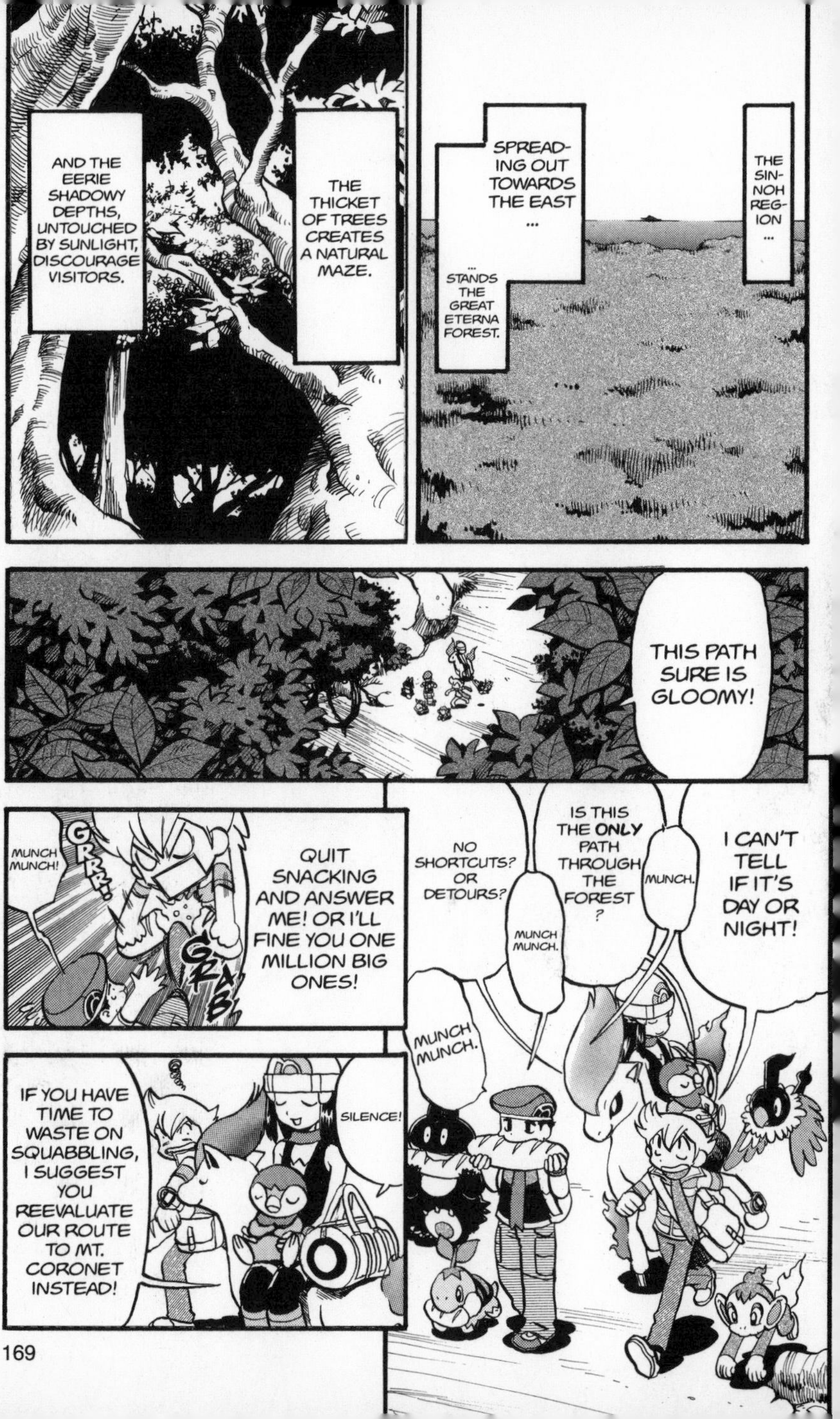
THE SINNOH REGION...
SPREADING OUT TOWARDS THE EAST...
...STANDS THE GREAT ETERNA FOREST.
THE THICKET OF TREES CREATES A NATURAL MAZE.
AND THE EERIE SHADOWY DEPTHS, UNTOUCHED BY SUNLIGHT, DISCOURAGE VISITORS.
THIS PATH SURE IS GLOOMY!
I CAN'T TELL IF IT'S DAY OR NIGHT!
MUNCH.
IS THIS THE **ONLY** PATH THROUGH THE FOREST?
MUNCH MUNCH.
NO SHORTCUTS? OR DETOURS?
MUNCH MUNCH.
GRRR!
MUNCH MUNCH!
QUIT SNACKING AND ANSWER ME! OR I'LL FINE YOU ONE MILLION BIG ONES!
GRAB
SILENCE!
IF YOU HAVE TIME TO WASTE ON SQUABBLING, I SUGGEST YOU REEVALUATE OUR ROUTE TO MT. CORONET INSTEAD!

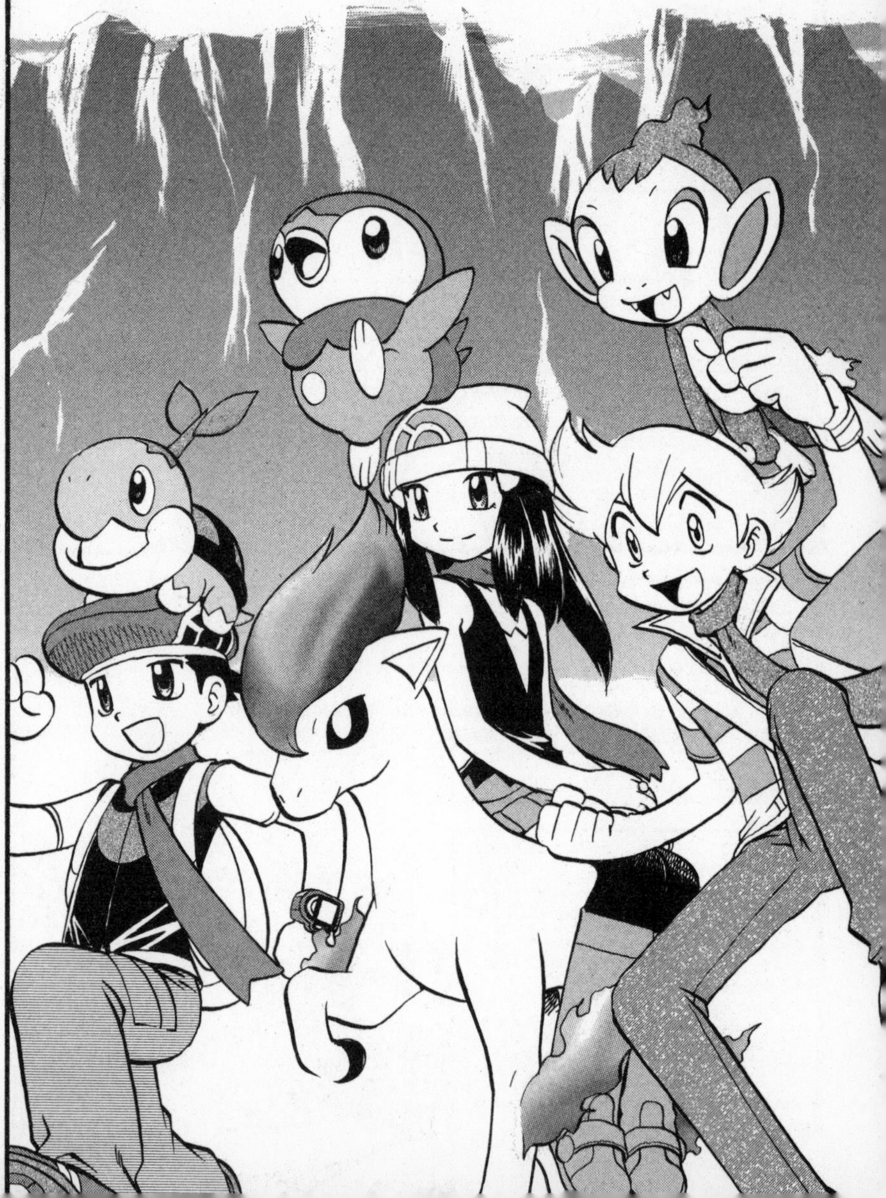

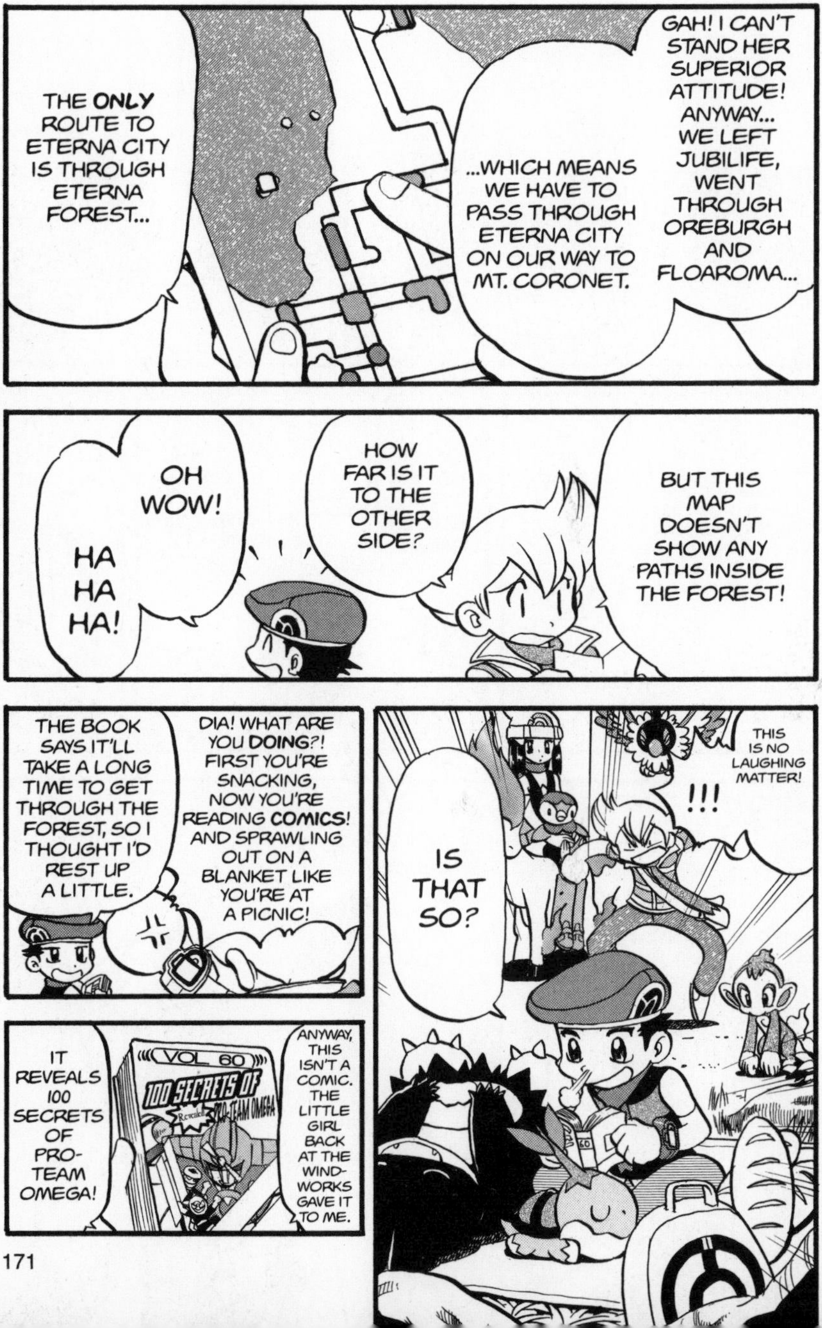
GAH! I CAN'T STAND HER SUPERIOR ATTITUDE! ANYWAY... WE LEFT JUBILIFE, WENT THROUGH OREBURGH AND FLOAROMA...
...WHICH MEANS WE HAVE TO PASS THROUGH ETERNA CITY ON OUR WAY TO MT. CORONET.
THE **ONLY** ROUTE TO ETERNA CITY IS THROUGH ETERNA FOREST...
BUT THIS MAP DOESN'T SHOW ANY PATHS INSIDE THE FOREST!
HOW FAR IS IT TO THE OTHER SIDE?
OH WOW!
HA HA HA!
THIS IS NO LAUGHING MATTER!
!!!
IS THAT SO?
DIA! WHAT ARE YOU **DOING**?! FIRST YOU'RE SNACKING, NOW YOU'RE READING **COMICS**! AND SPRAWLING OUT ON A BLANKET LIKE YOU'RE AT A PICNIC!
THE BOOK SAYS IT'LL TAKE A LONG TIME TO GET THROUGH THE FOREST, SO I THOUGHT I'D REST UP A LITTLE.
ANYWAY, THIS ISN'T A COMIC. THE LITTLE GIRL BACK AT THE WIND-WORKS GAVE IT TO ME.
VOL 60
100 SECRETS OF PRO-TEAM OMEGA
Revealed
IT REVEALS 100 SECRETS OF PRO-TEAM OMEGA!

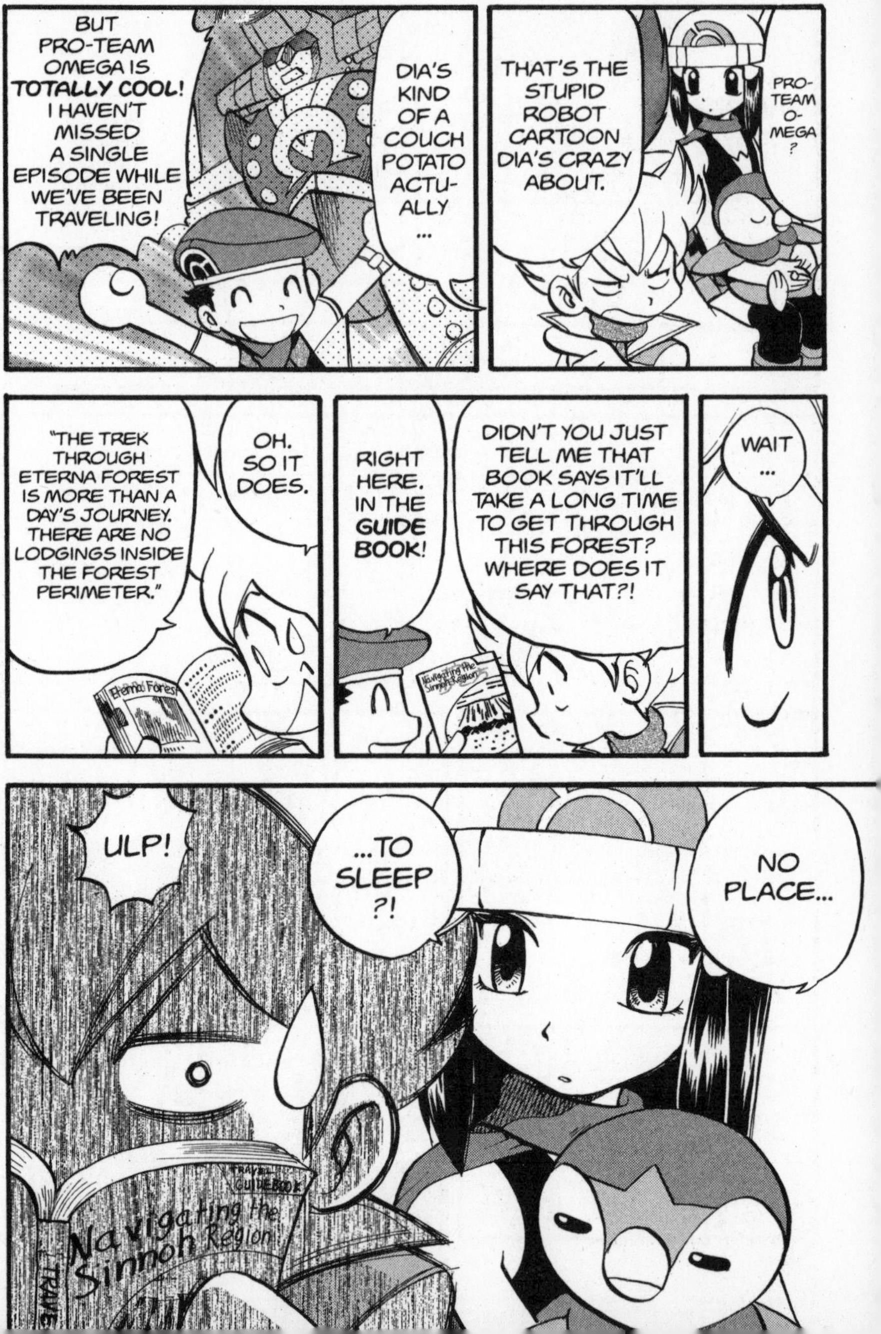
PRO-TEAM O-MEGA?
THAT'S THE STUPID ROBOT CARTOON DIA'S CRAZY ABOUT.
DIA'S KIND OF A COUCH POTATO ACTU-ALLY ...
BUT PRO-TEAM OMEGA IS **TOTALLY COOL**! I HAVEN'T MISSED A SINGLE EPISODE WHILE WE'VE BEEN TRAVELING!
WAIT ...
DIDN'T YOU JUST TELL ME THAT BOOK SAYS IT'LL TAKE A LONG TIME TO GET THROUGH THIS FOREST? WHERE DOES IT SAY THAT?!
RIGHT HERE. IN THE **GUIDE BOOK**!
Navigating the Sinnoh Region
"THE TREK THROUGH ETERNA FOREST IS MORE THAN A DAY'S JOURNEY. THERE ARE NO LODGINGS INSIDE THE FOREST PERIMETER."
OH. SO IT DOES.
Eterna Forest
NO PLACE...
...TO SLEEP ?!
ULP!
TRAVEL GUIDEBOOK
Navigating the Sinnoh Region

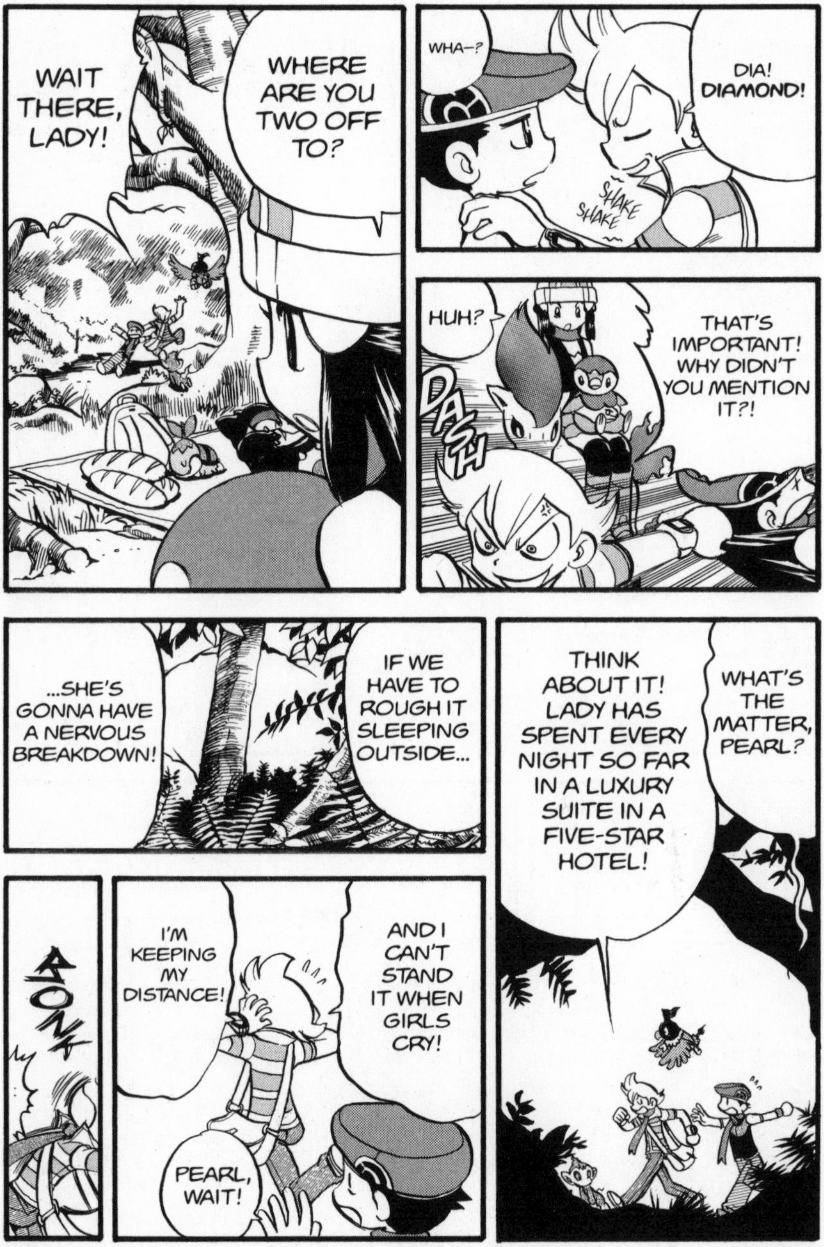
WAIT THERE, LADY!
WHERE ARE YOU TWO OFF TO?
WHA–?
DIA! DIAMOND!
SHAKE SHAKE
HUH?
THAT'S IMPORTANT! WHY DIDN'T YOU MENTION IT?!
DASH
WHAT'S THE MATTER, PEARL?
THINK ABOUT IT! LADY HAS SPENT EVERY NIGHT SO FAR IN A LUXURY SUITE IN A FIVE-STAR HOTEL!
IF WE HAVE TO ROUGH IT SLEEPING OUTSIDE...
...SHE'S GONNA HAVE A NERVOUS BREAKDOWN!
I'M KEEPING MY DISTANCE!
AND I CAN'T STAND IT WHEN GIRLS CRY!
PEARL, WAIT!
BONK

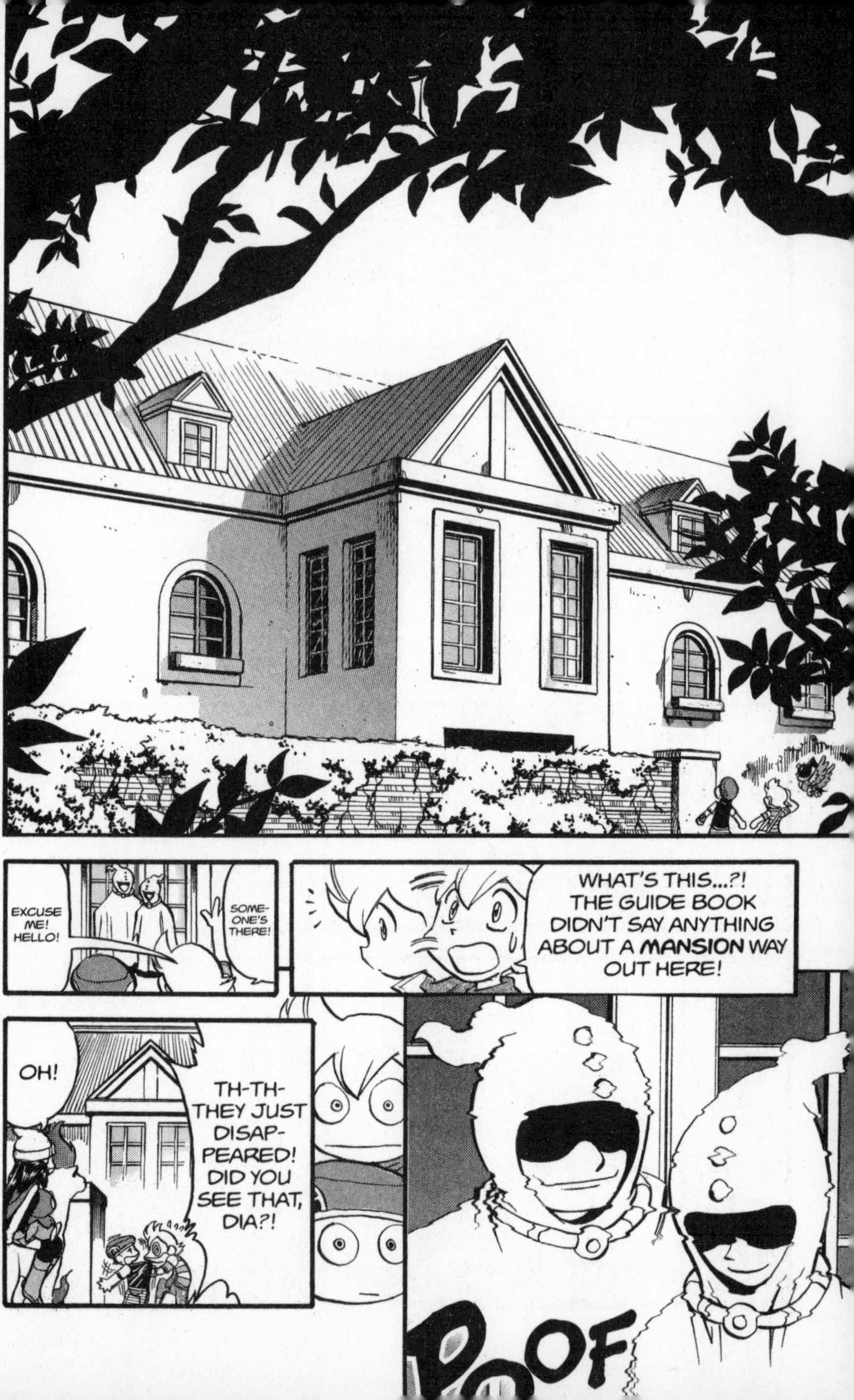
WHAT'S THIS...?! THE GUIDE BOOK DIDN'T SAY ANYTHING ABOUT A MANSION WAY OUT HERE!
SOME-ONE'S THERE!
EXCUSE ME! HELLO!
POOF
TH-TH-THEY JUST DISAP-PEARED! DID YOU SEE THAT, DIA?!
OH!

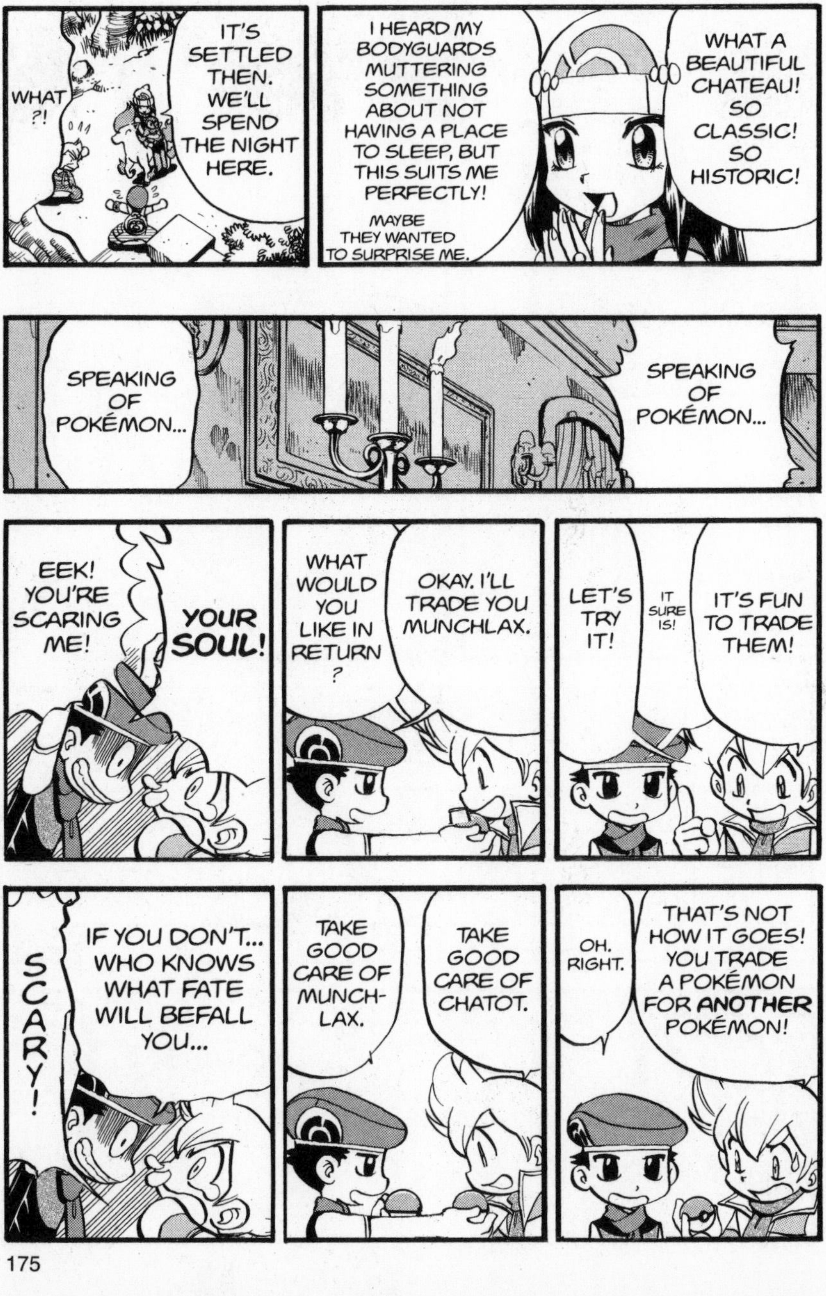
WHAT A BEAUTIFUL CHATEAU! SO CLASSIC! SO HISTORIC!
I HEARD MY BODYGUARDS MUTTERING SOMETHING ABOUT NOT HAVING A PLACE TO SLEEP, BUT THIS SUITS ME PERFECTLY!
MAYBE THEY WANTED TO SURPRISE ME.
IT'S SETTLED THEN. WE'LL SPEND THE NIGHT HERE.
WHAT ?!
SPEAKING OF POKÉMON...
SPEAKING OF POKÉMON...
IT'S FUN TO TRADE THEM!
IT SURE IS!
LET'S TRY IT!
OKAY. I'LL TRADE YOU MUNCHLAX.
WHAT WOULD YOU LIKE IN RETURN ?
YOUR SOUL!
EEK! YOU'RE SCARING ME!
THAT'S NOT HOW IT GOES! YOU TRADE A POKÉMON FOR ANOTHER POKÉMON!
OH. RIGHT.
TAKE GOOD CARE OF CHATOT.
TAKE GOOD CARE OF MUNCH-LAX.
IF YOU DON'T... WHO KNOWS WHAT FATE WILL BEFALL YOU...
SCARY!

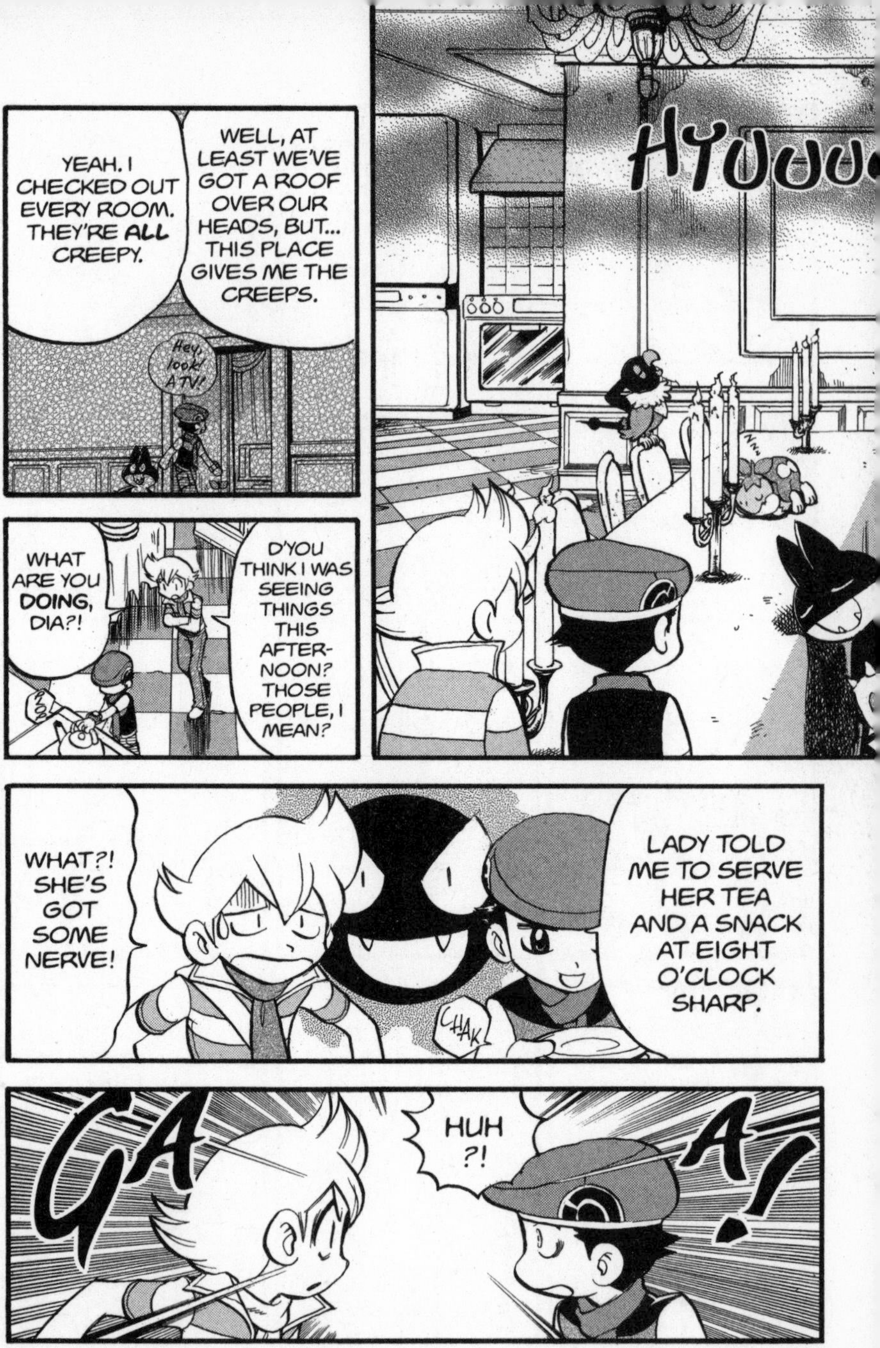
HYUUUU
WELL, AT LEAST WE'VE GOT A ROOF OVER OUR HEADS, BUT... THIS PLACE GIVES ME THE CREEPS.
YEAH. I CHECKED OUT EVERY ROOM. THEY'RE ALL CREEPY.
Hey, look! A TV!
D'YOU THINK I WAS SEEING THINGS THIS AFTER-NOON? THOSE PEOPLE, I MEAN?
WHAT ARE YOU DOING, DIA?!
LADY TOLD ME TO SERVE HER TEA AND A SNACK AT EIGHT O'CLOCK SHARP.
CHAK
WHAT?! SHE'S GOT SOME NERVE!
GA
A!
HUH ?!

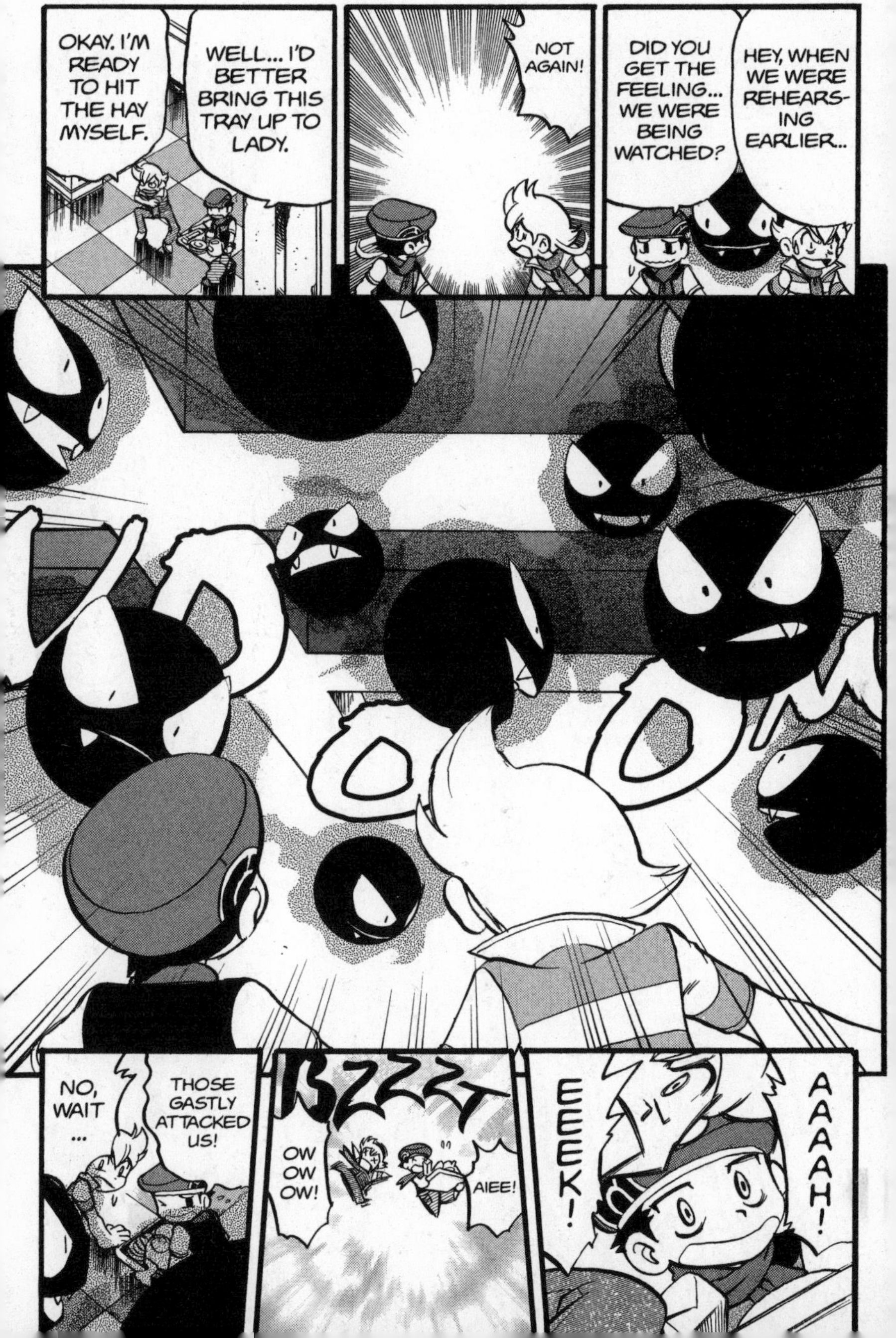

OKAY. I'M READY TO HIT THE HAY MYSELF.
WELL... I'D BETTER BRING THIS TRAY UP TO LADY.
NOT AGAIN!
HEY, WHEN WE WERE REHEARS-ING EARLIER...
DID YOU GET THE FEELING... WE WERE BEING WATCHED?
DOOM
NO, WAIT ...
THOSE GASTLY ATTACKED US!
BZZZT
OW OW OW!
AIEE!
EEEEK!
AAAAH!

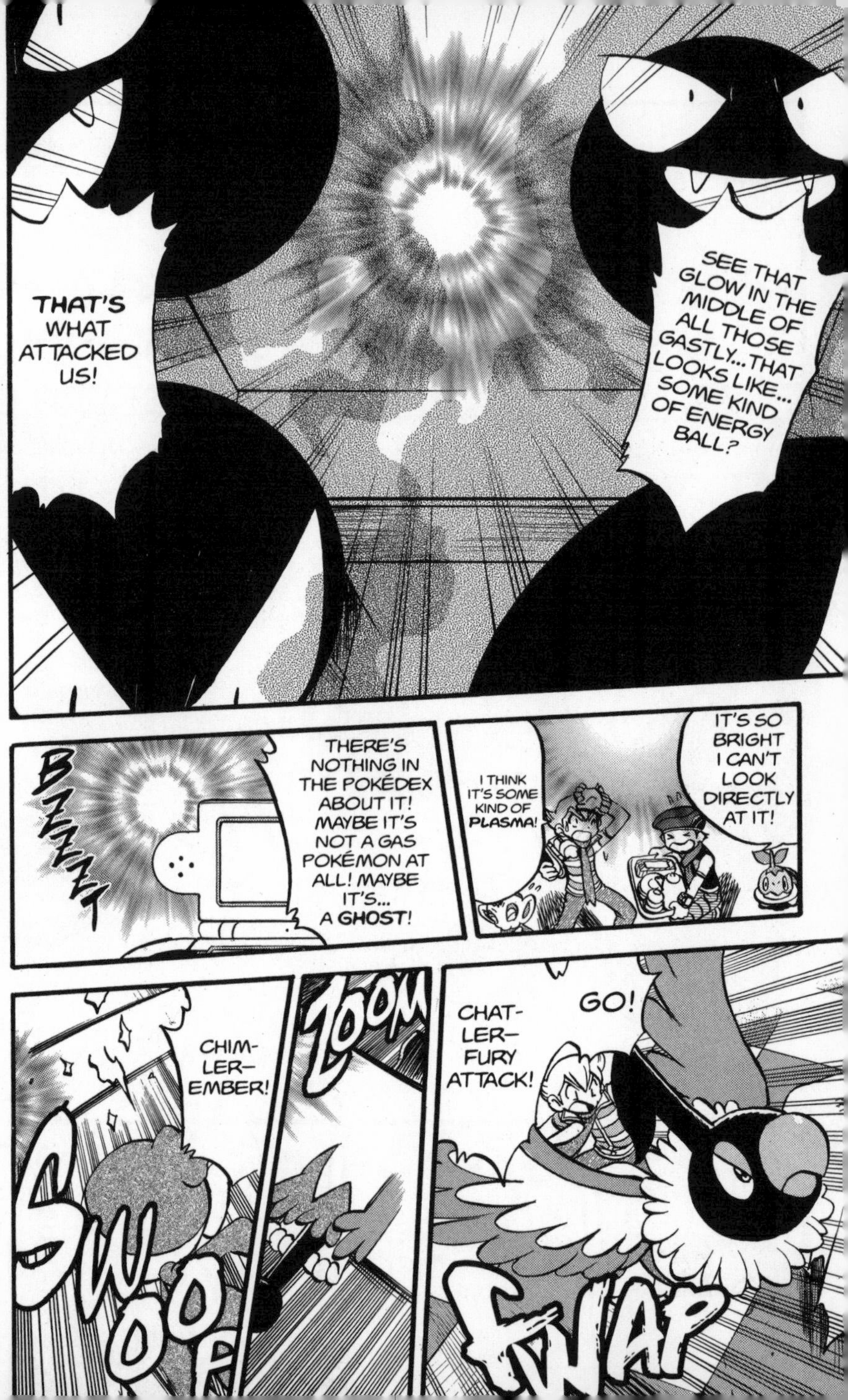
SEE THAT GLOW IN THE MIDDLE OF ALL THOSE GASTLY...THAT LOOKS LIKE... SOME KIND OF ENERGY BALL?
THAT'S WHAT ATTACKED US!
BZZZZZT
THERE'S NOTHING IN THE POKÉDEX ABOUT IT! MAYBE IT'S NOT A GAS POKÉMON AT ALL! MAYBE IT'S... A GHOST!
IT'S SO BRIGHT I CAN'T LOOK DIRECTLY AT IT!
I THINK IT'S SOME KIND OF PLASMA!
CHIM-LER-EMBER!
SWOOF
ZOOM
CHAT-LER-FURY ATTACK!
GO!
FWAP

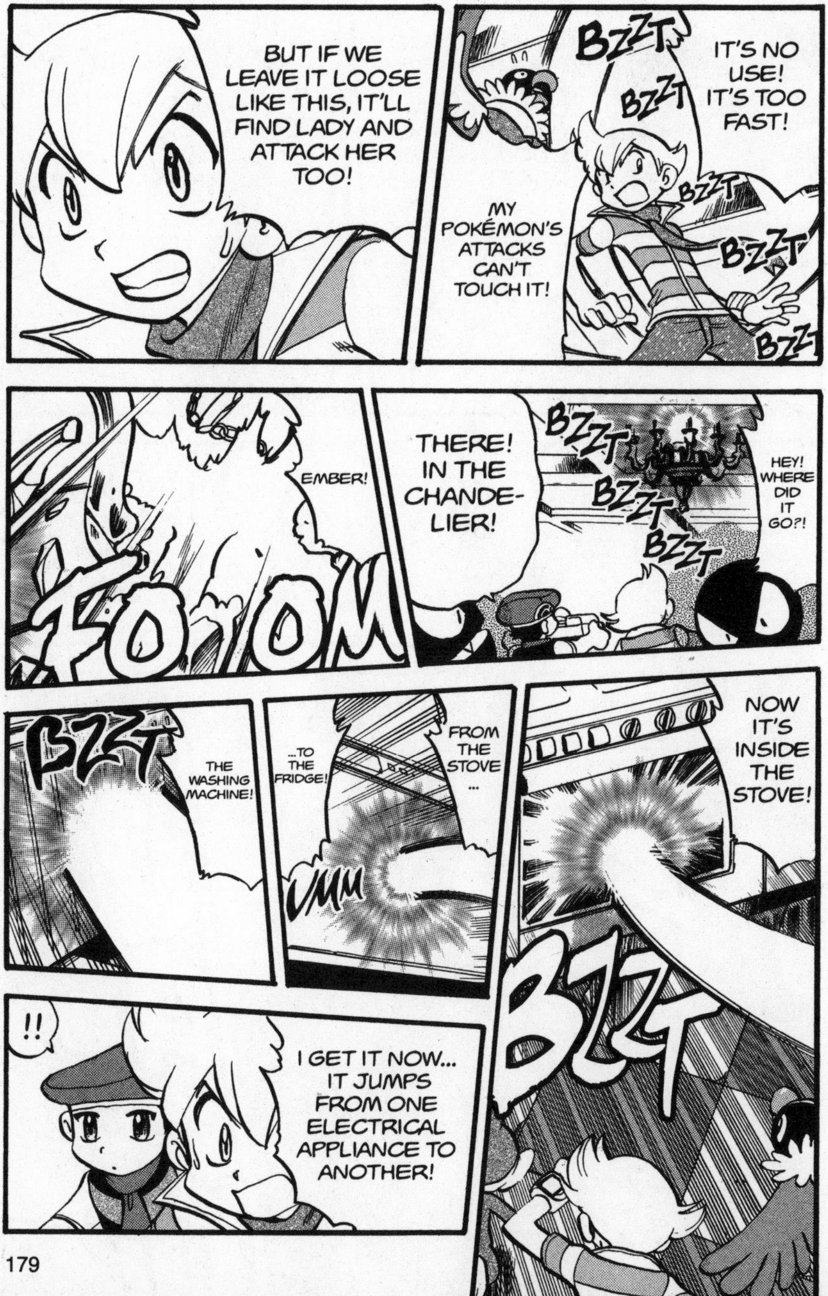
BUT IF WE LEAVE IT LOOSE LIKE THIS, IT'LL FIND LADY AND ATTACK HER TOO!
BZZT
IT'S NO USE! IT'S TOO FAST!
BZZT
MY POKéMON'S ATTACKS CAN'T TOUCH IT!
BZZT
BZZT
BZZT
EMBER!
FOOOM
THERE! IN THE CHANDE-LIER!
BZZT
BZZT
BZZT
HEY! WHERE DID IT GO?!
BZZT
THE WASHING MACHINE!
...TO THE FRIDGE!
VMM
FROM THE STOVE ...
NOW IT'S INSIDE THE STOVE!
BZZT
!!
I GET IT NOW... IT JUMPS FROM ONE ELECTRICAL APPLIANCE TO ANOTHER!

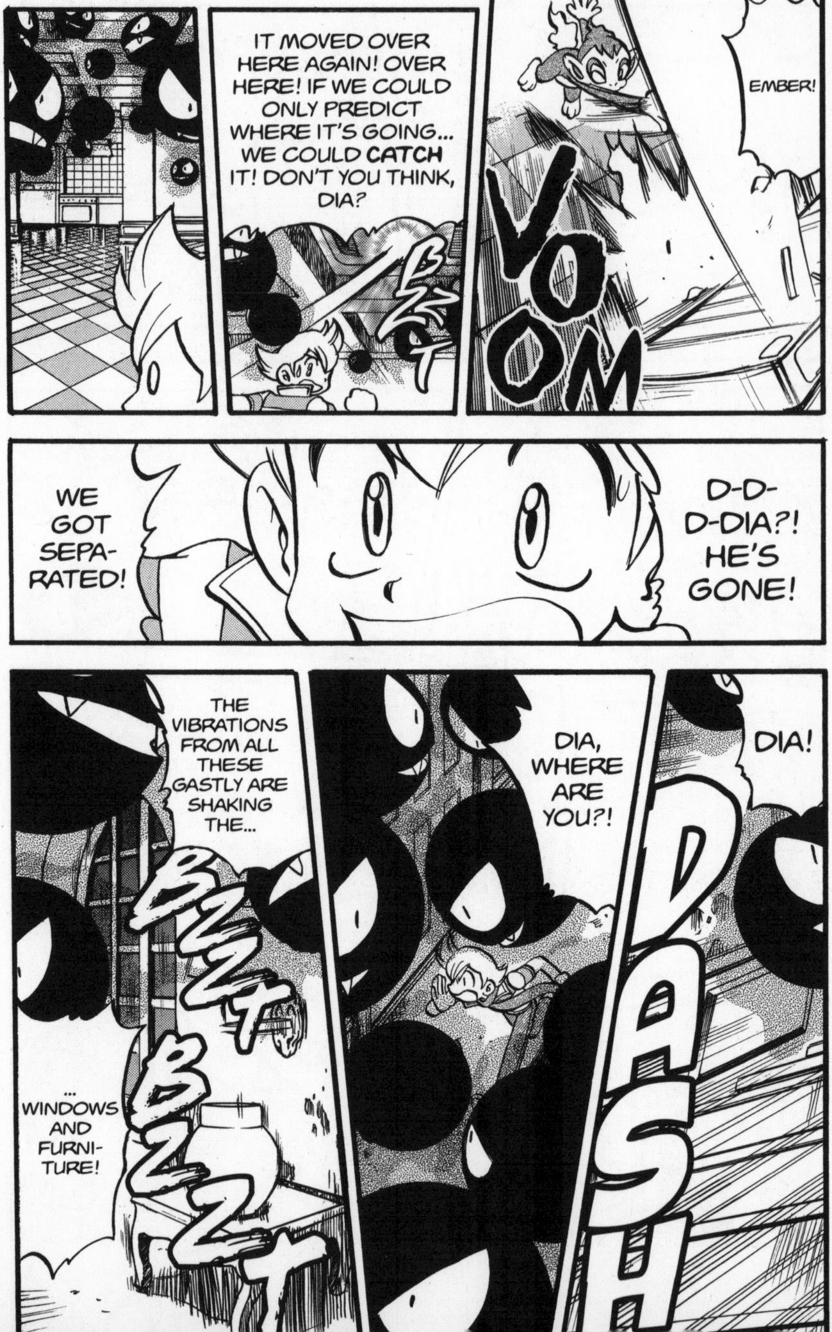
IT MOVED OVER HERE AGAIN! OVER HERE! IF WE COULD ONLY PREDICT WHERE IT'S GOING... WE COULD **CATCH** IT! DON'T YOU THINK, DIA?
BZZT
VOOM
EMBER!
WE GOT SEPA-RATED!
D-D-D-DIA?! HE'S GONE!
THE VIBRATIONS FROM ALL THESE GASTLY ARE SHAKING THE...
BZZZT
BZZZT
...WINDOWS AND FURNI-TURE!
DIA, WHERE ARE YOU?!
DIA!
DASH

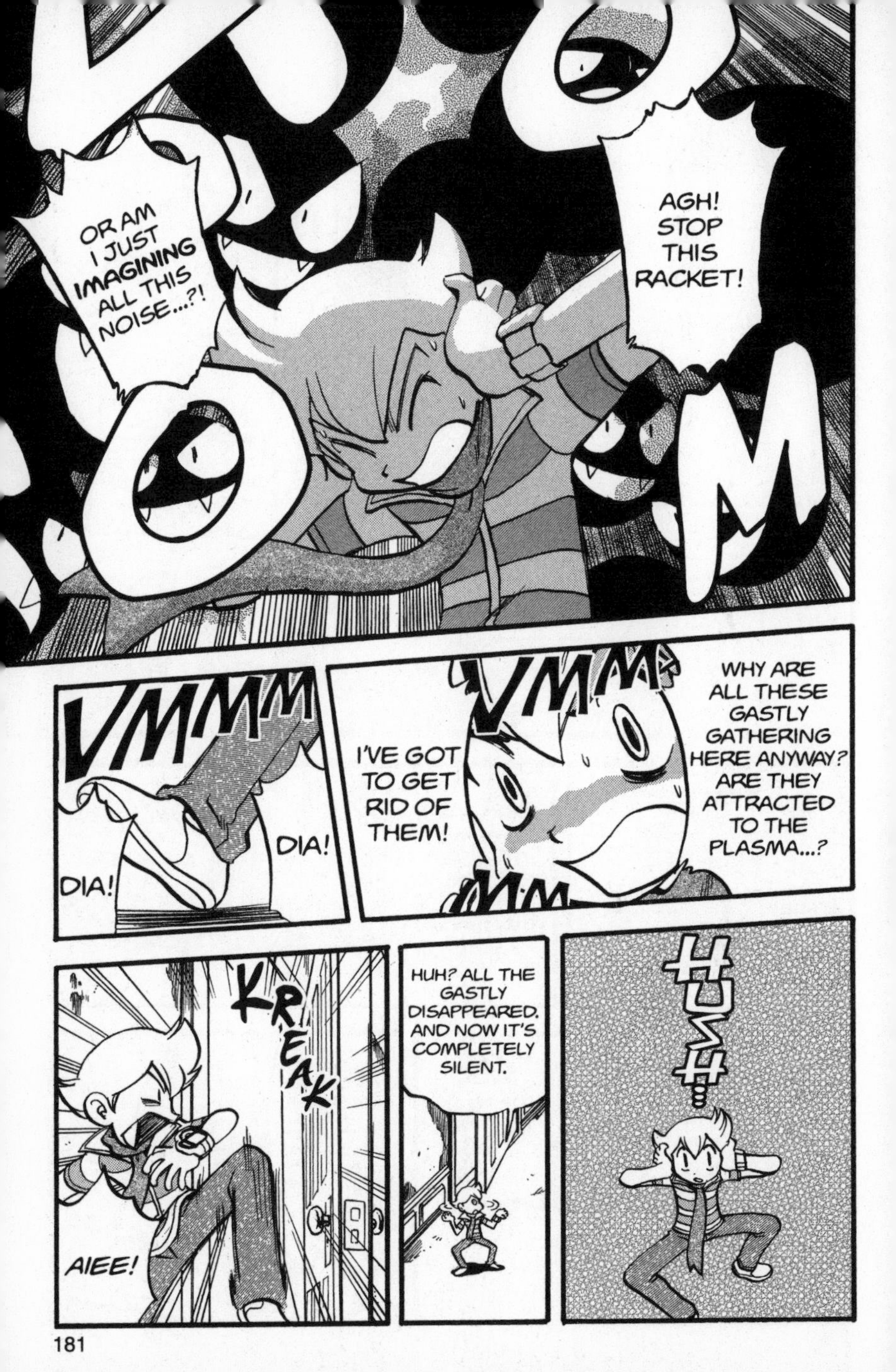
OR AM I JUST IMAGINING ALL THIS NOISE...?!
AGH! STOP THIS RACKET!
VMMM
DIA!
DIA!
VMMM
I'VE GOT TO GET RID OF THEM!
WHY ARE ALL THESE GASTLY GATHERING HERE ANYWAY? ARE THEY ATTRACTED TO THE PLASMA...?
KREAK
AIEE!
HUH? ALL THE GASTLY DISAPPEARED. AND NOW IT'S COMPLETELY SILENT.
HUSH

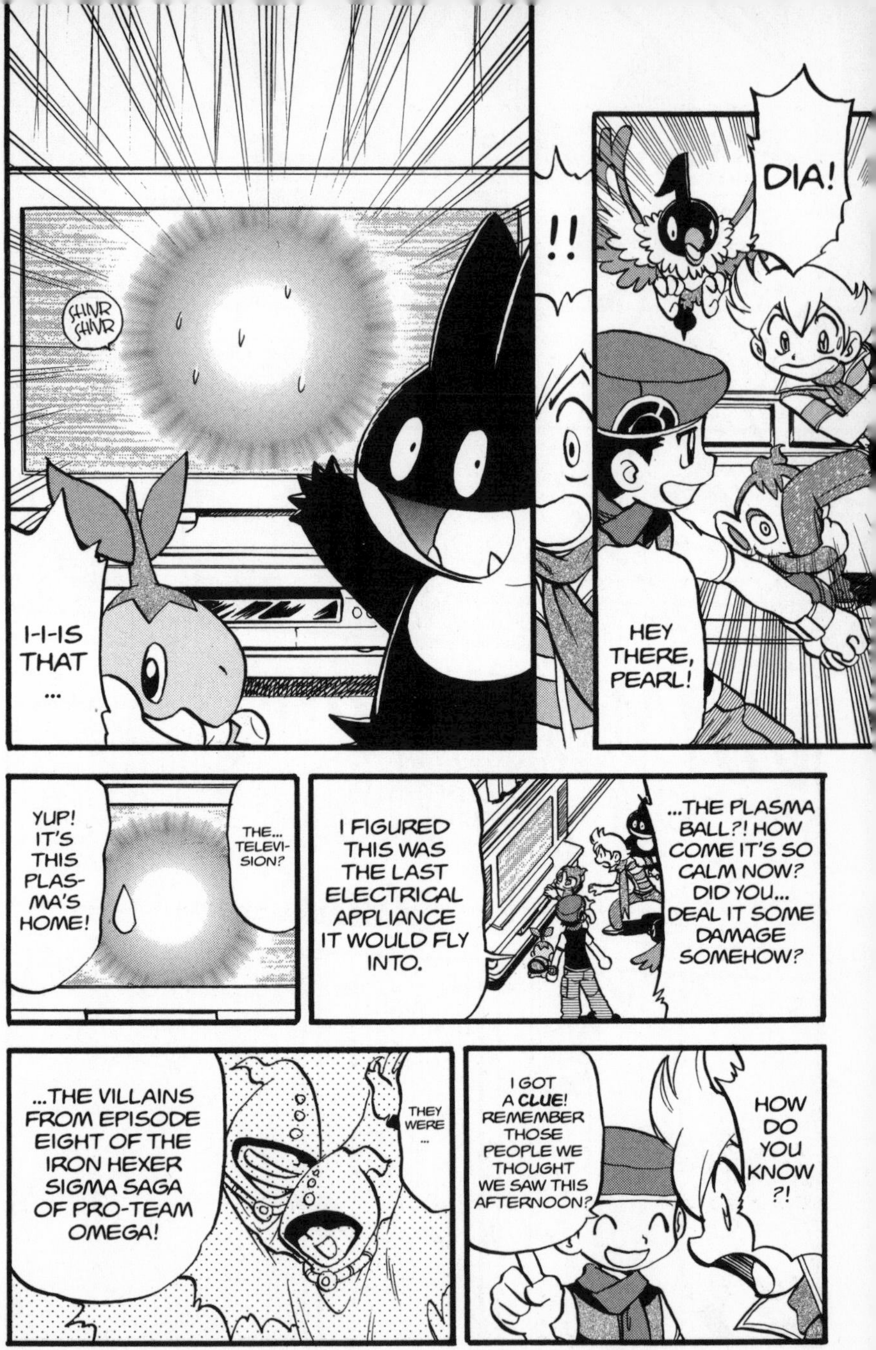
DIA!
HEY THERE, PEARL!
!!
SHIVR SHIVR
I-I-IS THAT ...
...THE PLASMA BALL?! HOW COME IT'S SO CALM NOW? DID YOU... DEAL IT SOME DAMAGE SOMEHOW?
I FIGURED THIS WAS THE LAST ELECTRICAL APPLIANCE IT WOULD FLY INTO.
THE... TELEVISION?
YUP! IT'S THIS PLASMA'S HOME!
HOW DO YOU KNOW?!
I GOT A **CLUE**! REMEMBER THOSE PEOPLE WE THOUGHT WE SAW THIS AFTERNOON?
THEY WERE ...
...THE VILLAINS FROM EPISODE EIGHT OF THE IRON HEXER SIGMA SAGA OF PRO-TEAM OMEGA!

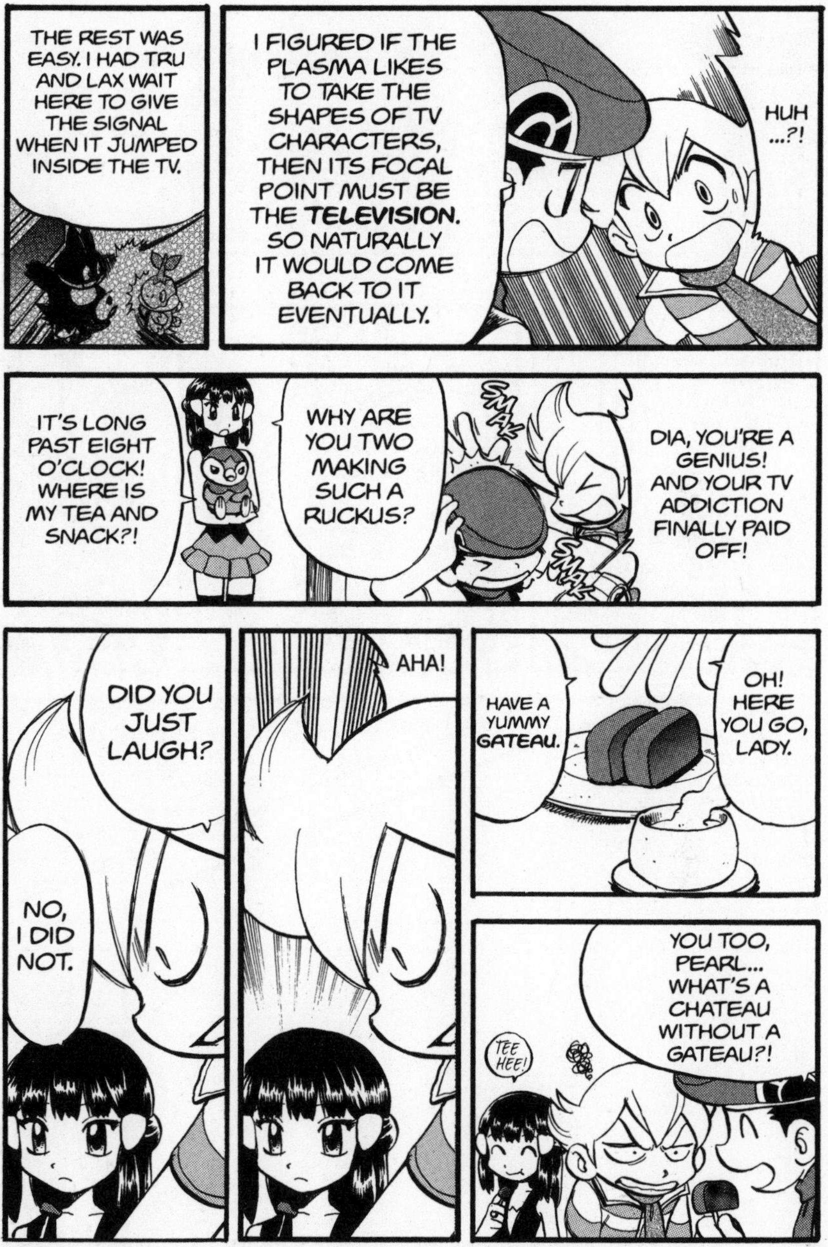
THE REST WAS EASY. I HAD TRU AND LAX WAIT HERE TO GIVE THE SIGNAL WHEN IT JUMPED INSIDE THE TV.
I FIGURED IF THE PLASMA LIKES TO TAKE THE SHAPES OF TV CHARACTERS, THEN ITS FOCAL POINT MUST BE THE **TELEVISION.** SO NATURALLY IT WOULD COME BACK TO IT EVENTUALLY.
HUH ...?!
DIA, YOU'RE A GENIUS! AND YOUR TV ADDICTION FINALLY PAID OFF!
SMAK
SMAK
WHY ARE YOU TWO MAKING SUCH A RUCKUS?
IT'S LONG PAST EIGHT O'CLOCK! WHERE IS MY TEA AND SNACK?!
OH! HERE YOU GO, LADY.
HAVE A YUMMY **GATEAU.**
YOU TOO, PEARL... WHAT'S A CHATEAU WITHOUT A GATEAU?!
TEE HEE!
DID YOU JUST LAUGH?
NO, I DID NOT.
AHA!

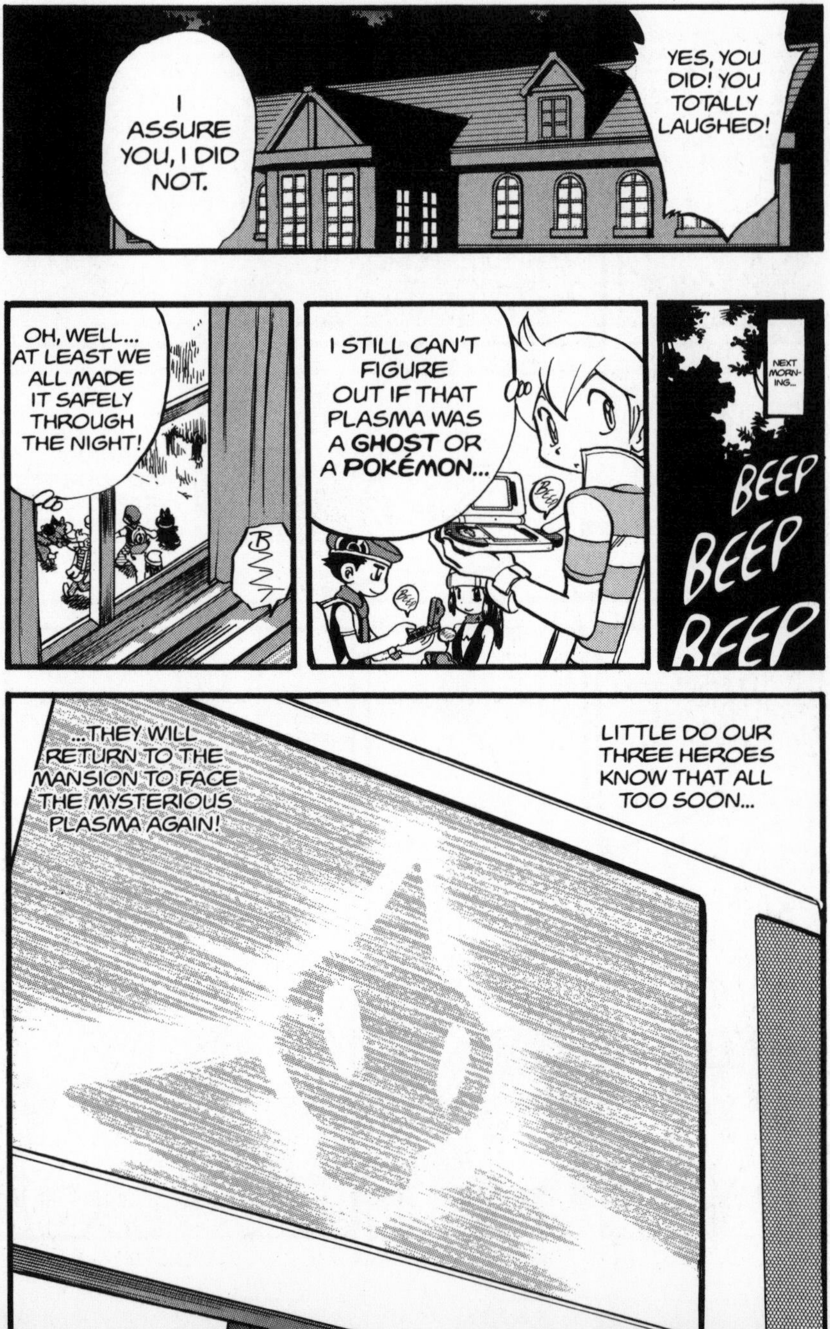
YES, YOU DID! YOU TOTALLY LAUGHED!
I ASSURE YOU, I DID NOT.
NEXT MORNING...
BEEP
BEEP
BEEP
I STILL CAN'T FIGURE OUT IF THAT PLASMA WAS A **GHOST** OR A **POKÉMON**...
OH, WELL... AT LEAST WE ALL MADE IT SAFELY THROUGH THE NIGHT!
LITTLE DO OUR THREE HEROES KNOW THAT ALL TOO SOON...
...THEY WILL RETURN TO THE MANSION TO FACE THE MYSTERIOUS PLASMA AGAIN!

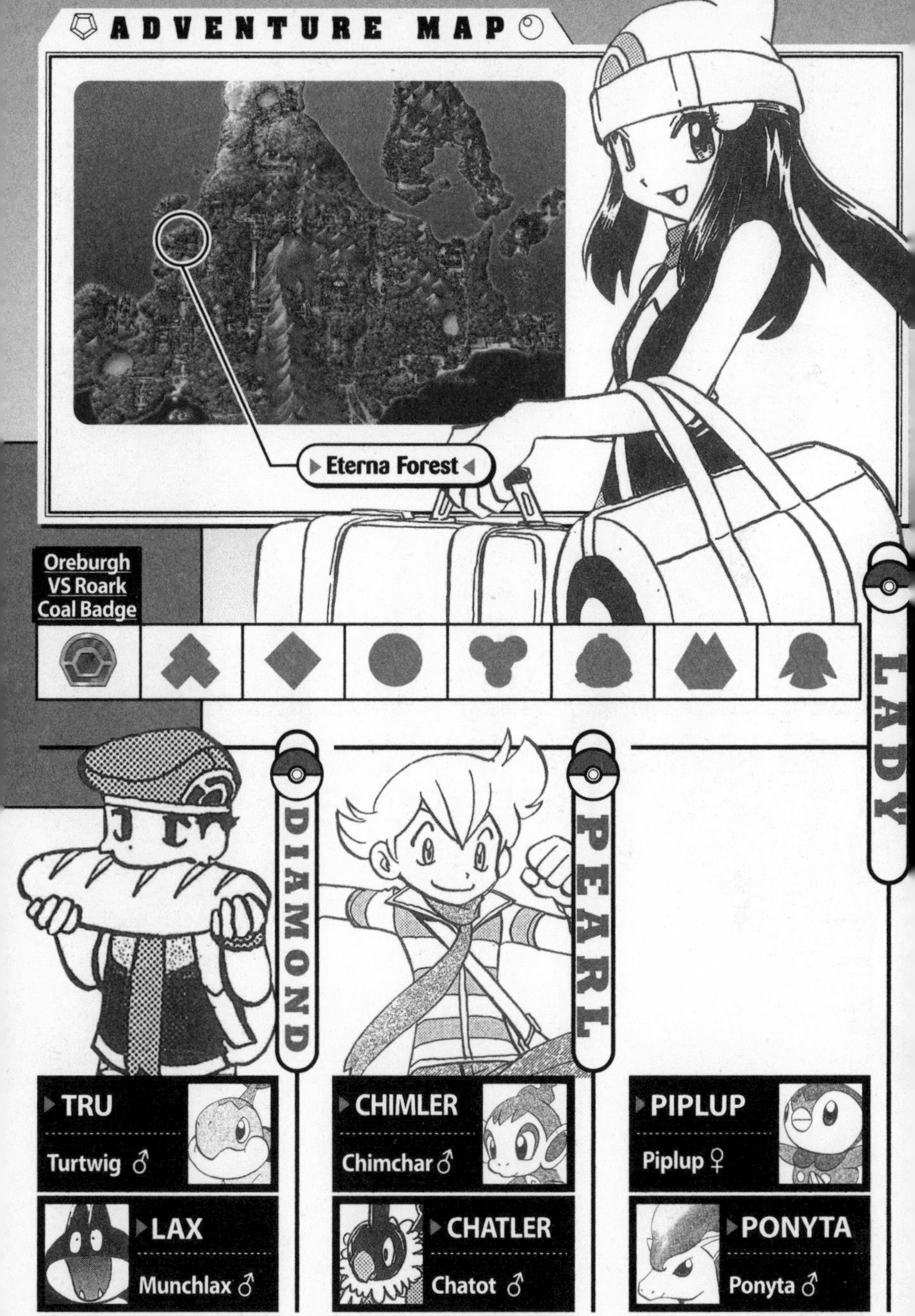
ADVENTURE MAP
Eterna Forest
Oreburgh
VS Roark
Coal Badge
LADY
DIAMOND
PEARL
TRU
Turtwig ♂
LAX
Munchlax ♂
CHIMLER
Chimchar ♂
CHATLER
Chatot ♂
PIPLUP
Piplup ♀
PONYTA
Ponyta ♂

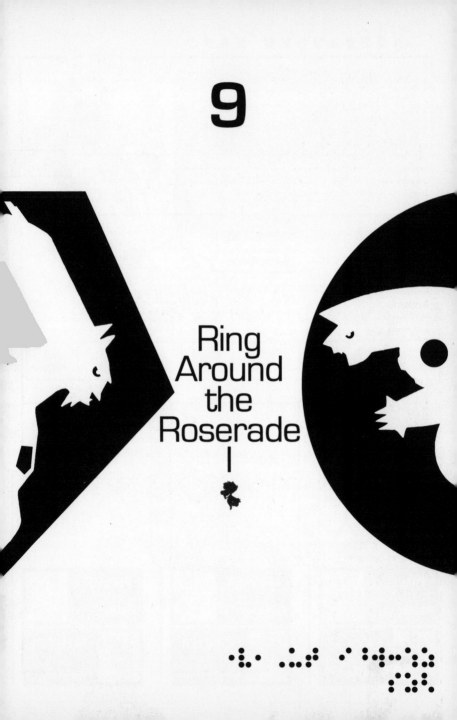

9

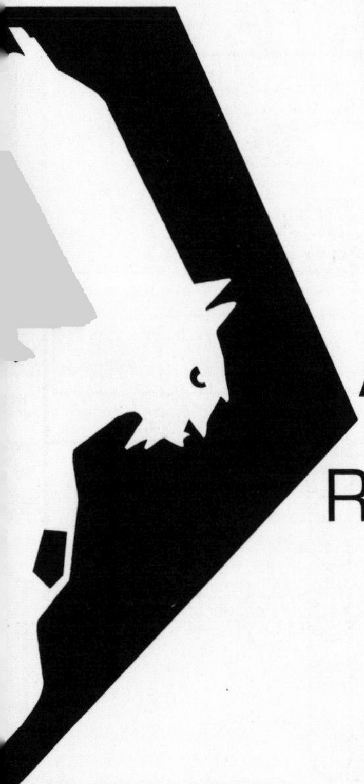

Ring Around the Roserade I

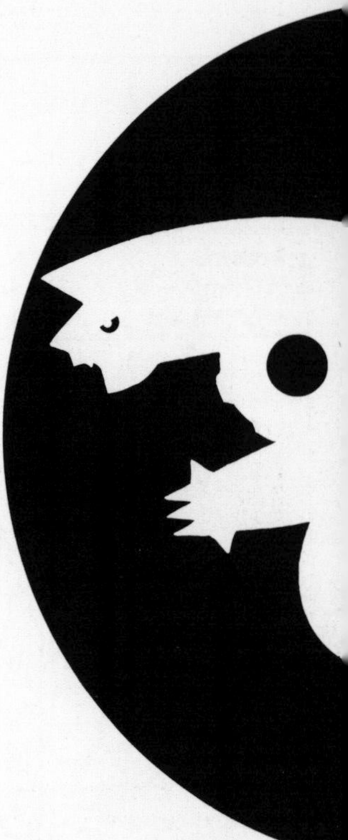

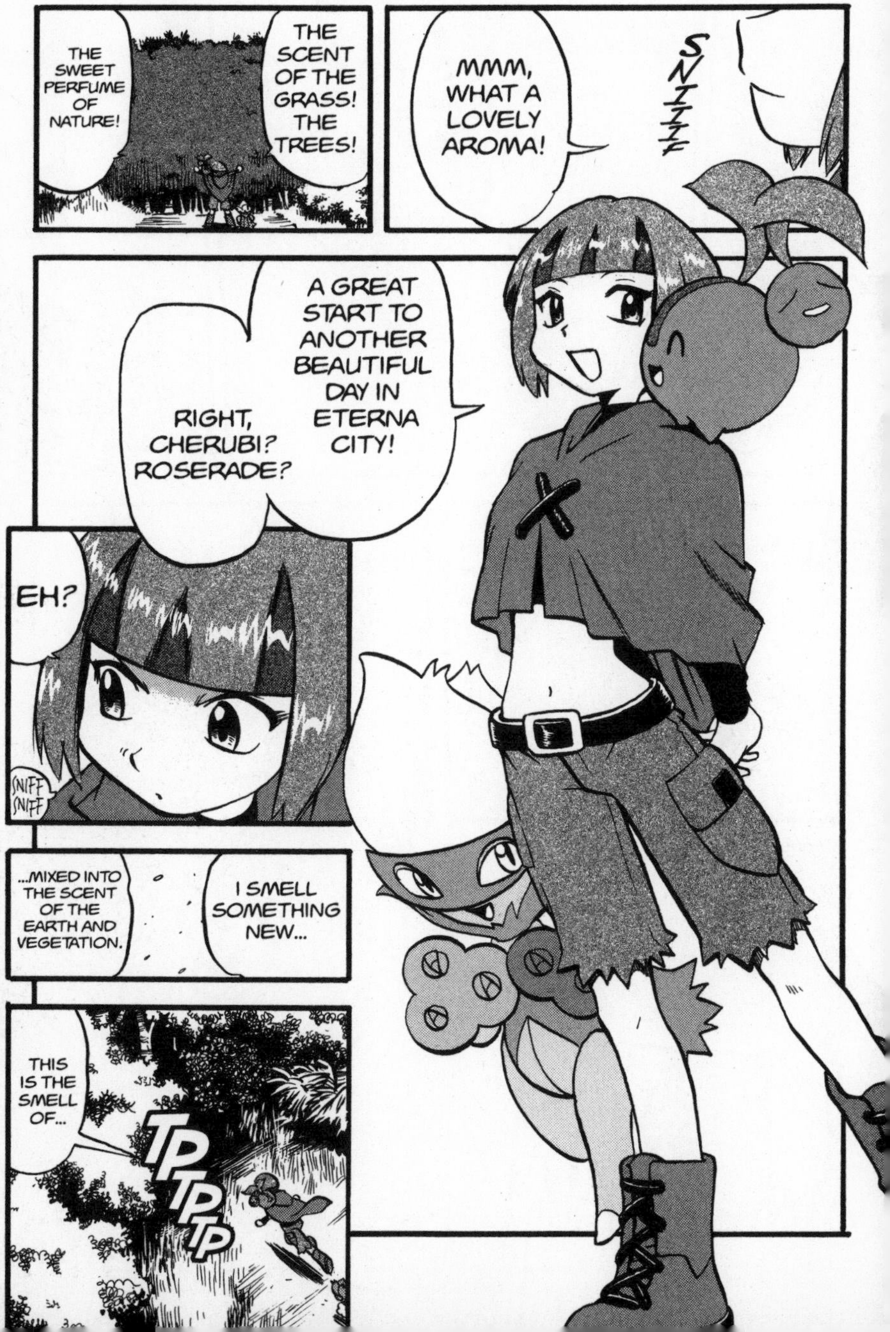
THE SWEET PERFUME OF NATURE!
THE SCENT OF THE GRASS! THE TREES!
MMM, WHAT A LOVELY AROMA!
SNIIIIFF
A GREAT START TO ANOTHER BEAUTIFUL DAY IN ETERNA CITY!
RIGHT, CHERUBI? ROSERADE?
EH?
SNIFF SNIFF
...MIXED INTO THE SCENT OF THE EARTH AND VEGETATION.
I SMELL SOMETHING NEW...
THIS IS THE SMELL OF...
TPTPTP

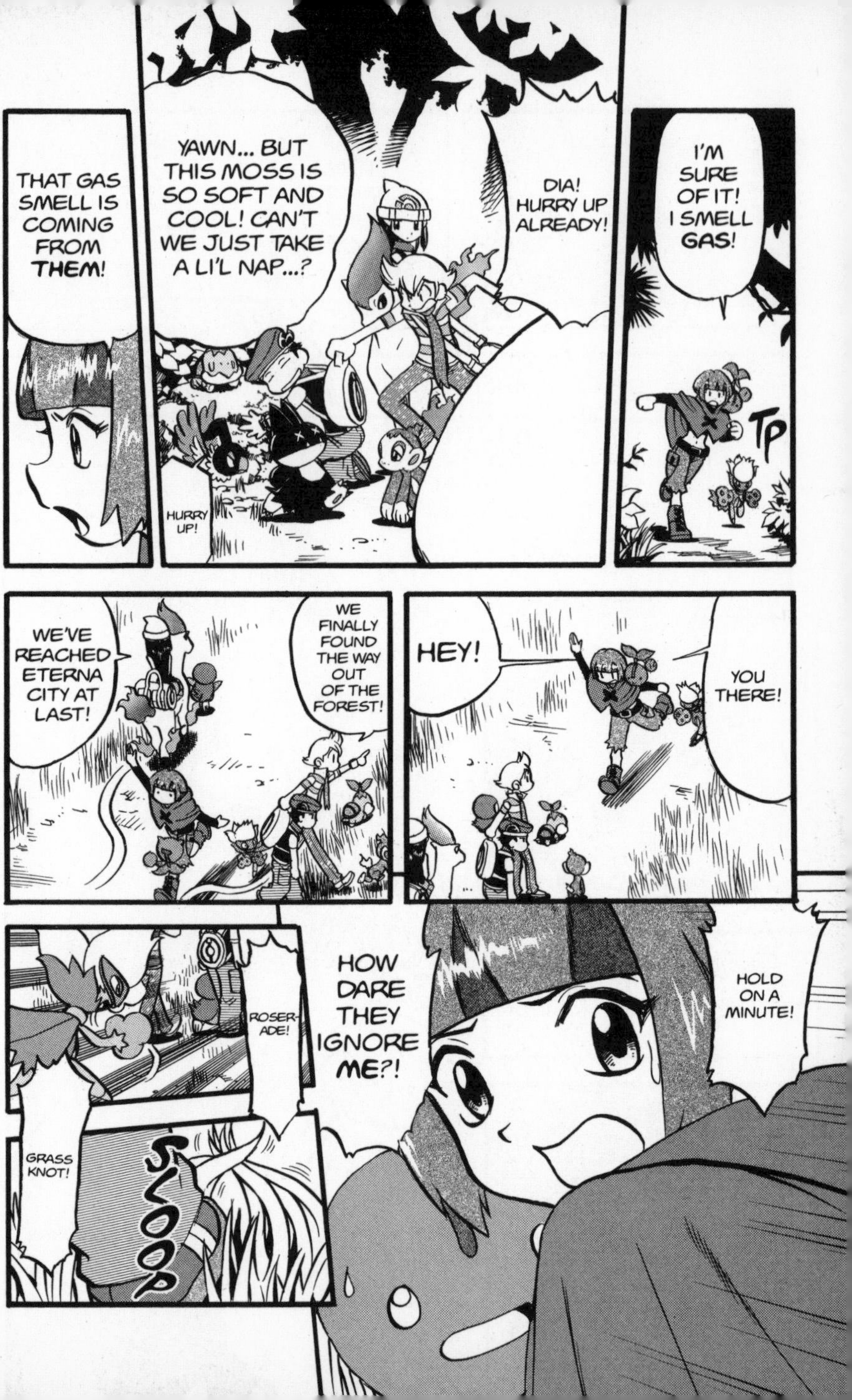
I'M SURE OF IT! I SMELL GAS!
DIA! HURRY UP ALREADY!
YAWN... BUT THIS MOSS IS SO SOFT AND COOL! CAN'T WE JUST TAKE A LI'L NAP...?
HURRY UP!
TP
THAT GAS SMELL IS COMING FROM THEM!
WE FINALLY FOUND THE WAY OUT OF THE FOREST!
WE'VE REACHED ETERNA CITY AT LAST!
YOU THERE!
HEY!
HOLD ON A MINUTE!
HOW DARE THEY IGNORE ME?!
ROSER-ADE!
GRASS KNOT!
SLOOP

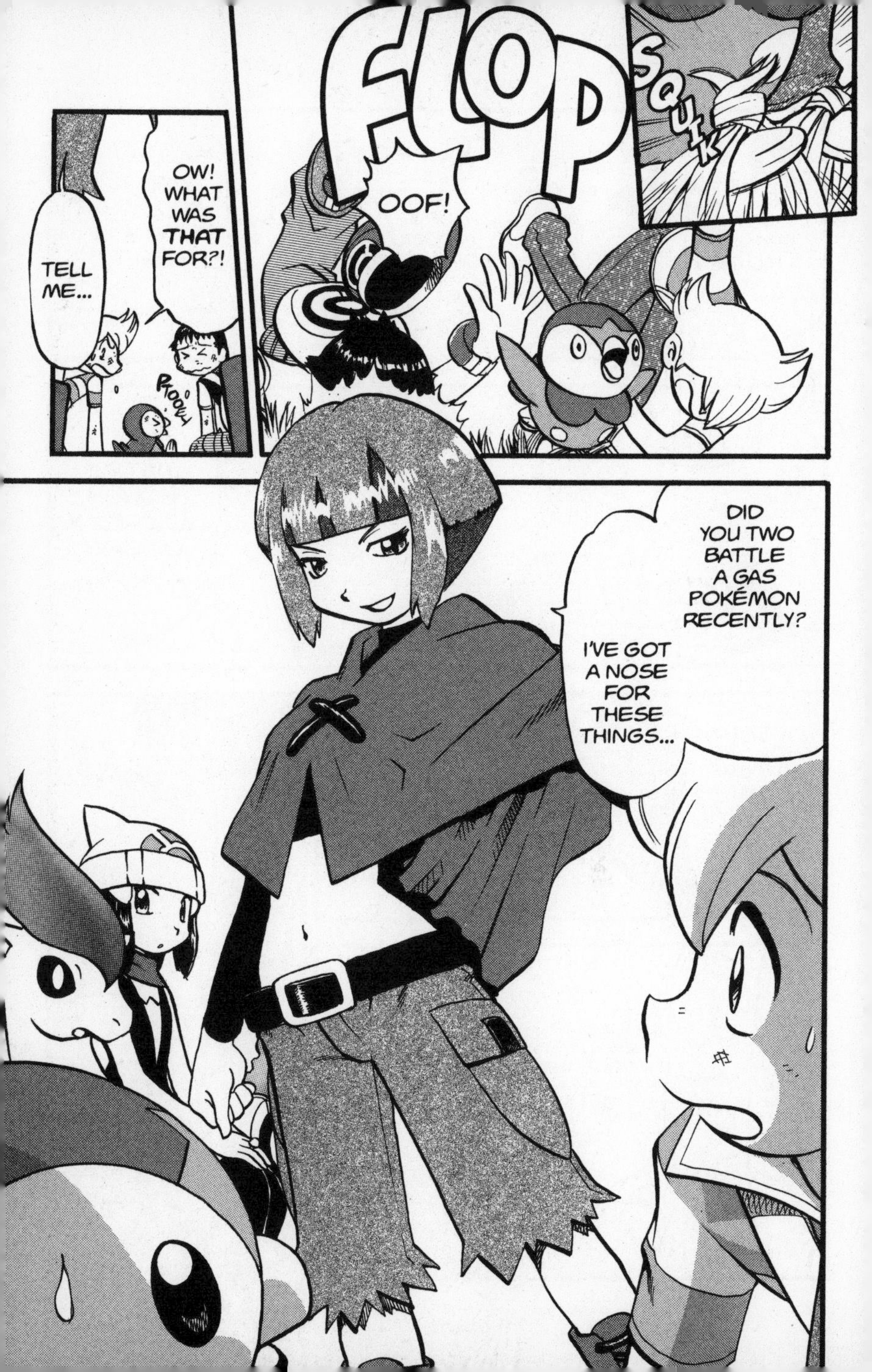

FLOP
SQUIK
OOF!
OW! WHAT WAS THAT FOR?!
TELL ME...
DID YOU TWO BATTLE A GAS POKÉMON RECENTLY?
I'VE GOT A NOSE FOR THESE THINGS...

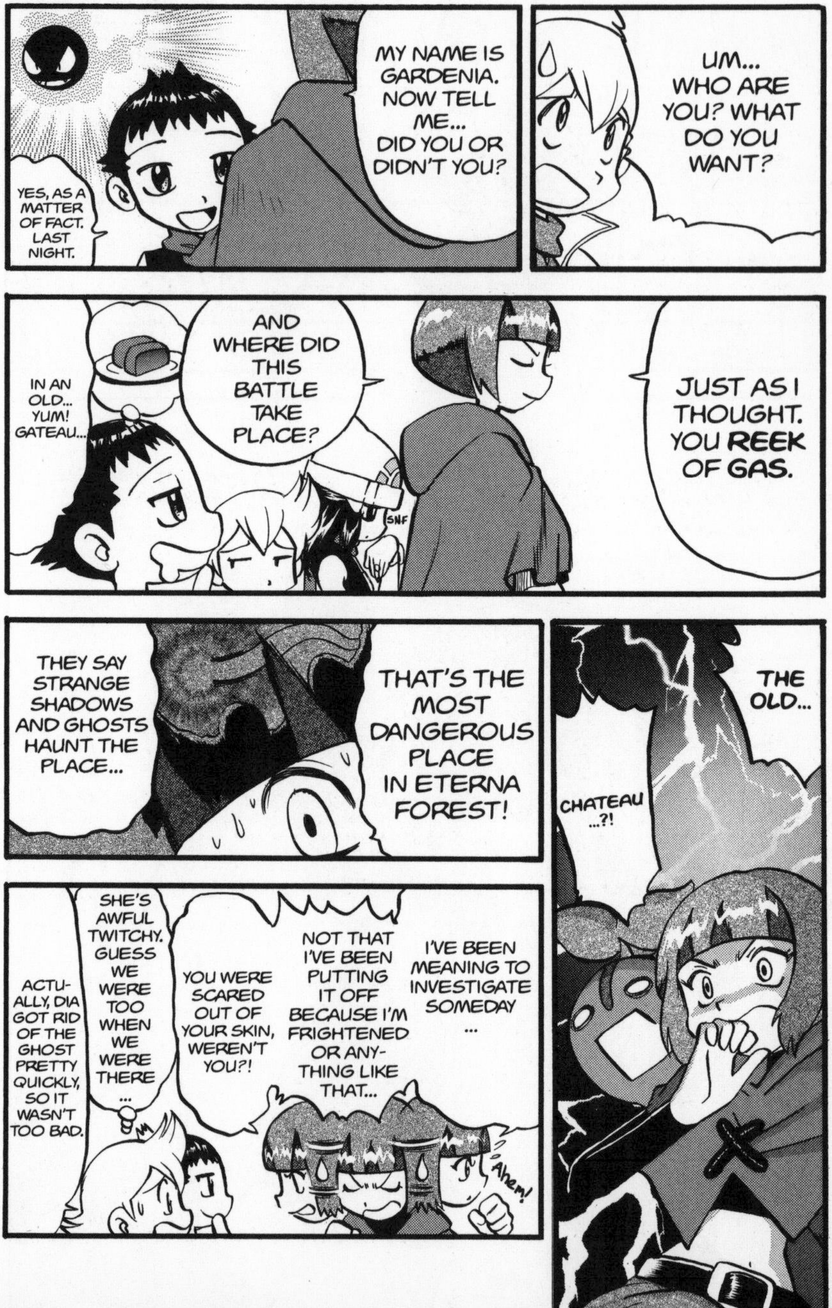

UM... WHO ARE YOU? WHAT DO YOU WANT?
MY NAME IS GARDENIA. NOW TELL ME... DID YOU OR DIDN'T YOU?
YES, AS A MATTER OF FACT. LAST NIGHT.
JUST AS I THOUGHT. YOU **REEK** OF **GAS.**
AND WHERE DID THIS BATTLE TAKE PLACE?
SNF
IN AN OLD... YUM! GATEAU...
THE OLD...
CHATEAU ...?!
THAT'S THE MOST DANGEROUS PLACE IN ETERNA FOREST!
THEY SAY STRANGE SHADOWS AND GHOSTS HAUNT THE PLACE...
I'VE BEEN MEANING TO INVESTIGATE SOMEDAY ...
NOT THAT I'VE BEEN PUTTING IT OFF BECAUSE I'M FRIGHTENED OR ANY-THING LIKE THAT...
Ahem!
YOU WERE SCARED OUT OF YOUR SKIN, WEREN'T YOU?!
SHE'S AWFUL TWITCHY. GUESS WE WERE TOO WHEN WE WERE THERE ...
ACTU-ALLY, DIA GOT RID OF THE GHOST PRETTY QUICKLY, SO IT WASN'T TOO BAD.

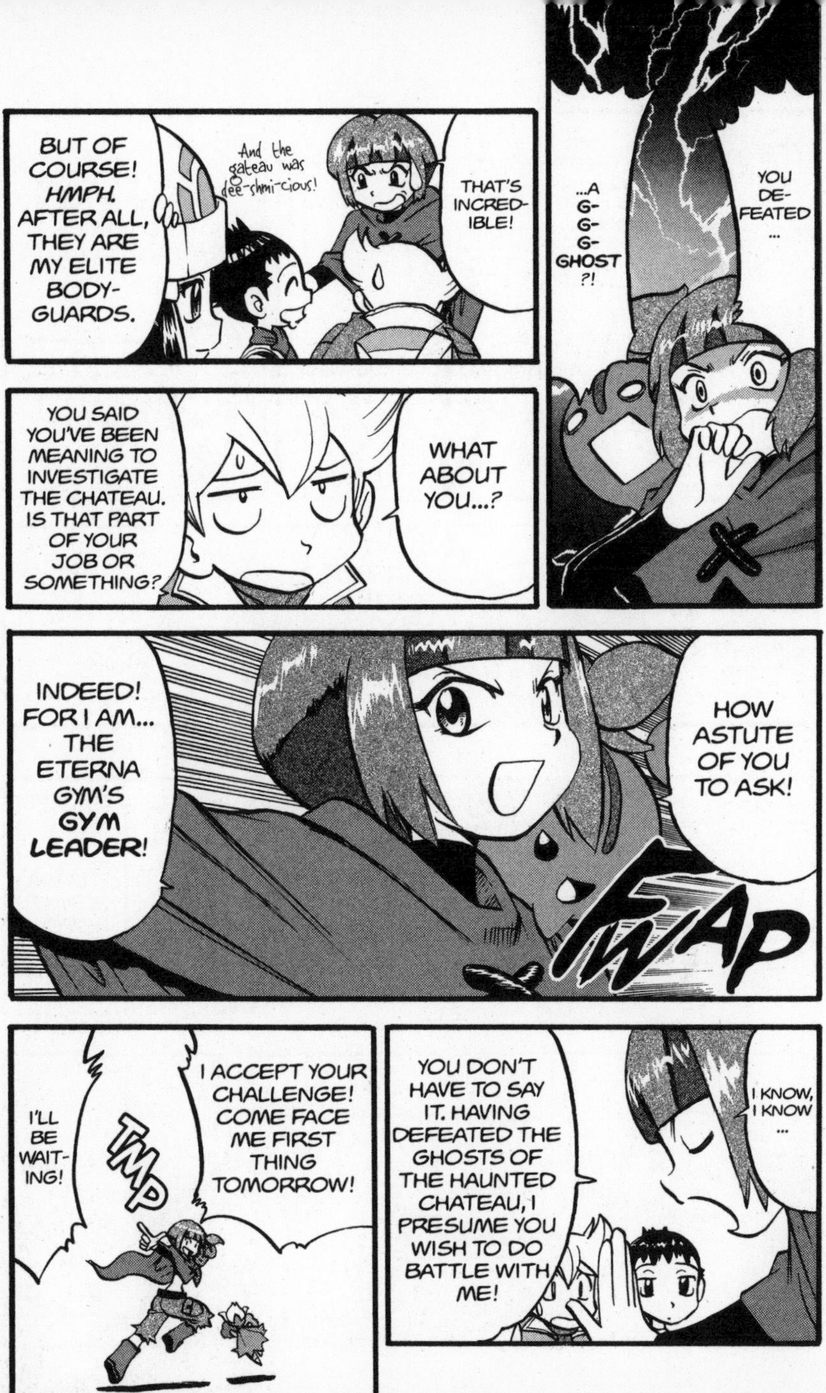
YOU DEFEATED ...
...A G-G-G-GHOST?!
THAT'S INCREDIBLE!
And the gateau was dee-shmi-cious!
BUT OF COURSE! HMPH. AFTER ALL, THEY ARE MY ELITE BODYGUARDS.
WHAT ABOUT YOU...?
YOU SAID YOU'VE BEEN MEANING TO INVESTIGATE THE CHATEAU. IS THAT PART OF YOUR JOB OR SOMETHING?
HOW ASTUTE OF YOU TO ASK!
INDEED! FOR I AM... THE ETERNA GYM'S GYM LEADER!
FWAP
I KNOW, I KNOW ...
YOU DON'T HAVE TO SAY IT. HAVING DEFEATED THE GHOSTS OF THE HAUNTED CHATEAU, I PRESUME YOU WISH TO DO BATTLE WITH ME!
I ACCEPT YOUR CHALLENGE! COME FACE ME FIRST THING TOMORROW!
TMP
I'LL BE WAITING!

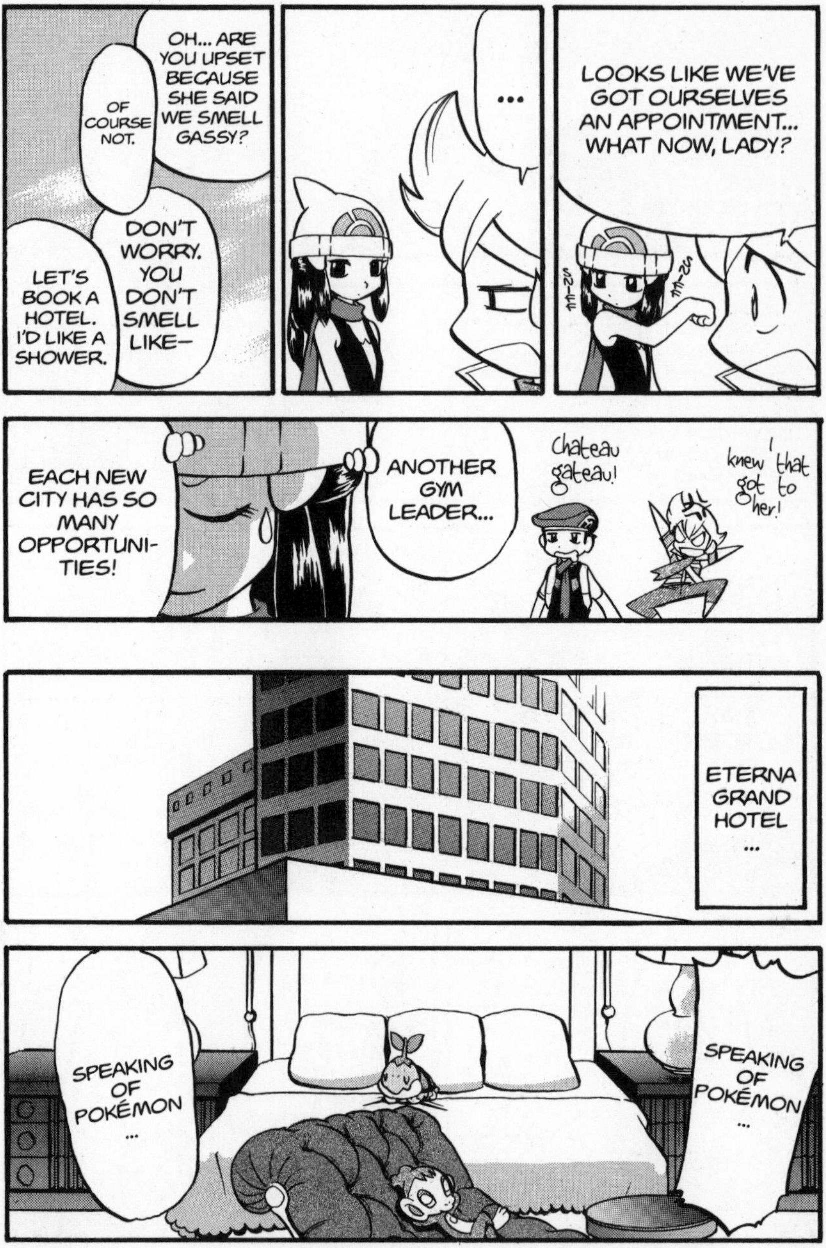
OH... ARE YOU UPSET BECAUSE SHE SAID WE SMELL GASSY?
OF COURSE NOT.
DON'T WORRY. YOU DON'T SMELL LIKE—
LET'S BOOK A HOTEL. I'D LIKE A SHOWER.
...
LOOKS LIKE WE'VE GOT OURSELVES AN APPOINTMENT... WHAT NOW, LADY?
EACH NEW CITY HAS SO MANY OPPORTUNITIES!
ANOTHER GYM LEADER...
Chateau gateau!
I knew that got to her!
ETERNA GRAND HOTEL ...
SPEAKING OF POKÉMON ...
SPEAKING OF POKÉMON ...

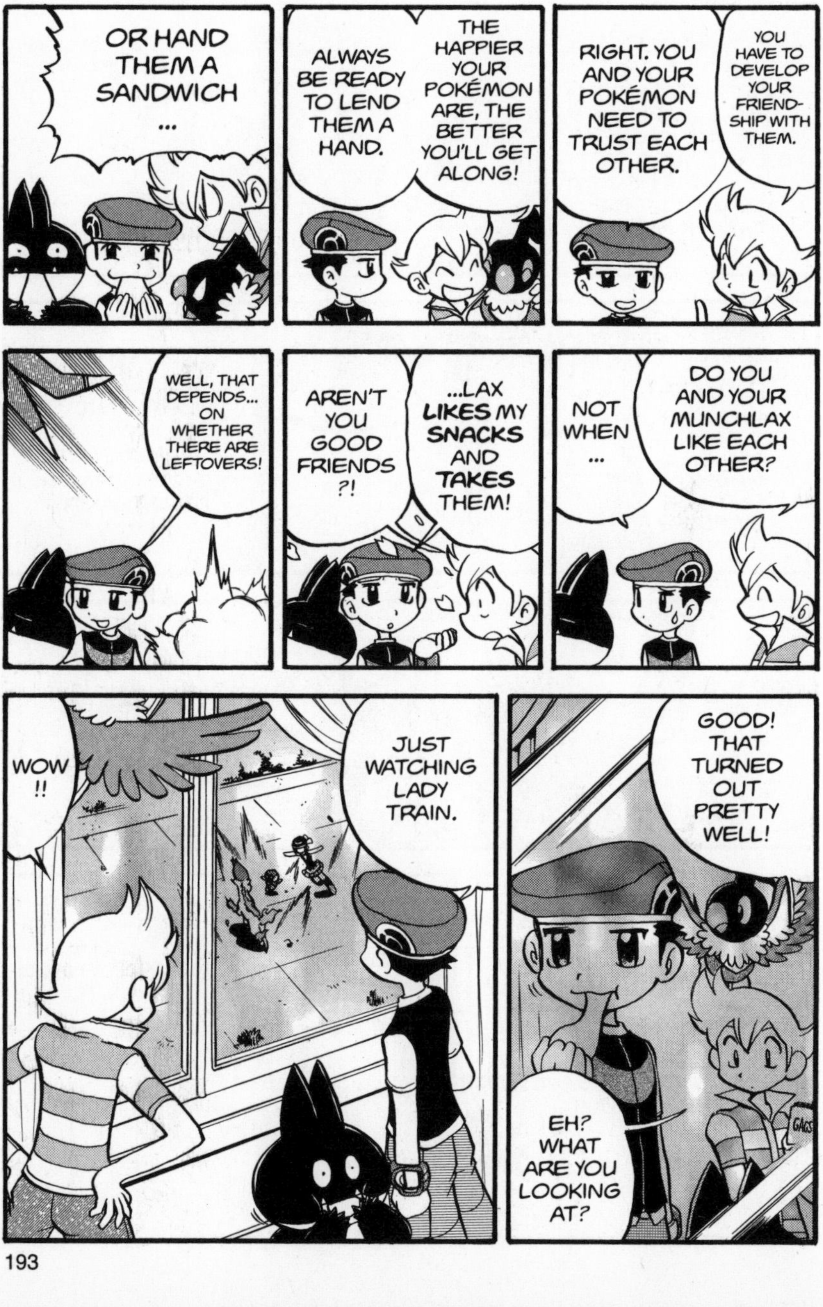
YOU HAVE TO DEVELOP YOUR FRIENDSHIP WITH THEM.
RIGHT. YOU AND YOUR POKÉMON NEED TO TRUST EACH OTHER.
THE HAPPIER YOUR POKÉMON ARE, THE BETTER YOU'LL GET ALONG!
ALWAYS BE READY TO LEND THEM A HAND.
OR HAND THEM A SANDWICH ...
DO YOU AND YOUR MUNCHLAX LIKE EACH OTHER?
NOT WHEN ...
...LAX **LIKES** MY **SNACKS** AND **TAKES** THEM!
AREN'T YOU GOOD FRIENDS ?!
WELL, THAT DEPENDS... ON WHETHER THERE ARE LEFTOVERS!
GOOD! THAT TURNED OUT PRETTY WELL!
EH? WHAT ARE YOU LOOKING AT?
JUST WATCHING LADY TRAIN.
WOW !!

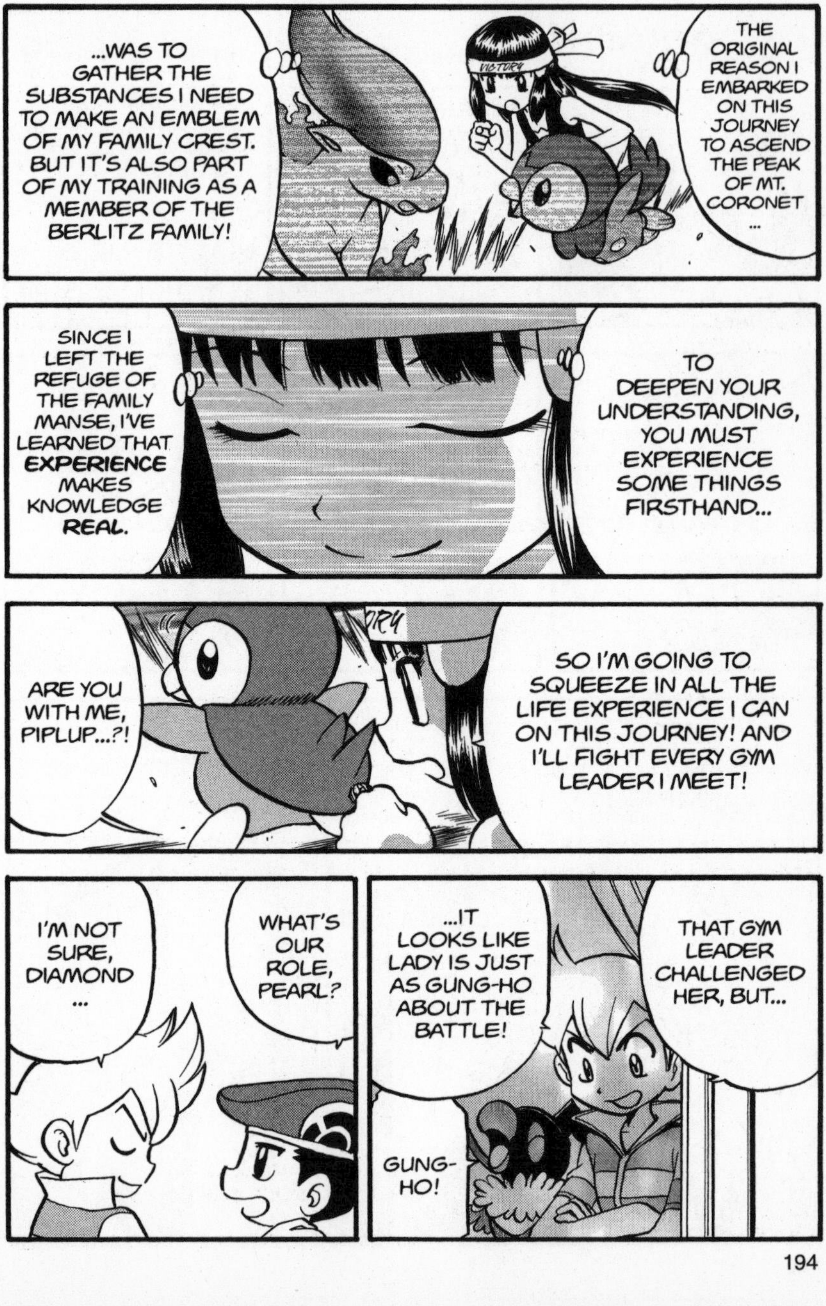
THE ORIGINAL REASON I EMBARKED ON THIS JOURNEY TO ASCEND THE PEAK OF MT. CORONET ...
...WAS TO GATHER THE SUBSTANCES I NEED TO MAKE AN EMBLEM OF MY FAMILY CREST. BUT IT'S ALSO PART OF MY TRAINING AS A MEMBER OF THE BERLITZ FAMILY!
VICTORY
TO DEEPEN YOUR UNDERSTANDING, YOU MUST EXPERIENCE SOME THINGS FIRSTHAND...
SINCE I LEFT THE REFUGE OF THE FAMILY MANSE, I'VE LEARNED THAT **EXPERIENCE** MAKES KNOWLEDGE **REAL.**
SO I'M GOING TO SQUEEZE IN ALL THE LIFE EXPERIENCE I CAN ON THIS JOURNEY! AND I'LL FIGHT EVERY GYM LEADER I MEET!
ARE YOU WITH ME, PIPLUP...?!
THAT GYM LEADER CHALLENGED HER, BUT...
...IT LOOKS LIKE LADY IS JUST AS GUNG-HO ABOUT THE BATTLE!
GUNG-HO!
WHAT'S OUR ROLE, PEARL?
I'M NOT SURE, DIAMOND ...

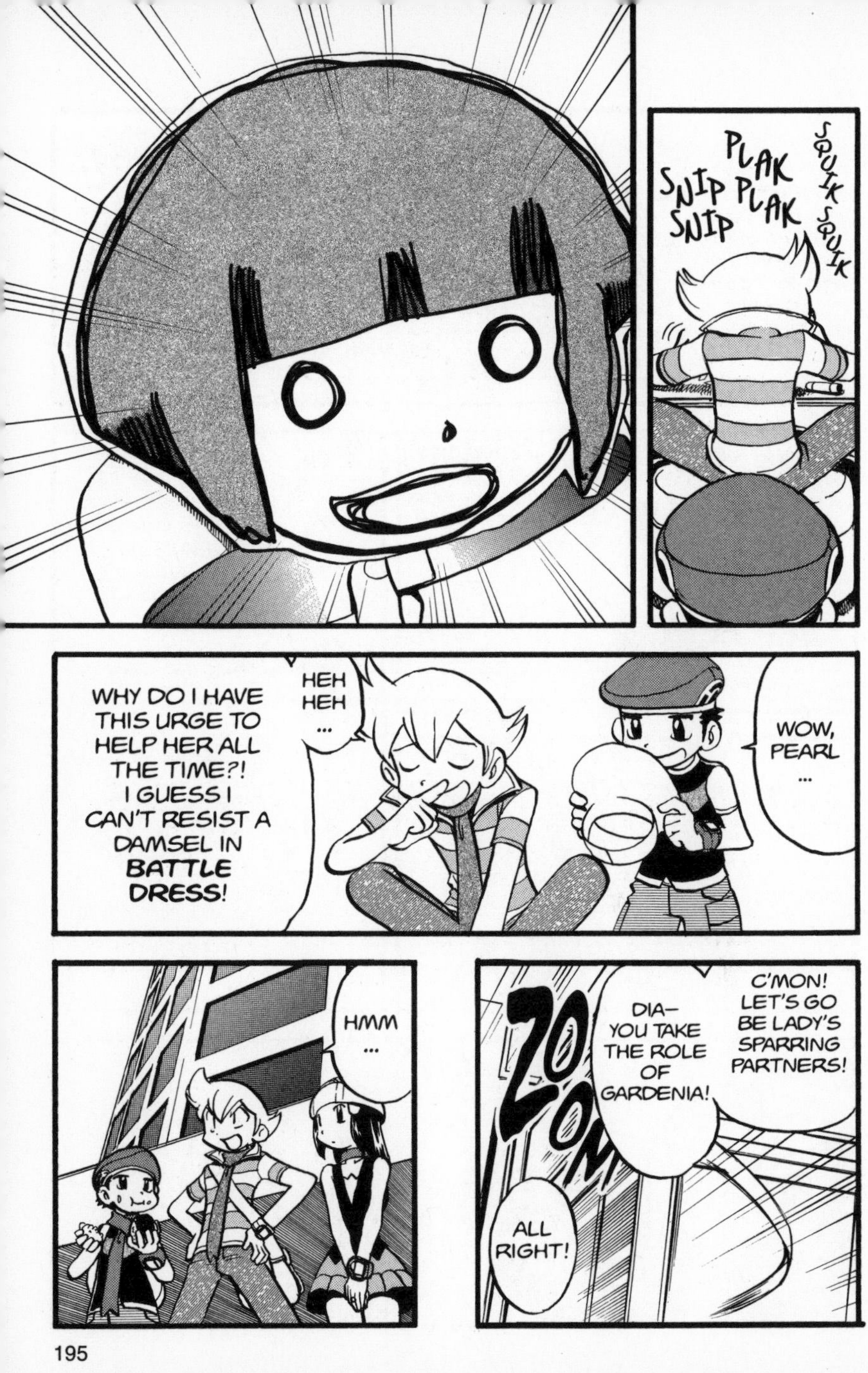
SNIP SNIP
PLAK PLAK
SQUIK SQUIK
WHY DO I HAVE THIS URGE TO HELP HER ALL THE TIME?! I GUESS I CAN'T RESIST A DAMSEL IN BATTLE DRESS!
HEH HEH ...
WOW, PEARL ...
HMM ...
ZOOM
DIA—YOU TAKE THE ROLE OF GARDENIA!
C'MON! LET'S GO BE LADY'S SPARRING PARTNERS!
ALL RIGHT!

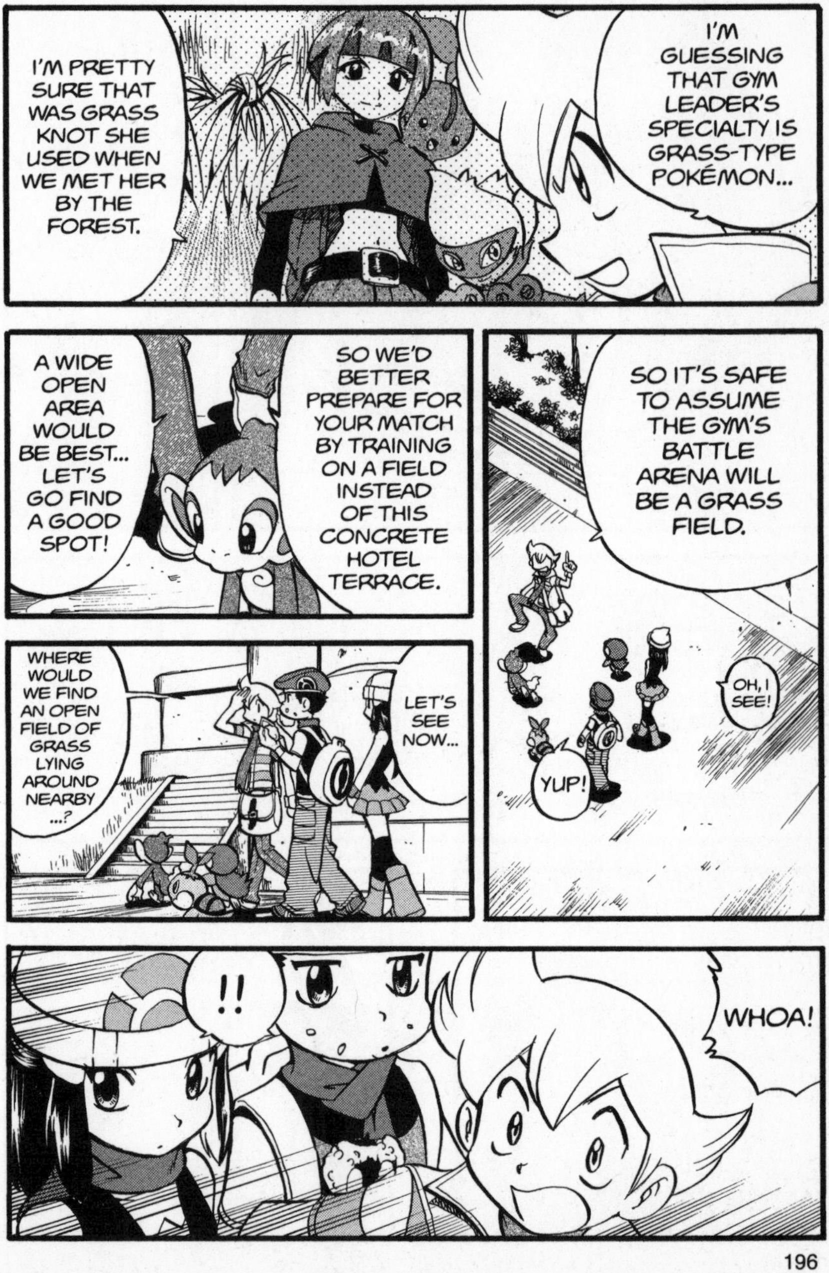
I'M GUESSING THAT GYM LEADER'S SPECIALTY IS GRASS-TYPE POKÉMON...
I'M PRETTY SURE THAT WAS GRASS KNOT SHE USED WHEN WE MET HER BY THE FOREST.
SO IT'S SAFE TO ASSUME THE GYM'S BATTLE ARENA WILL BE A GRASS FIELD.
OH, I SEE!
YUP!
SO WE'D BETTER PREPARE FOR YOUR MATCH BY TRAINING ON A FIELD INSTEAD OF THIS CONCRETE HOTEL TERRACE.
A WIDE OPEN AREA WOULD BE BEST... LET'S GO FIND A GOOD SPOT!
WHERE WOULD WE FIND AN OPEN FIELD OF GRASS LYING AROUND NEARBY ...?
LET'S SEE NOW...
!!
WHOA!

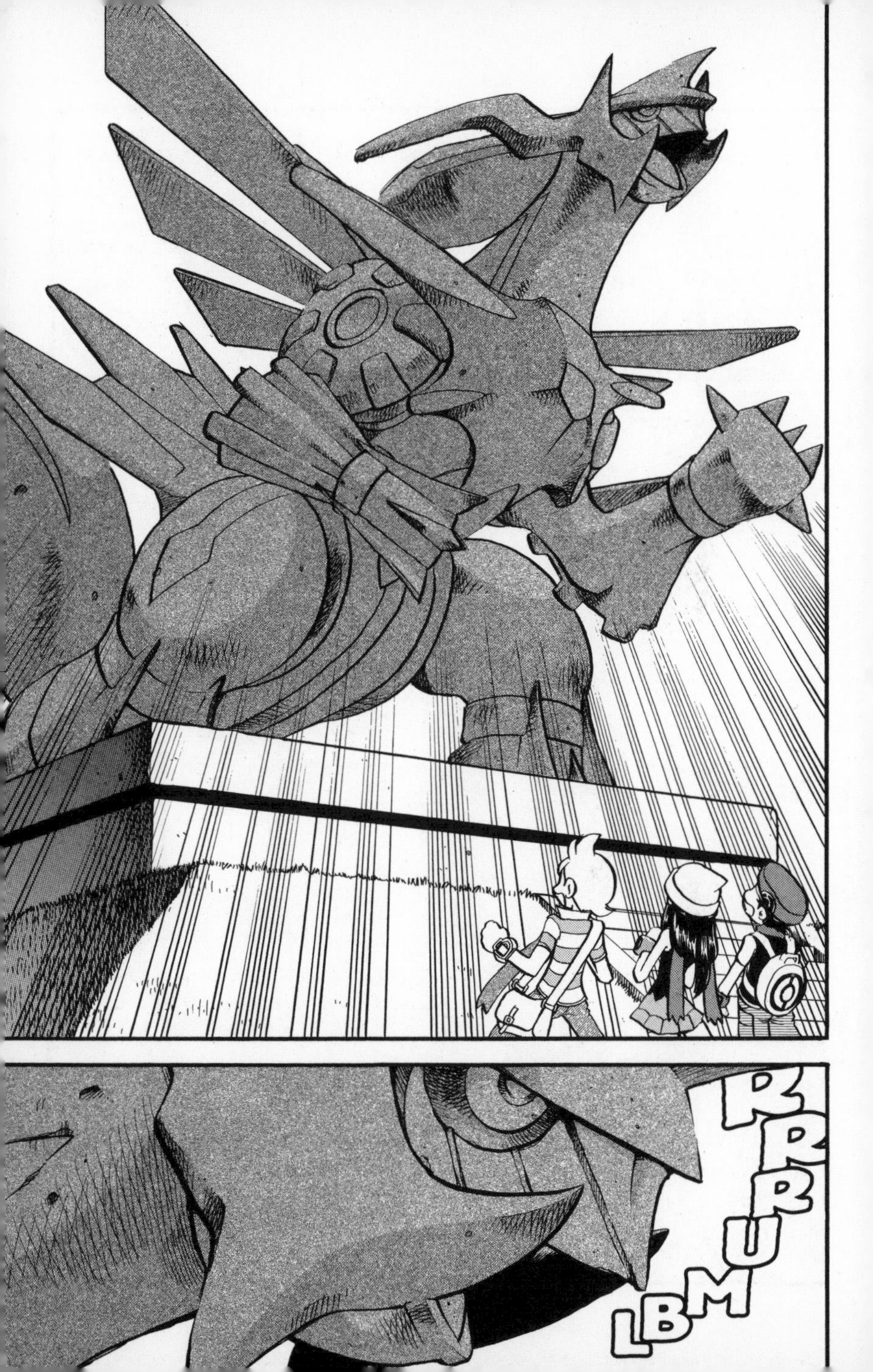
RRRUMBL

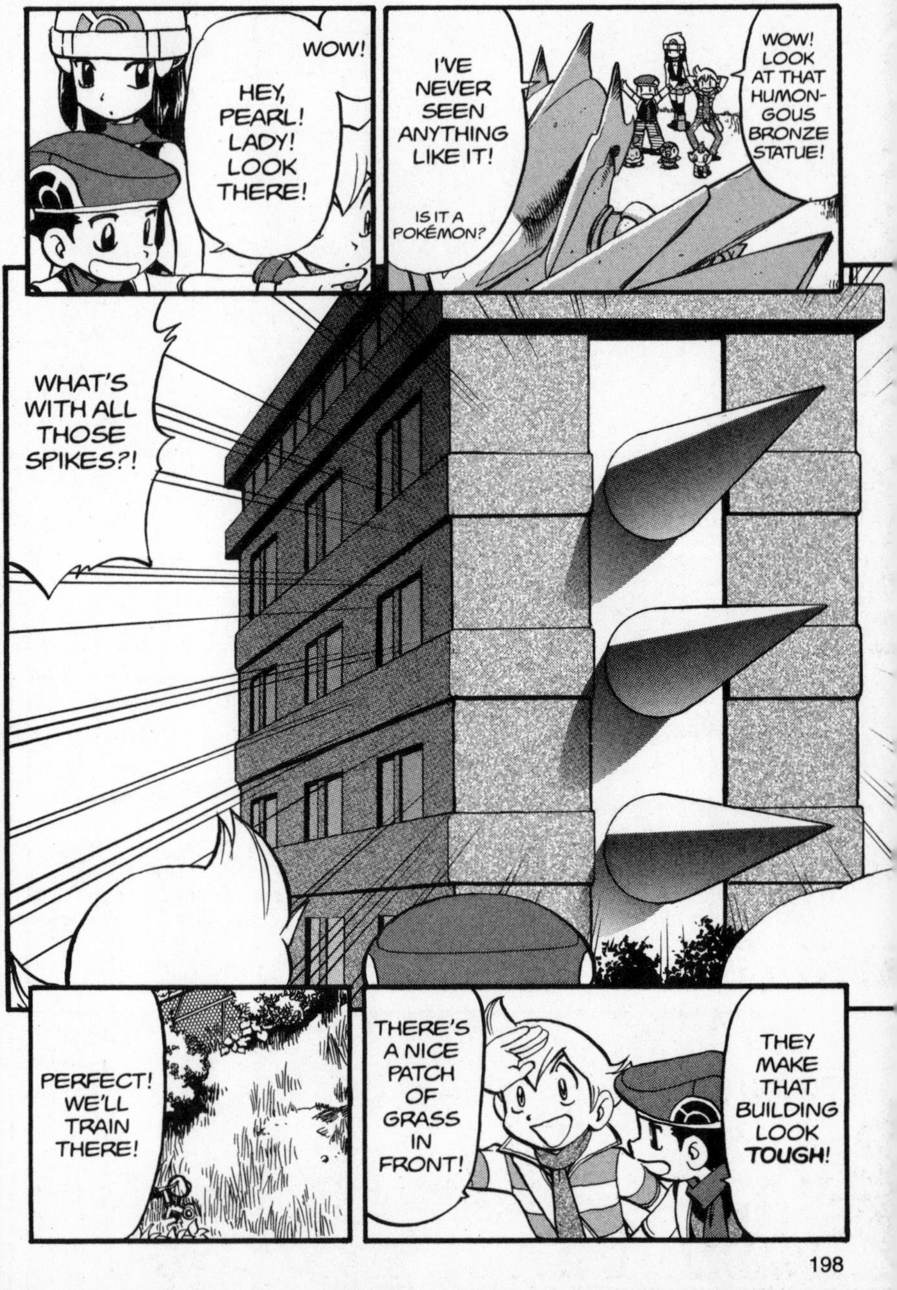
WOW!
HEY, PEARL! LADY! LOOK THERE!
I'VE NEVER SEEN ANYTHING LIKE IT!
IS IT A POKÉMON?
WOW! LOOK AT THAT HUMON-GOUS BRONZE STATUE!
WHAT'S WITH ALL THOSE SPIKES?!
PERFECT! WE'LL TRAIN THERE!
THERE'S A NICE PATCH OF GRASS IN FRONT!
THEY MAKE THAT BUILDING LOOK **TOUGH**!

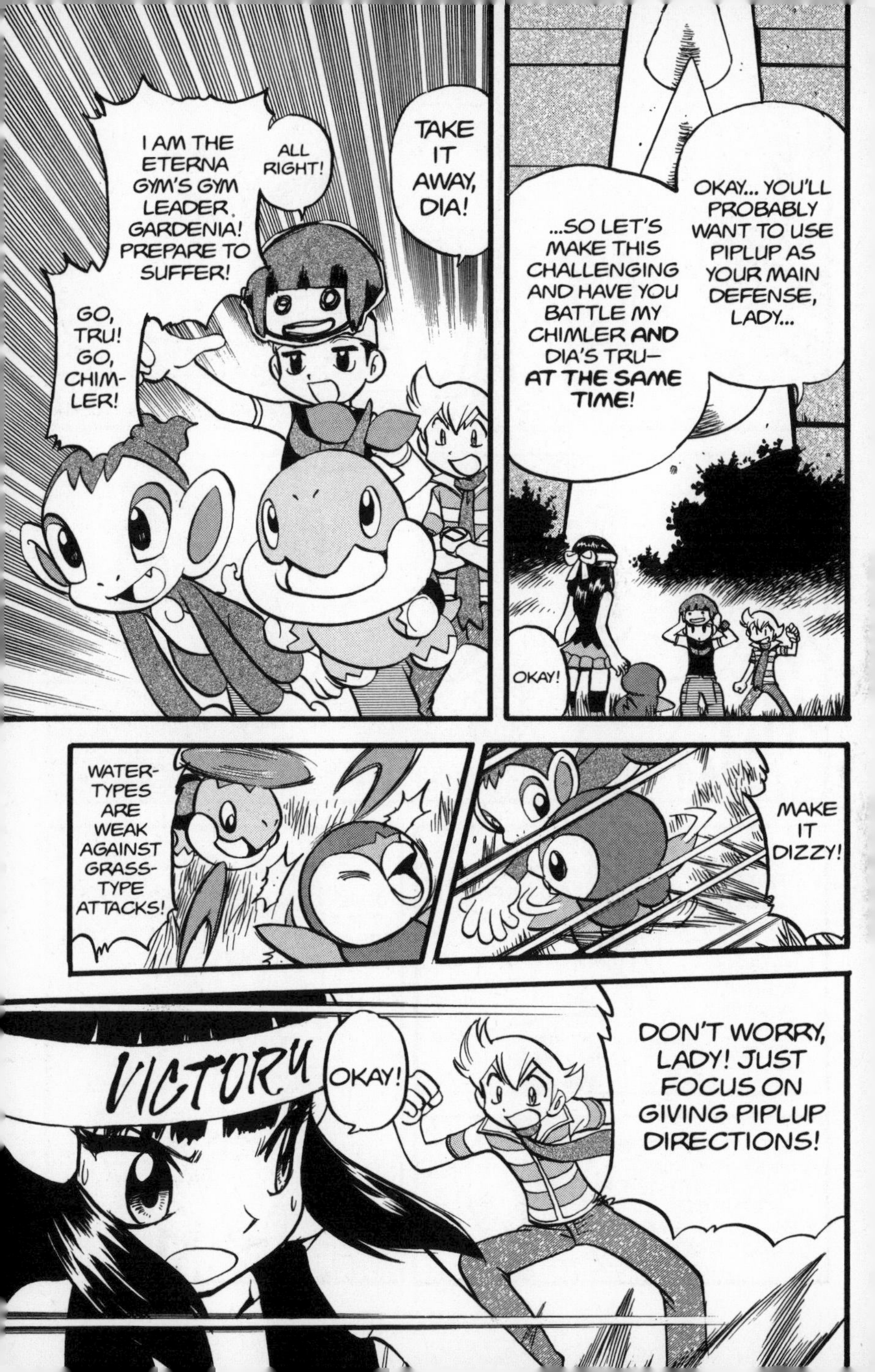
I AM THE ETERNA GYM'S GYM LEADER GARDENIA! PREPARE TO SUFFER!
ALL RIGHT!
TAKE IT AWAY, DIA!
GO, TRU! GO, CHIMLER!
OKAY... YOU'LL PROBABLY WANT TO USE PIPLUP AS YOUR MAIN DEFENSE, LADY...
...SO LET'S MAKE THIS CHALLENGING AND HAVE YOU BATTLE MY CHIMLER AND DIA'S TRU—AT THE SAME TIME!
OKAY!
WATER-TYPES ARE WEAK AGAINST GRASS-TYPE ATTACKS!
MAKE IT DIZZY!
VICTORY
DON'T WORRY, LADY! JUST FOCUS ON GIVING PIPLUP DIRECTIONS!
OKAY!

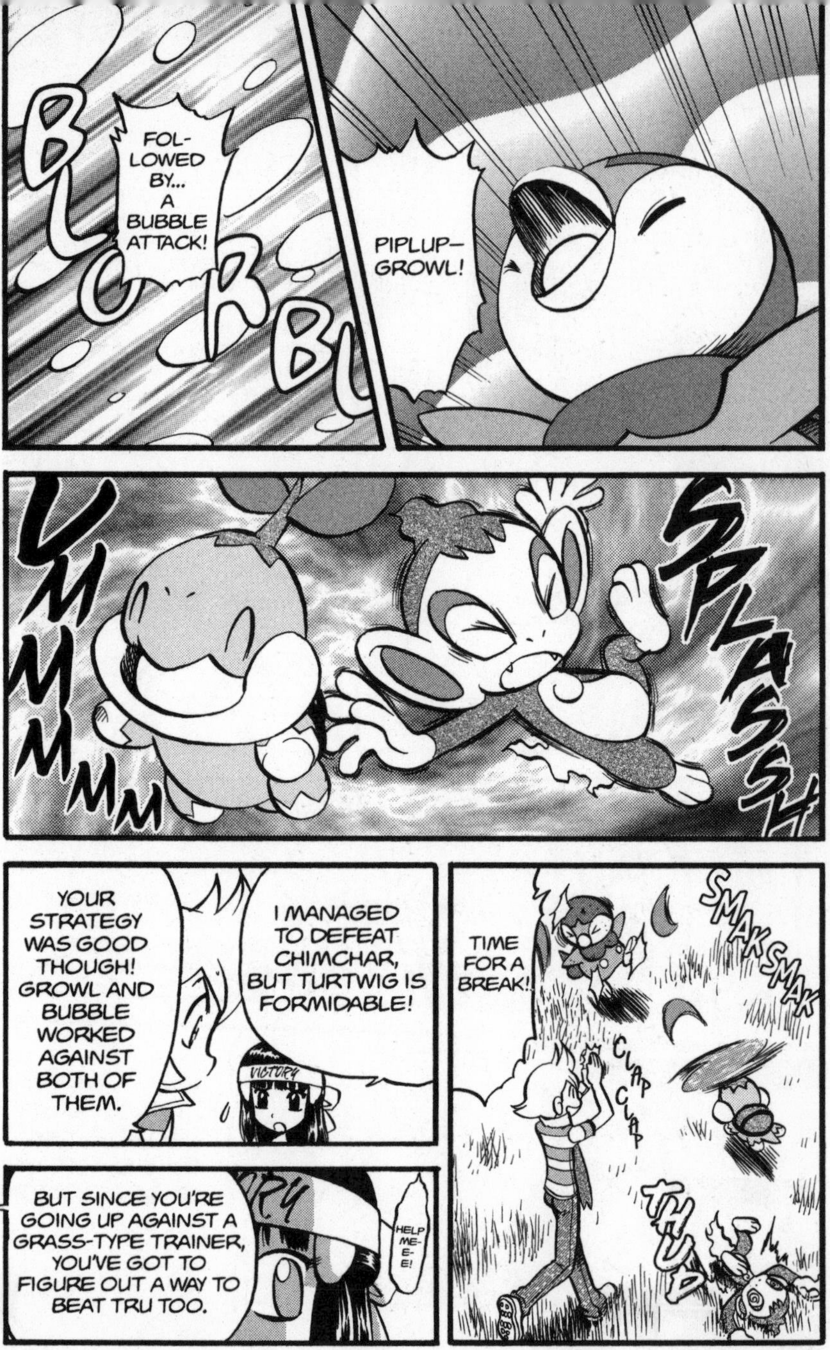
PIPLUP—
GROWL!
FOL-
LOWED
BY...
A
BUBBLE
ATTACK!
BLORBBL
SPLASH
I MANAGED
TO DEFEAT
CHIMCHAR,
BUT TURTWIG IS
FORMIDABLE!
YOUR
STRATEGY
WAS GOOD
THOUGH!
GROWL AND
BUBBLE
WORKED
AGAINST
BOTH OF
THEM.
VICTORY
BUT SINCE YOU'RE
GOING UP AGAINST A
GRASS-TYPE TRAINER,
YOU'VE GOT TO
FIGURE OUT A WAY TO
BEAT TRU TOO.
HELP
ME-
E-
E!
SMAKSMAK
TIME
FOR A
BREAK!
CLAP
CLAP
THUD

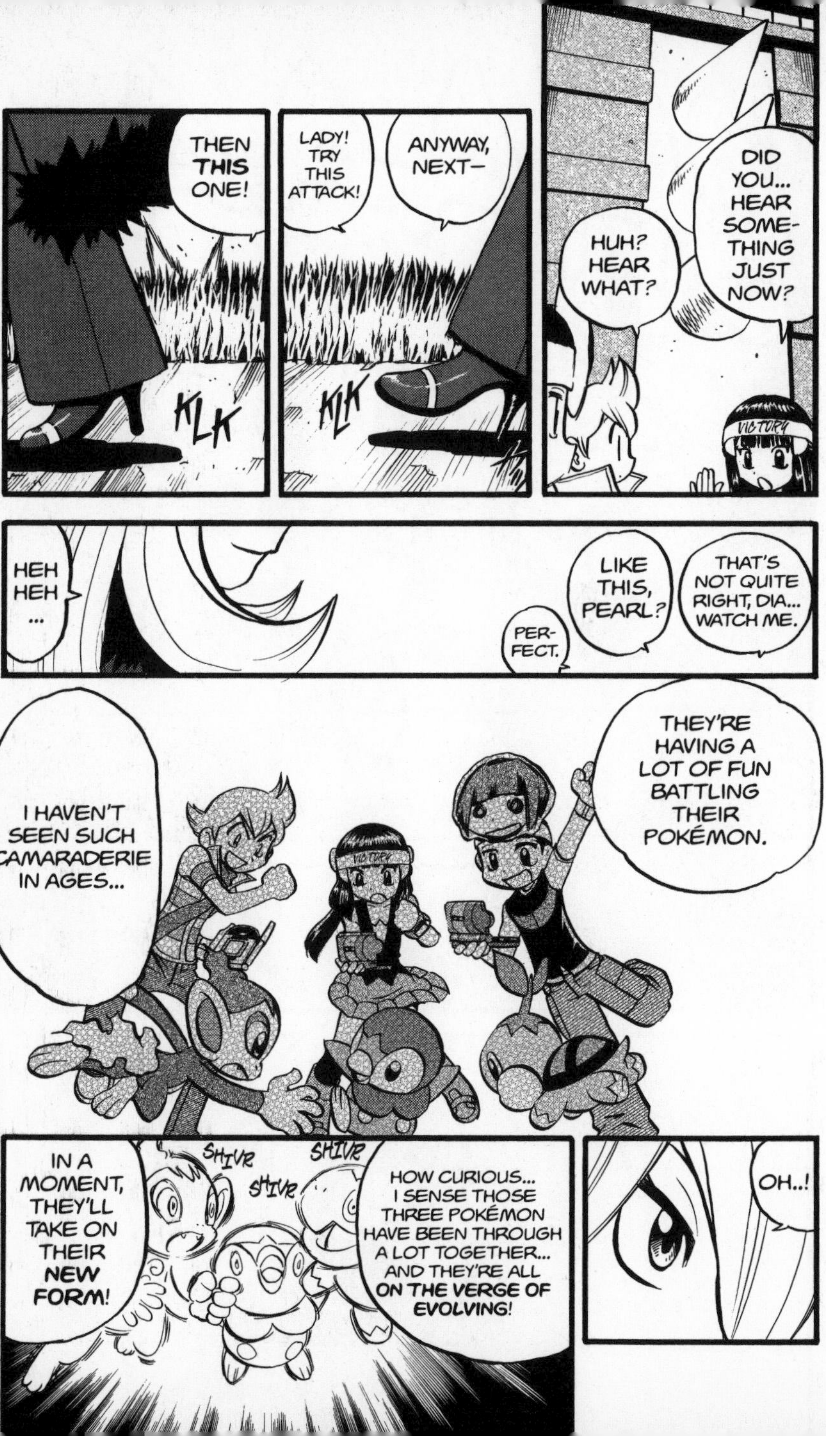

THEN THIS ONE!
KLK
LADY! TRY THIS ATTACK!
ANYWAY, NEXT—
KLK
DID YOU... HEAR SOME-THING JUST NOW?
HUH? HEAR WHAT?
VICTORY
HEH HEH ...
PER-FECT.
LIKE THIS, PEARL?
THAT'S NOT QUITE RIGHT, DIA... WATCH ME.
I HAVEN'T SEEN SUCH CAMARADERIE IN AGES...
THEY'RE HAVING A LOT OF FUN BATTLING THEIR POKÉMON.
VICTORY
IN A MOMENT, THEY'LL TAKE ON THEIR NEW FORM!
SHIVR
SHIVR
SHIVR
HOW CURIOUS... I SENSE THOSE THREE POKÉMON HAVE BEEN THROUGH A LOT TOGETHER... AND THEY'RE ALL ON THE VERGE OF EVOLVING!
OH...!

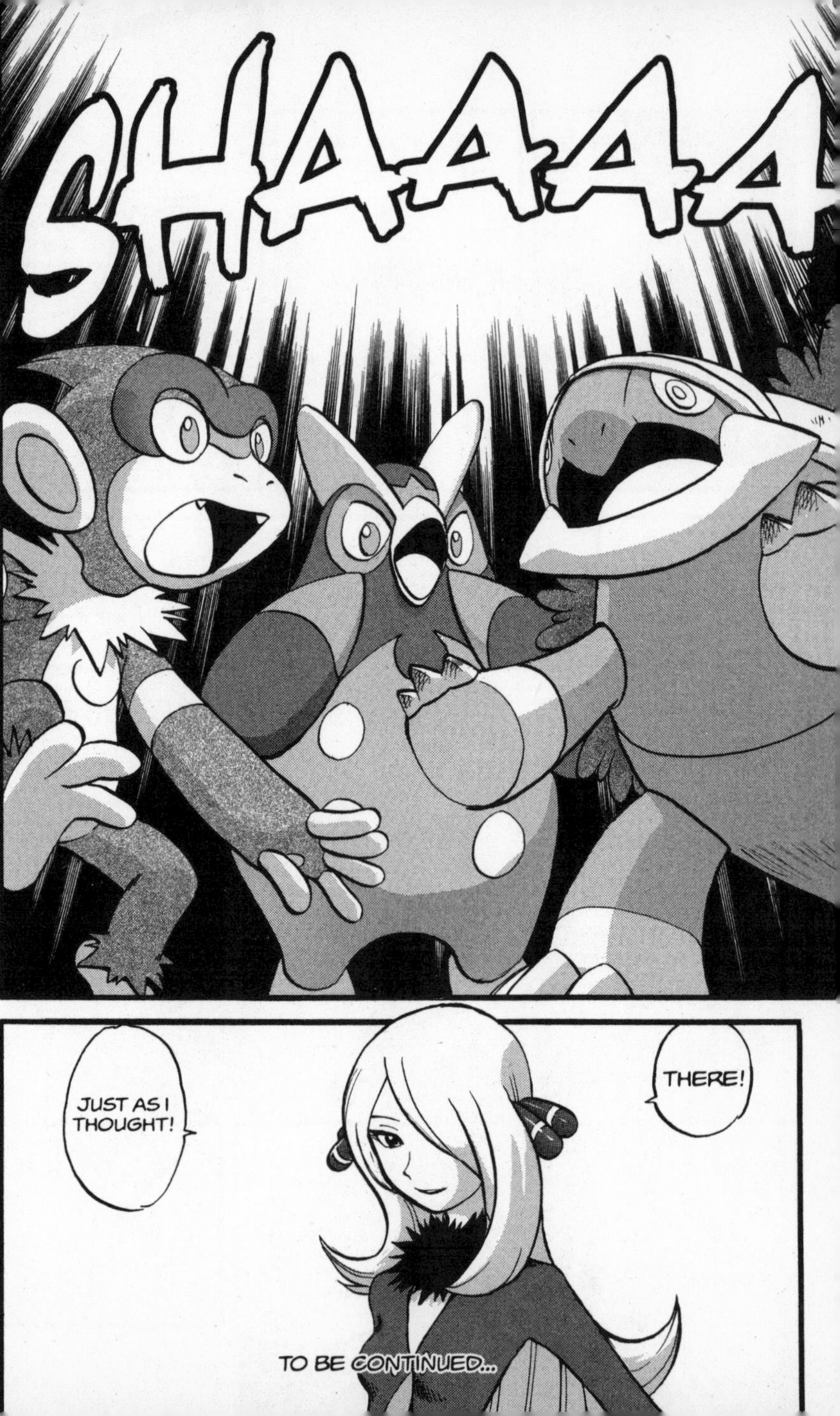
SHAAAA
THERE!
JUST AS I THOUGHT!
TO BE CONTINUED...

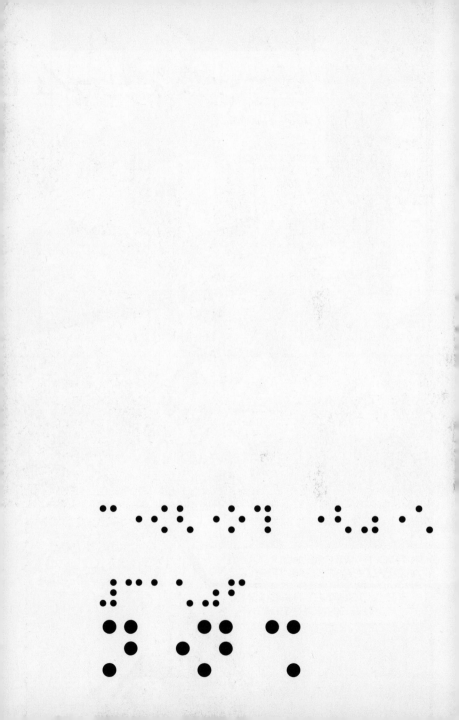

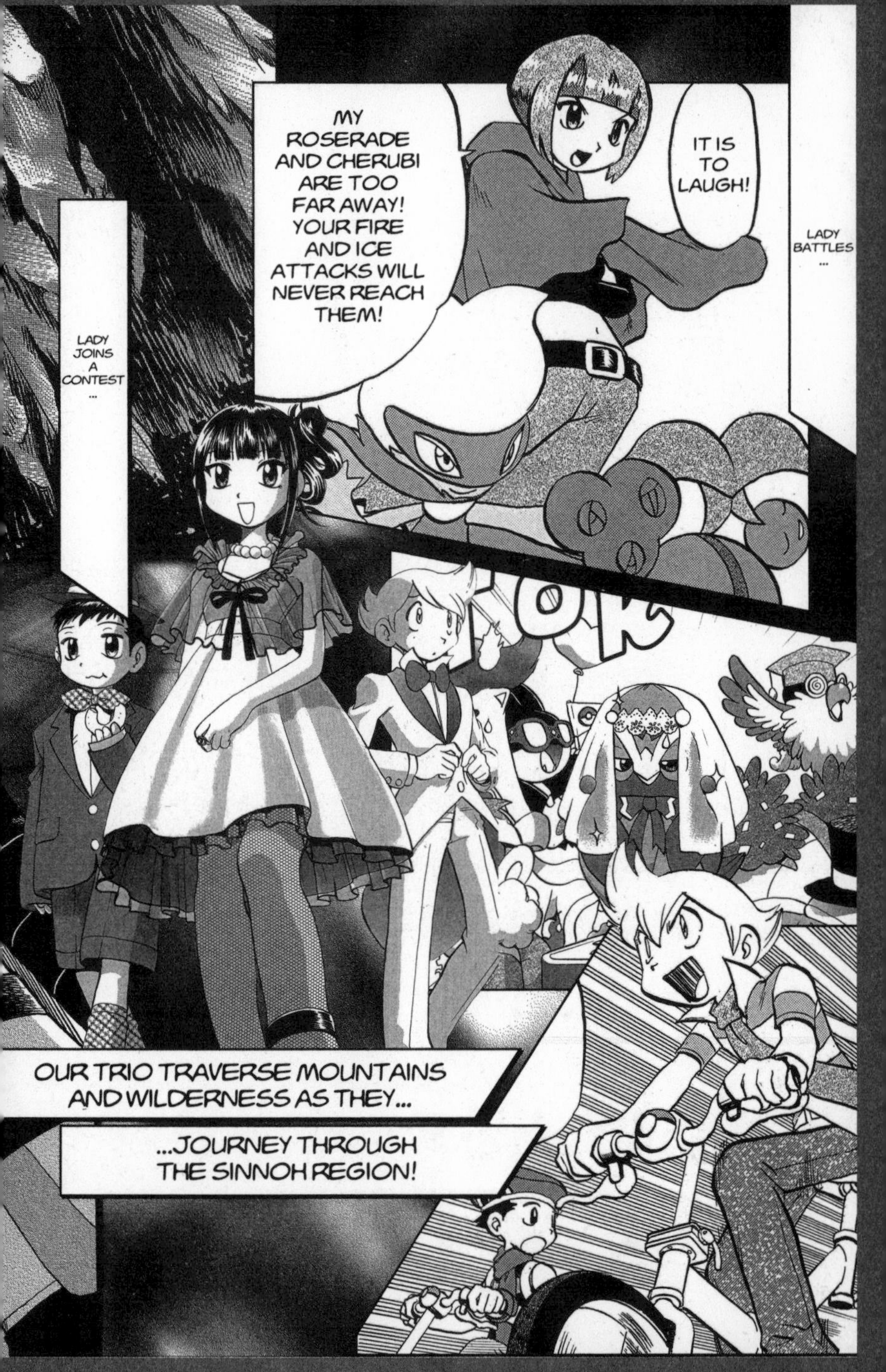

IT IS TO LAUGH!
MY ROSERADE AND CHERUBI ARE TOO FAR AWAY! YOUR FIRE AND ICE ATTACKS WILL NEVER REACH THEM!
LADY BATTLES ...
LADY JOINS A CONTEST ...
OUR TRIO TRAVERSE MOUNTAINS AND WILDERNESS AS THEY...
...JOURNEY THROUGH THE SINNOH REGION!

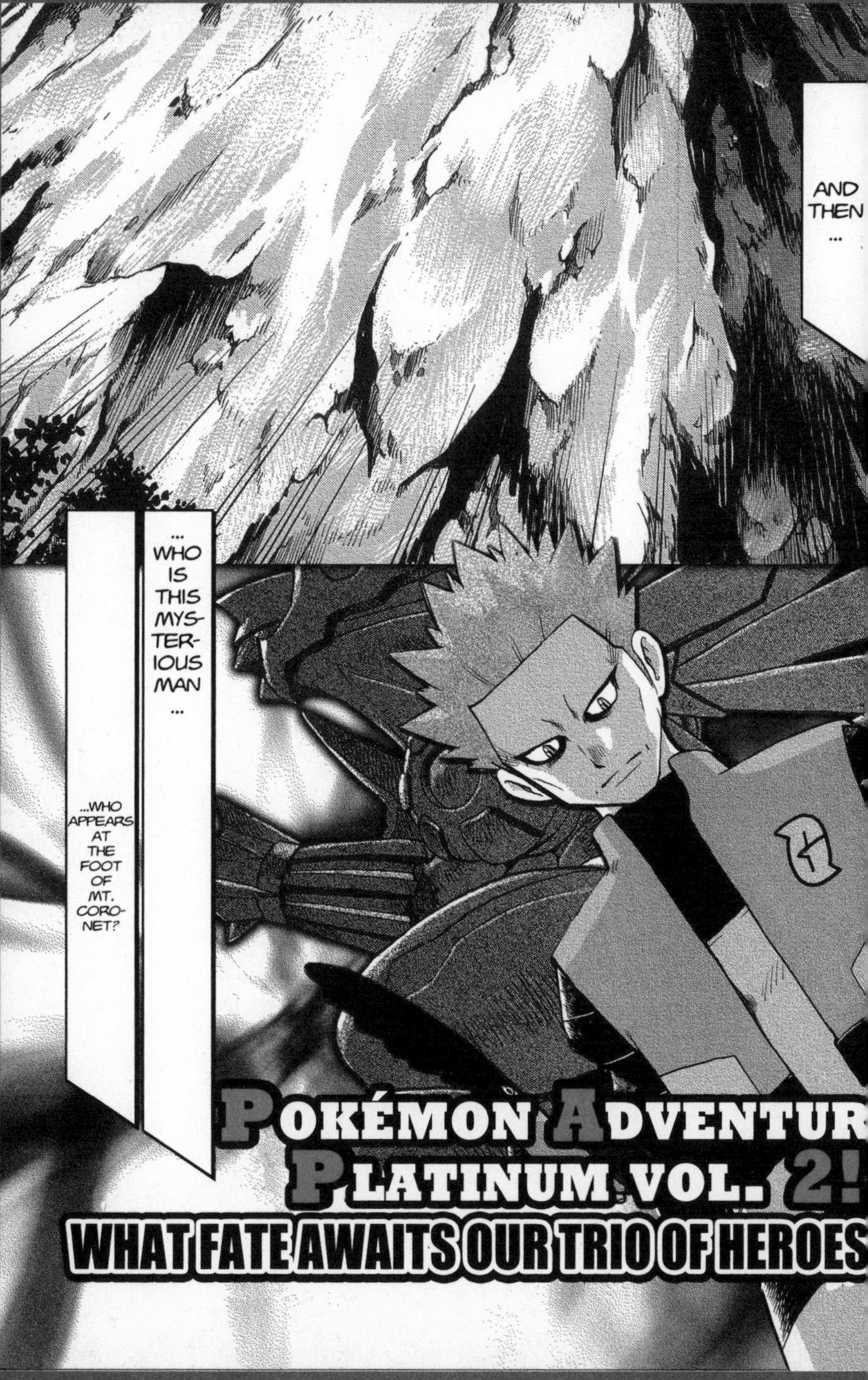

AND THEN ...
... WHO IS THIS MYS-TER-IOUS MAN ...
...WHO APPEARS AT THE FOOT OF MT. CORO-NET?
POKÉMON ADVENTUR
PLATINUM VOL. 2!
WHAT FATE AWAITS OUR TRIO OF HEROES

Message from
Hidenori Kusaka

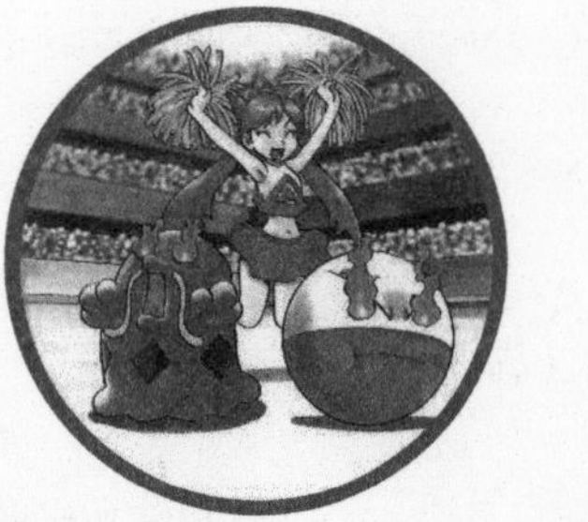

I've only been to the area in Japan known as "Snow Country" once, when I went to the Jisedai World Hobby Fair in Sapporo. That was my first and last visit. The *Pokémon Adventures* "Seventh Chapter" takes place in a similar setting. I don't have many images to work from, but I used my memories of the scenery I saw there as the setting for this new story arc.

The landscape in Hokkaido and Tohoku is vast and sweeping. The weather is cold, but the hearts of the people are warm. I hope this comes through in the story!

Message from
Satoshi Yamamoto

Thank you for your patience! The Pokémon Adventures "Seventh Chapter," the Diamond and Pearl story arc, has finally begun. There are lots of interesting characters in this series, but if I had to choose who I'd most like to go on an adventure with, I would have to answer–Diamond, Pearl, and Lady. It would be so much fun to stay in a suite at a fancy hotel, eat good food, get smacked by Pearl... Well not that last part, I guess. Ha, ha!

Enjoy your adventures with this terrific trio!

More Adventures Coming Soon...

Pearl, Diamond and Lady Berlitz finally reach the base of Mt. Coronet. They're all set to scale its cloudy peak, but first...there are dancing Contests to win, badges to compete for and enemies to evade!

Speaking of enemies, are those shadowy figures members of...*Team Galactic*?!

Plus, meet Stunky, Probopass, Buneary, Pachirisu, Croagunk and many more Sinnoh Pokémon friends!

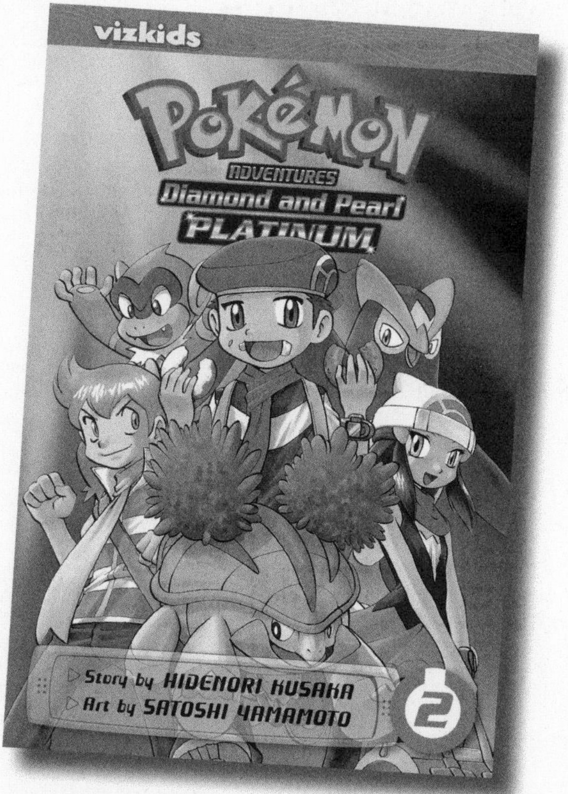
vizkids
POKéMON
ADVENTURES
Diamond and Pearl
PLATINUM
Story by HIDENORI KUSAKA
Art by SATOSHI YAMAMOTO
2

AVAILABLE JUNE 2011!

Pokémon ADVENTURES Diamond and Pearl PLATINUM™

Pokémon ADVENTURES: DIAMOND AND PEARL/ PLATINUM
Volume 1
VIZ Kids Edition

Story by HIDENORI KUSAKA
Art by SATOSHI YAMAMOTO

Original Japanese edition "POCKET MONSTER SPECIAL" published by SHOGAKUKAN Inc.

Translation/Katherine Schilling
Touch-up & Lettering/Annaliese Christman
Design/Yukiko Whitley
Editor/Annette Roman

Printed in the U.S.A.

Published by VIZ Media, LLC
P.O. Box 77010
San Francisco, CA 94107

10 9 8 7 6 5 4 3 2 1
First printing, March 2011